MW01089074

H.G. WELLS
THE WAR OF THE WORLDS
THE WORLDS
& OTHER TALES

FLAME TREE PUBLISHING
6 Melbray Mews, Fulham,
London SW6 3NS, United Kingdom
www.flametreepublishing.com

First published and copyright © 2021
Flame Tree Publishing Ltd

This edition of *The War of the Worlds* is based on the original publication by William
Heinemann (1898). 'A Dream of Armageddon' was published in *Black and White*
magazine in 1901. *The First Men in the Moon* was originally published in hardcover
by George Newnes (1901).

21 23 25 24 22
1 3 5 7 9 10 8 6 4 2

ISBN: 978-1-83964-479-5

Cover and pattern art is created by Flame Tree Studio, inspired by the posters and
advertisements for early black and white movie adaptations of classic gothic novels.
Some artwork elements courtesy of Shutterstock, (Delcarmat and Svekloid).

Judith John (Glossary) is a writer and editor specializing in literature and history. A former
secondary school English Language and Literature teacher, she has subsequently worked
as an editor on major educational projects, including *English A: Literature* for the Pearson
International Baccalaureate series. Judith's major research interests include Romantic and
Gothic literature, and Renaissance drama.

A copy of the CIP data for this book is available
from the British Library.

Designed and created in the UK | Printed and bound in China

COLLECTOR'S EDITIONS

H.G. WELLS

THE WAR OF THE WORLDS

& OTHER TALES

Reading List & Glossary of Terms
With a New Introduction by
DR. EMELYNE GODFREY

FLAME TREE PUBLISHING

CONTENTS

INTRODUCTION
& FURTHER READING

INTRODUCTION

ULLA! ULLA!

The **stylus** descends onto the vinyl which spins with a barely perceptible whirr of anticipation. Drawing back, we take our seats. Outside, the autumnal sky is darkening over the hills and somewhere in the house a kettle boils. And then the crackling static comes. We wait, and forthwith, the deep voice begins. It is a broadcast of sorts and its echo places it outside of time.

> *No one would have believed, in the last years of the nineteenth century, that human affairs were being watched from the timeless worlds of space. No one could have dreamed we were being scrutinized as someone with a microscope studies creatures that swarm and multiply in a drop of water. Few men even considered the possibility of life on other planets. And yet, across the gulf of space, minds immeasurably superior to ours regarded this Earth with envious eyes, and slowly and surely they drew their plans against us.*

To many, Richard Burton's opening words in *Jeff Wayne's The Musical Version of the War of the Worlds* (1978) are their first introduction to the works of Herbert George Wells, affectionately known as 'H.G.' I first heard Wayne's reworking of Well's words in the year of the tenth anniversary and the ninetieth anniversary of the publication of Wells's tale in novel form. The juxtaposition of weird, unearthly sounds and pulsing synthesizers against images of Victorian streets displayed in the album booklet was rivetingly apt. These sounds of mysterious origins were as strange and magical to my eight-year-old ears as the alien technology must have been to the Victorian residents of Wells's Woking when they saw the first cylinder fall on Horsell Common.

Like George Pal's 1960s film interpretation of Wells's earlier classic, *The Time Machine* (1895), Wayne's musical is of its time but still sounds fresh. Together with the instrumental that follows Burton's words, Mike Trim's front cover design draws the viewer into the tale with its horrifying green, bug-eyed tripods whose ovoid shoulders are a monstrous, metallic tribute to the gigot sleeves worn by women in the decade in which Wells wrote the novel. Against a night sky and a blaze of white steam, the alien destroyer directs its heat ray downwards and dissolves the heart of the *Thunder Child* warship, the vessel on which the narrator and the horrified bystanders around him have pinned all their hopes. This album cover inspires a warning that we should never be too complacent in the power and might of mankind.

Wells is widely credited as one of the founding fathers of modern science fiction. He predicted the world wide web in the form of an internationally updated dictionary which he called the 'world brain', commercial air travel and, it seems, some form of instant face-to-face connection such as the FaceTime or Zoom apps which offered an emotional lifeline to the rest of the world during the lockdown of 2020. As Wells speculated in 'Wanted – Professors of Foresight' (1932): 'There will be no more distance left and little separation. You will be able to see and talk to your friends anywhere in the world as easily and surely as you send a telegram today... Before another half-century has passed everybody, so to speak, will be on call next door.

You cannot doubt it.' His short story, 'A Dream of Armageddon' (1901) and the novels *The War of the Worlds* (1898) and *The First Men in the Moon* (1901) form his early imaginative investigations into the impact of this shrinkage of distance across the world and across space. 'Wanted – Professors of Foresight!' looked back across the expanse of the first three decades of the twentieth century, eerily warning radio listeners that:

> *Either we must make peace throughout the world, make one world-state, one world-pax, with one money, one police, one speech and one brotherhood, however hard that task may seem, or we must prepare to live with the voice of the stranger in our ears, with the eyes of the stranger in our homes, with the knife of the stranger always at our throats, in fear and in danger of death, enemy-neighbours with the rest of our species. Distance **was** protection, **was** safety, though it meant also ignorance and indifference and a narrow, unstimulated life. For good or evil, distance has been done away with.*

Wells, who wrote over eighty short stories and more than one hundred books, reaching international audiences with his radio broadcasts, predicted the atom bomb and aerial and tank warfare. His 'guns that could carry beyond sight' in 'A Dream of Armageddon' are highly suggestive of cruise missiles. He also warned throughout his life that scientific leaps, unaccompanied by social change, accountability and cooperation, could plunge humanity into the abyss. *The War of the Worlds*, 'A Dream of Armageddon' and *The First Men in the Moon* all offer visions of the end of the world unleashed through science: when Cavor tests Cavorite for the first time, for example, he unleashes a local cyclone and almost asphyxiates the world.

PART 1: THE YOUNG 'BERTIE' WELLS

The idea of *The War of the Worlds* came from Wells's brother, Frank. Out for a walk across the tranquil Surrey countryside, the two brothers discussed the fate of the Aboriginal population of Tasmania under European settlers in the early nineteenth century. Wells would return to the subject in his ground-breaking *The Outline of History* (1920) but for now, he was looking for a way to prompt the flag wavers at Queen Victoria's Diamond Jubilee of 1897 (the story was brazenly first serialized in the popular *Pearson's Magazine* during the celebrations), to relate to the victims of the imperial expansionist drive. Interestingly, anti-imperialism would also crop up in *The First Men in the Moon*, skilfully manifested through Bedford's prejudicial eyes as he dismissively assesses the first Selenites he meets. At the same time, Wells had been fascinated by images of dead London in literature and had explored a variety of catastrophes which might challenge British imperial hubris.

George Tomkyns Chesney's popular *The Battle of Dorking: Reminiscences of a Volunteer* (1871) begins with an ominous warning to readers to keep alert to international dangers. Feeding into anxieties about German military might, the novel was one of many invasion and disaster stories which fired the public imagination. Surveying the bucolic surroundings of Surrey, Frank mused about the possibility of aliens descending from the sky. Mars, named after the Roman god of war, had been the subject of much speculation. In 1877, Giovanni Schiaparelli observed *canali*, translated as channels or canals, the latter term suggestive of intelligent planning. Consequently, Percival Lowell's *Mars* (1895) documented the sightings at his observatory in Flagstaff, Arizona of a network of channels in the now dried out Mars. Wells had now pinpointed his method of narration and had identified a sufficiently powerful enemy desperate and intellectually powerful enough to stop at nothing in order to survive.

Life Underground

The War of the Worlds importantly owed its origins to Wells's early life. His writing was after all profoundly if not blatantly autobiographical. Wells was also fascinated by the role chance and crossroads played in his characters' lives. Bedford marvels at the 'purest accident' of meeting Cavor at Lympne, Kent in *The First Men in the Moon*, for example. In many ways, Wells's own life began at a confluence of passageways. In the early 1850s, his mother Sarah Neal was working as a lady's maid at Uppark, a seventeenth-century country house on the South Downs, when she encountered gardener and passionate cricket player, Joseph Wells. They may have walked to church or even almost collided in the property's service tunnels. A seemingly mismatched pair, Sarah was self-controlled and ardently believed in hellfire while Joe, quietly unconvinced, preferred to lie on the South Downs at night, marvelling at the majesty of space. When Sarah's parents died, she was left in debt and Joe stepped in with an offer of marriage. Sarah was permitted to cast off her black mourning garb for one hour during the ceremony.

Joe set up a shop at 47 High Street in Bromley, Kent, named Atlas House in honour of a lampstand on show in a shop window that was shaped like the Greek deity carrying the burden of the world (note the reference to Atlas near the end of *The First Men in the Moon*). Sarah's feeling of coming down in the world lay heavy on her own shoulders, too. After a career attending to ladies, she was now sweeping up coal dust and fighting off insects. She spent much of her time in the kitchen basement, where the only daylight came drifting down through a grate at street level. In fact, the subterranean kitchen and its image of class-based imprisonment became a prominent theme in Wells's work. This is particularly the case with his part-utopian, part science-fictional novel, *In the Days of the Comet* (1906), in which humanity falls under the spell of a comet's vapours and a utopian society emerges. Before the 'Change', we read many references to dark kitchens and dank sculleries but after the Earth has passed through the comet's tail, the roomier kitchens of stately homes are available to everyone.

'Geometrical Nightmares': the Narrator and the Curate

Wells was born on the afternoon of 21 September 1866. Before he could even talk, this future creator of utopias and parallel dimensions was constructing miniature worlds out of discarded eggshells and boxes that he found in his backyard. At nights he was beset with what he called 'geometrical nightmares' as if he were under attack from large kaleidoscopic images. When it came to territorial scraps with his older brothers, Frank and Freddy, Wells, who was a sickly child, turned to wit, kicking and biting. He also became aware of the brutality of life, hearing the sounds of animals awaiting slaughter over the fence next door. This morbid fascination with flesh is reflected in Bedford's detailed descriptions of the Selenites' butchering cave and his cravings for meat.

Early childhood influences also come together in *The War of the Worlds* where the narrator and the curate are stranded in a partly demolished house on the edge of a crater created by a newly fallen cylinder. The kitchen in which they are trapped becomes highly symbolic. It is decorated cheaply in the colours and accoutrements of the Aesthetic Movement. Wells did not subscribe to the idea of art for art's sake; he felt creative work ought to have social and political message. Later, the curate and the narrator are forced to move into the scullery and the grime of the coal cellar. As we often see in the novel, the Martians are indeed social levellers. The curate warns of hellfire but the narrator exercises his philosophical inquisitiveness and studies the Martians and their ways. It is not merely the curate's cries of woe which alarm the narrator but also the result of his lack of self-control: despite the narrator's attempts to ration their supplies and fight with him, the 'spoilt' curate is always begging for food.

Foods for Thought

A chance accident offered Wells a reprieve from his own insufficient childhood diet of mainly potatoes and cabbage and also launched him into the world of books. He was seven when an innkeeper's son playfully threw the slight boy in the air and missed his catch. Wells consequently fell onto a tent peg and broke his leg. The landlady took pity on him and he was given meats and desserts. During his recuperation Wells read nonfictional books about foreign lands and warfare including tales of Napoleon and the Wild West. Alongside his mother's required religious reading, he began devouring *Punch* and the works of Sir Walter Scott and did not dutifully avert his eyes from the busts of nude Greek statues that he saw at Sydenham's Crystal Palace. A photograph from around this time shows a blue-eyed boy interrupted in his reading, glancing up at the camera with a bright, impish expression on his face.

Dodging Drapery

When an injury meant that his father could no longer supplement the family income, Wells was drafted into the world of drapery as his two older brothers had been. The headstrong thirteen-year-old boy with a lust for knowledge and life hated the long hours, respectively keeping his body and brain active with fist fights and algebra under the cash desk. He felt as if he had become a 'drilled selling machine.' Wells's experiences and numerous attempts to break free from harness are reflected in his bicycling adventure and romance *The Wheels of Chance* (1896), *Kipps: The Story of a Simple Soul* (1905) and *The History of Mr Polly* (1910). Drapery and clerking were typical lower-middle-class professions and Wells's distaste for their lifestyle, bound by respectability and clock-watching, rings out bitterly through the words of the artilleryman whom the narrator of *The War of the Worlds* encounters in Dead London. The artilleryman's ravings are suggestive of the eugenic thinking that Wells was to explore in his writing – the weak and elderly in *The Days of the Comet* succumb to the poisonous vapours. Wells was by no means alone in his exploration of eugenics but there is no doubting that these passages make for uncomfortable reading.

On the death of Lady Fetherstonhaugh, her younger sister, Frances, whom Sarah had served, took over the running of Uppark House. Sarah was delighted by the opportunity to return to the estate as a housekeeper and her photograph from the time suggests a faint indulgent smile playing on her tight lips which offsets the severe appearance with her lace cap, black silk dress and brooch at her throat. Her youngest son visited her during a series of failed jobs as a draper, school teaching assistant, and trainee chemist in a shop in Midhurst – the last post inspiring his novel about a bogus medicinal wonder drink, *Tono-Bungay* (1909). Wells took evening classes at Horace Byatt's local grammar school, drawing sketches in the books of schoolmates and entertaining Uppark staff with his miniature theatre and his unofficial gazette, the *Up-Park Alarmist*. He would continue to document aspects of his life with loose, expressive doodles that he called his 'picshuas' in the years that followed, including, in 1898, a typed up manuscript page of *The War of the Worlds* with a sketch of his wife Jane in the form of a Martian tripod extending her tentacles towards a hatted, shivering stickman!

A Game of The Northwest Passage

Once again, Wells found himself pulled back into the drapery world, this time at the Southsea Drapery Emporium in Portsmouth. Now in his mid-teenage years, he was reading Darwin and asking himself 'what is space?' and 'what is matter?' Wells would gaze through the telescope at Uppark and read Plato's *Republic* and Thomas Paine's *Rights of Man* (1791) in the extensive library. He also walked the service tunnels, designed so that guests on the lawns would not see servants scuttling around. On damp days, the depressing air of these passageways with their fronds of mould around the walls would have been accentuated by the gloom but on bright, sunny days daylight and freedom would have been suggested by the ventilation shafts, full access to the sun being just out of reach. The modern visitor experience culminates in a pleasantly scented National Trust gift shop but when Wells's Time Traveller in *The Time Machine* (1895) encounters the tunnels of the year 802,701 that these passages were to inspire, he finds them full of manlike beasts in a world divided by the Eloi, the pampered descendants of the Victorian upper-classes and the Morlocks, the descendants of Victorian workers, who now both serve *and* devour their masters in the subterranean kitchens of the future.

Wells became Byatt's assistant teacher and accepted an offer to study as a teacher-in-training at the Normal School of Science (now Imperial College, part of the University of London). In 1884, an awestruck Wells entered the wrought iron gates of the institution and found himself nervously dissecting a rabbit under the gaze of 'Darwin's bulldog', T.H. Huxley. Another one of his teachers was Assistant Professor of Zoology Thomas Howes who receives a mention in *The War of the Worlds* when the narrator discusses research on Martians and their overdeveloped brains and hands. Howes also wrote the introduction to Wells's earliest published book, *Text-Book of Biology* (1893).

In Wells's short story, 'The Door in the Wall' (1906), cabinet minister Lionel Wallace spends his life searching West London for a green door against a white wall which hides a magical garden with playmates and panthers. On one occasion he glimpses the door during a game of The Northwest Passage in which the players have to find an alternative route to school. The purpose of the game was to become entangled in a maze of streets and reach the end goal just in time. Despite various setbacks and stumbles into the cul-de-sac of shopkeeping and drapery, Wells had finally made his circuitous way to university and, as it seemed, to the career of his dreams.

Wells's First Marriage: Isabel

The young student was easily distracted, however. He was drawn towards history, literature and socialism, inspired by lectures at William Morris's home in Hammersmith. Wells also began courting his cousin, Isabel Wells, a draper's daughter. Disliking the humdrum manual work of constructing apparatuses, he did not complete his degree and took up employment at Holt Academy, a private school in Wales. Wells returned to Uppark to convalesce after his kidney was crushed during a game of rugby, an incident that would permanently affect his health. A newfound sense of the fragility of his existence would serve to accelerate his writing and compel him to make some changes in his life.

In 1891 he was finally awarded his University of London B.Sc. with a First Class Honours in Zoology and Second in Geology. Wells and Isabel married. Although he would remain attracted to his wife – he even later sent a copy of *The War of the Worlds* to an impressed Isabel – Wells soon gravitated towards one of his science students, Amy Catherine Robbins. Divorce was on the cards. At the time a husband who applied for a divorce only needed to prove his wife's infidelity but a wife was required to show evidence of not only adultery but also desertion or cruelty or bigamy. Isabel's overly careful wording of the letter to Wells duly supplied in her affidavit suggests that the pair colluded to obtain the divorce, which was by no means unusual. The divorce granted, Wells began living with Amy, whom he called 'Jane', resisting the social pressure to marry.

Wells's Second Marriage: Duty versus Desire

Wells expresses his feelings about the tension between society's values and private desires in 'A Dream of Armageddon' which first appeared in the Boer War magazine, the *Black and White Budget*, from May to June in 1901 and was subsequently featured in *Twelve Stories and a Dream* (1903). The story is written in the first person, a technique Wells uses in *The War of the Worlds* and *The First Men in the Moon*. The effect creates immediacy and a confessional intimacy with the reader but, as Wells also wraps another narrative within the overall one, it invites us to question the narrator's perceptions. For instance, when Cavor's descriptions of events on the moon come to light, we start to wonder who is telling the truth. Wells likes to sustain the question in the reader's mind and he frequently accentuates this narrative confusion through the format of the dream.

'A Dream of Armageddon' takes place in a train compartment. Near the beginning of *The War of the Worlds*, Wells uses the shunting trains and the light signals to indicate normality and respectable routine. But trains were themselves considered to be liminal social spaces whose tight corridors and closed off compartments witnessed

assignations and crimes from thefts to murders. When a distracted and
wan solicitor from Liverpool named Cooper enters the compartment,
he brings with him forbidden love, world war and death. As the train
leaves Rugby and picks up speed so does the pace of the narrative.

Lover Shadows

In this closed space, we are party to a racy confession. Cooper, a married
man, has been having an affair. So, too, would Wells, throughout his
married life with Jane, with whom he had two sons. For Wells, sexual
satisfaction was key to his ability to write. While Jane managed his
home, family and manuscripts (her involvement in his work meant that
she did not finish her science degree) he embarked on a lifelong quest to
find what he termed his 'lover shadow.' Recent scholarship suggests that
rather than seeing her as a victim, a long suffering typist, Jane played a
significant part in the creative process. Her own fiction was published
early on in their marriage. After her death, Wells edited *The Book of
Catherine Wells* (1928). Within, her story 'The Dragon-Fly' with its quiet,
accidental tragedy matches the reveries of Katherine Mansfield.

Wells's many lovers included the authors Elizabeth von Arnim and
Rebecca West, as well as the spy Moura Budberg and Amber Reeves,
a young economics and politics student who later co-wrote *The Work,
Wealth and Happiness of Mankind* (1932) with Wells. His espousal of
free love was reflected in his work. In 'A Dream of Armageddon',
however, the infidelity is masked in the format of Cooper's recurring
dream. Cooper's revelation that 'my soul had beaten against the thing
forgiven'[1] is highly suggestive of Wells's mindset. But in the dream
Cooper's name changes to Hedon, a powerful political figure who

1. H.G. Wells, 'A Dream of Armageddon', *Twelve Stories
and a Dream* (Macmillan and Co., 1903) page 339.

has no memory of the nineteenth-century Cooper while Cooper's recollections are patchy in parts, too. This convenient breaking of the link of memory allows Cooper to travel almost guilt-free through the mental landscape of his desires. Significantly, Hedon's beloved is not referred to as his wife but as 'the girl' and 'that dear lady of mine.' The Northerners whom he feels compelled to protect from the tyrannical Evesham would disapprove and so he abandons them and offers himself up to love and passion.

PART 2: OF STRANGE LANDS

The War of the Worlds and *The First Men in the Moon* feature distinctive unearthly landscapes. Wells wrote *The War of Worlds* whilst living in Woking, Surrey, scoping out possible sites on his bicycle for Martian destruction. Today Woking proudly salutes Wells's efforts in choosing Horsell Common's distinctive sandy heathland and putting the town on the map with many tributes including Michael Condron's tripod which looms over shoppers in the town centre, a heritage trail, and Wesley W. Harland's statue of the young Wells holding a globe or Cavorite-like sphere up to the light.

Wells's tale of Martian destruction has lent itself well to local adaptations; red weed and heat rays are capable of covering surfaces the world over. Most famously, Orson Welles relocated the action to Grover's Mill and Princeton, New Jersey for his Halloween radio theatre play of 1938 which allegedly caught unawares those listeners who missed his address stating that this fake broadcast was a 'holiday offering.' Hot on the heels of the serialization of *The War of the Worlds* in *Cosmopolitan* magazine in 1897 came American versions of the story in the *New York Evening Journal* and the *Boston Post*. Film adaptations by George Pal and Steven Spielberg followed suit in 1953 and 2005.

There have been many interpretations of the story in multimedia formats chiming with the concerns of the day from Cold War tensions to the threat of terrorism but those that most notably bring the location back to turn-of-the-century London and the Home Counties are Jeff Wayne's version and the BBC's 2019 adaptation which sets the action in the early twentieth century and incorporates elements of Wells's personal life into the story of lovers George and Amy.

Wells uses the land and cityscape to convey a sense of invasion and the red weed indicates the Martians' colonization of Earth in strong visual terms. The contrast between the known and the lurid unearthly is brilliantly evoked in Geoff Taylor's album artwork for Jeff Wayne's *The War of the Worlds*. The aerial destruction predicted by Wells which was manifest during World War II provided an uncanny inspiration in the network of adaptations of his novel. It is little known that Taylor used a photograph taken by PC Fred Tibbs of the fall of the frontage of 23 Queen Victoria Street, City of London in 1941 during the London Blitz, five years before Wells's death. Taylor incorporated fleeing Victorian Londoners into the image and a Martian looms down from the top-right-hand corner[2]. This is history twisting back on itself through art.

'The Landscape of a Dream'

Wells set the Earth scenes in *The First Men in the Moon* on the dramatic area around coastal Lympne and Littlestone-on-Sea on the Romney Marshes, historically referred to as the Fifth Continent. A rather more otherworldly landscape was presented to readers of the *Strand Magazine* when the story was first serialized from 1900 to 1901, with exclusive photographs of the Moon inviting them to

---

2. www.ploddinthesquaremile.co.uk/people/fred-tibbs

challenge François Deloncle's comment that there is no life on the planet and instead imagine its blue depths, mountainous terrain and the erratic, lush growths it normally hides from the human eye.

The public fascination with the Swiss Alps, which Wells later explored with Jane, comes through frequently in the *First Men in the Moon*. The Alps clearly made a deep impression on the author to the extent that when we first glimpse his utopia in *A Modern Utopia*, we find ourselves in Switzerland. Bedford and Cavor marvel at the ease of lunar mountaineering but it comes with its challenges. Had he perused the *Alpine Journal* in the 1890s, Wells would have seen the latest advice on altitude sickness, which was still imperfectly understood. Wells's constitution struggled with the rarefied air and the rigour of intense walking and while Jane took their sons on walking holidays, he would write to her from the olive groves of Italy.

The Ruins of Utopia

Bedford narrates the story of his visit to the moon from his home in Southern Italy which is where Wells sets 'A Dream of Armageddon.' Wells and Jane visited the ruins at Paestum in 1898 and Wells was stirred into thought by the temple's still solemnity. The Wellses spent time with George Gissing in Rome, dining with Arthur Conan Doyle and E.W. Hornung, but their trip to Naples and Florence was backgrounded by bread riots and campaigns against Italy's deadly imperialistic drive. These experiences and impressions filtered through to his work.

Wells took great pains over the story which he wrote while he was living right at the water's edge at Beach Cottage in Sandgate, Kent. He tried out a number of titles, including 'A Vision of War to Come', 'The Battle of Armageddon' and 'Armageddon: A Story of the Days to Come.' Early drafts of the story made references to the 'legend' of the sleeper, closely linking it to Wells's social science fiction novel *When the Sleeper Wakes* of 1899 (later revised in 1910 as *The Sleeper Awakes*). In that tale, Graham, a Victorian radical, regains consciousness after two hundred years in a coma. He awakens to find that he rules half the world, and is later pitted against his political foe, Ostrog, in battle. George Orwell, Aldous Huxley and Ray Bradbury were among a number of writers inspired by the story.

Hedon's future world in 'A Dream of Armageddon' bears some resemblance to William Morris's utopian Nowhere in that the people who take their meals together wear flowing gowns – Wells hated restrictive Victorian clothes and boots. But this Pleasure City is visually different to Nowhere with its technology in the form of travelators and LED lighting. Hedon finds happiness in this place where war is unknown and these qualities might classify the settlement on Capri as a utopia. For Wells, who was now entering his utopian phase of writing, utopias should not be static but kinetic and subject to transformation. The influx of tourists to Capri brings new blood yet the island's overdevelopment and overly free connection with the world renders the stunning island unstable. As he wrote in *A Modern Utopia* (1905): 'I forget that a Utopia is a thing of the imagination that becomes more fragile with every added circumstance, that, like a soap-bubble, it is most brilliantly and variously coloured at the very instant of its dissolution.'[3] The bubble bursts when the planes no longer bring tourists but war and destruction the world over.

'This Alien Life'

In the narrator's description of the Martians in *The War of the Worlds*, Wells's lively essay, 'The Man of the Year Million' (1893), makes a

---

3. H.G. Wells, *A Modern Utopia* (Penguin, 2005), page 234.

cameo appearance. While Darwin looked back to mankind's origins, Wells posited that it was more important to consider where we are going. Technological advances and creature comforts will render some of our physical features obsolete, he writes. The dispassionate intellect of the Grand Lunar and the Martians have resulted in over-developed brains and consequently, large heads. Like humans one million years from now, the Martians move around on their giant 'hands' and instead of eating, they absorb liquids, which in the Martians' case is through intravenous methods. Bedford and indeed the reader may well express distaste towards these 'men of leather', sadness at the Selenite mothers' inability to love their offspring who are physically and psychologically shaped to perform various tasks required by the state (a passage which screams out Aldous Huxley's *Brave New World*), not to mention shock learning of the Martian's intravenous consumption of human blood. The novels warn that unless we monitor our relationship to science and technology, social arrangements which we consider monstrous may become part of our everyday life. The Martian technology that has been left behind has taught humans the 'Secret of Flying' thus bringing them a step closer to the Martians with their cool intellects which in turn threatens the international understanding that humans have developed since the Martian invasion.

As 'A Dream of Armageddon' shows, when it comes to technology and political power, we must tread carefully. And while Selenite society has its faults, the Grand Lunar is puzzled by mankind's lack of cooperation which is matched by the despair that Cavor feels about the impact of the knowledge of his trip to the moon will have given the havoc that humans have already wrought on their own planet Earth. Here, Wells points us towards the Martians invaders and invites us to draw parallels with them and us.

Six years before his death at Hanover Terrace, Regent's Park, Wells set out his ideas on human rights in *The Rights of Man, Or, What Are We Fighting For?*, which spurred on the campaign for the United Nations Universal Declaration of Human Rights. At this time, too, Winston Churchill, who greatly admired Wells's work, was testing out his thoughts on space. His early unpublished manuscript, 'Are We Alone in Space?' (1939) appeared in shortened form in 1942 titled 'Are There Men in the Moon?'. The original was revised in the decade in which George Pal's *The War of the Worlds* appeared. In his essays, Churchill expressed his belief in aliens on other planets, provided we are flexible in our definitions on what constitutes 'life.' And now, at the time of writing, the Perseverance Rover is on its way to Mars from where a quiet kind of pulsing alien music seems to emanate, like, as Bedford would say, the whisperings of a record needle.

Dr. Emelyne Godfrey

Emelyne Godfrey, PhD, is Chairperson of the H.G. Wells Society. She is author of *Femininity, Crime and Self-Defence in Victorian Literature and Society* (2012) and *Masculinity, Crime and Self-Defence in Victorian Literature* (2010). In 2014 she edited *The Convert*, the first suffragette novel, originally published in 1907. Most recently, she was editor of *Utopias and Dystopias in the Fiction of H.G. Wells and William Morris* (2016).

FURTHER READING

Beck, Peter J., *The War of the Worlds: From H.G. Wells to Orson Welles, Jeff Wayne, Steven Spielberg & Beyond* (Bloomsbury, 2016)

Cole, Sarah, *Inventing Tomorrow: H.G. Wells and the Twentieth Century* (Columbia University Press, 2019)

Deloncle, François, 'The First Moon-Photographs Taken with the Great Paris Telescope', *Strand Magazine*, 1900, volume 119, pages 493–497

Godfrey, Emelyne (ed.), *Utopias and Dystopias in the Fiction of H.G. Wells and William Morris* (Palgrave, 2016)

Hammond, John R., *H.G. Wells and the Short Story* (Palgrave MacMillan, 1992)

James, Simon J., *Maps of Utopia: H.G. Wells, Modernity, & the End of Culture* (Oxford University Press, 2012)

Parrinder, Patrick, 'Wells, Herbert George', *Oxford Dictionary of National Biography* (available online at www.oxforddnb.com)

Riley, Timothy, 'Universal Appeal: Churchill's Essay about Extraterrestrial Life', *Finest Hour: The Journal of Winston Churchill and his Times*, 176 (Spring 2017), pages 40–41

Sherborne, Michael, *H.G. Wells: Another Kind of Life* (Peter Owen, 2010)

Smith, David C., *The Journalism of H.G. Wells: An Annotated Bibliography* (Equilibris, 2012)

Wei-Haas, Maya, 'Mars is Humming. Scientists Aren't Sure Why', *National Geographic*, 24 February 2020

Wells, H.G., 'A Dream of Armageddon', *Twelve Stories and a Dream* (Macmillan and Co., 1903), pages 331–377

Wells, H.G., 'An Experiment in Illustration', *Strand Magazine*, Vol. 59, No. 350 (February 1920), page 154

Wells, H.G., *The First Men in the Moon* (Penguin, 2005)

Wells, H.G., 'The Holiday of a Draper's Assistant: Life in a Margin', *Pall Mall Gazette*, 5 June 1894, page 3

Wells, H.G., 'The Man of the Year Million: A Scientific Forecast', *Pall Mall Gazette*, Vol. 57 (6 November 1893), page 3

Wells, H.G., *A Modern Utopia* (Penguin, 2005)

Wells, H.G., 'Wanted – Professors of Foresight!', *The Listener*, 23 November 1932, pages 729–730

Wells, H.G., *The War of the Worlds* (shortened version), *Strand Magazine*, Vol. 59, No. 350 (February 1920), pages 155–63

The Martian theme also appears in the following stories by Wells, 'The Crystal Egg', (1897), 'The Star', (1897) and the novel, *Star-Begotten: A Biological Fantasia* (1937)

OTHER MEDIA

Wells's novel was lovingly adapted by Mark Gatiss, with a nod to Georges Méliès and Neil Armstrong, in *The First Men in the Moon* (BBC Four, 2010).

I particularly recommend the evocative readings of *The First Men in the Moon* and *The War of the Worlds* by Alexander Vlahos and David Tennant in *H.G. Wells: The Science Fiction Collection* (Audible, 2019).

Michael Sheen, who played Wells in the BBC drama, *H.G. Wells: War with the World* (2006) sounds uncannily like Richard Burton in Jeff Wayne's *The War of the Worlds: The Musical Drama, An Audible Original Drama* (2018).

H.G. WELLS
THE WAR OF THE WORLDS

BOOK ONE
THE COMING OF
THE MARTIANS

CHAPTER 1

The Eve of the War

No one would have believed in the last years of the nineteenth century that this world was being watched keenly and closely by intelligences greater than man's and yet as mortal as his own; that as men busied themselves about their various concerns they were scrutinised and studied, perhaps almost as narrowly as a man with a microscope might scrutinise the transient creatures that swarm and multiply in a drop of water. With infinite complacency men went to and fro over this globe about their little affairs, serene in their assurance of their empire over matter. It is possible that the infusoria under the microscope do the same. No one gave a thought to the older worlds of space as sources of human danger, or thought of them only to dismiss the idea of life upon them as impossible or improbable. It is curious to recall some of the mental habits of those departed days. At most terrestrial men fancied there might be other men upon Mars, perhaps inferior to themselves and ready to welcome a missionary enterprise. Yet across the gulf of space, minds that are to our minds as ours are to those of the beasts that perish, intellects vast and cool and unsympathetic, regarded this earth with envious eyes, and slowly and surely drew their plans against us. And early in the twentieth century came the great disillusionment.

The planet Mars, I scarcely need remind the reader, revolves about the sun at a mean distance of 140,000,000 miles, and the light and heat it receives from the sun is barely half of that received by this world. It must be, if the nebular hypothesis has any truth, older than our world; and long before this earth ceased to be molten, life upon its surface must have begun its course. The fact that it is scarcely one seventh of the volume of the earth must have accelerated its cooling to the temperature at which life could begin. It has air and water and all that is necessary for the support of animated existence.

Yet so vain is man, and so blinded by his vanity, that no writer, up to the very end of the nineteenth century, expressed any idea that intelligent life might have developed there far, or indeed at all, beyond its earthly level. Nor was it generally understood that since Mars is older than our earth, with scarcely a quarter of the superficial area and remoter from the sun, it necessarily follows that it is not only more distant from time's beginning but nearer its end.

The secular cooling that must someday overtake our planet has already gone far indeed with our neighbour. Its physical condition is still largely a mystery, but we know now that even in its equatorial region the midday temperature barely approaches that of our coldest winter. Its air is much more attenuated than ours, its oceans have shrunk until they cover but a third of its surface, and as its slow seasons change huge snowcaps gather and melt about either pole and periodically inundate its temperate zones. That last stage of exhaustion, which to us is still incredibly remote, has become a present-day problem for the inhabitants of Mars. The immediate pressure of necessity has brightened their intellects, enlarged their powers, and hardened their hearts. And looking across space with instruments, and intelligences such as we have scarcely dreamed of, they see, at its nearest distance only 35,000,000 of miles sunward of them, a morning star of hope, our own warmer planet, green with vegetation and grey with water, with a cloudy atmosphere eloquent of fertility, with glimpses through its drifting cloud wisps of broad stretches of populous country and narrow, navy-crowded seas.

And we men, the creatures who inhabit this earth, must be to them at least as alien and lowly as are the monkeys and lemurs to us. The intellectual side of man already admits that life is an incessant struggle for existence, and it would seem that this too is the belief of the minds upon Mars. Their world is far gone in its cooling and this world is still crowded with life, but crowded only with what they regard as inferior animals. To carry warfare sunward is, indeed, their only escape from the destruction that, generation after generation, creeps upon them.

And before we judge of them too harshly we must remember what ruthless and utter destruction our own species has wrought, not only upon animals, such as the vanished bison and the dodo, but upon its inferior races. The Tasmanians, in spite of their human likeness, were entirely swept out of existence in a war of extermination waged by European immigrants, in the space of fifty years. Are we such apostles of mercy as to complain if the Martians warred in the same spirit?

The Martians seem to have calculated their descent with amazing subtlety – their mathematical learning is evidently far in excess of ours – and to have carried out their preparations with a well-nigh perfect unanimity. Had our instruments permitted it, we might have seen the gathering trouble far back in the nineteenth century. Men like Schiaparelli watched the red planet – it is odd, by-the-bye, that for countless centuries Mars has been the star of war – but failed to interpret the fluctuating appearances of the markings they mapped so well. All that time the Martians must have been getting ready.

During the opposition of 1894 a great light was seen on the illuminated part of the disk, first at the Lick Observatory, then by Perrotin of Nice, and then by other observers. English readers heard of it first in the issue of *Nature* dated August 2. I am inclined to think that this blaze may have been the casting of the huge gun, in the vast pit sunk into their planet, from which their shots were fired at us. Peculiar markings, as yet unexplained, were seen near the site of that outbreak during the next two oppositions.

The storm burst upon us six years ago now. As Mars approached opposition, Lavelle of Java set the wires of the astronomical exchange palpitating with the amazing intelligence of a huge outbreak of incandescent gas upon the planet. It had occurred towards midnight of the twelfth; and the spectroscope, to which he had at once resorted, indicated a mass of flaming gas, chiefly hydrogen, moving with an enormous velocity towards this earth. This jet of fire had become invisible about a quarter past twelve. He compared it to a colossal puff of flame suddenly and violently squirted out of the planet, "as flaming gases rushed out of a gun."

A singularly appropriate phrase it proved. Yet the next day there was nothing of this in the papers except a little note in the *Daily Telegraph*, and the world went in ignorance of one of the gravest dangers that ever threatened the human race. I might not have heard of the eruption at all had I not met Ogilvy, the well-known astronomer, at Ottershaw. He was immensely excited at the news, and in the excess of his feelings invited me up to take a turn with him that night in a scrutiny of the red planet.

In spite of all that has happened since, I still remember that vigil very distinctly: the black and silent observatory, the shadowed lantern throwing a feeble glow upon the floor in the corner, the steady ticking of the clockwork of the telescope, the little slit in the roof – an oblong profundity with the stardust streaked across it. Ogilvy moved about, invisible but audible. Looking through the telescope, one saw a circle of deep blue and the little round planet swimming in the field. It seemed such a little thing, so bright and small and still, faintly marked with transverse stripes, and slightly flattened from the perfect round. But so little it was, so silvery warm – a pin's-head of light! It was as if it quivered, but really this was the telescope vibrating with the activity of the clockwork that kept the planet in view.

As I watched, the planet seemed to grow larger and smaller and to advance and recede, but that was simply that my eye was tired. Forty millions of miles it was from us – more than forty millions of miles of void. Few people realise the immensity of vacancy in which the dust of the material universe swims.

Near it in the field, I remember, were three faint points of light, three telescopic stars infinitely remote, and all around it was the unfathomable darkness of empty space. You know how that blackness looks on a frosty starlight night. In a telescope it seems far profounder. And invisible to me because it was so remote and small, flying swiftly and steadily towards me across that incredible distance, drawing nearer every minute by so many thousands of miles, came the Thing they were sending us, the Thing that was to bring so much struggle and calamity and death to the earth. I never dreamed of it then as I watched; no one on earth dreamed of that unerring missile.

That night, too, there was another jetting out of gas from the distant planet. I saw it. A reddish flash at the edge, the slightest projection of the outline just as the chronometer struck midnight; and at that I told Ogilvy and he took my place. The night was warm and I was thirsty, and I went stretching my legs clumsily and feeling my way in the darkness, to the little table where the siphon stood, while Ogilvy exclaimed at the streamer of gas that came out towards us.

That night another invisible missile started on its way to the earth from Mars, just a second or so under twenty-four hours after the first one. I remember how I sat on the table there in the blackness, with patches of green and crimson swimming before my eyes. I wished I had a light to smoke by, little suspecting the meaning of the minute gleam I had seen and all that it would presently bring me. Ogilvy watched till one, and then gave it up; and we lit the lantern and walked over to his house. Down below in the darkness were Ottershaw and Chertsey and all their hundreds of people, sleeping in peace.

He was full of speculation that night about the condition of Mars, and scoffed at the vulgar idea of its having inhabitants who were signalling us. His idea was that meteorites might be falling in a heavy shower upon the planet, or that a huge volcanic explosion was in progress. He pointed out to me how unlikely it was that organic evolution had taken the same direction in the two adjacent planets.

"The chances against anything manlike on Mars are a million to one," he said.

Hundreds of observers saw the flame that night and the night after about midnight, and again the night after; and so for ten nights, a flame each night. Why the shots ceased after the tenth no one on earth has attempted to explain. It may be the gases of the firing caused the Martians inconvenience. Dense clouds of smoke or dust, visible through a powerful telescope on earth as little grey, fluctuating patches, spread through the clearness of the planet's atmosphere and obscured its more familiar features.

Even the daily papers woke up to the disturbances at last, and popular notes appeared here, there, and everywhere concerning the volcanoes upon Mars. The seriocomic periodical *Punch*, I remember, made a happy use of it in the political cartoon. And, all unsuspected, those missiles the Martians had fired at us drew earthward, rushing now at a pace of many miles a second through the empty gulf of space, hour by hour and day by day, nearer and nearer. It seems to me now almost incredibly wonderful that, with that swift fate hanging over us, men could go about their petty concerns as they did. I remember how jubilant Markham was at securing a new photograph of the planet for the illustrated paper he edited in those days. People in these latter times scarcely realise the abundance and enterprise of our nineteenth-century papers. For my own part, I was much occupied in learning to ride the bicycle, and busy upon a series of papers discussing the probable developments of moral ideas as civilisation progressed.

One night (the first missile then could scarcely have been 10,000,000 miles away) I went for a walk with my wife. It was starlight and I explained the Signs of the Zodiac to her, and pointed out Mars, a bright dot of light creeping zenithward, towards which so many telescopes were pointed. It was a warm night. Coming home, a party of excursionists from Chertsey or Isleworth passed us singing and playing music. There were lights in the upper windows of the houses as the people went to bed. From the railway station in the distance came the sound of shunting trains, ringing and rumbling, softened almost into melody by the distance. My wife pointed out to me the brightness of the red, green, and yellow signal lights hanging in a framework against the sky. It seemed so safe and tranquil.

CHAPTER 2

The Falling Star

Then came the night of the first falling star. It was seen early in the morning, rushing over Winchester eastward, a line of flame high in the atmosphere. Hundreds must have seen it, and taken it for an ordinary falling star. Albin described it as leaving a greenish streak behind it that glowed for some seconds. Denning, our greatest authority on meteorites, stated that the height of its first appearance was about ninety or one hundred miles. It seemed to him that it fell to earth about one hundred miles east of him.

I was at home at that hour and writing in my study; and although my French windows face towards Ottershaw and the blind was up (for I loved in those days to look up at the night sky), I saw nothing of it. Yet this strangest of all things that ever came to earth from outer space must have fallen while I was sitting there, visible to me had I only looked up as it passed. Some of those who saw its flight say it travelled with a hissing sound. I myself heard nothing of that. Many people in Berkshire, Surrey, and Middlesex must have seen the fall of it, and, at most, have thought that another meteorite had descended. No one seems to have troubled to look for the fallen mass that night.

But very early in the morning poor Ogilvy, who had seen the shooting star and who was persuaded that a meteorite lay somewhere on the common between Horsell, Ottershaw, and Woking, rose early with the idea of finding it. Find it he did, soon after dawn, and not far from the sand pits. An enormous hole had been made by the impact of the projectile, and the sand and gravel had been flung violently in every direction over the heath, forming heaps visible a mile and a half away. The heather was on fire eastward, and a thin blue smoke rose against the dawn.

The Thing itself lay almost entirely buried in sand, amidst the scattered splinters of a fir tree it had shivered to fragments in its descent. The uncovered part had the appearance of a huge cylinder, caked over and its outline softened by a thick scaly dun-coloured incrustation. It had a diameter of about thirty yards. He approached the mass, surprised at the size and more so at the shape, since most meteorites are rounded more or less completely. It was, however, still so hot from its flight through the air as to forbid his near approach. A stirring noise within its cylinder he ascribed to the unequal cooling of its surface; for at that time it had not occurred to him that it might be hollow.

He remained standing at the edge of the pit that the Thing had made for itself, staring at its strange appearance, astonished chiefly at its unusual shape and colour, and dimly perceiving even then some evidence of design in its arrival. The early morning was wonderfully still, and the sun, just clearing the pine trees towards Weybridge, was already warm. He did not remember hearing any birds that morning, there was certainly no breeze stirring, and the only sounds were the faint movements from within the cindery cylinder. He was all alone on the common.

Then suddenly he noticed with a start that some of the grey clinker, the ashy incrustation that covered the meteorite, was falling off the circular edge of the end. It was dropping off in flakes and raining down upon the sand. A large piece suddenly came off and fell with a sharp noise that brought his heart into his mouth.

For a minute he scarcely realised what this meant, and, although the heat was excessive, he clambered down into the pit close to the bulk to see the Thing more clearly. He fancied even then that the cooling of the body might account for this, but what disturbed that idea was the fact that the ash was falling only from the end of the cylinder.

And then he perceived that, very slowly, the circular top of the cylinder was rotating on its body. It was such a gradual movement that he discovered it only through noticing that a black mark that had been near him five minutes ago was now at the other side of the circumference. Even then he scarcely understood what this indicated, until he heard a muffled grating sound and saw the black mark jerk forward an inch or so. Then the thing came upon him in a flash. The cylinder was artificial – hollow – with an end that screwed out! Something within the cylinder was unscrewing the top!

"Good heavens!" said Ogilvy. "There's a man in it – men in it! Half roasted to death! Trying to escape!"

At once, with a quick mental leap, he linked the Thing with the flash upon Mars.

The thought of the confined creature was so dreadful to him that he forgot the heat and went forward to the cylinder to help turn. But luckily the dull radiation arrested him before he could burn his hands on the still-glowing metal. At that he stood irresolute for a moment, then turned, scrambled out of the pit, and set off running wildly into Woking. The time then must have been somewhere about six o'clock. He met a waggoner and tried to make him understand, but the tale he told and his appearance were so wild – his hat had fallen off in the pit – that the man simply drove on. He was equally unsuccessful with the potman who was just unlocking the doors of the public-house by Horsell Bridge. The fellow thought

he was a lunatic at large and made an unsuccessful attempt to shut
him into the taproom. That sobered him a little; and when he saw
Henderson, the London journalist, in his garden, he called over the
palings and made himself understood.

"Henderson," he called, "you saw that shooting star last night?"

"Well?" said Henderson.

"It's out on Horsell Common now."

"Good Lord!" said Henderson. "Fallen meteorite! That's good."

"But it's something more than a meteorite. It's a cylinder – an
artificial cylinder, man! And there's something inside."

Henderson stood up with his spade in his hand.

"What's that?" he said. He was deaf in one ear.

Ogilvy told him all that he had seen. Henderson was a minute or
so taking it in. Then he dropped his spade, snatched up his jacket,
and came out into the road. The two men hurried back at once to the
common, and found the cylinder still lying in the same position. But
now the sounds inside had ceased, and a thin circle of bright metal
showed between the top and the body of the cylinder. Air was either
entering or escaping at the rim with a thin, sizzling sound.

They listened, rapped on the scaly burnt metal with a stick, and,
meeting with no response, they both concluded the man or men
inside must be insensible or dead.

Of course the two were quite unable to do anything. They shouted
consolation and promises, and went off back to the town again to
get help. One can imagine them, covered with sand, excited and
disordered, running up the little street in the bright sunlight just as the
shop folks were taking down their shutters and people were opening
their bedroom windows. Henderson went into the railway station
at once, in order to telegraph the news to London. The newspaper
articles had prepared men's minds for the reception of the idea.

By eight o'clock a number of boys and unemployed men had already started for the common to see the "dead men from Mars." That was the form the story took. I heard of it first from my newspaper boy about a quarter to nine when I went out to get my *Daily Chronicle*. I was naturally startled, and lost no time in going out and across the Ottershaw bridge to the sand pits.

CHAPTER 3

On Horsell Common

I found a little crowd of perhaps twenty people surrounding the huge hole in which the cylinder lay. I have already described the appearance of that colossal bulk, embedded in the ground. The turf and gravel about it seemed charred as if by a sudden explosion. No doubt its impact had caused a flash of fire. Henderson and Ogilvy were not there. I think they perceived that nothing was to be done for the present, and had gone away to breakfast at Henderson's house.

There were four or five boys sitting on the edge of the Pit, with their feet dangling, and amusing themselves – until I stopped them – by throwing stones at the giant mass. After I had spoken to them about it, they began playing at "touch" in and out of the group of bystanders.

Among these were a couple of cyclists, a jobbing gardener I employed sometimes, a girl carrying a baby, Gregg the butcher and his little boy, and two or three loafers and golf caddies who were accustomed to hang about the railway station. There was very little talking. Few of the common people in England had anything but the vaguest astronomical ideas in those days. Most of them were staring quietly at the big table like end of the cylinder, which was still as Ogilvy and Henderson had left it. I fancy the popular expectation of a heap of charred corpses was disappointed at this inanimate bulk. Some went away while I was there, and other people came. I clambered into the pit and fancied I heard a faint movement under my feet. The top had certainly ceased to rotate.

It was only when I got thus close to it that the strangeness of this object was at all evident to me. At the first glance it was really no more exciting than an overturned carriage or a tree blown across the road. Not so much so, indeed. It looked like a rusty gas float. It required a certain amount of scientific education to perceive that the grey scale of the Thing was no common oxide, that the yellowish-white metal that gleamed in the crack between the lid and the cylinder had an unfamiliar hue. "Extra-terrestrial" had no meaning for most of the onlookers.

At that time it was quite clear in my own mind that the Thing had come from the planet Mars, but I judged it improbable that it contained any living creature. I thought the unscrewing might be automatic. In spite of Ogilvy, I still believed that there were men in Mars. My mind ran fancifully on the possibilities of its containing manuscript, on the difficulties in translation that might arise, whether we should find coins and models in it, and so forth. Yet it was a little too large for assurance on this idea. I felt an impatience to see it opened. About eleven, as nothing seemed happening, I walked back, full of such thought, to my home in Maybury. But I found it difficult to get to work upon my abstract investigations.

In the afternoon the appearance of the common had altered very much. The early editions of the evening papers had startled London with enormous headlines:

A MESSAGE RECEIVED FROM MARS.
REMARKABLE STORY FROM WOKING,

...and so forth. In addition, Ogilvy's wire to the Astronomical Exchange had roused every observatory in the three kingdoms.

There were half a dozen flies or more from the Woking station standing in the road by the sand pits, a basket-chaise from Chobham, and a rather lordly carriage. Besides that, there was quite a heap of bicycles. In addition, a large number of people must have walked, in spite of the heat of the day, from Woking and Chertsey, so that there was altogether quite a considerable crowd – one or two gaily dressed ladies among the others.

It was glaringly hot, not a cloud in the sky nor a breath of wind, and the only shadow was that of the few scattered pine trees. The burning heather had been extinguished, but the level ground towards Ottershaw was blackened as far as one could see, and still giving off vertical streamers of smoke. An enterprising sweet-stuff dealer in the Chobham Road had sent up his son with a barrow-load of green apples and ginger beer.

Going to the edge of the pit, I found it occupied by a group of about half a dozen men – Henderson, Ogilvy, and a tall, fair-haired man that I afterwards learned was Stent, the Astronomer Royal, with several workmen wielding spades and pickaxes. Stent was giving directions in a clear, high-pitched voice. He was standing on the cylinder, which was now evidently much cooler; his face was crimson and streaming with perspiration, and something seemed to have irritated him.

A large portion of the cylinder had been uncovered, though its lower end was still embedded. As soon as Ogilvy saw me among the staring crowd on the edge of the pit he called to me to come down, and asked me if I would mind going over to see Lord Hilton, the lord of the manor.

The growing crowd, he said, was becoming a serious impediment to their excavations, especially the boys. They wanted a light railing put up, and help to keep the people back. He told me that a faint stirring was occasionally still audible within the case, but that the workmen had failed to unscrew the top, as it afforded no grip to them. The case appeared to be enormously thick, and it was possible that the faint sounds we heard represented a noisy tumult in the interior.

I was very glad to do as he asked, and so become one of the privileged spectators within the contemplated enclosure. I failed to find Lord Hilton at his house, but I was told he was expected from London by the six o'clock train from Waterloo; and as it was then about a quarter past five, I went home, had some tea, and walked up to the station to waylay him.

CHAPTER 4

The Cylinder Opens

When I returned to the common the sun was setting. Scattered groups were hurrying from the direction of Woking, and one or two persons were returning. The crowd about the pit had increased, and stood out black against the lemon yellow of the sky – a couple of hundred people, perhaps. There were raised voices, and some sort of struggle appeared to be going on about the pit. Strange imaginings passed through my mind. As I drew nearer I heard Stent's voice:

"Keep back! Keep back!"

A boy came running towards me.

"It's a-movin'," he said to me as he passed; "a-screwin' and a-screwin' out. I don't like it. I'm a-goin' 'ome, I am."

I went on to the crowd. There were really, I should think, two or three hundred people elbowing and jostling one another, the one or two ladies there being by no means the least active.

"He's fallen in the pit!" cried some one.

"Keep back!" said several.

The crowd swayed a little, and I elbowed my way through. Every one seemed greatly excited. I heard a peculiar humming sound from the pit.

"I say!" said Ogilvy; "help keep these idiots back. We don't know what's in the confounded thing, you know!"

I saw a young man, a shop assistant in Woking I believe he was, standing on the cylinder and trying to scramble out of the hole again. The crowd had pushed him in.

The end of the cylinder was being screwed out from within. Nearly two feet of shining screw projected. Somebody blundered against me, and I narrowly missed being pitched onto the top of the screw. I turned, and as I did so the screw must have come out, for the lid of the cylinder fell upon the gravel with a ringing concussion. I stuck my elbow into the person behind me, and turned my head towards the Thing again. For a moment that circular cavity seemed perfectly black. I had the sunset in my eyes.

I think everyone expected to see a man emerge – possibly something a little unlike us terrestrial men, but in all essentials a man. I know I did. But, looking, I presently saw something stirring within the shadow: greyish billowy movements, one above another, and then two luminous disks – like eyes. Then something resembling a little grey snake, about the thickness of a walking stick, coiled up out of the writhing middle, and wriggled in the air towards me – and then another.

A sudden chill came over me. There was a loud shriek from a woman behind. I half turned, keeping my eyes fixed upon the cylinder still, from which other tentacles were now projecting, and began pushing my way back from the edge of the pit. I saw astonishment giving place to horror on the faces of the people about me. I heard inarticulate exclamations on all sides. There was a general movement backwards. I saw the shopman struggling still on the edge of the pit. I found myself alone, and saw the people on the other side of the pit running off, Stent among them. I looked again at the cylinder, and ungovernable terror gripped me. I stood petrified and staring.

A big greyish rounded bulk, the size, perhaps, of a bear, was rising slowly and painfully out of the cylinder. As it bulged up and caught the light, it glistened like wet leather.

Two large dark-coloured eyes were regarding me steadfastly. The mass that framed them, the head of the thing, was rounded, and had, one might say, a face. There was a mouth under the eyes, the lipless brim of which quivered and panted, and dropped saliva. The whole creature heaved and pulsated convulsively. A lank tentacular appendage gripped the edge of the cylinder, another swayed in the air.

Those who have never seen a living Martian can scarcely imagine the strange horror of its appearance. The peculiar V-shaped mouth with its pointed upper lip, the absence of brow ridges, the absence of a chin beneath the wedgelike lower lip, the incessant quivering of this mouth, the Gorgon groups of tentacles, the tumultuous breathing of the lungs in a strange atmosphere, the evident heaviness and painfulness of movement due to the greater gravitational energy of the earth – above all, the extraordinary intensity of the immense eyes – were at once vital, intense, inhuman, crippled and monstrous. There was something fungoid in the oily brown skin, something in the clumsy deliberation of the tedious movements unspeakably nasty. Even at this first encounter, this first glimpse, I was overcome with disgust and dread.

Suddenly the monster vanished. It had toppled over the brim of the cylinder and fallen into the pit, with a thud like the fall of a great mass of leather. I heard it give a peculiar thick cry, and forthwith another of these creatures appeared darkly in the deep shadow of the aperture.

I turned and, running madly, made for the first group of trees, perhaps a hundred yards away; but I ran slantingly and stumbling, for I could not avert my face from these things.

There, among some young pine trees and furze bushes, I stopped, panting, and waited further developments. The common round the sand pits was dotted with people, standing like myself in a half-fascinated terror, staring at these creatures, or rather at the heaped gravel at the edge of the pit in which they lay. And then, with a renewed horror, I saw a round, black object bobbing up and down on the edge of the pit. It was the head of the shopman who had fallen in, but showing as a little black object against the hot western sun. Now he got his shoulder and knee up, and again he seemed to slip back until only his head was visible. Suddenly he vanished, and I could have fancied a faint shriek had reached me. I had a momentary impulse to go back and help him that my fears overruled.

Everything was then quite invisible, hidden by the deep pit and the heap of sand that the fall of the cylinder had made. Anyone coming along the road from Chobham or Woking would have been amazed at the sight – a dwindling multitude of perhaps a hundred people or more standing in a great irregular circle, in ditches, behind bushes, behind gates and hedges, saying little to one another and that in short, excited shouts, and staring, staring hard at a few heaps of sand. The barrow of ginger beer stood, a queer derelict, black against the burning sky, and in the sand pits was a row of deserted vehicles with their horses feeding out of nosebags or pawing the ground.

CHAPTER 5

The Heat Ray

After the glimpse I had had of the Martians emerging from the cylinder in which they had come to the earth from their planet, a kind of fascination paralysed my actions. I remained standing knee-deep in the heather, staring at the mound that hid them. I was a battleground of fear and curiosity.

I did not dare to go back towards the pit, but I felt a passionate longing to peer into it. I began walking, therefore, in a big curve, seeking some point of vantage and continually looking at the sand heaps that hid these new-comers to our earth. Once a leash of thin black whips, like the arms of an octopus, flashed across the sunset and was immediately withdrawn, and afterwards a thin rod rose up, joint by joint, bearing at its apex a circular disk that spun with a wobbling motion. What could be going on there?

Most of the spectators had gathered in one or two groups – one a little crowd towards Woking, the other a knot of people in the direction of Chobham. Evidently they shared my mental conflict. There were few near me. One man I approached – he was, I perceived, a neighbour of mine, though I did not know his name – and accosted. But it was scarcely a time for articulate conversation.

"What ugly *brutes*!" he said. "Good God! What ugly brutes!" He repeated this over and over again.

"Did you see a man in the pit?" I said; but he made no answer to that. We became silent, and stood watching for a time side by side, deriving, I fancy, a certain comfort in one another's company. Then I shifted my position to a little knoll that gave me the advantage of a yard or more of elevation and when I looked for him presently he was walking towards Woking.

The sunset faded to twilight before anything further happened. The crowd far away on the left, towards Woking, seemed to grow, and I heard now a faint murmur from it. The little knot of people towards Chobham dispersed. There was scarcely an intimation of movement from the pit.

It was this, as much as anything, that gave people courage, and I suppose the new arrivals from Woking also helped to restore confidence. At any rate, as the dusk came on a slow, intermittent movement upon the sand pits began, a movement that seemed to gather force as the stillness of the evening about the cylinder remained unbroken. Vertical black figures in twos and threes would advance, stop, watch, and advance again, spreading out as they did so in a thin irregular crescent that promised to enclose the pit in its attenuated horns. I, too, on my side began to move towards the pit.

Then I saw some cabmen and others had walked boldly into the sand pits, and heard the clatter of hoofs and the grind of wheels. I saw a lad trundling off the barrow of apples. And then, within thirty yards of the pit, advancing from the direction of Horsell, I noted a little black knot of men, the foremost of whom was waving a white flag.

This was the Deputation. There had been a hasty consultation, and since the Martians were evidently, in spite of their repulsive forms, intelligent creatures, it had been resolved to show them, by approaching them with signals, that we too were intelligent.

Flutter, flutter, went the flag, first to the right, then to the left. It was too far for me to recognise anyone there, but afterwards I learned that Ogilvy, Stent, and Henderson were with others in this attempt at communication. This little group had in its advance dragged inward, so to speak, the circumference of the now almost complete circle of people, and a number of dim black figures followed it at discreet distances.

Suddenly there was a flash of light, and a quantity of luminous greenish smoke came out of the pit in three distinct puffs, which drove up, one after the other, straight into the still air.

This smoke (or flame, perhaps, would be the better word for it) was so bright that the deep blue sky overhead and the hazy stretches of brown common towards Chertsey, set with black pine trees, seemed to darken abruptly as these puffs arose, and to remain the darker after their dispersal. At the same time a faint hissing sound became audible.

Beyond the pit stood the little wedge of people with the white flag at its apex, arrested by these phenomena, a little knot of small vertical black shapes upon the black ground. As the green smoke arose, their faces flashed out pallid green, and faded again as it vanished. Then slowly the hissing passed into a humming, into a long, loud, droning noise. Slowly a humped shape rose out of the pit, and the ghost of a beam of light seemed to flicker out from it.

Forthwith flashes of actual flame, a bright glare leaping from one to another, sprang from the scattered group of men. It was as if some invisible jet impinged upon them and flashed into white flame. It was as if each man were suddenly and momentarily turned to fire.

Then, by the light of their own destruction, I saw them staggering and falling, and their supporters turning to run.

I stood staring, not as yet realising that this was death leaping from man to man in that little distant crowd. All I felt was that it was something very strange. An almost noiseless and blinding flash of light, and a man fell headlong and lay still; and as the unseen shaft of heat passed over them, pine trees burst into fire, and every dry furze bush became with one dull thud a mass of flames. And far away towards Knaphill I saw the flashes of trees and hedges and wooden buildings suddenly set alight.

It was sweeping round swiftly and steadily, this flaming death, this invisible, inevitable sword of heat. I perceived it coming towards me by the flashing bushes it touched, and was too astounded and stupefied to stir. I heard the crackle of fire in the sand pits and the sudden squeal of a horse that was as suddenly stilled. Then it was as if an invisible yet intensely heated finger were drawn through the heather between me and the Martians, and all along a curving line beyond the sand pits the dark ground smoked and crackled. Something fell with a crash far away to the left where the road from Woking station opens out on the common. Forth-with the hissing and humming ceased, and the black, dome-like object sank slowly out of sight into the pit.

All this had happened with such swiftness that I had stood motionless, dumbfounded and dazzled by the flashes of light. Had that death swept through a full circle, it must inevitably have slain me in my surprise. But it passed and spared me, and left the night about me suddenly dark and unfamiliar.

The undulating common seemed now dark almost to blackness, except where its roadways lay grey and pale under the deep blue sky of the early night. It was dark, and suddenly void of men. Overhead the stars were mustering, and in the west the sky was still a pale, bright, almost greenish blue. The tops of the pine trees and the roofs of Horsell came out sharp and black against the western afterglow. The Martians and their appliances were altogether invisible, save for that thin mast upon which their restless mirror wobbled. Patches of bush and isolated trees here and there smoked and glowed still, and the houses towards Woking station were sending up spires of flame into the stillness of the evening air.

Nothing was changed save for that and a terrible astonishment. The little group of black specks with the flag of white had been swept out of existence, and the stillness of the evening, so it seemed to me, had scarcely been broken.

It came to me that I was upon this dark common, helpless, unprotected, and alone. Suddenly, like a thing falling upon me from without, came - fear.

With an effort I turned and began a stumbling run through the heather.

The fear I felt was no rational fear, but a panic terror not only of the Martians, but of the dusk and stillness all about me. Such an extraordinary effect in unmanning me it had that I ran weeping silently as a child might do. Once I had turned, I did not dare to look back.

I remember I felt an extraordinary persuasion that I was being played with, that presently, when I was upon the very verge of safety, this mysterious death - as swift as the passage of light - would leap after me from the pit about the cylinder and strike me down.

CHAPTER 6

The Heat Ray in Chobham Road

It is still a matter of wonder how the Martians are able to slay men so swiftly and so silently. Many think that in some way they are able to generate an intense heat in a chamber of practically absolute non-conductivity. This intense heat they project in a parallel beam against any object they choose, by means of a polished parabolic mirror of unknown composition, much as the parabolic mirror of a lighthouse projects a beam of light. But no one has absolutely proved these details. However it is done, it is certain that a beam of heat is the essence of the matter. Heat, and invisible, instead of visible, light. Whatever is combustible flashes into flame at its touch, lead runs like water, it softens iron, cracks and melts glass, and when it falls upon water, incontinently that explodes into steam.

That night nearly forty people lay under the starlight about the pit, charred and distorted beyond recognition, and all night long the common from Horsell to Maybury was deserted and brightly ablaze.

The news of the massacre probably reached Chobham, Woking, and Ottershaw about the same time. In Woking the shops had closed when the tragedy happened, and a number of people, shop people and so forth, attracted by the stories they had heard, were walking over the Horsell Bridge and along the road between the hedges that runs out at last upon the common. You may imagine the young people brushed up after the labours of the day, and making this novelty, as they would make any novelty, the excuse for walking together and enjoying a trivial flirtation. You may figure to yourself the hum of voices along the road in the gloaming...

As yet, of course, few people in Woking even knew that the cylinder had opened, though poor Henderson had sent a messenger on a bicycle to the post office with a special wire to an evening paper.

As these folks came out by twos and threes upon the open, they found little knots of people talking excitedly and peering at the spinning mirror over the sand pits, and the newcomers were, no doubt, soon infected by the excitement of the occasion.

By half past eight, when the Deputation was destroyed, there may have been a crowd of three hundred people or more at this place, besides those who had left the road to approach the Martians nearer. There were three policemen too, one of whom was mounted, doing their best, under instructions from Stent, to keep the people back and deter them from approaching the cylinder. There was some booing from those more thoughtless and excitable souls to whom a crowd is always an occasion for noise and horse-play.

Stent and Ogilvy, anticipating some possibilities of a collision, had telegraphed from Horsell to the barracks as soon as the Martians emerged, for the help of a company of soldiers to protect these strange creatures from violence. After that they returned to lead that ill-fated advance. The description of their death, as it was seen by the crowd, tallies very closely with my own impressions: the three puffs of green smoke, the deep humming note, and the flashes of flame.

But that crowd of people had a far narrower escape than mine. Only the fact that a hummock of heathery sand intercepted the lower part of the Heat-Ray saved them. Had the elevation of the parabolic mirror been a few yards higher, none could have lived to tell the tale.

They saw the flashes and the men falling and an invisible hand, as it were, lit the bushes as it hurried towards them through the twilight. Then, with a whistling note that rose above the droning of the pit, the beam swung close over their heads, lighting the tops of the beech trees that line the road, and splitting the bricks, smashing the windows, firing the window frames, and bringing down in crumbling ruin a portion of the gable of the house nearest the corner.

In the sudden thud, hiss, and glare of the igniting trees, the panic-stricken crowd seems to have swayed hesitatingly for some moments. Sparks and burning twigs began to fall into the road, and single leaves like puffs of flame. Hats and dresses caught fire. Then came a crying from the common. There were shrieks and shouts, and suddenly a mounted policeman came galloping through the confusion with his hands clasped over his head, screaming.

"They're coming!" a woman shrieked, and incontinently everyone was turning and pushing at those behind, in order to clear their way to Woking again. They must have bolted as blindly as a flock of sheep. Where the road grows narrow and black between the high banks the crowd jammed, and a desperate struggle occurred. All that crowd did not escape; three persons at least, two women and a little boy, were crushed and trampled there, and left to die amid the terror and the darkness.

CHAPTER 7

How I Reached Home

For my own part, I remember nothing of my flight except the stress of blundering against trees and stumbling through the heather. All about me gathered the invisible terrors of the Martians; that pitiless sword of heat seemed whirling to and fro, flourishing overhead before it descended and smote me out of life. I came into the road between the crossroads and Horsell, and ran along this to the crossroads.

At last I could go no further; I was exhausted with the violence of my emotion and of my flight, and I staggered and fell by the wayside. That was near the bridge that crosses the canal by the gasworks. I fell and lay still.

I must have remained there some time.

I sat up, strangely perplexed. For a moment, perhaps, I could not clearly understand how I came there. My terror had fallen from me like a garment. My hat had gone, and my collar had burst away from its fastener. A few minutes before, there had only been three real things before me – the immensity of the night and space and nature, my own feebleness and anguish, and the near approach of death. Now it was as if something turned over, and the point of view altered abruptly. There was no sensible transition from one state of mind to the other. I was immediately the self of every day again – a decent, ordinary citizen. The silent common, the impulse of my flight, the starting flames, were as if they had been in a dream. I asked myself had these latter things indeed happened? I could not credit it.

I rose and walked unsteadily up the steep incline of the bridge. My mind was blank wonder. My muscles and nerves seemed drained of their strength. I dare say I staggered drunkenly. A head rose over the arch, and the figure of a workman carrying a basket appeared. Beside him ran a little boy. He passed me, wishing me good night. I was minded to speak to him, but did not. I answered his greeting with a meaningless mumble and went on over the bridge.

Over the Maybury arch a train, a billowing tumult of white, firelit smoke, and a long caterpillar of lighted windows, went flying south – clatter, clatter, clap, rap, and it had gone. A dim group of people talked in the gate of one of the houses in the pretty little row of gables that was called Oriental Terrace. It was all so real and so familiar. And that behind me! It was frantic, fantastic! Such things, I told myself, could not be.

Perhaps I am a man of exceptional moods. I do not know how far my experience is common. At times I suffer from the strangest sense of detachment from myself and the world about me; I seem to watch it all from the outside, from somewhere inconceivably remote, out of time, out of space, out of the stress and tragedy of it all. This feeling was very strong upon me that night. Here was another side to my dream.

But the trouble was the blank incongruity of this serenity and the swift death flying yonder, not two miles away. There was a noise of business from the gasworks, and the electric lamps were all alight. I stopped at the group of people.

"What news from the common?" said I.

There were two men and a woman at the gate.

"Eh?" said one of the men, turning.

"What news from the common?" I said.

"'Ain't yer just *been* there?" asked the men.

"People seem fair silly about the common," said the woman over the gate. "What's it all abart?"

"Haven't you heard of the men from Mars?" said I; "the creatures from Mars?"

"Quite enough," said the woman over the gate. "Thenks"; and all three of them laughed.

I felt foolish and angry. I tried and found I could not tell them what I had seen. They laughed again at my broken sentences.

"You'll hear more yet," I said, and went on to my home.

I startled my wife at the doorway, so haggard was I. I went into the dining room, sat down, drank some wine, and so soon as I could collect myself sufficiently I told her the things I had seen. The dinner, which was a cold one, had already been served, and remained neglected on the table while I told my story.

"There is one thing," I said, to allay the fears I had aroused; "they are the most sluggish things I ever saw crawl. They may keep the pit and kill people who come near them, but they cannot get out of it.... But the horror of them!"

"Don't, dear!" said my wife, knitting her brows and putting her hand on mine.

"Poor Ogilvy!" I said. "To think he may be lying dead there!"

My wife at least did not find my experience incredible. When I saw how deadly white her face was, I ceased abruptly.

"They may come here," she said again and again.

I pressed her to take wine, and tried to reassure her.

"They can scarcely move," I said.

I began to comfort her and myself by repeating all that Ogilvy had told me of the impossibility of the Martians establishing themselves on the earth. In particular I laid stress on the gravitational difficulty. On the surface of the earth the force of gravity is three times what it is on the surface of Mars. A Martian, therefore, would weigh three times more than on Mars, albeit his muscular strength would be the same. His own body would be a cope of lead to him. That, indeed, was the general opinion. Both *The Times* and the *Daily Telegraph*, for instance, insisted on it the next morning, and both overlooked, just as I did, two obvious modifying influences.

The atmosphere of the earth, we now know, contains far more oxygen or far less argon (whichever way one likes to put it) than does Mars. The invigorating influences of this excess of oxygen upon the Martians indisputably did much to counterbalance the increased weight of their bodies. And, in the second place, we all overlooked the fact that such mechanical intelligence as the Martian possessed was quite able to dispense with muscular exertion at a pinch.

But I did not consider these points at the time, and so my reasoning was dead against the chances of the invaders. With wine and food, the confidence of my own table, and the necessity of reassuring my wife, I grew by insensible degrees courageous and secure.

"They have done a foolish thing," said I, fingering my wineglass. "They are dangerous because, no doubt, they are mad with terror. Perhaps they expected to find no living things – certainly no intelligent living things."

"A shell in the pit" said I, "if the worst comes to the worst will kill them all."

The intense excitement of the events had no doubt left my perceptive powers in a state of erethism. I remember that dinner table with extraordinary vividness even now. My dear wife's sweet anxious face peering at me from under the pink lamp shade, the white cloth with its silver and glass table furniture – for in those days even philosophical writers had many little luxuries – the crimson-purple wine in my glass, are photographically distinct. At the end of it I sat, tempering nuts with a cigarette, regretting Ogilvy's rashness, and denouncing the shortsighted timidity of the Martians.

So some respectable dodo in the Mauritius might have lorded it in his nest, and discussed the arrival of that shipful of pitiless sailors in want of animal food. "We will peck them to death tomorrow, my dear."

I did not know it, but that was the last civilised dinner I was to eat for very many strange and terrible days.

CHAPTER 8

Friday Night

The most extraordinary thing to my mind, of all the strange and wonderful things that happened upon that Friday, was the dovetailing of the commonplace habits of our social order with the first beginnings of the series of events that was to topple that social order headlong. If on Friday night you had taken a pair of compasses and drawn a circle with a radius of five miles round the Woking sand pits, I doubt if you would have had one human being outside it, unless it were some relation of Stent or of the three or four cyclists or London people lying dead on the common, whose emotions or habits were at all affected by the new-comers. Many people had heard of the cylinder, of course, and talked about it in their leisure, but it certainly did not make the sensation that an ultimatum to Germany would have done.

In London that night poor Henderson's telegram describing the gradual unscrewing of the shot was judged to be a canard, and his evening paper, after wiring for authentication from him and receiving no reply – the man was killed – decided not to print a special edition.

Even within the five-mile circle the great majority of people were inert. I have already described the behaviour of the men and women to whom I spoke. All over the district people were dining and supping; working men were gardening after the labours of the day, children were being put to bed, young people were wandering through the lanes love-making, students sat over their books.

Maybe there was a murmur in the village streets, a novel and dominant topic in the public-houses, and here and there a messenger, or even an eye-witness of the later occurrences, caused a whirl of excitement, a shouting, and a running to and fro; but for the most part the daily routine of working, eating, drinking, sleeping, went on as it had done for countless years – as though no planet Mars existed in the sky. Even at Woking station and Horsell and Chobham that was the case.

In Woking junction, until a late hour, trains were stopping and going on, others were shunting on the sidings, passengers were alighting and waiting, and everything was proceeding in the most ordinary way. A boy from the town, trenching on Smith's monopoly, was selling papers with the afternoon's news. The ringing impact of trucks, the sharp whistle of the engines from the junction, mingled with their shouts of "Men from Mars!" Excited men came into the station about nine o'clock with incredible tidings, and caused no more disturbance than drunkards might have done. People rattling Londonwards peered into the darkness outside the carriage windows, and saw only a rare, flickering, vanishing spark dance up from the direction of Horsell, a red glow and a thin veil of smoke driving across the stars, and thought that nothing more serious than a heath fire was happening. It was only round the edge of the common that any disturbance was perceptible. There were half a dozen villas burning on the Woking border. There were lights in all the houses on the common side of the three villages, and the people there kept awake till dawn.

A curious crowd lingered restlessly, people coming and going but the crowd remaining, both on the Chobham and Horsell bridges.

One or two adventurous souls, it was afterwards found, went into the darkness and crawled quite near the Martians; but they never returned, for now and again a light-ray, like the beam of a warship's searchlight swept the common, and the Heat-Ray was ready to follow. Save for such, that big area of common was silent and desolate, and the charred bodies lay about on it all night under the stars, and all the next day. A noise of hammering from the pit was heard by many people.

So you have the state of things on Friday night. In the centre, sticking into the skin of our old planet Earth like a poisoned dart, was this cylinder. But the poison was scarcely working yet. Around it was a patch of silent common, smouldering in places, and with a few dark, dimly seen objects lying in contorted attitudes here and there. Here and there was a burning bush or tree. Beyond was a fringe of excitement, and farther than that fringe the inflammation had not crept as yet. In the rest of the world the stream of life still flowed as it had flowed for immemorial years. The fever of war that would presently clog vein and artery, deaden nerve and destroy brain, had still to develop.

All night long the Martians were hammering and stirring, sleepless, indefatigable, at work upon the machines they were making ready, and ever and again a puff of greenish-white smoke whirled up to the starlit sky.

About eleven a company of soldiers came through Horsell, and deployed along the edge of the common to form a cordon. Later a second company marched through Chobham to deploy on the north side of the common. Several officers from the Inkerman barracks had been on the common earlier in the day, and one, Major Eden, was reported to be missing. The colonel of the regiment came to the Chobham bridge and was busy questioning the crowd at midnight.

The military authorities were certainly alive to the seriousness of the business. About eleven, the next morning's papers were able to say, a squadron of hussars, two Maxims, and about four hundred men of the Cardigan regiment started from Aldershot.

A few seconds after midnight the crowd in the Chertsey road, Woking, saw a star fall from heaven into the pine woods to the northwest. It had a greenish colour, and caused a silent brightness like summer lightning. This was the second cylinder.

CHAPTER 9

The Fighting Begins

Saturday lives in my memory as a day of suspense. It was a day of lassitude too, hot and close, with, I am told, a rapidly fluctuating barometer. I had slept but little, though my wife had succeeded in sleeping, and I rose early. I went into my garden before breakfast and stood listening, but towards the common there was nothing stirring but a lark.

The milkman came as usual. I heard the rattle of his chariot and I went round to the side gate to ask the latest news. He told me that during the night the Martians had been surrounded by troops, and that guns were expected. Then – a familiar, reassuring note – I heard a train running towards Woking.

"They aren't to be killed," said the milkman, "if that can possibly be avoided."

I saw my neighbour gardening, chatted with him for a time, and then strolled in to breakfast. It was a most unexceptional morning. My neighbour was of opinion that the troops would be able to capture or to destroy the Martians during the day.

"It's a pity they make themselves so unapproachable," he said. "It would be curious to know how they live on another planet; we might learn a thing or two."

He came up to the fence and extended a handful of strawberries, for his gardening was as generous as it was enthusiastic. At the same time he told me of the burning of the pine woods about the Byfleet Golf Links.

"They say," said he, "that there's another of those blessed things fallen there – number two. But one's enough, surely. This lot'll cost the insurance people a pretty penny before everything's settled." He laughed with an air of the greatest good humour as he said this. The woods, he said, were still burning, and pointed out a haze of smoke to me. "They will be hot under foot for days, on account of the thick soil of pine needles and turf," he said, and then grew serious over "poor Ogilvy."

After breakfast, instead of working, I decided to walk down towards the common. Under the railway bridge I found a group of soldiers – sappers, I think, men in small round caps, dirty red jackets unbuttoned, and showing their blue shirts, dark trousers, and boots coming to the calf. They told me no one was allowed over the canal, and, looking along the road towards the bridge, I saw one of the Cardigan men standing sentinel there. I talked with these soldiers for a time; I told them of my sight of the Martians on the previous evening. None of them had seen the Martians, and they had but the vaguest ideas of them, so that they plied me with questions. They said that they did not know who had authorised the movements of the troops; their idea was that a dispute had arisen at the Horse Guards. The ordinary sapper is a great deal better educated than the common soldier, and they discussed the peculiar conditions of the possible fight with some acuteness. I described the Heat-Ray to them, and they began to argue among themselves.

"Crawl up under cover and rush 'em, say I," said one.

"Get aht!" said another. "What's cover against this 'ere 'eat? Sticks to cook yer! What we got to do is to go as near as the ground'll let us, and then drive a trench."

"Blow yer trenches! You always want trenches; you ought to ha' been born a rabbit Snippy."

"Ain't they got any necks, then?" said a third, abruptly – a little, contemplative, dark man, smoking a pipe.

I repeated my description.

"Octopuses," said he, "that's what I calls 'em. Talk about fishers of men – fighters of fish it is this time!"

"It ain't no murder killing beasts like that," said the first speaker.

"Why not shell the darned things strite off and finish 'em?" said the little dark man. "You carn tell what they might do."

"Where's your shells?" said the first speaker. "There ain't no time. Do it in a rush, that's my tip, and do it at once."

So they discussed it. After a while I left them, and went on to the railway station to get as many morning papers as I could.

But I will not weary the reader with a description of that long morning and of the longer afternoon. I did not succeed in getting a glimpse of the common, for even Horsell and Chobham church towers were in the hands of the military authorities. The soldiers I addressed didn't know anything; the officers were mysterious as well as busy. I found people in the town quite secure again in the presence of the military, and I heard for the first time from Marshall, the tobacconist, that his son was among the dead on the common. The soldiers had made the people on the outskirts of Horsell lock up and leave their houses.

I got back to lunch about two, very tired for, as I have said, the day was extremely hot and dull; and in order to refresh myself I took a cold bath in the afternoon. About half past four I went up to the railway station to get an evening paper, for the morning papers had contained only a very inaccurate description of the killing of Stent, Henderson, Ogilvy, and the others. But there was little I didn't know.

The Martians did not show an inch of themselves. They seemed busy in their pit, and there was a sound of hammering and an almost continuous streamer of smoke. Apparently they were busy getting ready for a struggle. "Fresh attempts have been made to signal, but without success," was the stereotyped formula of the papers. A sapper told me it was done by a man in a ditch with a flag on a long pole. The Martians took as much notice of such advances as we should of the lowing of a cow.

I must confess the sight of all this armament, all this preparation, greatly excited me. My imagination became belligerent, and defeated the invaders in a dozen striking ways; something of my schoolboy dreams of battle and heroism came back. It hardly seemed a fair fight to me at that time. They seemed very helpless in that pit of theirs.

About three o'clock there began the thud of a gun at measured intervals from Chertsey or Addlestone. I learned that the smouldering pine wood into which the second cylinder had fallen was being shelled, in the hope of destroying that object before it opened. It was only about five, however, that a field gun reached Chobham for use against the first body of Martians.

About six in the evening, as I sat at tea with my wife in the summerhouse talking vigorously about the battle that was lowering upon us, I heard a muffled detonation from the common, and immediately after a gust of firing. Close on the heels of that came a violent rattling crash, quite close to us, that shook the ground; and, starting out upon the lawn, I saw the tops of the trees about the Oriental College burst into smoky red flame, and the tower of the little church beside it slide down into ruin. The pinnacle of the mosque had vanished, and the roof line of the college itself looked as if a hundred-ton gun had been at work upon it. One of our chimneys cracked as if a shot had hit it, flew, and a piece of it came clattering down the tiles and made a heap of broken red fragments upon the flower bed by my study window.

I and my wife stood amazed. Then I realised that the crest of Maybury Hill must be within range of the Martians' Heat-Ray now that the college was cleared out of the way.

At that I gripped my wife's arm, and without ceremony ran her out into the road. Then I fetched out the servant, telling her I would go upstairs myself for the box she was clamouring for.

"We can't possibly stay here," I said; and as I spoke the firing reopened for a moment upon the common.

"But where are we to go?" said my wife in terror.

I thought perplexed. Then I remembered her cousins at Leatherhead.

"Leatherhead!" I shouted above the sudden noise.

She looked away from me downhill. The people were coming out of their houses, astonished.

"How are we to get to Leatherhead?" she said.

Down the hill I saw a bevy of hussars ride under the railway bridge; three galloped through the open gates of the Oriental College; two others dismounted, and began running from house to house. The sun, shining through the smoke that drove up from the tops of the trees, seemed blood red, and threw an unfamiliar lurid light upon everything.

"Stop here," said I; "you are safe here"; and I started off at once for the Spotted Dog, for I knew the landlord had a horse and dog cart. I ran, for I perceived that in a moment everyone upon this side of the hill would be moving. I found him in his bar, quite unaware of what was going on behind his house. A man stood with his back to me, talking to him.

"I must have a pound," said the landlord, "and I've no one to drive it."

"I'll give you two," said I, over the stranger's shoulder.

"What for?"

"And I'll bring it back by midnight," I said.

"Lord!" said the landlord; "what's the hurry? I'm selling my bit of a pig. Two pounds, and you bring it back? What's going on now?"

I explained hastily that I had to leave my home, and so secured the dog cart. At the time it did not seem to me nearly so urgent that the landlord should leave his. I took care to have the cart there and then, drove it off down the road, and, leaving it in charge of my wife and servant, rushed into my house and packed a few valuables, such plate as we had, and so forth. The beech trees below the house were burning while I did this, and the palings up the road glowed red. While I was occupied in this way, one of the dismounted hussars came running up. He was going from house to house, warning people to leave. He was going on as I came out of my front door, lugging my treasures, done up in a tablecloth. I shouted after him:

"What news?"

He turned, stared, bawled something about "crawling out in a thing like a dish cover," and ran on to the gate of the house at the crest. A sudden whirl of black smoke driving across the road hid him for a moment. I ran to my neighbour's door and rapped to satisfy myself of what I already knew, that his wife had gone to London with him and had locked up their house. I went in again, according to my promise, to get my servant's box, lugged it out, clapped it beside her on the tail of the dog cart, and then caught the reins and jumped up into the driver's seat beside my wife. In another moment we were clear of the smoke and noise, and spanking down the opposite slope of Maybury Hill towards Old Woking.

In front was a quiet sunny landscape, a wheat field ahead on either side of the road, and the Maybury Inn with its swinging sign. I saw the doctor's cart ahead of me. At the bottom of the hill I turned my head to look at the hillside I was leaving. Thick streamers of black smoke shot with threads of red fire were driving up into the still air, and throwing dark shadows upon the green treetops eastward. The smoke already extended far away to the east and west – to the Byfleet pine woods eastward, and to Woking on the west. The road was dotted with people running towards us. And very faint now, but very distinct through the hot, quiet air, one heard the whirr of a machine-gun that was presently stilled, and an intermittent cracking of rifles. Apparently the Martians were setting fire to everything within range of their Heat-Ray.

I am not an expert driver, and I had immediately to turn my attention to the horse. When I looked back again the second hill had hidden the black smoke. I slashed the horse with the whip, and gave him a loose rein until Woking and Send lay between us and that quivering tumult. I overtook and passed the doctor between Woking and Send.

CHAPTER 10

In the Storm

Leatherhead is about twelve miles from Maybury Hill. The scent of hay was in the air through the lush meadows beyond Pyrford, and the hedges on either side were sweet and gay with multitudes of dog-roses. The heavy firing that had broken out while we were driving down Maybury Hill ceased as abruptly as it began, leaving the evening very peaceful and still. We got to Leatherhead without misadventure about nine o'clock, and the horse had an hour's rest while I took supper with my cousins and commended my wife to their care.

My wife was curiously silent throughout the drive, and seemed oppressed with forebodings of evil. I talked to her reassuringly, pointing out that the Martians were tied to the Pit by sheer heaviness, and at the utmost could but crawl a little out of it; but she answered only in monosyllables. Had it not been for my promise to the innkeeper, she would, I think, have urged me to stay in Leatherhead that night. Would that I had! Her face, I remember, was very white as we parted.

For my own part, I had been feverishly excited all day. Something very like the war fever that occasionally runs through a civilised community had got into my blood, and in my heart I was not so very sorry that I had to return to Maybury that night. I was even afraid that that last fusillade I had heard might mean the extermination of our invaders from Mars. I can best express my state of mind by saying that I wanted to be in at the death.

It was nearly eleven when I started to return. The night was unexpectedly dark; to me, walking out of the lighted passage of my cousins' house, it seemed indeed black, and it was as hot and close as the day. Overhead the clouds were driving fast, albeit not a breath stirred the shrubs about us. My cousins' man lit both lamps. Happily, I knew the road intimately. My wife stood in the light of the doorway, and watched me until I jumped up into the dog cart. Then abruptly she turned and went in, leaving my cousins side by side wishing me good hap.

I was a little depressed at first with the contagion of my wife's fears, but very soon my thoughts reverted to the Martians. At that time I was absolutely in the dark as to the course of the evening's fighting. I did not know even the circumstances that had precipitated the conflict. As I came through Ockham (for that was the way I returned, and not through Send and Old Woking) I saw along the western horizon a blood-red glow, which as I drew nearer, crept slowly up the sky. The driving clouds of the gathering thunderstorm mingled there with masses of black and red smoke.

Ripley Street was deserted, and except for a lighted window or so the village showed not a sign of life; but I narrowly escaped an accident at the corner of the road to Pyrford, where a knot of people stood with their backs to me. They said nothing to me as I passed. I do not know what they knew of the things happening beyond the hill, nor do I know if the silent houses I passed on my way were sleeping securely, or deserted and empty, or harassed and watching against the terror of the night.

From Ripley until I came through Pyrford I was in the valley of the Wey, and the red glare was hidden from me. As I ascended the little hill beyond Pyrford Church the glare came into view again, and the trees about me shivered with the first intimation of the storm that was upon me. Then I heard midnight pealing out from Pyrford Church behind me, and then came the silhouette of Maybury Hill, with its tree-tops and roofs black and sharp against the red.

Even as I beheld this a lurid green glare lit the road about me and showed the distant woods towards Addlestone. I felt a tug at the reins. I saw that the driving clouds had been pierced as it were by a thread of green fire, suddenly lighting their confusion and falling into the field to my left. It was the third falling star!

Close on its apparition, and blindingly violet by contrast, danced out the first lightning of the gathering storm, and the thunder burst like a rocket overhead. The horse took the bit between his teeth and bolted.

A moderate incline runs towards the foot of Maybury Hill, and down this we clattered. Once the lightning had begun, it went on in as rapid a succession of flashes as I have ever seen. The thunderclaps, treading one on the heels of another and with a strange crackling accompaniment, sounded more like the working of a gigantic electric machine than the usual detonating reverberations. The flickering light was blinding and confusing, and a thin hail smote gustily at my face as I drove down the slope.

At first I regarded little but the road before me, and then abruptly my attention was arrested by something that was moving rapidly down the opposite slope of Maybury Hill. At first I took it for the wet roof of a house, but one flash following another showed it to be in swift rolling movement. It was an elusive vision – a moment of bewildering darkness, and then, in a flash like daylight, the red masses of the Orphanage near the crest of the hill, the green tops of the pine trees, and this problematical object came out clear and sharp and bright.

And this Thing I saw! How can I describe it? A monstrous tripod, higher than many houses, striding over the young pine trees, and smashing them aside in its career; a walking engine of glittering metal, striding now across the heather; articulate ropes of steel dangling from it, and the clattering tumult of its passage mingling with the riot of the thunder. A flash, and it came out vividly, heeling over one way with two feet in the air, to vanish and reappear almost instantly as it seemed, with the next flash, a hundred yards nearer. Can you imagine a milking stool tilted and bowled violently along the ground? That was the impression those instant flashes gave. But instead of a milking stool imagine it a great body of machinery on a tripod stand.

Then suddenly the trees in the pine wood ahead of me were parted, as brittle reeds are parted by a man thrusting through them; they were snapped off and driven headlong, and a second huge tripod appeared, rushing, as it seemed, headlong towards me. And I was galloping hard to meet it! At the sight of the second monster my nerve went altogether. Not stopping to look again, I wrenched the horse's head hard round to the right and in another moment the dog cart had heeled over upon the horse; the shafts smashed noisily, and I was flung sideways and fell heavily into a shallow pool of water.

I crawled out almost immediately, and crouched, my feet still in the water, under a clump of furze. The horse lay motionless (his neck was broken, poor brute!) and by the lightning flashes I saw the black bulk of the overturned dog cart and the silhouette of the wheel still spinning slowly. In another moment the colossal mechanism went striding by me, and passed uphill towards Pyrford.

Seen nearer, the Thing was incredibly strange, for it was no mere insensate machine driving on its way. Machine it was, with a ringing metallic pace, and long, flexible, glittering tentacles (one of which gripped a young pine tree) swinging and rattling about its strange body. It picked its road as it went striding along, and the brazen hood that surmounted it moved to and fro with the inevitable suggestion of a head looking about. Behind the main body was a huge mass of white metal like a gigantic fisherman's basket, and puffs of green smoke squirted out from the joints of the limbs as the monster swept by me. And in an instant it was gone.

So much I saw then, all vaguely for the flickering of the lightning, in blinding highlights and dense black shadows.

As it passed it set up an exultant deafening howl that drowned the thunder – "Aloo! Aloo!" – and in another minute it was with its companion, half a mile away, stooping over something in the field. I have no doubt this Thing in the field was the third of the ten cylinders they had fired at us from Mars.

For some minutes I lay there in the rain and darkness watching, by the intermittent light, these monstrous beings of metal moving about in the distance over the hedge tops. A thin hail was now beginning, and as it came and went their figures grew misty and then flashed into clearness again. Now and then came a gap in the lightning, and the night swallowed them up.

I was soaked with hail above and puddle water below. It was some time before my blank astonishment would let me struggle up the bank to a drier position, or think at all of my imminent peril.

Not far from me was a little one-roomed squatter's hut of wood, surrounded by a patch of potato garden. I struggled to my feet at last, and, crouching and making use of every chance of cover, I made a run for this. I hammered at the door, but I could not make the people hear (if there were any people inside), and after a time I desisted, and, availing myself of a ditch for the greater part of the way, succeeded in crawling, unobserved by these monstrous machines, into the pine woods towards Maybury.

Under cover of this I pushed on, wet and shivering now, towards my own house. I walked among the trees trying to find the footpath. It was very dark indeed in the wood, for the lightning was now becoming infrequent, and the hail, which was pouring down in a torrent, fell in columns through the gaps in the heavy foliage.

If I had fully realised the meaning of all the things I had seen I should have immediately worked my way round through Byfleet to Street Cobham, and so gone back to rejoin my wife at Leatherhead. But that night the strangeness of things about me, and my physical wretchedness, prevented me, for I was bruised, weary, wet to the skin, deafened and blinded by the storm.

I had a vague idea of going on to my own house, and that was as much motive as I had. I staggered through the trees, fell into a ditch and bruised my knees against a plank, and finally splashed out into the lane that ran down from the College Arms. I say splashed, for the storm water was sweeping the sand down the hill in a muddy torrent. There in the darkness a man blundered into me and sent me reeling back.

He gave a cry of terror, sprang sideways, and rushed on before I could gather my wits sufficiently to speak to him. So heavy was the stress of the storm just at this place that I had the hardest task to win my way up the hill. I went close up to the fence on the left and worked my way along its palings.

Near the top I stumbled upon something soft, and, by a flash of lightning, saw between my feet a heap of black broadcloth and a pair of boots. Before I could distinguish clearly how the man lay, the flicker of light had passed. I stood over him waiting for the next flash. When it came, I saw that he was a sturdy man, cheaply but not shabbily dressed; his head was bent under his body, and he lay crumpled up close to the fence, as though he had been flung violently against it.

Overcoming the repugnance natural to one who had never before touched a dead body, I stooped and turned him over to feel for his heart. He was quite dead. Apparently his neck had been broken. The lightning flashed for a third time, and his face leaped upon me. I sprang to my feet. It was the landlord of the Spotted Dog, whose conveyance I had taken.

I stepped over him gingerly and pushed on up the hill. I made my way by the police station and the College Arms towards my own house. Nothing was burning on the hillside, though from the common there still came a red glare and a rolling tumult of ruddy smoke beating up against the drenching hail. So far as I could see by the flashes, the houses about me were mostly uninjured. By the College Arms a dark heap lay in the road.

Down the road towards Maybury Bridge there were voices and the sound of feet, but I had not the courage to shout or to go to them. I let myself in with my latchkey, closed, locked and bolted the door, staggered to the foot of the staircase, and sat down. My imagination was full of those striding metallic monsters, and of the dead body smashed against the fence.

I crouched at the foot of the staircase with my back to the wall, shivering violently.

CHAPTER 11

At the Window

I have already said that my storms of emotion have a trick of exhausting themselves. After a time I discovered that I was cold and wet, and with little pools of water about me on the stair carpet. I got up almost mechanically, went into the dining room and drank some whiskey, and then I was moved to change my clothes.

After I had done that I went upstairs to my study, but why I did so I do not know. The window of my study looks over the trees and the railway towards Horsell Common. In the hurry of our departure this window had been left open. The passage was dark, and, by contrast with the picture the window frame enclosed, the side of the room seemed impenetrably dark. I stopped short in the doorway.

The thunderstorm had passed. The towers of the Oriental College and the pine trees about it had gone, and very far away, lit by a vivid red glare, the common about the sand pits was visible. Across the light huge black shapes, grotesque and strange, moved busily to and fro.

It seemed indeed as if the whole country in that direction was on fire – a broad hillside set with minute tongues of flame, swaying and writhing with the gusts of the dying storm, and throwing a red reflection upon the cloud-scud above. Every now and then a haze of smoke from some nearer conflagration drove across the window and hid the Martian shapes. I could not see what they were doing, nor the clear form of them, nor recognise the black objects they were busied upon. Neither could I see the nearer fire, though the reflections of it danced on the wall and ceiling of the study. A sharp, resinous tang of burning was in the air.

I closed the door noiselessly and crept towards the window. As I did so, the view opened out until, on the one hand, it reached to the houses about Woking station, and on the other to the charred and blackened pine woods of Byfleet. There was a light down below the hill, on the railway, near the arch, and several of the houses along the Maybury road and the streets near the station were glowing ruins. The light upon the railway puzzled me at first; there were a black heap and a vivid glare, and to the right of that a row of yellow oblongs. Then I perceived this was a wrecked train, the fore part smashed and on fire, the hinder carriages still upon the rails.

Between these three main centres of light – the houses, the train, and the burning county towards Chobham – stretched irregular patches of dark country, broken here and there by intervals of dimly glowing and smoking ground. It was the strangest spectacle, that black expanse set with fire. It reminded me, more than anything else, of the Potteries at night. At first I could distinguish no people at all, though I peered intently for them. Later I saw against the light of Woking station a number of black figures hurrying one after the other across the line.

And this was the little world in which I had been living securely for years, this fiery chaos! What had happened in the last seven hours I still did not know; nor did I know, though I was beginning to guess, the relation between these mechanical colossi and the sluggish lumps I had seen disgorged from the cylinder. With a queer feeling of impersonal interest I turned my desk chair to the window, sat down, and stared at the blackened country, and particularly at the three gigantic black things that were going to and fro in the glare about the sand pits.

They seemed amazingly busy. I began to ask myself what they could be. Were they intelligent mechanisms? Such a thing I felt was impossible. Or did a Martian sit within each, ruling, directing, using, much as a man's brain sits and rules in his body? I began to compare the things to human machines, to ask myself for the first time in my life how an ironclad or a steam engine would seem to an intelligent lower animal.

The storm had left the sky clear, and over the smoke of the burning land the little fading pinpoint of Mars was dropping into the west, when a soldier came into my garden. I heard a slight scraping at the fence, and rousing myself from the lethargy that had fallen upon me, I looked down and saw him dimly, clambering over the palings. At the sight of another human being my torpor passed, and I leaned out of the window eagerly.

"Hist!" said I, in a whisper.

He stopped astride of the fence in doubt. Then he came over and across the lawn to the corner of the house. He bent down and stepped softly.

"Who's there?" he said, also whispering, standing under the window and peering up.

"Where are you going?" I asked.

"God knows."

"Are you trying to hide?"

"That's it."

"Come into the house," I said.

I went down, unfastened the door, and let him in, and locked the door again. I could not see his face. He was hatless, and his coat was unbuttoned.

"My God!" he said, as I drew him in.

"What has happened?" I asked.

"What hasn't?" In the obscurity I could see he made a gesture of despair. "They wiped us out – simply wiped us out," he repeated again and again.

He followed me, almost mechanically, into the dining room.

"Take some whiskey," I said, pouring out a stiff dose.

He drank it. Then abruptly he sat down before the table, put his head on his arms, and began to sob and weep like a little boy, in a perfect passion of emotion, while I, with a curious forgetfulness of my own recent despair, stood beside him, wondering.

It was a long time before he could steady his nerves to answer my questions, and then he answered perplexingly and brokenly. He was a driver in the artillery, and had only come into action about seven. At that time firing was going on across the common, and it was said the first party of Martians were crawling slowly towards their second cylinder under cover of a metal shield.

Later this shield staggered up on tripod legs and became the first of the fighting-machines I had seen. The gun he drove had been unlimbered near Horsell, in order to command the sand pits, and its arrival it was that had precipitated the action. As the limber gunners went to the rear, his horse trod in a rabbit hole and came down, throwing him into a depression of the ground. At the same moment the gun exploded behind him, the ammunition blew up, there was fire all about him, and he found himself lying under a heap of charred dead men and dead horses.

"I lay still," he said, "scared out of my wits, with the fore quarter of a horse atop of me. We'd been wiped out. And the smell – good God! Like burnt meat! I was hurt across the back by the fall of the horse, and there I had to lie until I felt better. Just like parade it had been a minute before – then stumble, bang, swish!"

"Wiped out!" he said.

He had hid under the dead horse for a long time, peeping out furtively across the common. The Cardigan men had tried a rush, in skirmishing order, at the pit, simply to be swept out of existence. Then the monster had risen to its feet and had begun to walk leisurely to and fro across the common among the few fugitives, with its headlike hood turning about exactly like the head of a cowled human being. A kind of arm carried a complicated metallic case, about which green flashes scintillated, and out of the funnel of this there smoked the Heat-Ray.

In a few minutes there was, so far as the soldier could see, not a living thing left upon the common, and every bush and tree upon it that was not already a blackened skeleton was burning. The hussars had been on the road beyond the curvature of the ground, and he saw nothing of them. He heard the Martians rattle for a time and then become still. The giant saved Woking station and its cluster of houses until the last; then in a moment the Heat-Ray was brought to bear, and the town became a heap of fiery ruins. Then the Thing shut off the Heat-Ray, and turning its back upon the artilleryman, began to waddle away towards the smouldering pine woods that sheltered the second cylinder. As it did so a second glittering Titan built itself up out of the pit.

The second monster followed the first, and at that the artilleryman began to crawl very cautiously across the hot heather ash towards Horsell. He managed to get alive into the ditch by the side of the road, and so escaped to Woking. There his story became ejaculatory. The place was impassable. It seems there were a few people alive there, frantic for the most part and many burned and scalded. He was turned aside by the fire, and hid among some almost scorching heaps of broken wall as one of the Martian giants returned. He saw this one pursue a man, catch him up in one of its steely tentacles, and knock his head against the trunk of a pine tree. At last, after nightfall, the artilleryman made a rush for it and got over the railway embankment.

Since then he had been skulking along towards Maybury, in the hope of getting out of danger Londonward. People were hiding in trenches and cellars, and many of the survivors had made off towards Woking village and Send. He had been consumed with thirst until he found one of the water mains near the railway arch smashed, and the water bubbling out like a spring upon the road.

That was the story I got from him, bit by bit. He grew calmer telling me and trying to make me see the things he had seen. He had eaten no food since midday, he told me early in his narrative, and I found some mutton and bread in the pantry and brought it into the room. We lit no lamp for fear of attracting the Martians, and ever and again our hands would touch upon bread or meat. As he talked, things about us came darkly out of the darkness, and the trampled bushes and broken rose trees outside the window grew distinct. It would seem that a number of men or animals had rushed across the lawn. I began to see his face, blackened and haggard, as no doubt mine was also.

When we had finished eating we went softly upstairs to my study, and I looked again out of the open window. In one night the valley had become a valley of ashes. The fires had dwindled now. Where flames had been there were now streamers of smoke; but the countless ruins of shattered and gutted houses and blasted and blackened trees that the night had hidden stood out now gaunt and terrible in the pitiless light of dawn. Yet here and there some object had had the luck to escape – a white railway signal here, the end of a greenhouse there, white and fresh amid the wreckage. Never before in the history of warfare had destruction been so indiscriminate and so universal. And shining with the growing light of the east, three of the metallic giants stood about the pit, their cowls rotating as though they were surveying the desolation they had made.

It seemed to me that the pit had been enlarged, and ever and again puffs of vivid green vapour streamed up and out of it towards the brightening dawn – streamed up, whirled, broke, and vanished.

Beyond were the pillars of fire about Chobham. They became pillars of bloodshot smoke at the first touch of day.

CHAPTER 12

What I Saw of the Destruction of Weybridge and Shepperton

As the dawn grew brighter we withdrew from the window from which we had watched the Martians, and went very quietly downstairs.

The artilleryman agreed with me that the house was no place to stay in. He proposed, he said, to make his way Londonward, and thence rejoin his battery – No. 12, of the Horse Artillery. My plan was to return at once to Leatherhead; and so greatly had the strength of the Martians impressed me that I had determined to take my wife to Newhaven, and go with her out of the country forthwith. For I already perceived clearly that the country about London must inevitably be the scene of a disastrous struggle before such creatures as these could be destroyed.

Between us and Leatherhead, however, lay the third cylinder, with its guarding giants. Had I been alone, I think I should have taken my chance and struck across country. But the artilleryman dissuaded me: "It's no kindness to the right sort of wife," he said, "to make her a widow"; and in the end I agreed to go with him, under cover of the woods, northward as far as Street Cobham before I parted with him. Thence I would make a big detour by Epsom to reach Leatherhead.

I should have started at once, but my companion had been in active service and he knew better than that. He made me ransack the house for a flask, which he filled with whiskey; and we lined every available pocket with packets of biscuits and slices of meat. Then we crept out of the house, and ran as quickly as we could down the ill-made road by which I had come overnight. The houses seemed deserted. In the road lay a group of three charred bodies close together, struck dead by the Heat-Ray; and here and there were things that people had dropped – a clock, a slipper, a silver spoon, and the like poor valuables. At the corner turning up towards the post office a little cart, filled with boxes and furniture, and horseless, heeled over on a broken wheel. A cash box had been hastily smashed open and thrown under the debris.

Except the lodge at the Orphanage, which was still on fire, none of the houses had suffered very greatly here. The Heat-Ray had shaved the chimney tops and passed. Yet, save ourselves, there did not seem to be a living soul on Maybury Hill. The majority of the inhabitants had escaped, I suppose, by way of the Old Woking road – the road I had taken when I drove to Leatherhead – or they had hidden.

We went down the lane, by the body of the man in black, sodden now from the overnight hail, and broke into the woods at the foot of the hill. We pushed through these towards the railway without meeting a soul. The woods across the line were but the scarred and blackened ruins of woods; for the most part the trees had fallen, but a certain proportion still stood, dismal grey stems, with dark brown foliage instead of green.

On our side the fire had done no more than scorch the nearer trees; it had failed to secure its footing. In one place the woodmen had been at work on Saturday; trees, felled and freshly trimmed, lay in a clearing, with heaps of sawdust by the sawing-machine and its engine. Hard by was a temporary hut, deserted. There was not a breath of wind this morning, and everything was strangely still. Even the birds were hushed, and as we hurried along I and the artilleryman talked in whispers and looked now and again over our shoulders. Once or twice we stopped to listen.

After a time we drew near the road, and as we did so we heard the clatter of hoofs and saw through the tree stems three cavalry soldiers riding slowly towards Woking. We hailed them, and they halted while we hurried towards them. It was a lieutenant and a couple of privates of the 8th Hussars, with a stand like a theodolite, which the artilleryman told me was a heliograph.

"You are the first men I've seen coming this way this morning," said the lieutenant. "What's brewing?"

His voice and face were eager. The men behind him stared curiously. The artilleryman jumped down the bank into the road and saluted.

"Gun destroyed last night, sir. Have been hiding. Trying to rejoin battery, sir. You'll come in sight of the Martians, I expect, about half a mile along this road."

"What the dickens are they like?" asked the lieutenant.

"Giants in armour, sir. Hundred feet high. Three legs and a body like 'luminium, with a mighty great head in a hood, sir."

"Get out!" said the lieutenant. "What confounded nonsense!"

"You'll see, sir. They carry a kind of box, sir, that shoots fire and strikes you dead."

"What d'ye mean – a gun?"

"No, sir," and the artilleryman began a vivid account of the Heat-Ray. Halfway through, the lieutenant interrupted him and looked up at me. I was still standing on the bank by the side of the road.

"It's perfectly true," I said.

"Well," said the lieutenant, "I suppose it's my business to see it too. Look here" – to the artilleryman – "we're detailed here clearing people out of their houses. You'd better go along and report yourself

89

to Brigadier-General Marvin, and tell him all you know. He's at Weybridge. Know the way?"

"I do," I said; and he turned his horse southward again.

"Half a mile, you say?" said he.

"At most," I answered, and pointed over the treetops southward. He thanked me and rode on, and we saw them no more.

Farther along we came upon a group of three women and two children in the road, busy clearing out a labourer's cottage. They had got hold of a little hand truck, and were piling it up with unclean-looking bundles and shabby furniture. They were all too assiduously engaged to talk to us as we passed.

By Byfleet station we emerged from the pine trees, and found the country calm and peaceful under the morning sunlight. We were far beyond the range of the Heat-Ray there, and had it not been for the silent desertion of some of the houses, the stirring movement of packing in others, and the knot of soldiers standing on the bridge over the railway and staring down the line towards Woking, the day would have seemed very like any other Sunday.

Several farm waggons and carts were moving creakily along the road to Addlestone, and suddenly through the gate of a field we saw, across a stretch of flat meadow, six twelve-pounders standing neatly at equal distances pointing towards Woking. The gunners stood by the guns waiting, and the ammunition waggons were at a business-like distance. The men stood almost as if under inspection.

"That's good!" said I. "They will get one fair shot, at any rate."

The artilleryman hesitated at the gate.

"I shall go on," he said.

Farther on towards Weybridge, just over the bridge, there were a number of men in white fatigue jackets throwing up a long rampart, and more guns behind.

"It's bows and arrows against the lightning, anyhow," said the artilleryman. "They 'aven't seen that fire-beam yet."

The officers who were not actively engaged stood and stared over the treetops southwestward, and the men digging would stop every now and again to stare in the same direction.

Byfleet was in a tumult; people packing, and a score of hussars, some of them dismounted, some on horseback, were hunting them about. Three or four black government waggons, with crosses in white circles, and an old omnibus, among other vehicles, were being loaded in the village street. There were scores of people, most of them sufficiently sabbatical to have assumed their best clothes. The soldiers were having the greatest difficulty in making them realise the gravity of their position. We saw one shrivelled old fellow with a huge box and a score or more of flower pots containing orchids, angrily expostulating with the corporal who would leave them behind. I stopped and gripped his arm.

"Do you know what's over there?" I said, pointing at the pine tops that hid the Martians.

"Eh?" said he, turning. "I was explainin' these is vallyble."

"Death!" I shouted. "Death is coming! Death!" and leaving him to digest that if he could, I hurried on after the artillery-man. At the corner I looked back. The soldier had left him, and he was still standing by his box, with the pots of orchids on the lid of it, and staring vaguely over the trees.

No one in Weybridge could tell us where the headquarters were established; the whole place was in such confusion as I had never seen in any town before. Carts, carriages everywhere, the most astonishing miscellany of conveyances and horseflesh. The respectable inhabitants of the place, men in golf and boating costumes, wives prettily dressed, were packing, river-side loafers energetically helping, children excited, and, for the most part, highly delighted at this astonishing variation of their Sunday experiences. In the midst of it all the worthy vicar was very pluckily holding an early celebration, and his bell was jangling out above the excitement.

I and the artilleryman, seated on the step of the drinking fountain, made a very passable meal upon what we had brought with us. Patrols of soldiers – here no longer hussars, but grenadiers in white – were warning people to move now or to take refuge in their cellars as soon as the firing began. We saw as we crossed the railway bridge that a growing crowd of people had assembled in and about the railway station, and the swarming platform was piled with boxes and packages. The ordinary traffic had been stopped, I believe, in order to allow of the passage of troops and guns to Chertsey, and I have heard since that a savage struggle occurred for places in the special trains that were put on at a later hour.

We remained at Weybridge until midday, and at that hour we found ourselves at the place near Shepperton Lock where the Wey and Thames join. Part of the time we spent helping two old women to pack a little cart. The Wey has a treble mouth, and at this point boats are to be hired, and there was a ferry across the river. On the Shepperton side was an inn with a lawn, and beyond that the tower of Shepperton Church – it has been replaced by a spire – rose above the trees.

Here we found an excited and noisy crowd of fugitives. As yet the flight had not grown to a panic, but there were already far more people than all the boats going to and fro could enable to cross. People came panting along under heavy burdens; one husband and wife were even carrying a small outhouse door between them, with some of their household goods piled thereon. One man told us he meant to try to get away from Shepperton station.

There was a lot of shouting, and one man was even jesting. The idea people seemed to have here was that the Martians were simply formidable human beings, who might attack and sack the town, to be certainly destroyed in the end. Every now and then people would glance nervously across the Wey, at the meadows towards Chertsey, but everything over there was still.

Across the Thames, except just where the boats landed, everything was quiet, in vivid contrast with the Surrey side. The people who landed there from the boats went tramping off down the lane. The big ferryboat had just made a journey. Three or four soldiers stood on the lawn of the inn, staring and jesting at the fugitives, without offering to help. The inn was closed, as it was now within prohibited hours.

"What's that?" cried a boatman, and "Shut up, you fool!" said a man near me to a yelping dog. Then the sound came again, this time from the direction of Chertsey, a muffled thud – the sound of a gun.

The fighting was beginning. Almost immediately unseen batteries across the river to our right, unseen because of the trees, took up the chorus, firing heavily one after the other. A woman screamed. Everyone stood arrested by the sudden stir of battle, near us and yet invisible to us. Nothing was to be seen save flat meadows, cows feeding unconcernedly for the most part, and silvery pollard willows motionless in the warm sunlight.

"The sojers'll stop 'em," said a woman beside me, doubtfully. A haziness rose over the treetops.

Then suddenly we saw a rush of smoke far away up the river, a puff of smoke that jerked up into the air and hung; and forthwith the ground heaved under foot and a heavy explosion shook the air, smashing two or three windows in the houses near, and leaving us astonished.

"Here they are!" shouted a man in a blue jersey. "Yonder! D'yer see them? Yonder!"

Quickly, one after the other, one, two, three, four of the armoured Martians appeared, far away over the little trees, across the flat meadows that stretched towards Chertsey, and striding hurriedly towards the river. Little cowled figures they seemed at first, going with a rolling motion and as fast as flying birds.

Then, advancing obliquely towards us, came a fifth. Their armoured bodies glittered in the sun as they swept swiftly forward upon the guns, growing rapidly larger as they drew nearer. One on the extreme left, the remotest that is, flourished a huge case high in the air, and the ghostly, terrible Heat-Ray I had already seen on Friday night smote towards Chertsey, and struck the town.

At sight of these strange, swift, and terrible creatures the crowd near the water's edge seemed to me to be for a moment horror-struck. There was no screaming or shouting, but a silence. Then a hoarse murmur and a movement of feet – a splashing from the water. A man, too frightened to drop the portmanteau he carried on his shoulder, swung round and sent me staggering with a blow from the corner of his burden. A woman thrust at me with her hand and rushed past me. I turned with the rush of the people, but I was not too terrified for thought. The terrible Heat-Ray was in my mind. To get under water! That was it!

"Get under water!" I shouted, unheeded.

I faced about again, and rushed towards the approaching Martian, rushed right down the gravelly beach and headlong into the water. Others did the same. A boatload of people putting back came leaping out as I rushed past. The stones under my feet were muddy and slippery, and the river was so low that I ran perhaps twenty feet scarcely waist-deep. Then, as the Martian towered overhead scarcely a couple of hundred yards away, I flung myself forward under the surface. The splashes of the people in the boats leaping into the river sounded like thunderclaps in my ears. People were landing hastily on both sides of the river. But the Martian machine took no more notice for the moment of the people running this way and that than a man would of the confusion of ants in a nest against which his foot has kicked. When, half suffocated, I raised my head above water, the Martian's hood pointed at the batteries that were still firing across the river, and as it advanced it swung loose what must have been the generator of the Heat-Ray.

In another moment it was on the bank, and in a stride wading halfway across. The knees of its foremost legs bent at the farther bank, and in another moment it had raised itself to its full height again, close to the village of Shepperton. Forthwith the six guns which, unknown to anyone on the right bank, had been hidden behind the outskirts of that village, fired simultaneously. The sudden near concussion, the last close upon the first, made my heart jump. The monster was already raising the case generating the Heat-Ray as the first shell burst six yards above the hood.

I gave a cry of astonishment. I saw and thought nothing of the other four Martian monsters; my attention was riveted upon the nearer incident. Simultaneously two other shells burst in the air near the body as the hood twisted round in time to receive, but not in time to dodge, the fourth shell.

The shell burst clean in the face of the Thing. The hood bulged, flashed, was whirled off in a dozen tattered fragments of red flesh and glittering metal.

"Hit!" shouted I, with something between a scream and a cheer.

I heard answering shouts from the people in the water about me. I could have leaped out of the water with that momentary exultation.

The decapitated colossus reeled like a drunken giant; but it did not fall over. It recovered its balance by a miracle, and, no longer heeding its steps and with the camera that fired the Heat-Ray now rigidly upheld, it reeled swiftly upon Shepperton. The living intelligence, the Martian within the hood, was slain and splashed to the four winds of heaven, and the Thing was now but a mere intricate device of metal whirling to destruction. It drove along in a straight line, incapable of guidance. It struck the tower of Shepperton Church, smashing it down as the impact of a battering ram might have done, swerved aside, blundered on and collapsed with tremendous force into the river out of my sight.

A violent explosion shook the air, and a spout of water, steam, mud, and shattered metal shot far up into the sky. As the camera of the Heat-Ray hit the water, the latter had immediately flashed into steam. In another moment a huge wave, like a muddy tidal bore but almost scaldingly hot, came sweeping round the bend upstream. I saw people struggling shorewards, and heard their screaming and shouting faintly above the seething and roar of the Martian's collapse.

For a moment I heeded nothing of the heat, forgot the patent need of self-preservation. I splashed through the tumultuous water, pushing aside a man in black to do so, until I could see round the bend. Half a dozen deserted boats pitched aimlessly upon the confusion of the waves. The fallen Martian came into sight downstream, lying across the river, and for the most part submerged.

Thick clouds of steam were pouring off the wreckage, and through the tumultuously whirling wisps I could see, intermittently and vaguely, the gigantic limbs churning the water and flinging a splash and spray of mud and froth into the air. The tentacles swayed and struck like living arms, and, save for the helpless purposelessness of these movements, it was as if some wounded thing were struggling for its life amid the waves. Enormous quantities of a ruddy-brown fluid were spurting up in noisy jets out of the machine.

My attention was diverted from this death flurry by a furious yelling, like that of the thing called a siren in our manufacturing towns. A man, knee-deep near the towing path, shouted inaudibly to me and pointed. Looking back, I saw the other Martians advancing with gigantic strides down the riverbank from the direction of Chertsey. The Shepperton guns spoke this time unavailingly.

At that I ducked at once under water, and, holding my breath until movement was an agony, blundered painfully ahead under the surface as long as I could. The water was in a tumult about me, and rapidly growing hotter.

When for a moment I raised my head to take breath and throw the hair and water from my eyes, the steam was rising in a whirling white fog that at first hid the Martians altogether. The noise was deafening. Then I saw them dimly, colossal figures of grey, magnified by the mist. They had passed by me, and two were stooping over the frothing, tumultuous ruins of their comrade.

The third and fourth stood beside him in the water, one perhaps two hundred yards from me, the other towards Laleham. The generators of the Heat-Rays waved high, and the hissing beams smote down this way and that.

The air was full of sound, a deafening and confusing conflict of noises – the clangorous din of the Martians, the crash of falling houses, the thud of trees, fences, sheds flashing into flame, and the crackling and roaring of fire. Dense black smoke was leaping up to mingle with the steam from the river, and as the Heat-Ray went to and fro over Weybridge its impact was marked by flashes of incandescent white, that gave place at once to a smoky dance of lurid flames. The nearer houses still stood intact, awaiting their fate, shadowy, faint and pallid in the steam, with the fire behind them going to and fro.

For a moment perhaps I stood there, breast-high in the almost boiling water, dumbfounded at my position, hopeless of escape. Through the reek I could see the people who had been with me in the river scrambling out of the water through the reeds, like little frogs hurrying through grass from the advance of a man, or running to and fro in utter dismay on the towing path.

Then suddenly the white flashes of the Heat-Ray came leaping towards me. The houses caved in as they dissolved at its touch, and darted out flames; the trees changed to fire with a roar. The Ray flickered up and down the towing path, licking off the people who ran this way and that, and came down to the water's edge not fifty yards from where I stood. It swept across the river to Shepperton, and the water in its track rose in a boiling weal crested with steam. I turned shoreward.

In another moment the huge wave, well-nigh at the boiling-point had rushed upon me. I screamed aloud, and scalded, half blinded, agonised, I staggered through the leaping, hissing water towards the shore. Had my foot stumbled, it would have been the end. I fell helplessly, in full sight of the Martians, upon the broad, bare gravelly spit that runs down to mark the angle of the Wey and Thames. I expected nothing but death.

I have a dim memory of the foot of a Martian coming down within a score of yards of my head, driving straight into the loose gravel, whirling it this way and that and lifting again; of a long suspense, and then of the four carrying the debris of their comrade between them, now clear and then presently faint through a veil of smoke, receding interminably, as it seemed to me, across a vast space of river and meadow. And then, very slowly, I realised that by a miracle I had escaped.

CHAPTER 13

How I Fell in with the Curate

After getting this sudden lesson in the power of terrestrial weapons, the Martians retreated to their original position upon Horsell Common; and in their haste, and encumbered with the debris of their smashed companion, they no doubt overlooked many such a stray and negligible victim as myself. Had they left their comrade and pushed on forthwith, there was nothing at that time between them and London but batteries of twelve-pounder guns, and they would certainly have reached the capital in advance of the tidings of their approach; as sudden, dreadful, and destructive their advent would have been as the earthquake that destroyed Lisbon a century ago.

But they were in no hurry. Cylinder followed cylinder on its interplanetary flight; every twenty-four hours brought them reinforcement. And meanwhile the military and naval authorities, now fully alive to the tremendous power of their antagonists, worked with furious energy. Every minute a fresh gun came into position until, before twilight, every copse, every row of suburban villas on the hilly slopes about Kingston and Richmond, masked an expectant black muzzle. And through the charred and desolated area – perhaps twenty square miles altogether – that encircled the Martian encampment on Horsell Common, through charred and ruined villages among the green trees, through the blackened and smoking arcades that had been but a day ago pine spinneys, crawled the devoted scouts with the heliographs that were presently to warn the gunners of the Martian approach. But the Martians now understood our command of artillery and the danger of human proximity, and not a man ventured within a mile of either cylinder, save at the price of his life.

It would seem that these giants spent the earlier part of the afternoon in going to and fro, transferring everything from the second and third cylinders – the second in Addlestone Golf Links and the third at Pyrford – to their original pit on Horsell Common. Over that, above the blackened heather and ruined buildings that stretched far and wide, stood one as sentinel, while the rest abandoned their vast fighting-machines and descended into the pit. They were hard at work there far into the night, and the towering pillar of dense green smoke that rose therefrom could be seen from the hills about Merrow, and even, it is said, from Banstead and Epsom Downs.

And while the Martians behind me were thus preparing for their next sally, and in front of me Humanity gathered for the battle, I made my way with infinite pains and labour from the fire and smoke of burning Weybridge towards London.

I saw an abandoned boat, very small and remote, drifting down-stream; and throwing off the most of my sodden clothes, I went after it, gained it, and so escaped out of that destruction. There were no oars in the boat, but I contrived to paddle, as well as my parboiled hands would allow, down the river towards Halliford and Walton, going very tediously and continually looking behind me, as you may well understand. I followed the river, because I considered that the water gave me my best chance of escape should these giants return.

The hot water from the Martian's overthrow drifted downstream with me, so that for the best part of a mile I could see little of either bank. Once, however, I made out a string of black figures hurrying across the meadows from the direction of Weybridge. Halliford, it seemed, was deserted, and several of the houses facing the river were on fire. It was strange to see the place quite tranquil, quite desolate under the hot blue sky, with the smoke and little threads of flame going straight up into the heat of the afternoon. Never before had I seen houses burning without the accompaniment of an obstructive crowd. A little farther on the dry reeds up the bank were smoking and glowing, and a line of fire inland was marching steadily across a late field of hay.

For a long time I drifted, so painful and weary was I after the violence I had been through, and so intense the heat upon the water. Then my fears got the better of me again, and I resumed my paddling. The sun scorched my bare back. At last, as the bridge at Walton was coming into sight round the bend, my fever and faintness overcame my fears, and I landed on the Middlesex bank and lay down, deadly sick, amid the long grass. I suppose the time was then about four or five o'clock. I got up presently, walked perhaps half a mile without meeting a soul, and then lay down again in the shadow of a hedge. I seem to remember talking, wanderingly, to myself during that last spurt. I was also very thirsty, and bitterly regretful I had drunk no more water. It is a curious thing that I felt angry with my wife; I cannot account for it, but my impotent desire to reach Leatherhead worried me excessively.

I do not clearly remember the arrival of the curate, so that probably I dozed. I became aware of him as a seated figure in soot-smudged shirt sleeves, and with his upturned, clean-shaven face staring at a faint flickering that danced over the sky. The sky was what is called a mackerel sky – rows and rows of faint down-plumes of cloud, just tinted with the midsummer sunset.

I sat up, and at the rustle of my motion he looked at me quickly.

"Have you any water?" I asked abruptly.

He shook his head.

"You have been asking for water for the last hour," he said.

For a moment we were silent, taking stock of each other. I dare say he found me a strange enough figure, naked, save for my water-soaked trousers and socks, scalded, and my face and shoulders blackened by the smoke. His face was a fair weakness, his chin retreated, and his hair lay in crisp, almost flaxen curls on his low forehead; his eyes were rather large, pale blue, and blankly staring. He spoke abruptly, looking vacantly away from me.

"What does it mean?" he said. "What do these things mean?"

I stared at him and made no answer.

He extended a thin white hand and spoke in almost a complaining tone.

"Why are these things permitted? What sins have we done? The morning service was over, I was walking through the roads to clear my brain for the afternoon, and then – fire, earthquake, death! As if it were Sodom and Gomorrah! All our work undone, all the work... What are these Martians?"

"What are we?" I answered, clearing my throat.

He gripped his knees and turned to look at me again. For half a minute, perhaps, he stared silently.

"I was walking through the roads to clear my brain," he said. "And suddenly – fire, earthquake, death!"

He relapsed into silence, with his chin now sunken almost to his knees.

Presently he began waving his hand.

"All the work – all the Sunday schools – What have we done – what has Weybridge done? Everything gone – everything destroyed. The church! We rebuilt it only three years ago. Gone! Swept out of existence! Why?"

Another pause, and he broke out again like one demented.

"The smoke of her burning goeth up for ever and ever!" he shouted.

His eyes flamed, and he pointed a lean finger in the direction of Weybridge.

By this time I was beginning to take his measure. The tremendous tragedy in which he had been involved – it was evident he was a fugitive from Weybridge – had driven him to the very verge of his reason.

"Are we far from Sunbury?" I said, in a matter-of-fact tone.

"What are we to do?" he asked. "Are these creatures everywhere? Has the earth been given over to them?"

"Are we far from Sunbury?"

"Only this morning I officiated at early celebration—"

"Things have changed," I said, quietly. "You must keep your head. There is still hope."

"Hope!"

"Yes. Plentiful hope – for all this destruction!"

I began to explain my view of our position. He listened at first, but as I went on the interest dawning in his eyes gave place to their former stare, and his regard wandered from me.

"This must be the beginning of the end," he said, interrupting me. "The end! The great and terrible day of the Lord! When men shall call upon the mountains and the rocks to fall upon them and hide them – hide them from the face of Him that sitteth upon the throne!"

I began to understand the position. I ceased my laboured reasoning, struggled to my feet, and, standing over him, laid my hand on his shoulder.

"Be a man!" said I. "You are scared out of your wits! What good is religion if it collapses under calamity? Think of what earthquakes and floods, wars and volcanoes, have done before to men! Did you think God had exempted Weybridge? He is not an insurance agent."

For a time he sat in blank silence.

"But how can we escape?" he asked, suddenly. "They are invulnerable, they are pitiless."

"Neither the one nor, perhaps, the other," I answered. "And the mightier they are the more sane and wary should we be. One of them was killed yonder not three hours ago."

"Killed!" he said, staring about him. "How can God's ministers be killed?"

"I saw it happen." I proceeded to tell him. "We have chanced to come in for the thick of it," said I, "and that is all."

"What is that flicker in the sky?" he asked abruptly.

I told him it was the heliograph signalling – that it was the sign of human help and effort in the sky.

"We are in the midst of it," I said, "quiet as it is. That flicker in the sky tells of the gathering storm. Yonder, I take it are the Martians, and Londonward, where those hills rise about Richmond and Kingston and the trees give cover, earthworks are being thrown up and guns are being placed. Presently the Martians will be coming this way again."

And even as I spoke he sprang to his feet and stopped me by a gesture.

"Listen!" he said.

From beyond the low hills across the water came the dull resonance of distant guns and a remote weird crying. Then everything was still. A cockchafer came droning over the hedge and past us. High in the west the crescent moon hung faint and pale above the smoke of Weybridge and Shepperton and the hot, still splendour of the sunset.

"We had better follow this path," I said, "northward."

CHAPTER 14

In London

My younger brother was in London when the Martians fell at Woking. He was a medical student working for an imminent examination, and he heard nothing of the arrival until Saturday morning. The morning papers on Saturday contained, in addition to lengthy special articles on the planet Mars, on life in the planets, and so forth, a brief and vaguely worded telegram, all the more striking for its brevity.

The Martians, alarmed by the approach of a crowd, had killed a number of people with a quick-firing gun, so the story ran. The telegram concluded with the words: "Formidable as they seem to be, the Martians have not moved from the pit into which they have fallen, and, indeed, seem incapable of doing so. Probably this is due to the relative strength of the earth's gravitational energy." On that last text their leader-writer expanded very comfortingly.

Of course all the students in the crammer's biology class, to which my brother went that day, were intensely interested, but there were no signs of any unusual excitement in the streets. The afternoon papers puffed scraps of news under big headlines. They had nothing to tell beyond the movements of troops about the common, and the burning of the pine woods between Woking and Weybridge, until eight. Then the *St. James's Gazette*, in an extra-special edition, announced the bare fact of the interruption of telegraphic communication. This was thought to be due to the falling of burning pine trees across the line. Nothing more of the fighting was known that night, the night of my drive to Leatherhead and back.

My brother felt no anxiety about us, as he knew from the description in the papers that the cylinder was a good two miles from my house. He made up his mind to run down that night to me, in order, as he says, to see the Things before they were killed. He dispatched a telegram, which never reached me, about four o'clock, and spent the evening at a music hall.

In London, also, on Saturday night there was a thunderstorm, and my brother reached Waterloo in a cab. On the platform from which the midnight train usually starts he learned, after some waiting, that an accident prevented trains from reaching Woking that night. The nature of the accident he could not ascertain; indeed, the railway authorities did not clearly know at that time. There was very little excitement in the station, as the officials, failing to realise that anything further than a breakdown between Byfleet and Woking junction had occurred, were running the theatre trains which usually passed through Woking round by Virginia Water or Guildford. They were busy making the necessary arrangements to alter the route of the Southampton and Portsmouth Sunday League excursions. A nocturnal newspaper reporter, mistaking my brother for the traffic manager, to whom he bears a slight resemblance, waylaid and tried to interview him. Few people, excepting the railway officials, connected the breakdown with the Martians.

I have read, in another account of these events, that on Sunday morning "all London was electrified by the news from Woking." As a matter of fact, there was nothing to justify that very extravagant phrase. Plenty of Londoners did not hear of the

Martians until the panic of Monday morning. Those who did took some time to realise all that the hastily worded telegrams in the Sunday papers conveyed. The majority of people in London do not read Sunday papers.

The habit of personal security, moreover, is so deeply fixed in the Londoner's mind, and startling intelligence so much a matter of course in the papers, that they could read without any personal tremors: "About seven o'clock last night the Martians came out of the cylinder, and, moving about under an armour of metallic shields, have completely wrecked Woking station with the adjacent houses, and massacred an entire battalion of the Cardigan Regiment. No details are known. Maxims have been absolutely useless against their armour; the field guns have been disabled by them. Flying hussars have been galloping into Chertsey. The Martians appear to be moving slowly towards Chertsey or Windsor. Great anxiety prevails in West Surrey, and earthworks are being thrown up to check the advance Londonward." That was how the Sunday *Sun* put it, and a clever and remarkably prompt "handbook" article in the *Referee* compared the affair to a menagerie suddenly let loose in a village.

No one in London knew positively of the nature of the armoured Martians, and there was still a fixed idea that these monsters must be sluggish: "crawling," "creeping painfully" – such expressions occurred in almost all the earlier reports. None of the telegrams could have been written by an eyewitness of their advance. The Sunday papers printed separate editions as further news came to hand, some even in default of it. But there was practically nothing more to tell people until late in the afternoon, when the authorities gave the press agencies the news in their possession. It was stated that the people of Walton and Weybridge, and all the district were pouring along the roads Londonward, and that was all.

My brother went to church at the Foundling Hospital in the morning, still in ignorance of what had happened on the previous night. There he heard allusions made to the invasion, and a special prayer for peace. Coming out, he bought a *Referee*. He became alarmed at the news in this, and went again to Waterloo station to find out if communication were restored. The omnibuses, carriages, cyclists, and innumerable people walking in their best clothes seemed scarcely affected by the strange intelligence that the news venders were disseminating. People were interested, or, if alarmed, alarmed only on account of the local residents. At the station he heard for the first time that the Windsor and Chertsey lines were now interrupted. The porters told him that several remarkable telegrams had been received in the morning from Byfleet and Chertsey stations, but that these had abruptly ceased. My brother could get very little precise detail out of them.

"There's fighting going on about Weybridge" was the extent of their information.

The train service was now very much disorganised. Quite a number of people who had been expecting friends from places on the South-Western network were standing about the station. One grey-headed old gentleman came and abused the South-Western Company bitterly to my brother. "It wants showing up," he said.

One or two trains came in from Richmond, Putney, and Kingston, containing people who had gone out for a day's boating and found the locks closed and a feeling of panic in the air. A man in a blue and white blazer addressed my brother, full of strange tidings.

"There's hosts of people driving into Kingston in traps and carts and things, with boxes of valuables and all that," he said. "They come from Molesey and Weybridge and Walton, and they say there's been guns heard at Chertsey, heavy firing, and that mounted soldiers have told them to get off at once because the Martians are coming. We heard guns firing at Hampton Court station, but we thought it was thunder. What the dickens does it all mean? The Martians can't get out of their pit, can they?"

My brother could not tell him.

Afterwards he found that the vague feeling of alarm had spread to the clients of the underground railway, and that the Sunday excursionists began to return from all over the South-Western "lung" – Barnes, Wimbledon, Richmond Park, Kew, and so forth – at unnaturally early hours; but not a soul had anything more than vague hearsay to tell of. Everyone connected with the terminus seemed ill-tempered.

About five o'clock the gathering crowd in the station was immensely excited by the opening of the line of communication, which is almost invariably closed, between the South-Eastern and the South-Western stations, and the passage of carriage trucks bearing huge guns and carriages crammed with soldiers. These were the guns that were brought up from Woolwich and Chatham to cover Kingston. There was an exchange of pleasantries: "You'll get eaten!" "We're the beast-tamers!" and so forth. A little while after that a squad of police came into the station and began to clear the public off the platforms, and my brother went out into the street again.

The church bells were ringing for evensong, and a squad of Salvation Army lassies came singing down Waterloo Road. On the bridge a number of loafers were watching a curious brown scum that came drifting down the stream in patches. The sun was just setting, and the Clock Tower and the Houses of Parliament rose against one of the most peaceful skies it is possible to imagine, a sky of gold, barred with long transverse stripes of reddish-purple cloud. There was talk of a floating body. One of the men there, a reservist he said he was, told my brother he had seen the heliograph flickering in the west.

In Wellington Street my brother met a couple of sturdy roughs who had just been rushed out of Fleet Street with still-wet newspapers and staring placards. "Dreadful catastrophe!" they bawled one to the other down Wellington Street. "Fighting at Weybridge! Full description! Repulse of the Martians! London in Danger!" He had to give threepence for a copy of that paper.

Then it was, and then only, that he realised something of the full power and terror of these monsters. He learned that they were not merely a handful of small sluggish creatures, but that they were minds swaying vast mechanical bodies; and that they could move swiftly and smite with such power that even the mightiest guns could not stand against them.

They were described as "vast spiderlike machines, nearly a hundred feet high, capable of the speed of an express train, and able to shoot out a beam of intense heat." Masked batteries, chiefly of field guns, had been planted in the country about Horsell Common, and especially between the Woking district and London. Five of the machines had been seen moving towards the Thames, and one, by a happy chance, had been destroyed. In the other cases the shells had missed, and the batteries had been at once annihilated by the Heat-Rays. Heavy losses of soldiers were mentioned, but the tone of the dispatch was optimistic.

The Martians had been repulsed; they were not invulnerable. They had retreated to their triangle of cylinders again, in the circle about Woking. Signallers with heliographs were pushing forward upon them from all sides. Guns were in rapid transit from Windsor, Portsmouth, Aldershot, Woolwich – even from the north; among others, long wire-guns of ninety-five tons from Woolwich. Altogether one hundred and sixteen were in position or being hastily placed, chiefly covering London. Never before in England had there been such a vast or rapid concentration of military material.

Any further cylinders that fell, it was hoped, could be destroyed at once by high explosives, which were being rapidly manufactured and distributed. No doubt, ran the report, the situation was of the strangest and gravest description, but the public was exhorted to avoid and discourage panic. No doubt the Martians were strange and terrible in the extreme, but at the outside there could not be more than twenty of them against our millions.

The authorities had reason to suppose, from the size of the cylinders, that at the outside there could not be more than five in each cylinder – fifteen altogether. And one at least was disposed of – perhaps more. The public would be fairly warned of the approach of danger, and elaborate measures were being taken for the protection of the people in the threatened southwestern suburbs. And so, with reiterated assurances of the safety of London and the ability of the authorities to cope with the difficulty, this quasi-proclamation closed.

This was printed in enormous type on paper so fresh that it was still wet, and there had been no time to add a word of comment. It was curious, my brother said, to see how ruthlessly the usual contents of the paper had been hacked and taken out to give this place.

All down Wellington Street people could be seen fluttering out the pink sheets and reading, and the Strand was suddenly noisy with the voices of an army of hawkers following these pioneers. Men came scrambling off buses to secure copies. Certainly this news excited people intensely, whatever their previous apathy. The shutters of a map shop in the Strand were being taken down, my brother said, and a man in his Sunday raiment, lemon-yellow gloves even, was visible inside the window hastily fastening maps of Surrey to the glass.

Going on along the Strand to Trafalgar Square, the paper in his hand, my brother saw some of the fugitives from West Surrey. There was a man with his wife and two boys and some articles of furniture in a cart such as greengrocers use. He was driving from the direction of Westminster Bridge; and close behind him came a hay waggon with five or six respectable-looking people in it, and some boxes and bundles. The faces of these people were haggard, and their entire appearance contrasted conspicuously with the Sabbath-best appearance of the people on the omnibuses. People in fashionable clothing peeped at them out of cabs. They stopped at the Square as if undecided which way to take, and finally turned eastward along the Strand. Some way behind these came a man in workday clothes, riding one of those old-fashioned tricycles with a small front wheel. He was dirty and white in the face.

My brother turned down towards Victoria, and met a number of such people. He had a vague idea that he might see something of me. He noticed an unusual number of police regulating the traffic. Some of the refugees were exchanging news with the people on the omnibuses. One was professing to have seen the Martians. "Boilers on stilts, I tell you, striding along like men." Most of them were excited and animated by their strange experience.

Beyond Victoria the public-houses were doing a lively trade with these arrivals. At all the street corners groups of people were reading papers, talking excitedly, or staring at these unusual Sunday visitors. They seemed to increase as night drew on, until at last the roads, my brother said, were like Epsom High Street on a Derby Day. My brother addressed several of these fugitives and got unsatisfactory answers from most.

None of them could tell him any news of Woking except one man, who assured him that Woking had been entirely destroyed on the previous night.

"I come from Byfleet," he said; "man on a bicycle came through the place in the early morning, and ran from door to door warning us to come away. Then came soldiers. We went out to look, and there were clouds of smoke to the south – nothing but smoke, and not a soul coming that way. Then we heard the guns at Chertsey, and folks coming from Weybridge. So I've locked up my house and come on."

At the time there was a strong feeling in the streets that the authorities were to blame for their incapacity to dispose of the invaders without all this inconvenience.

About eight o'clock a noise of heavy firing was distinctly audible all over the south of London. My brother could not hear it for the traffic in the main thoroughfares, but by striking through the quiet back streets to the river he was able to distinguish it quite plainly.

He walked from Westminster to his apartments near Regent's Park, about two. He was now very anxious on my account, and disturbed at the evident magnitude of the trouble. His mind was inclined to run, even as mine had run on Saturday, on military details. He thought of all those silent, expectant guns, of the suddenly nomadic countryside; he tried to imagine "boilers on stilts" a hundred feet high.

There were one or two cartloads of refugees passing along Oxford Street, and several in the Marylebone Road, but so slowly was the news spreading that Regent Street and Portland Place were full of their usual Sunday-night promenaders, albeit they talked in groups, and along the edge of Regent's Park there were as many silent couples "walking out" together under the scattered gas lamps as ever there had been. The night was warm and still, and a little oppressive; the sound of guns continued intermittently, and after midnight there seemed to be sheet lightning in the south.

He read and re-read the paper, fearing the worst had happened to me. He was restless, and after supper prowled out again aimlessly. He returned and tried in vain to divert his attention to his examination notes. He went to bed a little after midnight, and was awakened from lurid dreams in the small hours of Monday by the sound of door knockers, feet running in the street, distant drumming, and a clamour of bells. Red reflections danced on the ceiling. For a moment he lay astonished, wondering whether day had come or the world gone mad. Then he jumped out of bed and ran to the window.

His room was an attic and as he thrust his head out, up and down the street there were a dozen echoes to the noise of his window sash, and heads in every kind of night disarray appeared. Enquiries were being shouted. "They are coming!" bawled a policeman, hammering at the door; "the Martians are coming!" and hurried to the next door.

The sound of drumming and trumpeting came from the Albany Street Barracks, and every church within earshot was hard at work killing sleep with a vehement disorderly tocsin. There was a noise of doors opening, and window after window in the houses opposite flashed from darkness into yellow illumination.

Up the street came galloping a closed carriage, bursting abruptly into noise at the corner, rising to a clattering climax under the window, and dying away slowly in the distance. Close on the rear of this came a couple of cabs, the forerunners of a long procession of flying vehicles, going for the most part to Chalk Farm station, where the North-Western special trains were loading up, instead of coming down the gradient into Euston.

For a long time my brother stared out of the window in blank astonishment, watching the policemen hammering at door after door, and delivering their incomprehensible message. Then the door behind him opened, and the man who lodged across the landing came in, dressed only in shirt, trousers, and slippers, his braces loose about his waist, his hair disordered from his pillow.

"What the devil is it?" he asked. "A fire? What a devil of a row!"

They both craned their heads out of the window, straining to hear what the policemen were shouting. People were coming out of the side streets, and standing in groups at the corners talking.

"What the devil is it all about?" said my brother's fellow lodger.

My brother answered him vaguely and began to dress, running with each garment to the window in order to miss nothing of the growing excitement. And presently men selling unnaturally early newspapers came bawling into the street:

"London in danger of suffocation! The Kingston and Richmond defences forced! Fearful massacres in the Thames Valley!"

And all about him – in the rooms below, in the houses on each side and across the road, and behind in the Park Terraces and in the hundred other streets of that part of Marylebone, and the Westbourne Park district and St. Pancras, and westward and northward in Kilburn and St. John's Wood and Hampstead, and eastward in Shoreditch and Highbury and Haggerston and Hoxton, and, indeed, through all the vastness of London from Ealing to East Ham – people were rubbing their eyes, and opening windows to stare out and ask aimless questions, dressing hastily as the first breath of the coming storm of Fear blew through the streets. It was the dawn of the great panic. London, which had gone to bed on Sunday night oblivious and inert, was awakened, in the small hours of Monday morning, to a vivid sense of danger.

Unable from his window to learn what was happening, my brother went down and out into the street, just as the sky between the parapets of the houses grew pink with the early dawn. The flying people on foot and in vehicles grew more numerous every moment. "Black Smoke!" he heard people crying, and again "Black Smoke!" The contagion of such a unanimous fear was inevitable. As my brother hesitated on the door-step, he saw another news vender approaching, and got a paper forthwith. The man was running away with the rest, and selling his papers for a shilling each as he ran – a grotesque mingling of profit and panic.

And from this paper my brother read that catastrophic dispatch of the Commander-in-Chief:

"The Martians are able to discharge enormous clouds of a black and poisonous vapour by means of rockets. They have smothered our batteries, destroyed Richmond, Kingston, and Wimbledon, and are advancing slowly towards London, destroying everything on the way. It is impossible to stop them. There is no safety from the Black Smoke but in instant flight."

That was all, but it was enough. The whole population of the great six-million city was stirring, slipping, running; presently it would be pouring *en masse* northward.

"Black Smoke!" the voices cried. "Fire!"

The bells of the neighbouring church made a jangling tumult, a cart carelessly driven smashed, amid shrieks and curses, against the water trough up the street. Sickly yellow lights went to and fro in the houses, and some of the passing cabs flaunted unextinguished lamps. And overhead the dawn was growing brighter, clear and steady and calm.

He heard footsteps running to and fro in the rooms, and up and down stairs behind him. His landlady came to the door, loosely wrapped in dressing gown and shawl; her husband followed ejaculating.

As my brother began to realise the import of all these things, he turned hastily to his own room, put all his available money – some ten pounds altogether – into his pockets, and went out again into the streets.

CHAPTER 15

What Had Happened in Surrey

It was while the curate had sat and talked so wildly to me under the hedge in the flat meadows near Halliford, and while my brother was watching the fugitives stream over Westminster Bridge, that the Martians had resumed the offensive. So far as one can ascertain from the conflicting accounts that have been put forth, the majority of them remained busied with preparations in the Horsell pit until nine that night, hurrying on some operation that disengaged huge volumes of green smoke.

But three certainly came out about eight o'clock and, advancing slowly and cautiously, made their way through Byfleet and Pyrford towards Ripley and Weybridge, and so came in sight of the expectant batteries against the setting sun. These Martians did not advance in a body, but in a line, each perhaps a mile and a half from his nearest fellow. They communicated with one another by means of sirenlike howls, running up and down the scale from one note to another.

It was this howling and firing of the guns at Ripley and St. George's Hill that we had heard at Upper Halliford. The Ripley gunners, unseasoned artillery volunteers who ought never to have been placed in such a position, fired one wild, premature, ineffectual volley, and bolted on horse and foot through the deserted village, while the Martian, without using his Heat-Ray, walked serenely over their guns, stepped gingerly among them, passed in front of them, and so came unexpectedly upon the guns in Painshill Park, which he destroyed.

The St. George's Hill men, however, were better led or of a better mettle. Hidden by a pine wood as they were, they seem to have been quite unsuspected by the Martian nearest to them. They laid their guns as deliberately as if they had been on parade, and fired at about a thousand yards' range.

The shells flashed all round him, and he was seen to advance a few paces, stagger, and go down. Everybody yelled together, and the guns were reloaded in frantic haste. The overthrown Martian set up a prolonged ululation, and immediately a second glittering giant, answering him, appeared over the trees to the south. It would seem that a leg of the tripod had been smashed by one of the shells. The whole of the second volley flew wide of the Martian on the ground, and, simultaneously, both his companions brought their Heat-Rays to bear on the battery. The ammunition blew up, the pine trees all about the guns flashed into fire, and only one or two of the men who were already running over the crest of the hill escaped.

After this it would seem that the three took counsel together and halted, and the scouts who were watching them report that they remained absolutely stationary for the next half hour. The Martian who had been overthrown crawled tediously out of his hood, a small brown figure, oddly suggestive from that distance of a speck of blight, and apparently engaged in the repair of his support. About nine he had finished, for his cowl was then seen above the trees again.

It was a few minutes past nine that night when these three sentinels were joined by four other Martians, each carrying a thick black tube. A similar tube was handed to each of the three, and the seven proceeded to distribute themselves at equal distances along a curved line between St. George's Hill, Weybridge, and the village of Send, southwest of Ripley.

A dozen rockets sprang out of the hills before them so soon as they began to move, and warned the waiting batteries about Ditton and Esher. At the same time four of their fighting machines, similarly armed with tubes, crossed the river, and two of them, black against the western sky, came into sight of myself and the curate as we hurried wearily and painfully along the road that runs northward out of Halliford. They moved, as it seemed to us, upon a cloud, for a milky mist covered the fields and rose to a third of their height.

At this sight the curate cried faintly in his throat, and began running; but I knew it was no good running from a Martian, and I turned aside and crawled through dewy nettles and brambles into the broad ditch by the side of the road. He looked back, saw what I was doing, and turned to join me.

The two halted, the nearer to us standing and facing Sunbury, the remoter being a grey indistinctness towards the evening star, away towards Staines.

The occasional howling of the Martians had ceased; they took up their positions in the huge crescent about their cylinders in absolute silence. It was a crescent with twelve miles between its horns. Never since the devising of gunpowder was the beginning of a battle so still. To us and to an observer about Ripley it would have had precisely the same effect – the Martians seemed in solitary possession of the darkling night, lit only as it was by the slender moon, the stars, the afterglow of the daylight, and the ruddy glare from St. George's Hill and the woods of Painshill.

But facing that crescent everywhere – at Staines, Hounslow, Ditton, Esher, Ockham, behind hills and woods south of the river, and across the flat grass meadows to the north of it, wherever a cluster of trees or village houses gave sufficient cover – the guns were waiting. The signal rockets burst and rained their sparks through the night and vanished, and the spirit of all those watching batteries rose to a tense expectation. The Martians had but to advance into the line of fire, and instantly those motionless black forms of men, those guns glittering so darkly in the early night, would explode into a thunderous fury of battle.

No doubt the thought that was uppermost in a thousand of those vigilant minds, even as it was uppermost in mine, was the riddle – how much they understood of us. Did they grasp that we in our millions were organized, disciplined, working together? Or did they interpret our spurts of fire, the sudden stinging of our shells, our steady investment of their encampment, as we should the furious unanimity of onslaught in a disturbed hive of bees? Did they dream they might exterminate us? (At that time no one knew what food they needed.) A hundred such questions struggled together in my mind as I watched that vast sentinel shape. And in the back of my mind was the sense of all the huge unknown and hidden forces Londonward. Had they prepared pitfalls? Were the powder mills at Hounslow ready as a snare? Would the Londoners have the heart and courage to make a greater Moscow of their mighty province of houses?

Then, after an interminable time, as it seemed to us, crouching and peering through the hedge, came a sound like the distant concussion of a gun. Another nearer, and then another. And then the Martian beside us raised his tube on high and discharged it, gunwise, with a heavy report that made the ground heave. The one towards Staines answered him. There was no flash, no smoke, simply that loaded detonation.

I was so excited by these heavy minute-guns following one another that I so far forgot my personal safety and my scalded hands as to clamber up into the hedge and stare towards Sunbury. As I did so a second report followed, and a big projectile hurtled overhead towards Hounslow. I expected at least to see smoke or fire, or some such evidence of its work. But all I saw was the deep blue sky above, with one solitary star, and the white mist spreading wide and low beneath. And there had been no crash, no answering explosion. The silence was restored; the minute lengthened to three.

"What has happened?" said the curate, standing up beside me.

"Heaven knows!" said I.

A bat flickered by and vanished. A distant tumult of shouting began and ceased. I looked again at the Martian, and saw he was now moving eastward along the riverbank, with a swift, rolling motion.

Every moment I expected the fire of some hidden battery to spring upon him; but the evening calm was unbroken. The figure of the Martian grew smaller as he receded, and presently the mist and the gathering night had swallowed him up. By a common impulse we clambered higher. Towards Sunbury was a dark appearance, as though a conical hill had suddenly come into being there, hiding our view of the farther country; and then, remoter across the river, over Walton, we saw another such summit. These hill-like forms grew lower and broader even as we stared.

Moved by a sudden thought, I looked northward, and there I perceived a third of these cloudy black kopjes had risen.

Everything had suddenly become very still. Far away to the southeast, marking the quiet, we heard the Martians hooting to one another, and then the air quivered again with the distant thud of their guns. But the earthly artillery made no reply.

Now at the time we could not understand these things, but later I was to learn the meaning of these ominous kopjes that gathered in the twilight. Each of the Martians, standing in the great crescent I have described, had discharged, by means of the gunlike tube he carried, a huge canister over whatever hill, copse, cluster of houses, or other possible cover for guns, chanced to be in front of him. Some fired only one of these, some two – as in the case of the one we had seen; the one at Ripley is said to have discharged no fewer than five at that time. These canisters smashed on striking the ground – they did not explode – and incontinently disengaged an enormous volume of heavy, inky vapour, coiling and pouring upward in a huge and ebony cumulus cloud, a gaseous hill that sank and spread itself slowly over the surrounding country. And the touch of that vapour, the inhaling of its pungent wisps, was death to all that breathes.

It was heavy, this vapour, heavier than the densest smoke, so that, after the first tumultuous uprush and outflow of its impact, it sank down through the air and poured over the ground in a manner rather liquid than gaseous, abandoning the hills, and streaming into the valleys and ditches and watercourses even as I have heard the carbonic-acid gas that pours from volcanic clefts is wont to do. And where it came upon water some chemical action occurred, and the surface would be instantly covered with a powdery scum that sank slowly and made way for more. The scum was absolutely insoluble, and it is a strange thing, seeing the instant effect of the gas, that one could drink without hurt the water from which it had been strained. The vapour did not diffuse as a true gas would do. It hung together in banks, flowing sluggishly down the slope of the land and driving reluctantly before the wind, and very slowly it combined with the mist and moisture of the air, and sank to the earth in the form of dust. Save that an unknown element giving a group of four lines in the blue of the spectrum is concerned, we are still entirely ignorant of the nature of this substance.

Once the tumultuous upheaval of its dispersion was over, the black smoke clung so closely to the ground, even before its precipitation, that fifty feet up in the air, on the roofs and upper stories of high houses and on great trees, there was a chance of escaping its poison altogether, as was proved even that night at Street Cobham and Ditton.

The man who escaped at the former place tells a wonderful story of the strangeness of its coiling flow, and how he looked down from the church spire and saw the houses of the village rising like ghosts out of its inky nothingness. For a day and a half he remained there, weary, starving and sun-scorched, the earth under the blue sky and against the prospect of the distant hills a velvet-black expanse, with red roofs, green trees, and, later, black-veiled shrubs and gates, barns, outhouses, and walls, rising here and there into the sunlight.

But that was at Street Cobham, where the black vapour was allowed to remain until it sank of its own accord into the ground. As a rule the Martians, when it had served its purpose, cleared the air of it again by wading into it and directing a jet of steam upon it.

This they did with the vapour banks near us, as we saw in the starlight from the window of a deserted house at Upper Halliford, whither we had returned. From there we could see the searchlights on Richmond Hill and Kingston Hill going to and fro, and about eleven the windows rattled, and we heard the sound of the huge siege guns that had been put in position there. These continued intermittently for the space of a quarter of an hour, sending chance shots at the invisible Martians at Hampton and Ditton, and then the pale beams of the electric light vanished, and were replaced by a bright red glow.

Then the fourth cylinder fell – a brilliant green meteor – as I learned afterwards, in Bushey Park. Before the guns on the Richmond and Kingston line of hills began, there was a fitful cannonade far away in the southwest, due, I believe, to guns being fired haphazard before the black vapour could overwhelm the gunners.

So, setting about it as methodically as men might smoke out a wasps' nest, the Martians spread this strange stifling vapour over the

Londonward country. The horns of the crescent slowly moved apart, until at last they formed a line from Hanwell to Coombe and Malden. All night through their destructive tubes advanced. Never once, after the Martian at St. George's Hill was brought down, did they give the artillery the ghost of a chance against them. Wherever there was a possibility of guns being laid for them unseen, a fresh canister of the black vapour was discharged, and where the guns were openly displayed the Heat-Ray was brought to bear.

By midnight the blazing trees along the slopes of Richmond Park and the glare of Kingston Hill threw their light upon a network of black smoke, blotting out the whole valley of the Thames and extending as far as the eye could reach. And through this two Martians slowly waded, and turned their hissing steam jets this way and that.

They were sparing of the Heat-Ray that night, either because they had but a limited supply of material for its production or because they did not wish to destroy the country but only to crush and overawe the opposition they had aroused. In the latter aim they certainly succeeded. Sunday night was the end of the organised opposition to their movements. After that no body of men would stand against them, so hopeless was the enterprise. Even the crews of the torpedo-boats and destroyers that had brought their quick-firers up the Thames refused to stop, mutinied, and went down again. The only offensive operation men ventured upon after that night was the preparation of mines and pitfalls, and even in that their energies were frantic and spasmodic.

One has to imagine, as well as one may, the fate of those batteries towards Esher, waiting so tensely in the twilight. Survivors there were none. One may picture the orderly expectation, the officers alert and watchful, the gunners ready, the ammunition piled to hand, the limber gunners with their horses and waggons, the groups of civilian spectators standing as near as they were permitted, the evening stillness, the ambulances and hospital tents with the burned and wounded from Weybridge; then the dull resonance of the shots the Martians fired, and the clumsy projectile whirling over the trees and houses and smashing amid the neighbouring fields.

One may picture, too, the sudden shifting of the attention, the swiftly spreading coils and bellyings of that blackness advancing headlong, towering heavenward, turning the twilight to a palpable darkness, a strange and horrible antagonist of vapour striding upon its victims, men and horses near it seen dimly, running, shrieking, falling headlong, shouts of dismay, the guns suddenly abandoned, men choking and writhing on the ground, and the swift broadening-out of the opaque cone of smoke. And then night and extinction – nothing but a silent mass of impenetrable vapour hiding its dead.

Before dawn the black vapour was pouring through the streets of Richmond, and the disintegrating organism of government was, with a last expiring effort, rousing the population of London to the necessity of flight.

CHAPTER 16

The Exodus from London

So you understand the roaring wave of fear that swept through the greatest city in the world just as Monday was dawning – the stream of flight rising swiftly to a torrent, lashing in a foaming tumult round the railway stations, banked up into a horrible struggle about the shipping in the Thames, and hurrying by every available channel northward and eastward. By ten o'clock the police organisation, and by midday even the railway organisations, were losing coherency, losing shape and efficiency, guttering, softening, running at last in that swift liquefaction of the social body.

All the railway lines north of the Thames and the South-Eastern people at Cannon Street had been warned by midnight on Sunday, and trains were being filled. People were fighting savagely for standing-room in the carriages even at two o'clock. By three, people were being trampled and crushed even in Bishopsgate Street, a couple of hundred yards or more from Liverpool Street station; revolvers were fired, people stabbed, and the policemen who had been sent to direct the traffic, exhausted and infuriated, were breaking the heads of the people they were called out to protect.

And as the day advanced and the engine drivers and stokers refused to return to London, the pressure of the flight drove the people in an ever-thickening multitude away from the stations and

along the northward-running roads. By midday a Martian had been
seen at Barnes, and a cloud of slowly sinking black vapour drove along
the Thames and across the flats of Lambeth, cutting off all escape over
the bridges in its sluggish advance. Another bank drove over Ealing,
and surrounded a little island of survivors on Castle Hill, alive, but
unable to escape.

After a fruitless struggle to get aboard a North-Western train at
Chalk Farm – the engines of the trains that had loaded in the goods
yard there *ploughed* through shrieking people, and a dozen stalwart
men fought to keep the crowd from crushing the driver against his
furnace – my brother emerged upon the Chalk Farm road, dodged
across through a hurrying swarm of vehicles, and had the luck to be
foremost in the sack of a cycle shop. The front tire of the machine
he got was punctured in dragging it through the window, but he got
up and off, notwithstanding, with no further injury than a cut wrist.
The steep foot of Haverstock Hill was impassable owing to several
overturned horses, and my brother struck into Belsize Road.

So he got out of the fury of the panic, and, skirting the Edgware
Road, reached Edgware about seven, fasting and wearied, but well
ahead of the crowd. Along the road people were standing in the
roadway, curious, wondering. He was passed by a number of cyclists,
some horsemen, and two motor cars. A mile from Edgware the rim
of the wheel broke, and the machine became unridable. He left it
by the roadside and trudged through the village. There were shops
half opened in the main street of the place, and people crowded on
the pavement and in the doorways and windows, staring astonished
at this extraordinary procession of fugitives that was beginning. He
succeeded in getting some food at an inn.

For a time he remained in Edgware not knowing what next to
do. The flying people increased in number. Many of them, like my

brother, seemed inclined to loiter in the place. There was no fresh news of the invaders from Mars.

At that time the road was crowded, but as yet far from congested. Most of the fugitives at that hour were mounted on cycles, but there were soon motor cars, hansom cabs, and carriages hurrying along, and the dust hung in heavy clouds along the road to St. Albans.

It was perhaps a vague idea of making his way to Chelmsford, where some friends of his lived, that at last induced my brother to strike into a quiet lane running eastward. Presently he came upon a stile, and, crossing it, followed a footpath northeastward. He passed near several farmhouses and some little places whose names he did not learn. He saw few fugitives until, in a grass lane towards High Barnet, he happened upon two ladies who became his fellow travellers. He came upon them just in time to save them.

He heard their screams, and, hurrying round the corner, saw a couple of men struggling to drag them out of the little pony-chaise in which they had been driving, while a third with difficulty held the frightened pony's head. One of the ladies, a short woman dressed in white, was simply screaming; the other, a dark, slender figure, slashed at the man who gripped her arm with a whip she held in her disengaged hand.

My brother immediately grasped the situation, shouted, and hurried towards the struggle. One of the men desisted and turned towards him, and my brother, realising from his antagonist's face that a fight was unavoidable, and being an expert boxer, went into him forthwith and sent him down against the wheel of the chaise.

It was no time for pugilistic chivalry and my brother laid him quiet with a kick, and gripped the collar of the man who pulled at the slender lady's arm. He heard the clatter of hoofs, the whip stung across his face, a third antagonist struck him between the eyes, and the man he held wrenched himself free and made off down the lane in the direction from which he had come.

Partly stunned, he found himself facing the man who had held the horse's head, and became aware of the chaise receding from him down the lane, swaying from side to side, and with the women in it looking back. The man before him, a burly rough, tried to close, and he stopped him with a blow in the face. Then, realising that he was deserted, he dodged round and made off down the lane after the chaise, with the sturdy man close behind him, and the fugitive, who had turned now, following remotely.

Suddenly he stumbled and fell; his immediate pursuer went headlong, and he rose to his feet to find himself with a couple of antagonists again. He would have had little chance against them had not the slender lady very pluckily pulled up and returned to his help. It seems she had had a revolver all this time, but it had been under the seat when she and her companion were attacked. She fired at six yards' distance, narrowly missing my brother. The less courageous of the robbers made off, and his companion followed him, cursing his cowardice. They both stopped in sight down the lane, where the third man lay insensible.

"Take this!" said the slender lady, and she gave my brother her revolver.

"Go back to the chaise," said my brother, wiping the blood from his split lip.

She turned without a word – they were both panting – and they went back to where the lady in white struggled to hold back the frightened pony.

The robbers had evidently had enough of it. When my brother looked again they were retreating.

"I'll sit here," said my brother, "if I may"; and he got upon the empty front seat. The lady looked over her shoulder.

"Give me the reins," she said, and laid the whip along the pony's side. In another moment a bend in the road hid the three men from my brother's eyes.

So, quite unexpectedly, my brother found himself, panting, with a cut mouth, a bruised jaw, and bloodstained knuckles, driving along an unknown lane with these two women.

He learned they were the wife and the younger sister of a surgeon living at Stanmore, who had come in the small hours from a dangerous case at Pinner, and heard at some railway station on his way of the Martian advance. He had hurried home, roused the women – their servant had left them two days before – packed some provisions, put his revolver under the seat – luckily for my brother – and told them to drive on to Edgware, with the idea of getting a train there. He stopped behind to tell the neighbours. He would overtake them, he said, at about half past four in the morning, and now it was nearly nine and they had seen nothing of him. They could not stop in Edgware because of the growing traffic through the place, and so they had come into this side lane.

That was the story they told my brother in fragments when presently they stopped again, nearer to New Barnet. He promised to stay with them, at least until they could determine what to do, or until the missing man arrived, and professed to be an expert shot with the revolver – a weapon strange to him – in order to give them confidence.

They made a sort of encampment by the wayside, and the pony became happy in the hedge. He told them of his own escape out of London, and all that he knew of these Martians and their ways. The sun crept higher in the sky, and after a time their talk died out and gave place to an uneasy state of anticipation. Several wayfarers came along the lane, and of these my brother gathered such news as he could. Every broken answer he had deepened his impression of the great disaster that had come on humanity, deepened his persuasion of the immediate necessity for prosecuting this flight. He urged the matter upon them.

"We have money," said the slender woman, and hesitated.

Her eyes met my brother's, and her hesitation ended.

"So have I," said my brother.

She explained that they had as much as thirty pounds in gold, besides a five-pound note, and suggested that with that they might get upon a train at St. Albans or New Barnet. My brother thought that was hopeless, seeing the fury of the Londoners to crowd upon the trains, and broached his own idea of striking across Essex towards Harwich and thence escaping from the country altogether.

Mrs. Elphinstone – that was the name of the woman in white – would listen to no reasoning, and kept calling upon "George"; but her sister-in-law was astonishingly quiet and deliberate, and at last agreed to my brother's suggestion. So, designing to cross the Great North Road, they went on towards Barnet, my brother leading the pony to save it as much as possible. As the sun crept up the sky the day became excessively hot, and under foot a thick, whitish sand grew burning and blinding, so that they travelled only very slowly. The hedges were grey with dust. And as they advanced towards Barnet a tumultuous murmuring grew stronger.

They began to meet more people. For the most part these were staring before them, murmuring indistinct questions, jaded, haggard, unclean. One man in evening dress passed them on foot, his eyes on the ground. They heard his voice, and, looking back at him, saw one hand clutched in his hair and the other beating invisible things. His paroxysm of rage over, he went on his way without once looking back.

As my brother's party went on towards the crossroads to the south of Barnet they saw a woman approaching the road across some fields on their left, carrying a child and with two other children; and then passed a man in dirty black, with a thick stick in one hand and a small portmanteau in the other. Then round the corner of the lane, from between the villas that guarded it at its confluence with the high road, came a little cart drawn by a sweating black pony and driven by a sallow youth in a bowler hat, grey with dust. There were three girls, East End factory girls, and a couple of little children crowded in the cart.

"This'll tike us rahnd Edgware?" asked the driver, wild-eyed, white-faced; and when my brother told him it would if he turned to the left, he whipped up at once without the formality of thanks.

My brother noticed a pale grey smoke or haze rising among the houses in front of them, and veiling the white facade of a terrace beyond the road that appeared between the backs of the villas. Mrs. Elphinstone suddenly cried out at a number of tongues of smoky red flame leaping up above the houses in front of them against the hot, blue sky. The tumultuous noise resolved itself now into the disorderly mingling of many voices, the gride of many wheels, the creaking of waggons, and the staccato of hoofs. The lane came round sharply not fifty yards from the crossroads.

"Good heavens!" cried Mrs. Elphinstone. "What is this you are driving us into?"

My brother stopped.

For the main road was a boiling stream of people, a torrent of human beings rushing northward, one pressing on another. A great bank of dust, white and luminous in the blaze of the sun, made everything within twenty feet of the ground grey and indistinct and was perpetually renewed by the hurrying feet of a dense crowd of horses and of men and women on foot, and by the wheels of vehicles of every description.

"Way!" my brother heard voices crying. "Make way!"

It was like riding into the smoke of a fire to approach the meeting point of the lane and road; the crowd roared like a fire, and the dust was hot and pungent. And, indeed, a little way up the road a villa was burning and sending rolling masses of black smoke across the road to add to the confusion.

Two men came past them. Then a dirty woman, carrying a heavy bundle and weeping. A lost retriever dog, with hanging tongue, circled dubiously round them, scared and wretched, and fled at my brother's threat.

So much as they could see of the road Londonward between the houses to the right was a tumultuous stream of dirty, hurrying people, pent in between the villas on either side; the black heads, the crowded forms, grew into distinctness as they rushed towards the corner, hurried past, and merged their individuality again in a receding multitude that was swallowed up at last in a cloud of dust.

"Go on! Go on!" cried the voices. "Way! Way!"

One man's hands pressed on the back of another. My brother stood at the pony's head. Irresistibly attracted, he advanced slowly, pace by pace, down the lane.

Edgware had been a scene of confusion, Chalk Farm a riotous tumult, but this was a whole population in movement. It is hard to imagine that host. It had no character of its own. The figures poured out past the corner, and receded with their backs to the group in the lane. Along the margin came those who were on foot threatened by the wheels, stumbling in the ditches, blundering into one another.

The carts and carriages crowded close upon one another, making little way for those swifter and more impatient vehicles that darted forward every now and then when an opportunity showed itself of doing so, sending the people scattering against the fences and gates of the villas.

"Push on!" was the cry. "Push on! They are coming!"

In one cart stood a blind man in the uniform of the Salvation Army, gesticulating with his crooked fingers and bawling, "Eternity! Eternity!" His voice was hoarse and very loud so that my brother could hear him long after he was lost to sight in the dust. Some of the people who crowded in the carts whipped stupidly at their horses and quarrelled with other drivers; some sat motionless, staring at nothing with miserable eyes; some gnawed their hands with thirst, or lay prostrate in the bottoms of their conveyances. The horses' bits were covered with foam, their eyes bloodshot.

There were cabs, carriages, shop cars, waggons, beyond counting; a mail cart, a road-cleaner's cart marked "Vestry of St. Pancras," a huge timber waggon crowded with roughs. A brewer's dray rumbled by with its two near wheels splashed with fresh blood.

"Clear the way!" cried the voices. "Clear the way!"

"Eter-nity! Eter-nity!" came echoing down the road.

There were sad, haggard women tramping by, well dressed, with children that cried and stumbled, their dainty clothes smothered in dust, their weary faces smeared with tears. With many of these came men, sometimes helpful, sometimes lowering and savage. Fighting side by side with them pushed some weary street outcast in faded black rags, wide-eyed, loud-voiced, and foul-mouthed. There were sturdy workmen thrusting their way along, wretched, unkempt men, clothed like clerks or shopmen, struggling spasmodically; a wounded soldier my brother noticed, men dressed in the clothes of railway porters, one wretched creature in a nightshirt with a coat thrown over it.

But varied as its composition was, certain things all that host had in common. There were fear and pain on their faces, and fear behind them. A tumult up the road, a quarrel for a place in a waggon, sent the whole host of them quickening their pace; even a man so scared and broken that his knees bent under him was galvanised for a moment into renewed activity. The heat and dust had already been at work upon this multitude. Their skins were dry, their lips black and cracked. They were all thirsty, weary, and footsore. And amid the various cries one heard disputes, reproaches, groans of weariness and fatigue; the voices of most of them were hoarse and weak. Through it all ran a refrain:

"Way! Way! The Martians are coming!"

Few stopped and came aside from that flood. The lane opened slantingly into the main road with a narrow opening, and had a delusive appearance of coming from the direction of London. Yet a kind of eddy of people drove into its mouth; weaklings elbowed out of the stream, who for the most part rested but a moment before plunging into it again. A little way down the lane, with two friends bending over him, lay a man with a bare leg, wrapped about with bloody rags. He was a lucky man to have friends.

A little old man, with a grey military moustache and a filthy black frock coat, limped out and sat down beside the trap, removed his boot – his sock was blood-stained – shook out a pebble, and hobbled on again; and then a little girl of eight or nine, all alone, threw herself under the hedge close by my brother, weeping.

"I can't go on! I can't go on!"

My brother woke from his torpor of astonishment and lifted her up, speaking gently to her, and carried her to Miss Elphinstone. So soon as my brother touched her she became quite still, as if frightened.

"Ellen!" shrieked a woman in the crowd, with tears in her voice – "Ellen!" And the child suddenly darted away from my brother, crying "Mother!"

"They are coming," said a man on horseback, riding past along the lane.

"Out of the way, there!" bawled a coachman, towering high; and my brother saw a closed carriage turning into the lane.

The people crushed back on one another to avoid the horse. My brother pushed the pony and chaise back into the hedge, and the man drove by and stopped at the turn of the way. It was a carriage, with a pole for a pair of horses, but only one was in the traces. My brother saw dimly through the dust that two men lifted out something on a white stretcher and put it gently on the grass beneath the privet hedge.

One of the men came running to my brother.

"Where is there any water?" he said. "He is dying fast, and very thirsty. It is Lord Garrick."

"Lord Garrick!" said my brother; "the Chief Justice?"

"The water?" he said.

"There may be a tap," said my brother, "in some of the houses. We have no water. I dare not leave my people."

The man pushed against the crowd towards the gate of the corner house.

"Go on!" said the people, thrusting at him. "They are coming! Go on!"

Then my brother's attention was distracted by a bearded, eagle-faced man lugging a small handbag, which split even as my brother's eyes rested on it and disgorged a mass of sovereigns that seemed to break up into separate coins as it struck the ground. They rolled hither and thither among the struggling feet of men and horses. The man stopped and looked stupidly at the heap, and the shaft of a cab struck his shoulder and sent him reeling. He gave a shriek and dodged back, and a cartwheel shaved him narrowly.

"Way!" cried the men all about him. "Make way!"

So soon as the cab had passed, he flung himself, with both hands open, upon the heap of coins, and began thrusting handfuls in his pocket. A horse rose close upon him, and in another moment, half rising, he had been borne down under the horse's hoofs.

"Stop!" screamed my brother, and pushing a woman out of his way, tried to clutch the bit of the horse.

Before he could get to it, he heard a scream under the wheels, and saw through the dust the rim passing over the poor wretch's back. The driver of the cart slashed his whip at my brother, who ran round behind the cart. The multitudinous shouting confused his ears. The man was writhing in the dust among his scattered money, unable to rise, for the wheel had broken his back, and his lower limbs lay limp and dead. My brother stood up and yelled at the next driver, and a man on a black horse came to his assistance.

"Get him out of the road," said he; and, clutching the man's collar with his free hand, my brother lugged him sideways. But he still clutched after his money, and regarded my brother fiercely, hammering at his arm with a handful of gold. "Go on! Go on!" shouted angry voices behind.

"Way! Way!"

There was a smash as the pole of a carriage crashed into the cart that the man on horseback stopped. My brother looked up, and the man with the gold twisted his head round and bit the wrist that held his collar. There was a concussion, and the black horse came staggering sideways, and the carthorse pushed beside it. A hoof missed my brother's foot by a hair's breadth. He released his grip on the fallen man and jumped back. He saw anger change to terror on the face of the poor wretch on the ground, and in a moment he was hidden and my brother was borne backward and carried past the entrance of the lane, and had to fight hard in the torrent to recover it.

He saw Miss Elphinstone covering her eyes, and a little child, with all a child's want of sympathetic imagination, staring with dilated eyes at a dusty something that lay black and still, ground and crushed under the rolling wheels. "Let us go back!" he shouted, and began turning the pony round. "We cannot cross this – hell," he said and they went back a hundred yards the way they had come, until the fighting crowd was hidden. As they passed the bend in the lane my brother saw the face of the dying man in the ditch under the privet, deadly white and drawn, and shining with perspiration. The two women sat silent, crouching in their seat and shivering.

Then beyond the bend my brother stopped again. Miss Elphinstone was white and pale, and her sister-in-law sat weeping, too wretched even to call upon "George." My brother was horrified and perplexed. So soon as they had retreated he realised how urgent and unavoidable it was to attempt this crossing. He turned to Miss Elphinstone, suddenly resolute.

"We must go that way," he said, and led the pony round again.

For the second time that day this girl proved her quality. To force their way into the torrent of people, my brother plunged into the traffic and held back a cab horse, while she drove the pony across its head. A waggon locked wheels for a moment and ripped a long splinter from the chaise. In another moment they were caught and swept forward by the stream. My brother, with the cabman's whip marks red across his face and hands, scrambled into the chaise and took the reins from her.

"Point the revolver at the man behind," he said, giving it to her, "if he presses us too hard. No! – point it at his horse."

Then he began to look out for a chance of edging to the right across the road. But once in the stream he seemed to lose volition, to become a part of that dusty rout. They swept through Chipping Barnet with the torrent; they were nearly a mile beyond the centre of the town before they had fought across to the opposite side of the way. It was din and confusion indescribable; but in and beyond the town the road forks repeatedly, and this to some extent relieved the stress.

They struck eastward through Hadley, and there on either side of the road, and at another place farther on they came upon a great multitude of people drinking at the stream, some fighting to come at the water. And farther on, from a lull near East Barnet, they saw two trains running slowly one after the other without signal or order – trains swarming with people, with men even among the coals behind the engines – going northward along the Great Northern Railway. My brother supposes they must have filled outside London, for at that time the furious terror of the people had rendered the central termini impossible.

Near this place they halted for the rest of the afternoon, for the violence of the day had already utterly exhausted all three of them. They began to suffer the beginnings of hunger; the night was cold, and none of them dared to sleep. And in the evening many people came hurrying along the road nearby their stopping place, fleeing from unknown dangers before them, and going in the direction from which my brother had come.

CHAPTER 17

The "Thunder Child"

Had the Martians aimed only at destruction, they might on Monday have annihilated the entire population of London, as it spread itself slowly through the home counties. Not only along the road through Barnet, but also through Edgware and Waltham Abbey, and along the roads eastward to Southend and Shoeburyness, and south of the Thames to Deal and Broadstairs, poured the same frantic rout. If one could have hung that June morning in a balloon in the blazing blue above London every northward and eastward road running out of the tangled maze of streets would have seemed stippled black with the streaming fugitives, each dot a human agony of terror and physical distress. I have set forth at length in the last chapter my brother's account of the road through Chipping Barnet, in order that my readers may realise how that swarming of black dots appeared to one of those concerned. Never before in the history of the world had such a mass of human beings moved and suffered together. The legendary hosts of Goths and Huns, the hugest armies Asia has ever seen, would have been but a drop in that current. And this was no disciplined march; it was a stampede – a stampede gigantic and terrible – without order and without a goal, six million people unarmed and unprovisioned, driving headlong. It was the beginning of the rout of civilisation, of the massacre of mankind.

Directly below him the balloonist would have seen the network of streets far and wide, houses, churches, squares, crescents, gardens – already derelict – spread out like a huge map, and in the southward *blotted*. Over Ealing, Richmond, Wimbledon, it would have seemed as if some monstrous pen had flung ink upon the chart. Steadily, incessantly, each black splash grew and spread, shooting out ramifications this way and that, now banking itself against rising ground, now pouring swiftly over a crest into a new-found valley, exactly as a gout of ink would spread itself upon blotting paper.

And beyond, over the blue hills that rise southward of the river, the glittering Martians went to and fro, calmly and methodically spreading their poison cloud over this patch of country and then over that, laying it again with their steam jets when it had served its purpose, and taking possession of the conquered country. They do not seem to have aimed at extermination so much as at complete demoralisation and the destruction of any opposition. They exploded any stores of powder they came upon, cut every telegraph, and wrecked the railways here and there. They were hamstringing mankind. They seemed in no hurry to extend the field of their operations, and did not come beyond the central part of London all that day. It is possible that a very considerable number of people in London stuck to their houses through Monday morning. Certain it is that many died at home suffocated by the Black Smoke.

Until about midday the Pool of London was an astonishing scene. Steamboats and shipping of all sorts lay there, tempted by the enormous sums of money offered by fugitives, and it is said that many who swam out to these vessels were thrust off with boathooks and drowned. About one o'clock in the afternoon the thinning remnant of a cloud of the black vapour appeared between the arches of Blackfriars Bridge. At that the Pool became a scene of mad confusion, fighting, and collision, and for some time a multitude of boats and barges jammed in the northern arch of the Tower Bridge, and the sailors and lightermen had to fight savagely against the people who swarmed upon them from the riverfront. People were actually clambering down the piers of the bridge from above.

When, an hour later, a Martian appeared beyond the Clock Tower and waded down the river, nothing but wreckage floated above Limehouse.

Of the falling of the fifth cylinder I have presently to tell. The sixth star fell at Wimbledon. My brother, keeping watch beside the women in the chaise in a meadow, saw the green flash of it far beyond the hills. On Tuesday the little party, still set upon getting across the sea, made its way through the swarming country towards Colchester. The news that the Martians were now in possession of the whole of London was confirmed. They had been seen at Highgate, and even, it was said, at Neasden. But they did not come into my brother's view until the morrow.

That day the scattered multitudes began to realise the urgent need of provisions. As they grew hungry the rights of property ceased to be regarded. Farmers were out to defend their cattle-sheds, granaries, and ripening root crops with arms in their hands. A number of people now, like my brother, had their faces eastward, and there were some desperate souls even going back towards London to get food. These were chiefly people from the northern suburbs, whose knowledge of the Black Smoke came by hearsay. He heard that about half the members of the government had gathered at Birmingham, and that enormous quantities of high explosives were being prepared to be used in automatic mines across the Midland counties.

He was also told that the Midland Railway Company had replaced the desertions of the first day's panic, had resumed traffic, and was running northward trains from St. Albans to relieve the congestion of the home counties. There was also a placard in Chipping Ongar announcing that large stores of flour were available in the northern towns and that within twenty-four hours bread would be distributed among the starving people in the neighbourhood. But this intelligence did not deter him from the plan of escape he had formed, and the three pressed eastward all day, and heard no more of the bread distribution than this promise. Nor, as a matter of fact, did anyone else hear more of it. That night fell the seventh star, falling upon Primrose Hill. It fell while Miss Elphinstone was watching, for she took that duty alternately with my brother. She saw it.

On Wednesday the three fugitives – they had passed the night in a field of unripe wheat – reached Chelmsford, and there a body of the inhabitants, calling itself the Committee of Public Supply, seized the pony as provisions, and would give nothing in exchange for it but the promise of a share in it the next day. Here there were rumours of Martians at Epping, and news of the destruction of Waltham Abbey Powder Mills in a vain attempt to blow up one of the invaders.

People were watching for Martians here from the church towers. My brother, very luckily for him as it chanced, preferred to push on at once to the coast rather than wait for food, although all three of them were very hungry. By midday they passed through Tillingham, which, strangely enough, seemed to be quite silent and deserted, save for a few furtive plunderers hunting for food. Near Tillingham they suddenly came in sight of the sea, and the most amazing crowd of shipping of all sorts that it is possible to imagine.

For after the sailors could no longer come up the Thames, they came on to the Essex coast, to Harwich and Walton and Clacton, and afterwards to Foulness and Shoebury, to bring off the people. They lay in a huge sickle-shaped curve that vanished into mist at last

towards the Naze. Close inshore was a multitude of fishing smacks –
English, Scotch, French, Dutch, and Swedish; steam launches from the
Thames, yachts, electric boats; and beyond were ships of large burden,
a multitude of filthy colliers, trim merchantmen, cattle ships, passenger
boats, petroleum tanks, ocean tramps, an old white transport even, neat
white and grey liners from Southampton and Hamburg; and along the
blue coast across the Blackwater my brother could make out dimly a
dense swarm of boats chaffering with the people on the beach, a swarm
which also extended up the Blackwater almost to Maldon.

About a couple of miles out lay an ironclad, very low in the water,
almost, to my brother's perception, like a water-logged ship. This was
the ram *Thunder Child*. It was the only warship in sight, but far away
to the right over the smooth surface of the sea – for that day there was
a dead calm – lay a serpent of black smoke to mark the next ironclads
of the Channel Fleet, which hovered in an extended line, steam up
and ready for action, across the Thames estuary during the course of
the Martian conquest, vigilant and yet powerless to prevent it.

At the sight of the sea, Mrs. Elphinstone, in spite of the assurances of
her sister-in-law, gave way to panic. She had never been out of England
before, she would rather die than trust herself friendless in a foreign
country, and so forth. She seemed, poor woman, to imagine that the
French and the Martians might prove very similar. She had been growing
increasingly hysterical, fearful, and depressed during the two days'
journeyings. Her great idea was to return to Stanmore. Things had been
always well and safe at Stanmore. They would find George at Stanmore.

It was with the greatest difficulty they could get her down to
the beach, where presently my brother succeeded in attracting the
attention of some men on a paddle steamer from the Thames.
They sent a boat and drove a bargain for thirty-six pounds for the
three. The steamer was going, these men said, to Ostend.

It was about two o'clock when my brother, having paid their fares at the gangway, found himself safely aboard the steamboat with his charges. There was food aboard, albeit at exorbitant prices, and the three of them contrived to eat a meal on one of the seats forward.

There were already a couple of score of passengers aboard, some of whom had expended their last money in securing a passage, but the captain lay off the Blackwater until five in the afternoon, picking up passengers until the seated decks were even dangerously crowded. He would probably have remained longer had it not been for the sound of guns that began about that hour in the south. As if in answer, the ironclad seaward fired a small gun and hoisted a string of flags. A jet of smoke sprang out of her funnels.

Some of the passengers were of opinion that this firing came from Shoeburyness, until it was noticed that it was growing louder. At the same time, far away in the southeast the masts and upperworks of three ironclads rose one after the other out of the sea, beneath clouds of black smoke. But my brother's attention speedily reverted to the distant firing in the south. He fancied he saw a column of smoke rising out of the distant grey haze.

The little steamer was already flapping her way eastward of the big crescent of shipping, and the low Essex coast was growing blue and hazy, when a Martian appeared, small and faint in the remote distance, advancing along the muddy coast from the direction of Foulness. At that the captain on the bridge swore at the top of his voice with fear and anger at his own delay, and the paddles seemed infected with his terror. Every soul aboard stood at the bulwarks or on the seats of the steamer and stared at that distant shape, higher than the trees or church towers inland, and advancing with a leisurely parody of a human stride.

It was the first Martian my brother had seen, and he stood, more amazed than terrified, watching this Titan advancing deliberately towards the shipping, wading farther and farther into the water as the coast fell away. Then, far away beyond the Crouch, came another, striding over some stunted trees, and then yet another, still farther off, wading deeply through a shiny mudflat that seemed to hang halfway up between sea and sky. They were all stalking seaward, as if to intercept the escape of the multitudinous vessels that were crowded between Foulness and the Naze. In spite of the throbbing exertions of the engines of the little paddle-boat, and the pouring foam that her wheels flung behind her, she receded with terrifying slowness from this ominous advance.

Glancing northwestward, my brother saw the large crescent of shipping already writhing with the approaching terror; one ship passing behind another, another coming round from broadside to end on, steamships whistling and giving off volumes of steam, sails being let out, launches rushing hither and thither. He was so fascinated by this and by the creeping danger away to the left that he had no eyes for anything seaward. And then a swift movement of the steamboat (she had suddenly come round to avoid being run down) flung him headlong from the seat upon which he was standing. There was a shouting all about him, a trampling of feet, and a cheer that seemed to be answered faintly. The steamboat lurched and rolled him over upon his hands.

He sprang to his feet and saw to starboard, and not a hundred yards from their heeling, pitching boat, a vast iron bulk like the blade of a plough tearing through the water, tossing it on either side in huge waves of foam that leaped towards the steamer, flinging her paddles helplessly in the air, and then sucking her deck down almost to the waterline.

A douche of spray blinded my brother for a moment. When his eyes were clear again he saw the monster had passed and was rushing landward. Big iron upperworks rose out of this headlong structure, and from that twin funnels projected and spat a smoking blast shot with fire. It was the torpedo ram, *Thunder Child*, steaming headlong, coming to the rescue of the threatened shipping.

Keeping his footing on the heaving deck by clutching the bulwarks, my brother looked past this charging leviathan at the Martians again, and he saw the three of them now close together, and standing so far out to sea that their tripod supports were almost entirely submerged. Thus sunken, and seen in remote perspective, they appeared far less formidable than the huge iron bulk in whose wake the steamer was pitching so helplessly. It would seem they were regarding this new antagonist with astonishment. To their intelligence, it may be, the giant was even such another as themselves. The *Thunder Child* fired no gun, but simply drove full speed towards them. It was probably her not firing that enabled her to get so near the enemy as she did. They did not know what to make of her. One shell, and they would have sent her to the bottom forthwith with the Heat-Ray.

She was steaming at such a pace that in a minute she seemed halfway between the steamboat and the Martians – a diminishing black bulk against the receding horizontal expanse of the Essex coast.

Suddenly the foremost Martian lowered his tube and discharged a canister of the black gas at the ironclad. It hit her larboard side and glanced off in an inky jet that rolled away to seaward, an unfolding torrent of Black Smoke, from which the ironclad drove clear. To the watchers from the steamer, low in the water and with the sun in their eyes, it seemed as though she were already among the Martians.

They saw the gaunt figures separating and rising out of the water as they retreated shoreward, and one of them raised the camera-like generator of the Heat-Ray. He held it pointing obliquely downward, and a bank of steam sprang from the water at its touch. It must have driven through the iron of the ship's side like a white-hot iron rod through paper.

A flicker of flame went up through the rising steam, and then the Martian reeled and staggered. In another moment he was cut down, and a great body of water and steam shot high in the air. The guns of the *Thunder Child* sounded through the reek, going off one after the other, and one shot splashed the water high close by the steamer, ricocheted towards the other flying ships to the north, and smashed a smack to matchwood.

But no one heeded that very much. At the sight of the Martian's collapse the captain on the bridge yelled inarticulately, and all the crowding passengers on the steamer's stern shouted together. And then they yelled again. For, surging out beyond the white tumult, drove something long and black, the flames streaming from its middle parts, its ventilators and funnels spouting fire.

She was alive still; the steering gear, it seems, was intact and her engines working. She headed straight for a second Martian, and was within a hundred yards of him when the Heat-Ray came to bear. Then with a violent thud, a blinding flash, her decks, her funnels, leaped upward. The Martian staggered with the violence of her explosion, and in another moment the flaming wreckage, still driving forward with the impetus of its pace, had struck him and crumpled him up like a thing of cardboard. My brother shouted involuntarily. A boiling tumult of steam hid everything again.

"Two!" yelled the captain.

Everyone was shouting. The whole steamer from end to end rang with frantic cheering that was taken up first by one and then by all in the crowding multitude of ships and boats that was driving out to sea.

The steam hung upon the water for many minutes, hiding the third Martian and the coast altogether. And all this time the boat was paddling steadily out to sea and away from the fight; and when at last the confusion cleared, the drifting bank of black vapour intervened, and nothing of the *Thunder Child* could be made out, nor could the third Martian be seen. But the ironclads to seaward were now quite close and standing in towards shore past the steamboat.

The little vessel continued to beat its way seaward, and the ironclads receded slowly towards the coast, which was hidden still by a marbled bank of vapour, part steam, part black gas, eddying and combining in the strangest way. The fleet of refugees was scattering to the northeast; several smacks were sailing between the ironclads and the steamboat. After a time, and before they reached the sinking cloud bank, the warships turned northward, and then abruptly went about and passed into the thickening haze of evening southward. The coast grew faint, and at last indistinguishable amid the low banks of clouds that were gathering about the sinking sun.

Then suddenly out of the golden haze of the sunset came the vibration of guns, and a form of black shadows moving. Everyone struggled to the rail of the steamer and peered into the blinding furnace of the west, but nothing was to be distinguished clearly. A mass of smoke rose slanting and barred the face of the sun. The steamboat throbbed on its way through an interminable suspense.

The sun sank into grey clouds, the sky flushed and darkened, the evening star trembled into sight. It was deep twilight when the captain cried out and pointed. My brother strained his eyes. Something rushed up into the sky out of the greyness – rushed slantingly upward and very swiftly into the luminous clearness above the clouds in the western sky; something flat and broad, and very large, that swept round in a vast curve, grew smaller, sank slowly, and vanished again into the grey mystery of the night. And as it flew it rained down darkness upon the land.

BOOK TWO
THE EARTH UNDER
THE MARTIANS

CHAPTER 1

Under Foot

In the first book I have wandered so much from my own adventures to tell of the experiences of my brother that all through the last two chapters I and the curate have been lurking in the empty house at Halliford whither we fled to escape the Black Smoke. There I will resume. We stopped there all Sunday night and all the next day – the day of the panic – in a little island of daylight, cut off by the Black Smoke from the rest of the world. We could do nothing but wait in aching inactivity during those two weary days.

My mind was occupied by anxiety for my wife. I figured her at Leatherhead, terrified, in danger, mourning me already as a dead man. I paced the rooms and cried aloud when I thought of how I was cut off from her, of all that might happen to her in my absence. My cousin I knew was brave enough for any emergency, but he was not the sort of man to realise danger quickly, to rise promptly. What was needed now was not bravery, but circumspection. My only consolation was to believe that the Martians were moving London-ward and away from her. Such vague anxieties keep the mind sensitive and painful. I grew very weary and irritable with the curate's perpetual ejaculations; I tired of the sight of his selfish despair. After some ineffectual remonstrance I kept away from him, staying in a room – evidently a children's schoolroom – containing globes, forms, and copybooks. When he followed me thither, I went to a box room at the top of the house and, in order to be alone with my aching miseries, locked myself in.

We were hopelessly hemmed in by the Black Smoke all that day and the morning of the next. There were signs of people in the next house on Sunday evening – a face at a window and moving lights, and later the slamming of a door. But I do not know who these people were, nor what became of them. We saw nothing of them next day. The Black Smoke drifted slowly riverward all through Monday morning, creeping nearer and nearer to us, driving at last along the roadway outside the house that hid us.

A Martian came across the fields about midday, laying the stuff with a jet of superheated steam that hissed against the walls, smashed all the windows it touched, and scalded the curate's hand as he fled out of the front room. When at last we crept across the sodden rooms and looked out again, the country northward was as though a black snowstorm had passed over it. Looking towards the river, we were astonished to see an unaccountable redness mingling with the black of the scorched meadows.

For a time we did not see how this change affected our position, save that we were relieved of our fear of the Black Smoke. But later I perceived that we were no longer hemmed in, that now we might get away. So soon as I realised that the way of escape was open, my dream of action returned. But the curate was lethargic, unreasonable.

"We are safe here," he repeated; "safe here."

I resolved to leave him – would that I had! Wiser now for the artilleryman's teaching, I sought out food and drink. I had found oil and rags for my burns, and I also took a hat and a flannel shirt that I found in one of the bedrooms. When it was clear to him that I meant to go alone – had reconciled myself to going alone – he suddenly roused himself to come. And all being quiet throughout the afternoon, we started about five o'clock, as I should judge, along the blackened road to Sunbury.

In Sunbury, and at intervals along the road, were dead bodies lying in contorted attitudes, horses as well as men, overturned carts and luggage, all covered thickly with black dust. That pall of cindery powder made me think of what I had read of the destruction of Pompeii. We got to Hampton Court without misadventure, our minds full of strange and unfamiliar appearances, and at Hampton Court our eyes were relieved to find a patch of green that had escaped the suffocating drift. We went through Bushey Park, with its deer going to and fro under the chestnuts, and some men and women hurrying in the distance towards Hampton, and so we came to Twickenham. These were the first people we saw.

Away across the road the woods beyond Ham and Petersham were still afire. Twickenham was uninjured by either Heat-Ray or Black Smoke, and there were more people about here, though none could give us news. For the most part they were like ourselves, taking advantage of a lull to shift their quarters. I have an impression that many of the houses here were still occupied by scared inhabitants, too frightened even for flight. Here too the evidence of a hasty rout was abundant along the road. I remember most vividly three smashed bicycles in a heap, pounded into the road by the wheels of subsequent carts. We crossed Richmond Bridge about half past eight. We hurried across the exposed bridge, of course, but I noticed floating down the stream a number of red masses, some many feet across. I did not know what these were – there was no time for scrutiny – and I put a more horrible interpretation on them than they deserved. Here again on the Surrey side were black dust that had once been smoke, and dead bodies – a heap near the approach to the station; but we had no glimpse of the Martians until we were some way towards Barnes.

We saw in the blackened distance a group of three people running down a side street towards the river, but otherwise it seemed deserted. Up the hill Richmond town was burning briskly; outside the town of Richmond there was no trace of the Black Smoke.

Then suddenly, as we approached Kew, came a number of people running, and the upperworks of a Martian fighting-machine loomed in sight over the housetops, not a hundred yards away from us. We stood aghast at our danger, and had the Martian looked down we must immediately have perished. We were so terrified that we dared not go on, but turned aside and hid in a shed in a garden. There the curate crouched, weeping silently, and refusing to stir again.

But my fixed idea of reaching Leatherhead would not let me rest, and in the twilight I ventured out again. I went through a shrubbery, and along a passage beside a big house standing in its own grounds, and so emerged upon the road towards Kew. The curate I left in the shed, but he came hurrying after me.

That second start was the most foolhardy thing I ever did. For it was manifest the Martians were about us. No sooner had the curate overtaken me than we saw either the fighting-machine we had seen before or another, far away across the meadows in the direction of Kew Lodge. Four or five little black figures hurried before it across the green-grey of the field, and in a moment it was evident this Martian pursued them. In three strides he was among them, and they ran radiating from his feet in all directions. He used no Heat-Ray to destroy them, but picked them up one by one. Apparently he tossed them into the great metallic carrier which projected behind him, much as a workman's basket hangs over his shoulder.

It was the first time I realised that the Martians might have any other purpose than destruction with defeated humanity. We stood for a moment petrified, then turned and fled through a gate behind us into a walled garden, fell into, rather than found, a fortunate ditch, and lay there, scarce daring to whisper to each other until the stars were out.

I suppose it was nearly eleven o'clock before we gathered courage to start again, no longer venturing into the road, but sneaking along hedgerows and through plantations, and watching keenly through the darkness, he on the right and I on the left, for the Martians, who seemed to be all about us. In one place we blundered upon a scorched and blackened area, now cooling and ashen, and a number of scattered dead bodies of men, burned horribly about the heads and trunks but with their legs and boots mostly intact; and of dead horses, fifty feet, perhaps, behind a line of four ripped guns and smashed gun carriages.

Sheen, it seemed, had escaped destruction, but the place was silent and deserted. Here we happened on no dead, though the night was too dark for us to see into the side roads of the place. In Sheen my companion suddenly complained of faintness and thirst, and we decided to try one of the houses.

The first house we entered, after a little difficulty with the window, was a small semi-detached villa, and I found nothing eatable left in the place but some mouldy cheese. There was, however, water to drink; and I took a hatchet, which promised to be useful in our next house-breaking.

We then crossed to a place where the road turns towards Mortlake. Here there stood a white house within a walled garden, and in the pantry of this domicile we found a store of food – two loaves of bread in a pan, an uncooked steak, and the half of a ham. I give this catalogue so precisely because, as it happened, we were destined to subsist upon this store for the next fortnight. Bottled beer stood under a shelf, and there were two bags of haricot beans and some limp lettuces. This pantry opened into a kind of wash-up kitchen, and in this was firewood; there was also a cupboard, in which we found nearly a dozen of burgundy, tinned soups and salmon, and two tins of biscuits.

We sat in the adjacent kitchen in the dark – for we dared not strike a light – and ate bread and ham, and drank beer out of the same bottle. The curate, who was still timorous and restless, was now, oddly enough, for pushing on, and I was urging him to keep up his strength by eating when the thing happened that was to imprison us.

"It can't be midnight yet," I said, and then came a blinding glare of vivid green light. Everything in the kitchen leaped out, clearly visible in green and black, and vanished again. And then followed such a concussion as I have never heard before or since. So close on the heels of this as to seem instantaneous came a thud behind me, a clash of glass, a crash and rattle of falling masonry all about us, and the plaster of the ceiling came down upon us, smashing into a multitude of fragments upon our heads. I was knocked headlong across the floor against the oven handle and stunned. I was insensible for a long time, the curate told me, and when I came to we were in darkness again, and he, with a face wet, as I found afterwards, with blood from a cut forehead, was dabbing water over me.

For some time I could not recollect what had happened. Then things came to me slowly. A bruise on my temple asserted itself.

"Are you better?" asked the curate in a whisper.

At last I answered him. I sat up.

"Don't move," he said. "The floor is covered with smashed crockery from the dresser. You can't possibly move without making a noise, and I fancy *they* are outside."

We both sat quite silent, so that we could scarcely hear each other breathing. Everything seemed deadly still, but once something near us, some plaster or broken brickwork, slid down with a rumbling sound. Outside and very near was an intermittent, metallic rattle.

"That!" said the curate, when presently it happened again.

"Yes," I said. "But what is it?"

"A Martian!" said the curate.

I listened again.

"It was not like the Heat-Ray," I said, and for a time I was inclined to think one of the great fighting-machines had stumbled against the house, as I had seen one stumble against the tower of Shepperton Church.

Our situation was so strange and incomprehensible that for three or four hours, until the dawn came, we scarcely moved. And then the light filtered in, not through the window, which remained black, but through a triangular aperture between a beam and a heap of broken bricks in the wall behind us. The interior of the kitchen we now saw greyly for the first time.

The window had been burst in by a mass of garden mould, which flowed over the table upon which we had been sitting and lay about our feet. Outside, the soil was banked high against the house. At the top of the window frame we could see an uprooted drainpipe. The floor was littered with smashed hardware; the end of the kitchen towards the house was broken into, and since the daylight shone in there, it was evident the greater part of the house had collapsed. Contrasting vividly with this ruin was the neat dresser, stained in the fashion, pale green, and with a number of copper and tin vessels below it, the wallpaper imitating blue and white tiles, and a couple of coloured supplements fluttering from the walls above the kitchen range.

As the dawn grew clearer, we saw through the gap in the wall the body of a Martian, standing sentinel, I suppose, over the still glowing cylinder. At the sight of that we crawled as circumspectly as possible out of the twilight of the kitchen into the darkness of the scullery.

Abruptly the right interpretation dawned upon my mind.

"The fifth cylinder," I whispered, "the fifth shot from Mars, has struck this house and buried us under the ruins!"

For a time the curate was silent, and then he whispered:

"God have mercy upon us!"

I heard him presently whimpering to himself.

Save for that sound we lay quite still in the scullery; I for my part scarce dared breathe, and sat with my eyes fixed on the faint light of the kitchen door. I could just see the curate's face, a dim, oval shape, and his collar and cuffs. Outside there began a metallic hammering, then a violent hooting, and then again, after a quiet interval, a hissing like the hissing of an engine. These noises, for the most part problematical, continued intermittently, and seemed if anything to increase in number as time wore on. Presently a measured thudding and a vibration that made everything about us quiver and the vessels in the pantry ring and shift, began and continued. Once the light was eclipsed, and the ghostly kitchen doorway became absolutely dark. For many hours we must have crouched there, silent and shivering, until our tired attention failed...

At last I found myself awake and very hungry. I am inclined to believe we must have spent the greater portion of a day before that awakening. My hunger was at a stride so insistent that it moved me to action. I told the curate I was going to seek food, and felt my way towards the pantry. He made me no answer, but so soon as I began eating the faint noise I made stirred him up and I heard him crawling after me.

CHAPTER 2

What We Saw from the Ruined House

After eating we crept back to the scullery, and there I must have dozed again, for when presently I looked round I was alone. The thudding vibration continued with wearisome persistence. I whispered for the curate several times, and at last felt my way to the door of the kitchen. It was still daylight, and I perceived him across the room, lying against the triangular hole that looked out upon the Martians. His shoulders were hunched, so that his head was hidden from me.

I could hear a number of noises almost like those in an engine shed; and the place rocked with that beating thud. Through the aperture in the wall I could see the top of a tree touched with gold and the warm blue of a tranquil evening sky. For a minute or so I remained watching the curate, and then I advanced, crouching and stepping with extreme care amid the broken crockery that littered the floor.

I touched the curate's leg, and he started so violently that a mass of plaster went sliding down outside and fell with a loud impact. I gripped his arm, fearing he might cry out, and for a long time we crouched motionless. Then I turned to see how much of our rampart remained. The detachment of the plaster had left a vertical slit open in the debris, and by raising myself cautiously across a beam I was able to see out of this gap into what had been overnight a quiet suburban roadway. Vast, indeed, was the change that we beheld.

The fifth cylinder must have fallen right into the midst of the house we had first visited. The building had vanished, completely smashed, pulverised, and dispersed by the blow. The cylinder lay now far beneath the original foundations – deep in a hole, already vastly larger than the pit I had looked into at Woking. The earth all round it had splashed under that tremendous impact – "splashed" is the only word – and lay in heaped piles that hid the masses of the adjacent houses. It had behaved exactly like mud under the violent blow of a hammer. Our house had collapsed backward; the front portion, even on the ground floor, had been destroyed completely; by a chance the kitchen and scullery had escaped, and stood buried now under soil and ruins, closed in by tons of earth on every side save towards the cylinder. Over that aspect we hung now on the very edge of the great circular pit the Martians were engaged in making. The heavy beating sound was evidently just behind us, and ever and again a bright green vapour drove up like a veil across our peephole.

The cylinder was already opened in the centre of the pit, and on the farther edge of the pit, amid the smashed and gravel-heaped shrubbery, one of the great fighting-machines, deserted by its occupant, stood stiff and tall against the evening sky. At first I scarcely noticed the pit and the cylinder, although it has been convenient to describe them first, on account of the extraordinary glittering mechanism I saw busy in the excavation, and on account of the strange creatures that were crawling slowly and painfully across the heaped mould near it.

The mechanism it certainly was that held my attention first. It was one of those complicated fabrics that have since been called handling-machines, and the study of which has already given such an enormous impetus to terrestrial invention. As it dawned upon me first, it presented a sort of metallic spider with five jointed, agile legs, and with an extraordinary number of jointed levers, bars, and reaching and clutching tentacles about its body. Most of its arms were retracted, but with three long tentacles it was fishing out a number of rods, plates, and bars which lined the covering and apparently strengthened the walls of the cylinder. These, as it extracted them, were lifted out and deposited upon a level surface of earth behind it.

Its motion was so swift, complex, and perfect that at first I did not see it as a machine, in spite of its metallic glitter. The fighting-machines were coordinated and animated to an extraordinary pitch, but nothing to compare with this. People who have never seen these structures, and have only the ill-imagined efforts of artists or the imperfect descriptions of such eye-witnesses as myself to go upon, scarcely realise that living quality.

I recall particularly the illustration of one of the first pamphlets to give a consecutive account of the war. The artist had evidently made a hasty study of one of the fighting-machines, and there his knowledge ended. He presented them as tilted, stiff tripods, without either flexibility or subtlety, and with an altogether misleading monotony of effect. The pamphlet containing these renderings had a considerable vogue, and I mention them here simply to warn the reader against the impression they may have created. They were no more like the Martians I saw in action than a Dutch doll is like a human being. To my mind, the pamphlet would have been much better without them.

At first, I say, the handling-machine did not impress me as a machine, but as a crablike creature with a glittering integument, the controlling Martian whose delicate tentacles actuated its movements seeming to be simply the equivalent of the crab's cerebral portion. But then I perceived the resemblance of its grey-brown, shiny, leathery integument to that of the other sprawling bodies beyond, and the true nature of this dexterous workman dawned upon me. With that realisation my interest shifted to those other creatures, the real

Martians. Already I had had a transient impression of these, and the first nausea no longer obscured my observation. Moreover, I was concealed and motionless, and under no urgency of action.

They were, I now saw, the most unearthly creatures it is possible to conceive. They were huge round bodies – or, rather, heads – about four feet in diameter, each body having in front of it a face. This face had no nostrils – indeed, the Martians do not seem to have had any sense of smell, but it had a pair of very large dark-coloured eyes, and just beneath this a kind of fleshy beak. In the back of this head or body – I scarcely know how to speak of it – was the single tight tympanic surface, since known to be anatomically an ear, though it must have been almost useless in our dense air. In a group round the mouth were sixteen slender, almost whiplike tentacles, arranged in two bunches of eight each. These bunches have since been named rather aptly, by that distinguished anatomist, Professor Howes, the *hands*. Even as I saw these Martians for the first time they seemed to be endeavouring to raise themselves on these hands, but of course, with the increased weight of terrestrial conditions, this was impossible. There is reason to suppose that on Mars they may have progressed upon them with some facility.

The internal anatomy, I may remark here, as dissection has since shown, was almost equally simple. The greater part of the structure was the brain, sending enormous nerves to the eyes, ear, and tactile tentacles. Besides this were the bulky lungs, into which the mouth opened, and the heart and its vessels. The pulmonary distress caused by the denser atmosphere and greater gravitational attraction was only too evident in the convulsive movements of the outer skin.

And this was the sum of the Martian organs. Strange as it may seem to a human being, all the complex apparatus of digestion, which makes up the bulk of our bodies, did not exist in the Martians. They were heads – merely heads. Entrails they had none. They did not eat, much less digest. Instead, they took the fresh, living blood of other creatures, and *injected* it into their own veins. I have myself seen this being done, as I shall mention in its place. But, squeamish as I may seem, I cannot bring myself to describe what I could not endure even to continue watching. Let it suffice to say, blood obtained from a still living animal, in most cases from a human being, was run directly by means of a little pipette into the recipient canal...

The bare idea of this is no doubt horribly repulsive to us, but at the same time I think that we should remember how repulsive our carnivorous habits would seem to an intelligent rabbit.

The physiological advantages of the practice of injection are undeniable, if one thinks of the tremendous waste of human time and energy occasioned by eating and the digestive process. Our bodies are half made up of glands and tubes and organs, occupied in turning heterogeneous food into blood. The digestive processes and their reaction upon the nervous system sap our strength and colour our minds. Men go happy or miserable as they have healthy or unhealthy livers, or sound gastric glands. But the Martians were lifted above all these organic fluctuations of mood and emotion.

Their undeniable preference for men as their source of nourishment is partly explained by the nature of the remains of the victims they had brought with them as provisions from Mars. These creatures, to judge from the shrivelled remains that have fallen into human hands, were bipeds with flimsy, silicious skeletons (almost like those of the silicious sponges) and feeble musculature, standing about six feet high and having round, erect heads, and large eyes in flinty sockets. Two or three of these seem to have been brought in each cylinder, and all were killed before earth was reached. It was just as well for them, for the mere attempt to stand upright upon our planet would have broken every bone in their bodies.

And while I am engaged in this description, I may add in this place certain further details which, although they were not all evident to us at the time, will enable the reader who is unacquainted with them to form a clearer picture of these offensive creatures.

In three other points their physiology differed strangely from ours. Their organisms did not sleep, any more than the heart of man sleeps. Since they had no extensive muscular mechanism to recuperate, that periodical extinction was unknown to them. They had little or no sense of fatigue, it would seem. On earth they could never have moved without effort, yet even to the last they kept in action. In twenty-four hours they did twenty-four hours of work, as even on earth is perhaps the case with the ants.

In the next place, wonderful as it seems in a sexual world, the Martians were absolutely without sex, and therefore without any of the tumultuous emotions that arise from that difference among men. A young Martian, there can now be no dispute, was really born upon earth during the war, and it was found attached to its parent, partially *budded* off, just as young lilybulbs bud off, or like the young animals in the fresh-water polyp.

In man, in all the higher terrestrial animals, such a method of increase has disappeared; but even on this earth it was certainly the primitive method. Among the lower animals, up even to those first cousins of the vertebrated animals, the Tunicates, the two processes occur side by side, but finally the sexual method superseded its competitor altogether. On Mars, however, just the reverse has apparently been the case.

It is worthy of remark that a certain speculative writer of quasi-scientific repute, writing long before the Martian invasion, did forecast for man a final structure not unlike the actual Martian condition. His prophecy, I remember, appeared in November or

December, 1893, in a long-defunct publication, the *Pall Mall Budget*, and I recall a caricature of it in a pre-Martian periodical called *Punch*. He pointed out – writing in a foolish, facetious tone – that the perfection of mechanical appliances must ultimately supersede limbs; the perfection of chemical devices, digestion; that such organs as hair, external nose, teeth, ears, and chin were no longer essential parts of the human being, and that the tendency of natural selection would lie in the direction of their steady diminution through the coming ages. The brain alone remained a cardinal necessity. Only one other part of the body had a strong case for survival, and that was the hand, "teacher and agent of the brain." While the rest of the body dwindled, the hands would grow larger.

There is many a true word written in jest, and here in the Martians we have beyond dispute the actual accomplishment of such a suppression of the animal side of the organism by the intelligence. To me it is quite credible that the Martians may be descended from beings not unlike ourselves, by a gradual development of brain and hands (the latter giving rise to the two bunches of delicate tentacles at last) at the expense of the rest of the body. Without the body the brain would, of course, become a mere selfish intelligence, without any of the emotional substratum of the human being.

The last salient point in which the systems of these creatures differed from ours was in what one might have thought a very trivial particular. Micro-organisms, which cause so much disease and pain on earth, have either never appeared upon Mars or Martian sanitary science eliminated them ages ago. A hundred diseases, all the fevers and contagions of human life, consumption, cancers, tumours and such morbidities, never enter the scheme of their life. And speaking of the differences between the life on Mars and terrestrial life, I may allude here to the curious suggestions of the red weed.

Apparently the vegetable kingdom in Mars, instead of having green for a dominant colour, is of a vivid blood-red tint. At any rate, the seeds which the Martians (intentionally or accidentally) brought with them gave rise in all cases to red-coloured growths. Only that known popularly as the red weed, however, gained any footing in competition with terrestrial forms. The red creeper was quite a transitory growth, and few people have seen it growing. For a time, however, the red weed grew with astonishing vigour and luxuriance. It spread up the sides of the pit by the third or fourth day of our imprisonment, and its cactus-like branches formed a carmine fringe to the edges of our triangular window. And afterwards I found it broadcast throughout the country, and especially wherever there was a stream of water.

The Martians had what appears to have been an auditory organ, a single round drum at the back of the head-body, and eyes with a visual range not very different from ours except that, according to Philips, blue and violet were as black to them. It is commonly supposed that they communicated by sounds and tentacular gesticulations; this is asserted, for instance, in the able but hastily compiled pamphlet (written evidently by someone not an eye-witness of Martian actions) to which I have already alluded, and which, so far, has been the chief source of information concerning them. Now no surviving human being saw so much of the Martians in action as I did. I take no credit to myself for an accident, but the fact is so. And I assert that I watched them closely time after time, and that I have seen four, five, and (once) six of them sluggishly performing the most elaborately complicated operations together without either sound or gesture. Their peculiar hooting invariably preceded feeding; it had no modulation, and was, I believe, in no sense a signal, but merely the expiration of air preparatory to the suctional operation. I have a certain claim to at least an elementary knowledge of psychology, and in this matter I am convinced – as firmly as I am convinced of anything – that the Martians interchanged thoughts without any physical intermediation. And I have been convinced of this in spite of strong preconceptions. Before the Martian invasion, as an occasional reader here or there may remember, I had written with some little vehemence against the telepathic theory.

The Martians wore no clothing. Their conceptions of ornament and decorum were necessarily different from ours; and not only were they evidently much less sensible of changes of temperature than we are, but changes of pressure do not seem to have affected their health at all seriously. Yet though they wore no clothing, it was in the other artificial additions to their bodily resources that their great superiority over man lay. We men, with our bicycles and road-skates, our Lilienthal soaring-machines, our guns and sticks and so forth, are just in the beginning of the evolution that the Martians have worked out. They have become practically mere brains, wearing different bodies according to their needs just as men wear suits of clothes and take a bicycle in a hurry or an umbrella in the wet. And of their appliances, perhaps nothing is more wonderful to a man than the curious fact that what is the dominant feature of almost all human devices in mechanism is absent – the *wheel* is absent; among all the things they brought to earth there is no trace or suggestion of their use of wheels. One would have at least expected it in locomotion. And in this connection it is curious to remark that even on this earth Nature has never hit upon the wheel, or has preferred other expedients to its development. And not only did the Martians either not know of (which is incredible), or abstain from, the wheel, but in their apparatus singularly little use is made of the fixed pivot or relatively fixed pivot, with circular motions thereabout confined to one plane. Almost all the joints of the machinery present a complicated system of sliding parts moving over small but beautifully curved friction bearings. And while upon this matter of detail, it is remarkable that the long leverages of their machines are in most cases actuated by a sort of sham musculature of the disks in an elastic sheath; these disks become polarised and drawn closely and powerfully together when traversed by a current of electricity. In this way the curious parallelism to animal motions, which was so striking and disturbing to the human beholder, was attained. Such quasi-muscles abounded in the crablike handling-machine which, on my first peeping out of the slit, I watched unpacking the cylinder. It seemed infinitely more alive than the actual Martians lying beyond it in the sunset light, panting, stirring ineffectual tentacles, and moving feebly after their vast journey across space.

While I was still watching their sluggish motions in the sunlight, and noting each strange detail of their form, the curate reminded me of his presence by pulling violently at my arm. I turned to a scowling face, and silent, eloquent lips. He wanted the slit, which permitted only one of us to peep through; and so I had to forego watching them for a time while he enjoyed that privilege.

When I looked again, the busy handling-machine had already put together several of the pieces of apparatus it had taken out of the cylinder into a shape having an unmistakable likeness to its own; and down on the left a busy little digging mechanism had come into view, emitting jets of green vapour and working its way round the pit, excavating and embanking in a methodical and discriminating manner. This it was which had caused the regular beating noise, and the rhythmic shocks that had kept our ruinous refuge quivering. It piped and whistled as it worked. So far as I could see, the thing was without a directing Martian at all.

CHAPTER 3

The Days of Imprisonment

The arrival of a second fighting-machine drove us from our peephole into the scullery, for we feared that from his elevation the Martian might see down upon us behind our barrier. At a later date we began to feel less in danger of their eyes, for to an eye in the dazzle of the sunlight outside our refuge must have been blank blackness, but at first the slightest suggestion of approach drove us into the scullery in heart-throbbing retreat. Yet terrible as was the danger we incurred, the attraction of peeping was for both of us irresistible. And I recall now with a sort of wonder that, in spite of the infinite danger in which we were between starvation and a still more terrible death, we could yet struggle bitterly for that horrible privilege of sight. We would race across the kitchen in a grotesque way between eagerness and the dread of making a noise, and strike each other, and thrust and kick, within a few inches of exposure.

The fact is that we had absolutely incompatible dispositions and habits of thought and action, and our danger and isolation only accentuated the incompatibility. At Halliford I had already come to hate the curate's trick of helpless exclamation, his stupid rigidity of mind. His endless muttering monologue vitiated every effort I made to think out a line of action, and drove me at times, thus pent up and intensified, almost to the verge of craziness. He was as lacking in restraint as a silly woman. He would weep for hours together, and I verily believe that to the very end this spoiled child of life thought his weak tears in some way efficacious. And I would sit in the darkness unable to keep my mind off him by reason of his importunities. He ate more than I did, and it was in vain I pointed out that our only chance of life was to stop in the house until the Martians had done with their pit, that in that long patience a time might presently come when we should need food. He ate and drank impulsively in heavy meals at long intervals. He slept little.

As the days wore on, his utter carelessness of any consideration so intensified our distress and danger that I had, much as I loathed doing it, to resort to threats, and at last to blows. That brought him to reason for a time. But he was one of those weak creatures, void of pride, timorous, anaemic, hateful souls, full of shifty cunning, who face neither God nor man, who face not even themselves.

It is disagreeable for me to recall and write these things, but I set them down that my story may lack nothing. Those who have escaped the dark and terrible aspects of life will find my brutality, my flash of rage in our final tragedy, easy enough to blame; for they know what is wrong as well as any, but not what is possible to tortured men. But those who have been under the shadow, who have gone down at last to elemental things, will have a wider charity.

And while within we fought out our dark, dim contest of whispers, snatched food and drink, and gripping hands and blows, without, in the pitiless sunlight of that terrible June, was the strange wonder, the unfamiliar routine of the Martians in the pit. Let me return to those first new experiences of mine. After a long time I ventured back to the peephole, to find that the new-comers had been reinforced by the occupants of no fewer than three of the fighting-machines. These last had brought with them certain fresh appliances that stood in an orderly manner about the cylinder. The second handling-machine was now completed, and was busied in serving one of the novel contrivances the big machine had brought. This was a body resembling a milk can in its general form, above which oscillated a pear-shaped receptacle, and from which a stream of white powder flowed into a circular basin below.

The oscillatory motion was imparted to this by one tentacle of the handling-machine. With two spatulate hands the handling-machine was digging out and flinging masses of clay into the pear-shaped receptacle above, while with another arm it periodically opened a door and removed rusty and blackened clinkers from the middle part of the machine. Another steely tentacle directed the powder from the basin along a ribbed channel towards some receiver that was hidden from me by the mound of bluish dust. From this unseen receiver a little thread of green smoke rose vertically into the quiet air. As I looked, the handling-machine, with a faint and musical clinking, extended, telescopic fashion, a tentacle that had been a moment before a mere blunt projection, until its end was hidden behind the mound of clay. In another second it had lifted a bar of white aluminium into sight, untarnished as yet, and shining dazzlingly, and deposited it in a growing stack of bars that stood at the side of the pit. Between sunset and starlight this dexterous machine must have made more than a hundred such bars out of the crude clay, and the mound of bluish dust rose steadily until it topped the side of the pit.

The contrast between the swift and complex movements of these contrivances and the inert panting clumsiness of their masters was acute, and for days I had to tell myself repeatedly that these latter were indeed the living of the two things.

The curate had possession of the slit when the first men were brought to the pit. I was sitting below, huddled up, listening with all my ears. He made a sudden movement backward, and I, fearful that we were observed, crouched in a spasm of terror. He came sliding down the rubbish and crept beside me in the darkness, inarticulate, gesticulating, and for a moment I shared his panic. His gesture suggested a resignation of the slit, and after a little while my curiosity gave me courage, and I rose up, stepped across him, and clambered up to it. At first I could see no reason for his frantic behaviour. The twilight had now come, the stars were little and faint, but the pit was illuminated by the flickering green fire that came from the aluminium-making. The whole picture was a flickering scheme of green gleams and shifting rusty black shadows, strangely trying to the eyes. Over and through it all went the bats, heeding it not at all. The sprawling Martians were no longer to be seen, the mound of blue-green powder had risen to cover them from sight, and a fighting-machine, with its legs contracted, crumpled, and abbreviated, stood across the corner of the pit. And then, amid the clangour of the machinery, came a drifting suspicion of human voices, that I entertained at first only to dismiss.

I crouched, watching this fighting-machine closely, satisfying myself now for the first time that the hood did indeed contain a Martian. As the green flames lifted I could see the oily gleam of his integument and the brightness of his eyes. And suddenly I heard a yell, and saw a long tentacle reaching over the shoulder of the machine to the little cage that hunched upon its back. Then something – something struggling violently – was lifted high against the sky, a black, vague enigma against the starlight; and as this black object came down again, I saw by the green brightness that it was a man. For an instant he was clearly visible. He was a stout, ruddy, middle-aged man, well dressed; three days before, he must have been walking the world, a man of considerable consequence. I could see his staring eyes and gleams of light on his studs and watch chain. He vanished behind the mound, and for a moment there was silence. And then began a shrieking and a sustained and cheerful hooting from the Martians.

I slid down the rubbish, struggled to my feet, clapped my hands over my ears, and bolted into the scullery. The curate, who had been crouching silently with his arms over his head, looked up as I passed, cried out quite loudly at my desertion of him, and came running after me.

That night, as we lurked in the scullery, balanced between our horror and the terrible fascination this peeping had, although I felt an urgent need of action I tried in vain to conceive some plan of escape; but afterwards, during the second day, I was able to consider our position with great clearness. The curate, I found, was quite incapable of discussion; this new and culminating atrocity had robbed him of all vestiges of reason or forethought. Practically he had already sunk to the level of an animal. But as the saying goes, I gripped myself with both hands. It grew upon my mind, once I could face the facts, that terrible as our position was, there was as yet no justification for absolute despair. Our chief chance lay in the possibility of the Martians making the pit nothing more than a temporary encampment. Or even if they kept it permanently, they might not consider it necessary to guard it, and a chance of escape might be afforded us. I also weighed very carefully the possibility of our digging a way out in a direction away from the pit, but the chances of our emerging within sight of some sentinel fighting-machine seemed at first too great. And I should have had to do all the digging myself. The curate would certainly have failed me.

It was on the third day, if my memory serves me right, that I saw the lad killed. It was the only occasion on which I actually saw the Martians feed. After that experience I avoided the hole in the wall for the better part of a day. I went into the scullery, removed the door, and spent some hours digging with my hatchet as silently as possible; but when I had made a hole about a couple of feet deep the loose earth collapsed noisily, and I did not dare continue. I lost heart, and lay down on the scullery floor for a long time, having no spirit even to move. And after that I abandoned altogether the idea of escaping by excavation.

It says much for the impression the Martians had made upon me that at first I entertained little or no hope of our escape being brought about by their overthrow through any human effort. But on the fourth or fifth night I heard a sound like heavy guns.

It was very late in the night, and the moon was shining brightly. The Martians had taken away the excavating-machine, and, save for a fighting-machine that stood in the remoter bank of the pit and a handling-machine that was buried out of my sight in a corner of the pit immediately beneath my peephole, the place was deserted by them. Except for the pale glow from the handling-machine and the bars and patches of white moonlight the pit was in darkness, and, except for the clinking of the handling-machine, quite still. That night was a beautiful serenity; save for one planet, the moon seemed to have the sky to herself. I heard a dog howling, and that familiar sound it was that made me listen. Then I heard quite distinctly a booming exactly like the sound of great guns. Six distinct reports I counted, and after a long interval six again. And that was all.

CHAPTER 4

The Death of the Curate

It was on the sixth day of our imprisonment that I peeped for the last time, and presently found myself alone. Instead of keeping close to me and trying to oust me from the slit, the curate had gone back into the scullery. I was struck by a sudden thought. I went back quickly and quietly into the scullery. In the darkness I heard the curate drinking. I snatched in the darkness, and my fingers caught a bottle of burgundy.

For a few minutes there was a tussle. The bottle struck the floor and broke, and I desisted and rose. We stood panting and threatening each other. In the end I planted myself between him and the food, and told him of my determination to begin a discipline. I divided the food in the pantry, into rations to last us ten days. I would not let him eat any more that day. In the afternoon he made a feeble effort to get at the food. I had been dozing, but in an instant I was awake. All day and all night we sat face to face, I weary but resolute, and he weeping and complaining of his immediate hunger. It was, I know, a night and a day, but to me it seemed – it seems now – an interminable length of time.

And so our widened incompatibility ended at last in open conflict. For two vast days we struggled in undertones and wrestling contests. There were times when I beat and kicked him madly, times when I cajoled and persuaded him, and once I tried to bribe him with the last bottle of burgundy, for there was a rain-water pump from which I could get water. But neither force nor kindness availed; he was indeed beyond reason. He would neither desist from his attacks on the food nor from his noisy babbling to himself. The rudimentary precautions to keep our imprisonment endurable he would not observe. Slowly I began to realise the complete overthrow of his intelligence, to perceive that my sole companion in this close and sickly darkness was a man insane.

From certain vague memories I am inclined to think my own mind wandered at times. I had strange and hideous dreams whenever I slept. It sounds paradoxical, but I am inclined to think that the weakness and insanity of the curate warned me, braced me, and kept me a sane man.

On the eighth day he began to talk aloud instead of whispering, and nothing I could do would moderate his speech.

"It is just, O God!" he would say, over and over again. "It is just. On me and mine be the punishment laid. We have sinned, we have fallen short. There was poverty, sorrow; the poor were trodden in the dust, and I held my peace. I preached acceptable folly – my God, what folly! – when I should have stood up, though I died for it, and called upon them to repent – repent!...Oppressors of the poor and needy...! The wine press of God!"

Then he would suddenly revert to the matter of the food I withheld from him, praying, begging, weeping, at last threatening. He began to raise his voice – I prayed him not to. He perceived a hold on me – he threatened he would shout and bring the Martians upon us. For a time that scared me; but any concession would have shortened our chance of escape beyond estimating. I defied him, although I felt no assurance that he might not do this thing. But that day, at any rate, he did not. He talked with his voice rising slowly, through the greater part of the eighth and ninth days – threats, entreaties, mingled with a torrent of half-sane and always frothy repentance for his vacant sham of God's service, such as made me pity him. Then he slept awhile, and began again with renewed strength, so loudly that I must needs make him desist.

"Be still!" I implored.

He rose to his knees, for he had been sitting in the darkness near the copper.

"I have been still too long," he said, in a tone that must have reached the pit, "and now I must bear my witness. Woe unto this unfaithful city! Woe! Woe! Woe! Woe! Woe! To the inhabitants of the earth by reason of the other voices of the trumpet—"

"Shut up!" I said, rising to my feet, and in a terror lest the Martians should hear us. "For God's sake—"

"Nay," shouted the curate, at the top of his voice, standing likewise and extending his arms. "Speak! The word of the Lord is upon me!"

In three strides he was at the door leading into the kitchen.

"I must bear my witness! I go! It has already been too long delayed."

I put out my hand and felt the meat chopper hanging to the wall. In a flash I was after him. I was fierce with fear. Before he was halfway across the kitchen I had overtaken him. With one last touch of humanity I turned the blade back and struck him with the butt. He went headlong forward and lay stretched on the ground. I stumbled over him and stood panting. He lay still.

Suddenly I heard a noise without, the run and smash of slipping plaster, and the triangular aperture in the wall was darkened. I looked up and saw the lower surface of a handling-machine coming slowly across the hole. One of its gripping limbs curled amid the debris; another limb appeared, feeling its way over the fallen beams. I stood petrified, staring. Then I saw through a sort of glass plate near the edge of the body the face, as we may call it, and the large dark eyes of a Martian, peering, and then a long metallic snake of tentacle came feeling slowly through the hole.

I turned by an effort, stumbled over the curate, and stopped at the scullery door. The tentacle was now some way, two yards or more, in the room, and twisting and turning, with queer sudden movements, this way and that. For a while I stood fascinated by that slow, fitful advance. Then, with a faint, hoarse cry, I forced myself across the scullery. I trembled violently; I could scarcely stand upright. I opened the door of the coal cellar, and stood there in the darkness staring at the faintly lit doorway into the kitchen, and listening. Had the Martian seen me? What was it doing now?

Something was moving to and fro there, very quietly; every now and then it tapped against the wall, or started on its movements with a faint metallic ringing, like the movements of keys on a split-ring. Then a heavy body – I knew too well what – was dragged across the floor of the kitchen towards the opening. Irresistibly attracted, I crept to the door and peeped into the kitchen. In the triangle of bright outer sunlight I saw the Martian, in its Briareus of a handling-machine, scrutinizing the curate's head. I thought at once that it would infer my presence from the mark of the blow I had given him.

I crept back to the coal cellar, shut the door, and began to cover myself up as much as I could, and as noiselessly as possible in the darkness, among the firewood and coal therein. Every now and then I paused, rigid, to hear if the Martian had thrust its tentacles through the opening again.

Then the faint metallic jingle returned. I traced it slowly feeling over the kitchen. Presently I heard it nearer – in the scullery, as I judged. I thought that its length might be insufficient to reach me. I prayed copiously. It passed, scraping faintly across the cellar door. An age of almost intolerable suspense intervened; then I heard it fumbling at the latch! It had found the door! The Martians understood doors!

It worried at the catch for a minute, perhaps, and then the door opened.

In the darkness I could just see the thing – like an elephant's trunk more than anything else – waving towards me and touching and examining the wall, coals, wood and ceiling. It was like a black worm swaying its blind head to and fro.

Once, even, it touched the heel of my boot. I was on the verge of screaming; I bit my hand. For a time the tentacle was silent. I could have fancied it had been withdrawn. Presently, with an abrupt click, it gripped something – I thought it had me! – and seemed to go out of the cellar again. For a minute I was not sure. Apparently it had taken a lump of coal to examine.

I seized the opportunity of slightly shifting my position, which had become cramped, and then listened. I whispered passionate prayers for safety.

Then I heard the slow, deliberate sound creeping towards me again. Slowly, slowly it drew near, scratching against the walls and tapping the furniture.

While I was still doubtful, it rapped smartly against the cellar door and closed it. I heard it go into the pantry, and the biscuit-tins rattled and a bottle smashed, and then came a heavy bump against the cellar door. Then silence that passed into an infinity of suspense.

Had it gone?

At last I decided that it had.

It came into the scullery no more; but I lay all the tenth day in the close darkness, buried among coals and firewood, not daring even to crawl out for the drink for which I craved. It was the eleventh day before I ventured so far from my security.

CHAPTER 5

The Stillness

My first act before I went into the pantry was to fasten the door between the kitchen and the scullery. But the pantry was empty; every scrap of food had gone. Apparently, the Martian had taken it all on the previous day. At that discovery I despaired for the first time. I took no food, or no drink either, on the eleventh or the twelfth day.

At first my mouth and throat were parched, and my strength ebbed sensibly. I sat about in the darkness of the scullery, in a state of despondent wretchedness. My mind ran on eating. I thought I had become deaf, for the noises of movement I had been accustomed to hear from the pit had ceased absolutely. I did not feel strong enough to crawl noiselessly to the peephole, or I would have gone there.

On the twelfth day my throat was so painful that, taking the chance of alarming the Martians, I attacked the creaking rain-water pump that stood by the sink, and got a couple of glassfuls of blackened and tainted rain water. I was greatly refreshed by this, and emboldened by the fact that no enquiring tentacle followed the noise of my pumping.

During these days, in a rambling, inconclusive way, I thought much of the curate and of the manner of his death.

On the thirteenth day I drank some more water, and dozed and thought disjointedly of eating and of vague impossible plans of escape. Whenever I dozed I dreamt of horrible phantasms, of the death of the curate, or of sumptuous dinners; but, asleep or awake, I felt a keen pain that urged me to drink again and again. The light that came into the scullery was no longer grey, but red. To my disordered imagination it seemed the colour of blood.

On the fourteenth day I went into the kitchen, and I was surprised to find that the fronds of the red weed had grown right across the hole in the wall, turning the half-light of the place into a crimson-coloured obscurity.

It was early on the fifteenth day that I heard a curious, familiar sequence of sounds in the kitchen, and, listening, identified it as the snuffing and scratching of a dog. Going into the kitchen, I saw a dog's nose peering in through a break among the ruddy fronds. This greatly surprised me. At the scent of me he barked shortly.

I thought if I could induce him to come into the place quietly I should be able, perhaps, to kill and eat him; and in any case, it would be advisable to kill him, lest his actions attracted the attention of the Martians.

I crept forward, saying "Good dog!" very softly; but he suddenly withdrew his head and disappeared.

I listened – I was not deaf – but certainly the pit was still. I heard a sound like the flutter of a bird's wings, and a hoarse croaking, but that was all.

For a long while I lay close to the peephole, but not daring to move aside the red plants that obscured it. Once or twice I heard a faint pitter-patter like the feet of the dog going hither and thither on the sand far below me, and there were more birdlike sounds, but that was all. At length, encouraged by the silence, I looked out.

Except in the corner, where a multitude of crows hopped and fought over the skeletons of the dead the Martians had consumed, there was not a living thing in the pit.

I stared about me, scarcely believing my eyes. All the machinery had gone. Save for the big mound of greyish-blue powder in one corner, certain bars of aluminium in another, the black birds, and the skeletons of the killed, the place was merely an empty circular pit in the sand.

Slowly I thrust myself out through the red weed, and stood upon the mound of rubble. I could see in any direction save behind me, to the north, and neither Martians nor sign of Martians were to be seen. The pit dropped sheerly from my feet, but a little way along the rubbish afforded a practicable slope to the summit of the ruins. My chance of escape had come. I began to tremble.

I hesitated for some time, and then, in a gust of desperate resolution, and with a heart that throbbed violently, I scrambled to the top of the mound in which I had been buried so long.

I looked about again. To the northward, too, no Martian was visible.

When I had last seen this part of Sheen in the daylight it had been a straggling street of comfortable white and red houses, interspersed with abundant shady trees. Now I stood on a mound of smashed brickwork, clay, and gravel, over which spread a multitude of red cactus-shaped plants, knee-high, without a solitary terrestrial growth to dispute their footing. The trees near me were dead and brown, but further a network of red thread scaled the still living stems.

The neighbouring houses had all been wrecked, but none had been burned; their walls stood, sometimes to the second story, with smashed windows and shattered doors. The red weed grew tumultuously in their roofless rooms. Below me was the great pit, with the crows struggling for its refuse. A number of other birds hopped about among the ruins. Far away I saw a gaunt cat slink crouchingly along a wall, but traces of men there were none.

The day seemed, by contrast with my recent confinement, dazzlingly bright, the sky a glowing blue. A gentle breeze kept the red weed that covered every scrap of unoccupied ground gently swaying. And oh! the sweetness of the air!

CHAPTER 6

The Work of Fifteen Days

For some time I stood tottering on the mound regardless of my safety. Within that noisome den from which I had emerged I had thought with a narrow intensity only of our immediate security. I had not realised what had been happening to the world, had not anticipated this startling vision of unfamiliar things. I had expected to see Sheen in ruins – I found about me the landscape, weird and lurid, of another planet.

For that moment I touched an emotion beyond the common range of men, yet one that the poor brutes we dominate know only too well. I felt as a rabbit might feel returning to his burrow and suddenly confronted by the work of a dozen busy navvies digging the foundations of a house. I felt the first inkling of a thing that presently grew quite clear in my mind, that oppressed me for many days, a sense of dethronement, a persuasion that I was no longer a master, but an animal among the animals, under the Martian heel. With us it would be as with them, to lurk and watch, to run and hide; the fear and empire of man had passed away.

But so soon as this strangeness had been realised it passed, and my dominant motive became the hunger of my long and dismal fast. In the direction away from the pit I saw, beyond a red-covered wall, a patch of garden ground unburied. This gave me a hint, and I went knee-deep, and sometimes neck-deep, in the red weed. The density of the weed gave me a reassuring sense of hiding. The wall was some six feet high, and when I attempted to clamber it I found I could not lift my feet to the crest. So I went along by the side of it, and came to a corner and a rockwork that enabled me to get to the top, and tumble into the garden I coveted. Here I found some young onions, a couple of gladiolus bulbs, and a quantity of immature carrots, all of which I secured, and, scrambling over a ruined wall, went on my way through scarlet and crimson trees towards Kew – it was like walking through an avenue of gigantic blood drops – possessed with two ideas: to get more food, and to limp, as soon and as far as my strength permitted, out of this accursed unearthly region of the pit.

Some way farther, in a grassy place, was a group of mushrooms which also I devoured, and then I came upon a brown sheet of flowing shallow water, where meadows used to be. These fragments of nourishment served only to whet my hunger. At first I was surprised at this flood in a hot, dry summer, but afterwards I discovered that it was caused by the tropical exuberance of the red weed. Directly this extraordinary growth encountered water it straightway became gigantic and of unparalleled fecundity. Its seeds were simply poured down into the water of the Wey and Thames, and its swiftly growing and Titanic water fronds speedily choked both those rivers.

At Putney, as I afterwards saw, the bridge was almost lost in a tangle of this weed, and at Richmond, too, the Thames water poured in a broad and shallow stream across the meadows of Hampton and Twickenham. As the water spread the weed followed them, until the ruined villas of the Thames valley were for a time lost in this red swamp, whose margin I explored, and much of the desolation the Martians had caused was concealed.

In the end the red weed succumbed almost as quickly as it had spread. A cankering disease, due, it is believed, to the action of certain bacteria, presently seized upon it. Now by the action of natural selection, all terrestrial plants have acquired a resisting power against bacterial diseases – they never succumb without a severe struggle, but the red weed rotted like a thing already dead. The fronds became bleached, and then shrivelled and brittle. They broke off at the least touch, and the waters that had stimulated their early growth carried their last vestiges out to sea.

My first act on coming to this water was, of course, to slake my thirst. I drank a great deal of it and, moved by an impulse, gnawed some fronds of red weed; but they were watery, and had a sickly, metallic taste. I found the water was sufficiently shallow for me to wade securely, although the red weed impeded my feet a little; but the flood evidently got deeper towards the river, and I turned back to Mortlake. I managed to make out the road by means of occasional ruins of its villas and fences and lamps, and so presently I got out of this spate and made my way to the hill going up towards Roehampton and came out on Putney Common.

Here the scenery changed from the strange and unfamiliar to the wreckage of the familiar: patches of ground exhibited the devastation of a cyclone, and in a few score yards I would come upon perfectly undisturbed spaces, houses with their blinds trimly drawn and doors closed, as if they had been left for a day by the owners, or as if their inhabitants slept within. The red weed was less abundant; the tall trees along the lane were free from the red creeper. I hunted for food among the trees, finding nothing, and I also raided a couple of silent houses, but they had already been broken into and ransacked. I rested for the remainder of the daylight in a shrubbery, being, in my enfeebled condition, too fatigued to push on.

All this time I saw no human beings, and no signs of the Martians. I encountered a couple of hungry-looking dogs, but both hurried circuitously away from the advances I made them. Near Roehampton I had seen two human skeletons – not bodies, but skeletons, picked clean – and in the wood by me I found the crushed and scattered bones of several cats and rabbits and the skull of a sheep. But though I gnawed parts of these in my mouth, there was nothing to be got from them.

After sunset I struggled on along the road towards Putney, where I think the Heat-Ray must have been used for some reason. And in the garden beyond Roehampton I got a quantity of immature potatoes, sufficient to stay my hunger. From this garden one looked down upon Putney and the river. The aspect of the place in the dusk was singularly desolate: blackened trees, blackened, desolate ruins, and down the hill the sheets of the flooded river, red-tinged with the weed. And over all – silence. It filled me with indescribable terror to think how swiftly that desolating change had come.

For a time I believed that mankind had been swept out of existence, and that I stood there alone, the last man left alive. Hard by the top of Putney Hill I came upon another skeleton, with the arms dislocated and removed several yards from the rest of the body. As I proceeded I became more and more convinced that the extermination of mankind was, save for such stragglers as myself, already accomplished in this part of the world. The Martians, I thought, had gone on and left the country desolated, seeking food elsewhere. Perhaps even now they were destroying Berlin or Paris, or it might be they had gone northward.

CHAPTER 7

The Man on Putney Hill

I spent that night in the inn that stands at the top of Putney Hill, sleeping in a made bed for the first time since my flight to Leatherhead. I will not tell the needless trouble I had breaking into that house – afterwards I found the front door was on the latch – nor how I ransacked every room for food, until just on the verge of despair, in what seemed to me to be a servant's bedroom, I found a rat-gnawed crust and two tins of pineapple. The place had been already searched and emptied. In the bar I afterwards found some biscuits and sandwiches that had been overlooked. The latter I could not eat, they were too rotten, but the former not only stayed my hunger, but filled my pockets. I lit no lamps, fearing some Martian might come beating that part of London for food in the night. Before I went to bed I had an interval of restlessness, and prowled from window to window, peering out for some sign of these monsters. I slept little. As I lay in bed I found myself thinking consecutively – a thing I do not remember to have done since my last argument with the curate. During all the intervening time my mental condition had been a hurrying succession of vague emotional states or a sort of stupid receptivity. But in the night my brain, reinforced, I suppose, by the food I had eaten, grew clear again, and I thought.

Three things struggled for possession of my mind: the killing of the curate, the whereabouts of the Martians, and the possible fate of my wife. The former gave me no sensation of horror or remorse to recall; I saw it simply as a thing done, a memory infinitely disagreeable but quite without the quality of remorse. I saw myself then as I see myself now, driven step by step towards that hasty blow, the creature of a sequence of accidents leading inevitably to that. I felt no condemnation; yet the memory, static, unprogressive, haunted me. In the silence of the night, with that sense of the nearness of God that sometimes comes into the stillness and the darkness, I stood my trial, my only trial, for that moment of wrath and fear. I retraced every step of our conversation from the moment when I had found him crouching beside me, heedless of my thirst, and pointing to the fire and smoke that streamed up from the ruins of Weybridge. We had been incapable of co-operation – grim chance had taken no heed of that. Had I foreseen, I should have left him at Halliford. But I did not foresee; and crime is to foresee and do. And I set this down as I have set all this story down, as it was. There were no witnesses – all these things I might have concealed. But I set it down, and the reader must form his judgment as he will.

And when, by an effort, I had set aside that picture of a prostrate body, I faced the problem of the Martians and the fate of my wife. For the former I had no data; I could imagine a hundred things, and so, unhappily, I could for the latter. And suddenly that night became terrible. I found myself sitting up in bed, staring at the dark. I found myself praying that the Heat-Ray might have suddenly and painlessly struck her out of being. Since the night of my return from Leatherhead I had not prayed. I had uttered prayers, fetish prayers, had prayed as heathens mutter charms when I was in extremity; but now I prayed indeed, pleading steadfastly and sanely, face to face with the darkness of God. Strange night! Strangest in this, that so soon as dawn had come, I, who had talked with God, crept out of the house like a rat leaving its hiding place – a creature scarcely larger, an inferior animal, a thing that for any passing whim of our masters might be hunted and killed. Perhaps they also prayed confidently to God. Surely, if we have learned nothing else, this war has taught us pity – pity for those witless souls that suffer our dominion.

The morning was bright and fine, and the eastern sky glowed pink, and was fretted with little golden clouds. In the road that runs from the top of Putney Hill to Wimbledon was a number of poor vestiges of the panic torrent that must have poured Londonward on the Sunday night after the fighting began. There was a little two-wheeled cart inscribed with the name of Thomas Lobb, Greengrocer, New Malden, with a smashed wheel and an abandoned tin trunk; there was a straw hat trampled into the now hardened mud, and at the top of West Hill a lot of blood-stained glass about the overturned water trough. My movements were languid, my plans of the vaguest. I had an idea of going to Leatherhead, though knew that there I had the poorest chance of finding my wife. Certainly, unless death had overtaken them suddenly, my cousins and she would have fled thence; but it seemed to me I might find or learn there whither the Surrey people had fled. I knew I wanted to find my wife, that my heart ached for her and the world of men, but I had no clear idea how the finding might be done. I was also sharply aware now of my intense loneliness. From the corner I went, under cover of a thicket of trees and bushes, to the edge of Wimbledon Common, stretching wide and far.

That dark expanse was lit in patches by yellow gorse and broom; there was no red weed to be seen, and as I prowled, hesitating, on the verge of the open, the sun rose, flooding it all with light and vitality. I came upon a busy swarm of little frogs in a swampy place among the trees. I stopped to look at them, drawing a lesson from their stout resolve to live. And presently, turning suddenly, with an odd feeling of being watched, I beheld something crouching amid a clump of bushes. I stood regarding this. I made a step towards it, and it rose up and became a man armed with a cutlass. I approached him slowly. He stood silent and motionless, regarding me.

As I drew nearer I perceived he was dressed in clothes as dusty and filthy as my own; he looked, indeed, as though he had been dragged through a culvert. Nearer, I distinguished the green slime of ditches mixing with the pale drab of dried clay and shiny, coaly patches. His black hair fell over his eyes, and his face was dark and dirty and sunken, so that at first I did not recognise him. There was a red cut across the lower part of his face.

"Stop!" he cried, when I was within ten yards of him, and I stopped. His voice was hoarse. "Where do you come from?" he said.

I thought, surveying him.

"I come from Mortlake," I said. "I was buried near the pit the Martians made about their cylinder. I have worked my way out and escaped."

"There is no food about here," he said. "This is my country. All this hill down to the river, and back to Clapham, and up to the edge of the common. There is only food for one. Which way are you going?"

I answered slowly.

"I don't know," I said. "I have been buried in the ruins of a house thirteen or fourteen days. I don't know what has happened."

He looked at me doubtfully, then started, and looked with a changed expression.

"I've no wish to stop about here," said I. "I think I shall go to Leatherhead, for my wife was there."

He shot out a pointing finger.

"It is you," said he; "the man from Woking. And you weren't killed at Weybridge?"

I recognised him at the same moment.

"You are the artilleryman who came into my garden."

"Good luck!" he said. "We are lucky ones! Fancy *you*!" He put out a hand, and I took it. "I crawled up a drain," he said. "But they didn't kill everyone. And after they went away I got off towards Walton across the fields. But— It's not sixteen days altogether – and your hair is grey." He looked over his shoulder suddenly. "Only a rook," he said. "One gets to know that birds have shadows these days. This is a bit open. Let us crawl under those bushes and talk."

"Have you seen any Martians?" I said. "Since I crawled out—"

"They've gone away across London," he said. "I guess they've got a bigger camp there. Of a night, all over there, Hampstead way, the sky is alive with their lights. It's like a great city, and in the glare you can just see them moving. By daylight you can't. But nearer – I haven't seen them—" (he counted on his fingers) "five days. Then I saw a couple across Hammersmith way carrying something big. And the night before last" – he stopped and spoke impressively – "it was just a matter of lights, but it was something up in the air. I believe they've built a flying-machine, and are learning to fly."

I stopped, on hands and knees, for we had come to the bushes.

"Fly!"

"Yes," he said, "fly."

I went on into a little bower, and sat down.

"It is all over with humanity," I said. "If they can do that they will simply go round the world."

He nodded.

"They will. But— It will relieve things over here a bit. And besides—" He looked at me. "Aren't you satisfied it *is* up with humanity? I am. We're down; we're beat."

I stared. Strange as it may seem, I had not arrived at this fact – a fact perfectly obvious so soon as he spoke. I had still held a vague hope; rather, I had kept a lifelong habit of mind. He repeated his words, "We're beat." They carried absolute conviction.

"It's all over," he said. "They've lost *one* – just *one*. And they've made their footing good and crippled the greatest power in the world. They've walked over us. The death of that one at Weybridge was an accident. And these are only pioneers. They kept on coming. These green stars – I've seen none these five or six days, but I've no doubt they're falling somewhere every night. Nothing's to be done. We're under! We're beat!"

I made him no answer. I sat staring before me, trying in vain to devise some countervailing thought.

"This isn't a war," said the artilleryman. "It never was a war, any more than there's war between man and ants."

Suddenly I recalled the night in the observatory.

"After the tenth shot they fired no more – at least, until the first cylinder came."

"How do you know?" said the artilleryman. I explained. He thought. "Something wrong with the gun," he said. "But what if there is? They'll get it right again. And even if there's a delay, how can it alter the end? It's just men and ants. There's the ants builds their cities, live their lives, have wars, revolutions, until the men want them out of the way, and then they go out of the way. That's what we are now – just ants. Only—"

"Yes," I said.

"We're eatable ants."

We sat looking at each other.

"And what will they do with us?" I said.

"That's what I've been thinking," he said; "that's what I've been thinking. After Weybridge I went south – thinking. I saw what was up. Most of the people were hard at it squealing and exciting themselves. But I'm not so fond of squealing. I've been in sight of death once or twice; I'm not an ornamental soldier, and at the best and worst, death – it's just death. And it's the man that keeps on thinking comes through. I saw everyone tracking away south. Says I, 'Food won't last this way,' and I turned right back. I went for the Martians like a sparrow goes for man. All round" – he waved a hand to the horizon – "they're starving in heaps, bolting, treading on each other—"

He saw my face, and halted awkwardly.

"No doubt lots who had money have gone away to France," he said. He seemed to hesitate whether to apologise, met my eyes, and went on: "There's food all about here. Canned things in shops; wines, spirits, mineral waters; and the water mains and drains are empty. Well, I was telling you what I was thinking. 'Here's intelligent things,' I said, 'and it seems they want us for food. First, they'll smash us up – ships, machines, guns, cities, all the order and organisation. All that will go. If we were the size of ants we might pull through. But we're not. It's all too bulky to stop. That's the first certainty.' Eh?"

I assented.

"It is; I've thought it out. Very well, then – next; at present we're caught as we're wanted. A Martian has only to go a few miles to get a crowd on the run. And I saw one, one day, out by Wandsworth, picking houses to pieces and routing among the wreckage. But they won't keep on doing that. So soon as they've settled all our guns and ships, and smashed our railways, and done all the things they are doing over there, they will begin catching us systematic, picking the best and storing us in cages and things. That's what they will start doing in a bit. Lord! They haven't begun on us yet. Don't you see that?"

"Not begun!" I exclaimed.

"Not begun. All that's happened so far is through our not having the sense to keep quiet – worrying them with guns and such foolery. And losing our heads, and rushing off in crowds to where there wasn't any more safety than where we were. They don't want to bother us yet. They're making their things – making all the things they couldn't bring with them, getting things ready for the rest of their people. Very likely that's why the cylinders have stopped for a bit, for fear of hitting those who are here. And instead of our rushing about blind, on the howl, or getting dynamite on the chance of busting them up, we've got to fix ourselves up according to the new state of affairs. That's how I figure it out. It isn't quite according to what a man wants for his species, but it's about what the facts point to. And that's the principle I acted upon. Cities, nations, civilisation, progress – it's all over. That game's up. We're beat."

"But if that is so, what is there to live for?"

The artilleryman looked at me for a moment.

"There won't be any more blessed concerts for a million years or so; there won't be any Royal Academy of Arts, and no nice little feeds at restaurants. If it's amusement you're after, I reckon the game is up. If you've got any drawing-room manners or a dislike to eating peas with a knife or dropping aitches, you'd better chuck 'em away. They ain't no further use."

"You mean—"

"I mean that men like me are going on living – for the sake of the breed. I tell you, I'm grim set on living. And if I'm not mistaken, you'll show what insides *you've* got, too, before long. We aren't going to be exterminated. And I don't mean to be caught either, and tamed and fattened and bred like a thundering ox. Ugh! Fancy those brown creepers!"

"You don't mean to say—"

"I do. I'm going on, under their feet. I've got it planned; I've thought it out. We men are beat. We don't know enough. We've got to learn before we've got a chance. And we've got to live and keep independent while we learn. See! That's what has to be done."

I stared, astonished, and stirred profoundly by the man's resolution.

"Great God!" cried I. "But you are a man indeed!" And suddenly I gripped his hand.

"Eh!" he said, with his eyes shining. "I've thought it out, eh?"

"Go on," I said.

"Well, those who mean to escape their catching must get ready. I'm getting ready. Mind you, it isn't all of us that are made for wild beasts; and that's what it's got to be. That's why I watched you. I had my doubts. You're slender. I didn't know that it was you, you see, or just how you'd been buried. All these – the sort of people that lived in these houses, and all those damn little clerks that used to live down that way – they'd be no good. They haven't any spirit in them – no proud dreams and no proud lusts; and a man who hasn't one or the other – Lord! What is he but funk and precautions? They just used to skedaddle off to work – I've seen hundreds of 'em, bit of breakfast in hand, running wild and shining to catch their little season-ticket train, for fear they'd get dismissed if they didn't; working at businesses they were afraid to take the trouble to understand; skedaddling back for fear they wouldn't be in time for dinner; keeping indoors after dinner for fear of the back streets, and sleeping with the wives they married, not because they wanted them, but because they had a bit of money that would make for safety in their one little miserable skedaddle through the world. Lives insured and a bit invested for fear of accidents. And on Sundays – fear of the hereafter. As if hell was built for rabbits! Well, the Martians will just be a godsend to these. Nice roomy cages, fattening food, careful breeding, no worry. After a week or so chasing about the fields and lands on empty stomachs, they'll come and be caught cheerful. They'll be quite glad after a bit. They'll wonder what people did before there were Martians to take care of them. And the bar loafers, and mashers, and singers – I can imagine them. I can imagine them," he said, with a sort of sombre gratification. "There'll be any amount of sentiment and religion loose among them. There's hundreds of things I saw with my eyes that I've only begun to see clearly these last few days. There's lots will take things as they are – fat and stupid; and lots will be worried by a sort of feeling that it's all wrong, and that they ought to be doing something. Now whenever things are so that a lot of people feel they ought to be doing something, the weak, and those who go weak with a lot of complicated thinking, always make for a sort of do-nothing religion, very pious and superior, and submit to persecution and the will of the Lord. Very likely you've seen the same thing. It's energy in a gale of funk, and turned clean inside out. These cages will be full of psalms and hymns and piety. And those of a less simple sort will work in a bit of – what is it? – eroticism."

He paused.

"Very likely these Martians will make pets of some of them; train them to do tricks – who knows? – get sentimental over the pet boy who grew up and had to be killed. And some, maybe, they will train to hunt us."

"No," I cried, "that's impossible! No human being—"

"What's the good of going on with such lies?" said the artilleryman. "There's men who'd do it cheerful. What nonsense to pretend there isn't!"

And I succumbed to his conviction.

"If they come after me," he said; "Lord, if they come after me!" and subsided into a grim meditation.

I sat contemplating these things. I could find nothing to bring against this man's reasoning. In the days before the invasion no one would have questioned my intellectual superiority to his – I, a professed and recognised writer on philosophical themes, and he, a common soldier; and yet he had already formulated a situation that I had scarcely realised.

"What are you doing?" I said presently. "What plans have you made?"

He hesitated.

"Well, it's like this," he said. "What have we to do? We have to invent a sort of life where men can live and breed, and be sufficiently secure to bring the children up. Yes – wait a bit, and I'll make it clearer what I think ought to be done. The tame ones will go like all tame beasts; in a few generations they'll be big, beautiful, rich-blooded, stupid – rubbish! The risk is that we who keep wild will go savage – degenerate into a sort of big, savage rat... You see, how I mean to live is underground. I've been thinking about the drains. Of course those who don't know drains think horrible things; but under this London are miles and miles – hundreds of miles – and a few days rain and London empty will leave them sweet and clean. The main drains are big enough and airy enough for anyone. Then there's cellars, vaults, stores, from which bolting passages may be made to the drains. And the railway tunnels and subways. Eh? You begin to see? And we form a band – able-bodied, clean-minded men. We're not going to pick up any rubbish that drifts in. Weaklings go out again."

"As you meant me to go?"

"Well – I parleyed, didn't I?"

"We won't quarrel about that. Go on."

"Those who stop obey orders. Able-bodied, clean-minded women we want also – mothers and teachers. No lackadaisical ladies – no

THE   WAR   OF   THE   WORLDS

blasted rolling eyes. We can't have any weak or silly. Life is real again, and the useless and cumbersome and mischievous have to die. They ought to die. They ought to be willing to die. It's a sort of disloyalty, after all, to live and taint the race. And they can't be happy. Moreover, dying's none so dreadful; it's the funking makes it bad. And in all those places we shall gather. Our district will be London. And we may even be able to keep a watch, and run about in the open when the Martians keep away. Play cricket, perhaps. That's how we shall save the race. Eh? It's a possible thing? But saving the race is nothing in itself. As I say, that's only being rats. It's saving our knowledge and adding to it is the thing. There men like you come in. There's books, there's models. We must make great safe places down deep, and get all the books we can; not novels and poetry swipes, but ideas, science books. That's where men like you come in. We must go to the British Museum and pick all those books through. Especially we must keep up our science – learn more. We must watch these Martians. Some of us must go as spies. When it's all working, perhaps I will. Get caught, I mean. And the great thing is, we must leave the Martians alone. We mustn't even steal. If we get in their way, we clear out. We must show them we mean no harm. Yes, I know. But they're intelligent things, and they won't hunt us down if they have all they want, and think we're just harmless vermin."

The artilleryman paused and laid a brown hand upon my arm.

"After all, it may not be so much we may have to learn before – Just imagine this: four or five of their fighting machines suddenly starting off – Heat-Rays right and left, and not a Martian in 'em. Not a Martian in 'em, but men – men who have learned the way how. It may be in my time, even – those men. Fancy having one of them lovely things, with its Heat-Ray wide and free! Fancy having it in control! What would it matter if you smashed to smithereens at the

199

end of the run, after a bust like that? I reckon the Martians'll open their beautiful eyes! Can't you see them, man? Can't you see them hurrying, hurrying – puffing and blowing and hooting to their other mechanical affairs? Something out of gear in every case. And swish, bang, rattle, swish! Just as they are fumbling over it, *swish* comes the Heat-Ray, and, behold! man has come back to his own."

For a while the imaginative daring of the artilleryman, and the tone of assurance and courage he assumed, completely dominated my mind. I believed unhesitatingly both in his forecast of human destiny and in the practicability of his astonishing scheme, and the reader who thinks me susceptible and foolish must contrast his position, reading steadily with all his thoughts about his subject, and mine, crouching fearfully in the bushes and listening, distracted by apprehension. We talked in this manner through the early morning time, and later crept out of the bushes, and, after scanning the sky for Martians, hurried precipitately to the house on Putney Hill where he had made his lair. It was the coal cellar of the place, and when I saw the work he had spent a week upon – it was a burrow scarcely ten yards long, which he designed to reach to the main drain on Putney Hill – I had my first inkling of the gulf between his dreams and his powers. Such a hole I could have dug in a day. But I believed in him sufficiently to work with him all that morning until past midday at his digging. We had a garden barrow and shot the earth we removed against the kitchen range. We refreshed ourselves with a tin of mock-turtle soup and wine from the neighbouring pantry. I found a curious relief from the aching strangeness of the world in this steady labour. As we worked, I turned his project over in my mind, and presently objections and doubts began to arise; but I worked there all the morning, so glad was I to find myself with a purpose again. After working an hour I began to speculate on the distance one had to go before the cloaca was reached, the chances we had of missing it altogether. My immediate trouble was why we should dig this long tunnel, when it was possible to get into the drain at once down one of the manholes, and work back to the house. It seemed to me, too, that the house was inconveniently chosen, and required a needless length of tunnel. And just as I was beginning to face these things, the artilleryman stopped digging, and looked at me.

"We're working well," he said. He put down his spade. "Let us knock off a bit" he said. "I think it's time we reconnoitred from the roof of the house."

I was for going on, and after a little hesitation he resumed his spade; and then suddenly I was struck by a thought. I stopped, and so did he at once.

"Why were you walking about the common," I said, "instead of being here?"

"Taking the air," he said. "I was coming back. It's safer by night."

"But the work?"

"Oh, one can't always work," he said, and in a flash I saw the man plain. He hesitated, holding his spade. "We ought to reconnoitre now," he said, "because if any come near they may hear the spades and drop upon us unawares."

I was no longer disposed to object. We went together to the roof and stood on a ladder peeping out of the roof door. No Martians were to be seen, and we ventured out on the tiles, and slipped down under shelter of the parapet.

From this position a shrubbery hid the greater portion of Putney, but we could see the river below, a bubbly mass of red weed, and the low parts of Lambeth flooded and red. The red creeper swarmed up the trees about the old palace, and their branches stretched gaunt and dead, and set with shrivelled leaves, from amid its clusters. It was strange how entirely dependent both these things were upon flowing water for their propagation. About us neither had gained a footing; laburnums, pink mays, snowballs, and trees of arbor-vitae, rose out of laurels and hydrangeas, green and brilliant into the sunlight. Beyond Kensington dense smoke was rising, and that and a blue haze hid the northward hills.

The artilleryman began to tell me of the sort of people who still remained in London.

"One night last week," he said, "some fools got the electric light in order, and there was all Regent Street and the Circus ablaze, crowded with painted and ragged drunkards, men and women, dancing and shouting till dawn. A man who was there told me. And as the day came they became aware of a fighting-machine standing near by the Langham and looking down at them. Heaven knows how long he had been there. It must have given some of them a nasty turn. He came down the road towards them, and picked up nearly a hundred too drunk or frightened to run away."

Grotesque gleam of a time no history will ever fully describe!

From that, in answer to my questions, he came round to his grandiose plans again. He grew enthusiastic. He talked so eloquently of the possibility of capturing a fighting-machine that I more than half believed in him again. But now that I was beginning to understand something of his quality, I could divine the stress he laid on doing nothing precipitately. And I noted that now there was no question that he personally was to capture and fight the great machine.

After a time we went down to the cellar. Neither of us seemed disposed to resume digging, and when he suggested a meal, I was nothing loath. He became suddenly very generous, and when we had eaten he went away and returned with some excellent cigars. We lit these, and his optimism glowed. He was inclined to regard my coming as a great occasion.

"There's some champagne in the cellar," he said.

"We can dig better on this Thames-side burgundy," said I.

"No," said he; "I am host today. Champagne! Great God! We've a heavy enough task before us! Let us take a rest and gather strength while we may. Look at these blistered hands!"

And pursuant to this idea of a holiday, he insisted upon playing cards after we had eaten. He taught me euchre, and after dividing London between us, I taking the northern side and he the southern, we played for parish points. Grotesque and foolish as this will seem to the sober reader, it is absolutely true, and what is more remarkable, I found the card game and several others we played extremely interesting.

Strange mind of man! that, with our species upon the edge of extermination or appalling degradation, with no clear prospect before us but the chance of a horrible death, we could sit following the chance of this painted pasteboard, and playing the "joker" with vivid delight. Afterwards he taught me poker, and I beat him at three tough chess games. When dark came we decided to take the risk, and lit a lamp.

After an interminable string of games, we supped, and the artilleryman finished the champagne. We went on smoking the cigars. He was no longer the energetic regenerator of his species I had encountered in the morning. He was still optimistic, but it was a less kinetic, a more thoughtful optimism. I remember he wound up with my health, proposed in a speech of small variety and considerable intermittence. I took a cigar, and went upstairs to look at the lights of which he had spoken that blazed so greenly along the Highgate hills.

At first I stared unintelligently across the London valley. The northern hills were shrouded in darkness; the fires near Kensington glowed redly, and now and then an orange-red tongue of flame flashed up and vanished in the deep blue night. All the rest of London was black. Then, nearer, I perceived a strange light, a pale, violet-purple fluorescent glow, quivering under the night breeze. For a space I could not understand it, and then I knew that it must be the red weed from which this faint irradiation proceeded. With that realisation my dormant sense of wonder, my sense of the proportion of things, awoke again. I glanced from that to Mars, red and clear, glowing high in the west, and then gazed long and earnestly at the darkness of Hampstead and Highgate.

I remained a very long time upon the roof, wondering at the grotesque changes of the day. I recalled my mental states from the midnight prayer to the foolish card-playing. I had a violent revulsion of feeling. I remember I flung away the cigar with a certain wasteful symbolism. My folly came to me with glaring exaggeration. I seemed a traitor to my wife and to my kind; I was filled with remorse. I resolved to leave this strange undisciplined dreamer of great things to his drink and gluttony, and to go on into London. There, it seemed to me, I had the best chance of learning what the Martians and my fellowmen were doing. I was still upon the roof when the late moon rose.

CHAPTER 8

Dead London

After I had parted from the artilleryman, I went down the hill, and by the High Street across the bridge to Fulham. The red weed was tumultuous at that time, and nearly choked the bridge roadway; but its fronds were already whitened in patches by the spreading disease that presently removed it so swiftly.

At the corner of the lane that runs to Putney Bridge station I found a man lying. He was as black as a sweep with the black dust, alive, but helplessly and speechlessly drunk. I could get nothing from him but curses and furious lunges at my head. I think I should have stayed by him but for the brutal expression of his face.

There was black dust along the roadway from the bridge onwards, and it grew thicker in Fulham. The streets were horribly quiet. I got food – sour, hard, and mouldy, but quite eatable – in a baker's shop here. Some way towards Walham Green the streets became clear of powder, and I passed a white terrace of houses on fire; the noise of the burning was an absolute relief. Going on towards Brompton, the streets were quiet again.

Here I came once more upon the black powder in the streets and upon dead bodies. I saw altogether about a dozen in the length of the Fulham Road. They had been dead many days, so that I hurried quickly past them. The black powder covered them over, and softened their outlines. One or two had been disturbed by dogs.

Where there was no black powder, it was curiously like a Sunday in the City, with the closed shops, the houses locked up and the blinds drawn, the desertion, and the stillness. In some places plunderers had been at work, but rarely at other than the provision and wine shops. A jeweller's window had been broken open in one place, but apparently the thief had been disturbed, and a number of gold chains and a watch lay scattered on the pavement. I did not trouble to touch them. Farther on was a tattered woman in a heap on a doorstep; the hand that hung over her knee was gashed and bled down her rusty brown dress, and a smashed magnum of champagne formed a pool across the pavement. She seemed asleep, but she was dead.

The farther I penetrated into London, the profounder grew the stillness. But it was not so much the stillness of death – it was the stillness of suspense, of expectation. At any time the destruction that had already singed the northwestern borders of the metropolis, and had annihilated Ealing and Kilburn, might strike among these houses and leave them smoking ruins. It was a city condemned and derelict...

In South Kensington the streets were clear of dead and of black powder. It was near South Kensington that I first heard the howling. It crept almost imperceptibly upon my senses. It was a sobbing alternation of two notes, "Ulla, ulla, ulla, ulla," keeping on perpetually. When I passed streets that ran northward it grew in volume, and houses and buildings seemed to deaden and cut it off again. It came in a full tide down Exhibition Road. I stopped, staring towards Kensington Gardens, wondering at this strange, remote wailing. It was as if that mighty desert of houses had found a voice for its fear and solitude.

"Ulla, ulla, ulla, ulla," wailed that superhuman note – great waves of sound sweeping down the broad, sunlit roadway, between the tall buildings on each side. I turned northwards, marvelling, towards the iron gates of Hyde Park. I had half a mind to break into the Natural History Museum and find my way up to the summits of the towers, in order to see across the park. But I decided to keep to the ground, where quick hiding was possible, and so went on up the Exhibition Road. All the large mansions on each side of the road were empty and still, and my footsteps echoed against the sides of the houses. At the top, near the park gate, I came upon a strange sight – a bus overturned, and the skeleton of a horse picked clean. I puzzled over this for a time, and then went on to the bridge over the Serpentine. The voice grew stronger and stronger, though I could see nothing above the housetops on the north side of the park, save a haze of smoke to the northwest.

"Ulla, ulla, ulla, ulla," cried the voice, coming, as it seemed to me, from the district about Regent's Park. The desolating cry worked upon my mind. The mood that had sustained me passed. The wailing took possession of me. I found I was intensely weary, footsore, and now again hungry and thirsty.

It was already past noon. Why was I wandering alone in this city of the dead? Why was I alone when all London was lying in state, and in its black shroud? I felt intolerably lonely. My mind ran on old friends that I had forgotten for years. I thought of the poisons in the chemists' shops, of the liquors the wine merchants stored; I recalled the two sodden creatures of despair, who so far as I knew, shared the city with myself...

I came into Oxford Street by the Marble Arch, and here again were black powder and several bodies, and an evil, ominous smell from the gratings of the cellars of some of the houses. I grew very thirsty after the heat of my long walk. With infinite trouble I managed to break into a public-house and get food and drink. I was weary after eating, and went into the parlour behind the bar, and slept on a black horsehair sofa I found there.

I awoke to find that dismal howling still in my ears, "Ulla, ulla, ulla, ulla." It was now dusk, and after I had routed out some biscuits and a cheese in the bar – there was a meat safe, but it contained nothing but maggots – I wandered on through the silent residential squares to Baker Street – Portman Square is the only one I can name – and so came out at last upon Regent's Park. And as I emerged from the top of Baker Street, I saw far away over the trees in the clearness of the sunset the hood of the Martian giant from which this howling proceeded. I was not terrified. I came upon him as if it were a matter of course. I watched him for some time, but he did not move. He appeared to be standing and yelling, for no reason that I could discover.

I tried to formulate a plan of action. That perpetual sound of "Ulla, ulla, ulla, ulla," confused my mind. Perhaps I was too tired to be very fearful. Certainly I was more curious to know the reason of this monotonous crying than afraid. I turned back away from the park and struck into Park Road, intending to skirt the park, went along under the shelter of the terraces, and got a view of this stationary, howling Martian from the direction of St. John's Wood. A couple of hundred yards out of Baker Street I heard a yelping chorus, and saw, first a dog with a piece of putrescent red meat in his jaws coming headlong towards me, and then a pack of starving mongrels in pursuit of him. He made a wide curve to avoid me, as though he feared I might prove a fresh competitor. As the yelping died away down the silent road, the wailing sound of "Ulla, ulla, ulla, ulla," reasserted itself.

I came upon the wrecked handling-machine halfway to St. John's Wood station. At first I thought a house had fallen across the road. It was only as I clambered among the ruins that I saw, with a start, this mechanical Samson lying, with its tentacles bent and smashed and twisted, among the ruins it had made. The forepart was shattered. It seemed as if it had driven blindly straight at the house, and had been overwhelmed in its overthrow. It seemed to me then that this might have happened by a handling-machine escaping from the guidance of its Martian. I could not clamber among the ruins to see it, and the twilight was now so far advanced that the blood with which its seat was smeared, and the gnawed gristle of the Martian that the dogs had left, were invisible to me.

Wondering still more at all that I had seen, I pushed on towards Primrose Hill. Far away, through a gap in the trees, I saw a second Martian, as motionless as the first, standing in the park towards the Zoological Gardens, and silent. A little beyond the ruins about the smashed handling-machine I came upon the red weed again, and found the Regent's Canal, a spongy mass of dark-red vegetation.

As I crossed the bridge, the sound of "Ulla, ulla, ulla, ulla," ceased. It was, as it were, cut off. The silence came like a thunderclap.

The dusky houses about me stood faint and tall and dim; the trees towards the park were growing black. All about me the red weed clambered among the ruins, writhing to get above me in the dimness. Night, the mother of fear and mystery, was coming upon me. But while that voice sounded the solitude, the desolation, had been endurable; by virtue of it London had still seemed alive, and the sense of life about me had upheld me. Then suddenly a change, the passing of something – I knew not what – and then a stillness that could be felt. Nothing but this gaunt quiet.

London about me gazed at me spectrally. The windows in the white houses were like the eye sockets of skulls. About me my imagination found a thousand noiseless enemies moving. Terror seized me, a horror of my temerity. In front of me the road became pitchy black as though it was tarred, and I saw a contorted shape lying across the pathway. I could not bring myself to go on. I turned down St. John's Wood Road, and ran headlong from this unendurable stillness towards Kilburn. I hid from the night and the silence, until long after midnight, in a cabmen's shelter in Harrow Road. But before the dawn my courage returned, and while the stars were still in the sky I turned once more towards Regent's Park. I missed my way among the streets, and presently saw down a long avenue, in the half-light of the early dawn, the curve of Primrose Hill. On the summit, towering up to the fading stars, was a third Martian, erect and motionless like the others.

An insane resolve possessed me. I would die and end it. And I would save myself even the trouble of killing myself. I marched on recklessly towards this Titan, and then, as I drew nearer and the light grew, I saw that a multitude of black birds was circling and clustering about the hood. At that my heart gave a bound, and I began running along the road.

I hurried through the red weed that choked St. Edmund's Terrace (I waded breast-high across a torrent of water that was rushing down from the waterworks towards the Albert Road), and emerged upon the grass before the rising of the sun. Great mounds had been heaped about the crest of the hill, making a huge redoubt of it – it was the final and largest place the Martians had made – and from behind these heaps there rose a thin smoke against the sky. Against the sky line an eager dog ran and disappeared. The thought that had flashed into my mind grew real, grew credible. I felt no fear, only a wild, trembling exultation, as I ran up the hill towards the motionless monster. Out of the hood hung lank shreds of brown, at which the hungry birds pecked and tore.

In another moment I had scrambled up the earthen rampart and stood upon its crest, and the interior of the redoubt was below me.

A mighty space it was, with gigantic machines here and there within it, huge mounds of material and strange shelter places. And scattered about it, some in their overturned war-machines, some in the now rigid handling-machines, and a dozen of them stark and silent and laid in a row, were the Martians – *dead*! – slain by the putrefactive and disease bacteria against which their systems were unprepared; slain as the red weed was being slain; slain, after all man's devices had failed, by the humblest things that God, in his wisdom, has put upon this earth.

For so it had come about, as indeed I and many men might have foreseen had not terror and disaster blinded our minds. These germs of disease have taken toll of humanity since the beginning of things – taken toll of our prehuman ancestors since life began here. But by virtue of this natural selection of our kind we have developed resisting power; to no germs do we succumb without a struggle, and to many – those that cause putrefaction in dead matter, for instance – our living frames are altogether immune. But there are no bacteria in Mars, and directly these invaders arrived, directly they drank and fed, our microscopic allies began to work their overthrow. Already when I watched them they were irrevocably doomed, dying and rotting even as they went to and fro. It was inevitable. By the toll of a billion deaths man has bought his birthright of the earth, and it is his against all comers; it would still be his were the Martians ten times as mighty as they are. For neither do men live nor die in vain.

Here and there they were scattered, nearly fifty altogether, in that great gulf they had made, overtaken by a death that must have seemed to them as incomprehensible as any death could be. To me also at that time this death was incomprehensible. All I knew was that these things that had been alive and so terrible to men were dead. For a moment I believed that the destruction of Sennacherib had been repeated, that God had repented, that the Angel of Death had slain them in the night.

I stood staring into the pit, and my heart lightened gloriously, even as the rising sun struck the world to fire about me with his rays. The pit was still in darkness; the mighty engines, so great and wonderful in their power and complexity, so unearthly in their tortuous forms, rose weird and vague and strange out of the shadows towards the light. A multitude of dogs, I could hear, fought over the bodies that lay darkly in the depth of the pit, far below me. Across the pit on its farther lip, flat and vast and strange, lay the great flying-machine with which they had been experimenting upon our denser atmosphere when decay and death arrested them. Death had come not a day too soon. At the sound of a cawing overhead I looked up at the huge fighting-machine that would fight no more for ever, at the tattered red shreds of flesh that dripped down upon the overturned seats on the summit of Primrose Hill.

I turned and looked down the slope of the hill to where, enhaloed now in birds, stood those other two Martians that I had seen overnight, just as death had overtaken them. The one had died, even as it had been crying to its companions; perhaps it was the last to die, and its voice had gone on perpetually until the force of its machinery was exhausted. They glittered now, harmless tripod towers of shining metal, in the brightness of the rising sun.

All about the pit, and saved as by a miracle from everlasting destruction, stretched the great Mother of Cities. Those who have only seen London veiled in her sombre robes of smoke can scarcely imagine the naked clearness and beauty of the silent wilderness of houses.

Eastward, over the blackened ruins of the Albert Terrace and the splintered spire of the church, the sun blazed dazzling in a clear sky, and here and there some facet in the great wilderness of roofs caught the light and glared with a white intensity.

Northward were Kilburn and Hampsted, blue and crowded with houses; westward the great city was dimmed; and southward, beyond the Martians, the green waves of Regent's Park, the Langham Hotel, the dome of the Albert Hall, the Imperial Institute, and the giant mansions of the Brompton Road came out clear and little in the sunrise, the jagged ruins of Westminster rising hazily beyond. Far away and blue were the Surrey hills, and the towers of the Crystal Palace glittered like two silver rods. The dome of St. Paul's was dark against the sunrise, and injured, I saw for the first time, by a huge gaping cavity on its western side.

And as I looked at this wide expanse of houses and factories and churches, silent and abandoned; as I thought of the multitudinous hopes and efforts, the innumerable hosts of lives that had gone to build this human reef, and of the swift and ruthless destruction that had hung over it all; when I realised that the shadow had been rolled back, and that men might still live in the streets, and this dear vast dead city of mine be once more alive and powerful, I felt a wave of emotion that was near akin to tears.

The torment was over. Even that day the healing would begin. The survivors of the people scattered over the country – leaderless, lawless, foodless, like sheep without a shepherd – the thousands who had fled by sea, would begin to return; the pulse of life, growing stronger and stronger, would beat again in the empty streets and pour across the vacant squares. Whatever destruction was done, the hand of the destroyer was stayed. All the gaunt wrecks, the blackened skeletons of houses that stared so dismally at the sunlit grass of the hill, would presently be echoing with the hammers of the restorers and ringing with the tapping of their trowels. At the thought I extended my hands towards the sky and began thanking God. In a year, thought I – in a year...

With overwhelming force came the thought of myself, of my wife, and the old life of hope and tender helpfulness that had ceased for ever.

CHAPTER 9

Wreckage

And now comes the strangest thing in my story. Yet, perhaps, it is not altogether strange. I remember, clearly and coldly and vividly, all that I did that day until the time that I stood weeping and praising God upon the summit of Primrose Hill. And then I forget.

Of the next three days I know nothing. I have learned since that, so far from my being the first discoverer of the Martian overthrow, several such wanderers as myself had already discovered this on the previous night. One man – the first – had gone to St. Martin's-le-Grand, and, while I sheltered in the cabmen's hut, had contrived to telegraph to Paris. Thence the joyful news had flashed all over the world; a thousand cities, chilled by ghastly apprehensions, suddenly flashed into frantic illuminations; they knew of it in Dublin, Edinburgh, Manchester, Birmingham, at the time when I stood upon the verge of the pit. Already men, weeping with joy, as I have heard, shouting and staying their work to shake hands and shout, were making up trains, even as near as Crewe, to descend upon London. The church bells that had ceased a fortnight since suddenly caught the news, until all England was bell-ringing. Men on cycles, lean-faced, unkempt, scorched along every country lane shouting of unhoped deliverance, shouting to gaunt, staring figures of despair. And for the food! Across the Channel, across the Irish Sea, across the Atlantic, corn, bread, and

H . G . W E L L S

meat were tearing to our relief. All the shipping in the world seemed going Londonward in those days. But of all this I have no memory. I drifted – a demented man. I found myself in a house of kindly people, who had found me on the third day wandering, weeping, and raving through the streets of St. John's Wood. They have told me since that I was singing some insane doggerel about "The Last Man Left Alive! Hurrah! The Last Man Left Alive!" Troubled as they were with their own affairs, these people, whose name, much as I would like to express my gratitude to them, I may not even give here, nevertheless cumbered themselves with me, sheltered me, and protected me from myself. Apparently they had learned something of my story from me during the days of my lapse.

Very gently, when my mind was assured again, did they break to me what they had learned of the fate of Leatherhead. Two days after I was imprisoned it had been destroyed, with every soul in it, by a Martian. He had swept it out of existence, as it seemed, without any provocation, as a boy might crush an ant hill, in the mere wantonness of power.

I was a lonely man, and they were very kind to me. I was a lonely man and a sad one, and they bore with me. I remained with them four days after my recovery. All that time I felt a vague, a growing craving to look once more on whatever remained of the little life that seemed so happy and bright in my past. It was a mere hopeless desire to feast upon my misery. They dissuaded me. They did all they could to divert me from this morbidity. But at last I could resist the impulse no longer, and, promising faithfully to return to them, and parting, as I will confess, from these four-day friends with tears, I went out again into the streets that had lately been so dark and strange and empty.

Already they were busy with returning people; in places even there were shops open, and I saw a drinking fountain running water.

I remember how mockingly bright the day seemed as I went back on my melancholy pilgrimage to the little house at Woking, how busy the streets and vivid the moving life about me. So many people were abroad everywhere, busied in a thousand activities, that it seemed incredible that any great proportion of the population could have been slain. But then I noticed how yellow were the skins of the people I met, how shaggy the hair of the men, how large and bright their eyes, and that every other man still wore his dirty rags. Their faces seemed all with one of two expressions – a leaping exultation and energy or a grim resolution. Save for the expression of the faces, London seemed a city of tramps. The vestries were indiscriminately distributing bread sent us by the French government. The ribs of the few horses showed dismally. Haggard special constables with white badges stood at the corners of every street. I saw little of the mischief wrought by the Martians until I reached Wellington Street, and there I saw the red weed clambering over the buttresses of Waterloo Bridge.

At the corner of the bridge, too, I saw one of the common contrasts of that grotesque time – a sheet of paper flaunting against a thicket of the red weed, transfixed by a stick that kept it in place. It was the placard of the first newspaper to resume publication – the *Daily Mail*. I bought a copy for a blackened shilling I found in my pocket. Most of it was in blank, but the solitary compositor who did the thing had amused himself by making a grotesque scheme of advertisement stereo on the back page. The matter he printed was emotional; the news organisation had not as yet found its way back. I learned nothing fresh except that already in one week the examination of the Martian mechanisms had yielded astonishing results. Among other things, the article assured me what I did not believe at the time, that the "Secret of Flying," was discovered. At Waterloo I found the free trains that were taking people to their homes. The first rush was already over.

There were few people in the train, and I was in no mood for casual conversation. I got a compartment to myself, and sat with folded arms, looking greyly at the sunlit devastation that flowed past the windows. And just outside the terminus the train jolted over temporary rails, and on either side of the railway the houses were blackened ruins. To Clapham Junction the face of London was grimy with powder of the Black Smoke, in spite of two days of thunderstorms and rain, and at Clapham Junction the line had been wrecked again; there were hundreds of out-of-work clerks and shopmen working side by side with the customary navvies, and we were jolted over a hasty relaying.

All down the line from there the aspect of the country was gaunt and unfamiliar; Wimbledon particularly had suffered. Walton, by virtue of its unburned pine woods, seemed the least hurt of any place along the line. The Wandle, the Mole, every little stream, was a heaped mass of red weed, in appearance between butcher's meat and pickled cabbage. The Surrey pine woods were too dry, however, for the festoons of the red climber. Beyond Wimbledon, within sight of the line, in certain nursery grounds, were the heaped masses of earth about the sixth cylinder. A number of people were standing about it, and some sappers were busy in the midst of it. Over it flaunted a Union Jack, flapping cheerfully in the morning breeze. The nursery grounds were everywhere crimson with the weed, a wide expanse of livid colour cut with purple shadows, and very painful to the eye. One's gaze went with infinite relief from the scorched greys and sullen reds of the foreground to the blue-green softness of the eastward hills.

The line on the London side of Woking station was still undergoing repair, so I descended at Byfleet station and took the road to Maybury, past the place where I and the artilleryman had talked to the hussars, and on by the spot where the Martian had appeared to me in the thunderstorm. Here, moved by curiosity, I turned aside to find, among a tangle of red fronds, the warped and broken dog cart with the whitened bones of the horse scattered and gnawed. For a time I stood regarding these vestiges...

Then I returned through the pine wood, neck-high with red weed here and there, to find the landlord of the Spotted Dog had already found burial, and so came home past the College Arms. A man standing at an open cottage door greeted me by name as I passed.

I looked at my house with a quick flash of hope that faded immediately. The door had been forced; it was unfast and was opening slowly as I approached.

It slammed again. The curtains of my study fluttered out of the open window from which I and the artilleryman had watched the dawn. No one had closed it since. The smashed bushes were just as I had left them nearly four weeks ago. I stumbled into the hall, and the house felt empty. The stair carpet was ruffled and discoloured where I had crouched, soaked to the skin from the thunderstorm the night of the catastrophe. Our muddy footsteps I saw still went up the stairs.

I followed them to my study, and found lying on my writing-table still, with the selenite paper weight upon it, the sheet of work I had left on the afternoon of the opening of the cylinder. For a space I stood reading over my abandoned arguments. It was a paper on the probable development of Moral Ideas with the development of the civilising process; and the last sentence was the opening of a prophecy: "In about two hundred years," I had written, "we may expect—" The sentence ended abruptly. I remembered my inability to fix my mind that morning, scarcely a month gone by, and how I had broken off to get my *Daily Chronicle* from the newsboy. I remembered how I went down the garden gate as he came along, and how I had listened to his odd story of "Men from Mars."

I came down and went into the dining room. There were the mutton and the bread, both far gone now in decay, and a beer bottle overturned, just as I and the artilleryman had left them. My home was desolate. I perceived the folly of the faint hope I had cherished so long. And then a strange thing occurred. "It is no use," said a voice. "The house is deserted. No one has been here these ten days. Do not stay here to torment yourself. No one escaped but you."

I was startled. Had I spoken my thought aloud? I turned, and the French window was open behind me. I made a step to it, and stood looking out.

And there, amazed and afraid, even as I stood amazed and afraid, were my cousin and my wife – my wife white and tearless. She gave a faint cry.

"I came," she said. "I knew – knew—"

She put her hand to her throat – swayed. I made a step forward, and caught her in my arms.

CHAPTER 10

The Epilogue

I cannot but regret, now that I am concluding my story, how little I am able to contribute to the discussion of the many debatable questions which are still unsettled. In one respect I shall certainly provoke criticism. My particular province is speculative philosophy. My knowledge of comparative physiology is confined to a book or two, but it seems to me that Carver's suggestions as to the reason of the rapid death of the Martians is so probable as to be regarded almost as a proven conclusion. I have assumed that in the body of my narrative.

At any rate, in all the bodies of the Martians that were examined after the war, no bacteria except those already known as terrestrial species were found. That they did not bury any of their dead, and the reckless slaughter they perpetrated, point also to an entire ignorance of the putrefactive process. But probable as this seems, it is by no means a proven conclusion.

Neither is the composition of the Black Smoke known, which the Martians used with such deadly effect, and the generator of the Heat-Rays remains a puzzle. The terrible disasters at the Ealing and South Kensington laboratories have disinclined analysts for further investigations upon the latter. Spectrum analysis of the black powder points unmistakably to the presence of an unknown element with a brilliant group of three lines in the green, and it is possible that it combines with argon to form a compound which acts at once with deadly effect upon some constituent in the blood. But such unproven speculations will scarcely be of interest to the general reader, to whom this story is addressed. None of the brown scum that drifted down the Thames after the destruction of Shepperton was examined at the time, and now none is forthcoming.

The results of an anatomical examination of the Martians, so far as the prowling dogs had left such an examination possible, I have already given. But everyone is familiar with the magnificent and almost complete specimen in spirits at the Natural History Museum, and the countless drawings that have been made from it; and beyond that the interest of their physiology and structure is purely scientific.

A question of graver and universal interest is the possibility of another attack from the Martians. I do not think that nearly enough attention is being given to this aspect of the matter. At present the planet Mars is in conjunction, but with every return to opposition I, for one, anticipate a renewal of their adventure. In any case, we should be prepared. It seems to me that it should be possible to define the position of the gun from which the shots are discharged, to keep a sustained watch upon this part of the planet, and to anticipate the arrival of the next attack.

In that case the cylinder might be destroyed with dynamite or artillery before it was sufficiently cool for the Martians to emerge, or they might be butchered by means of guns so soon as the screw opened. It seems to me that they have lost a vast advantage in the failure of their first surprise. Possibly they see it in the same light.

Lessing has advanced excellent reasons for supposing that the Martians have actually succeeded in effecting a landing on the planet Venus. Seven months ago now, Venus and Mars were in alignment with the sun; that is to say, Mars was in opposition from the point of view of an observer on Venus. Subsequently a peculiar luminous and sinuous marking appeared on the unillumined half of the inner planet, and almost simultaneously a faint dark mark of a similar sinuous character was detected upon a photograph of the Martian disk. One needs to see the drawings of these appearances in order to appreciate fully their remarkable resemblance in character.

At any rate, whether we expect another invasion or not, our views of the human future must be greatly modified by these events. We have learned now that we cannot regard this planet as being fenced in and a secure abiding place for Man; we can never anticipate the unseen good or evil that may come upon us suddenly out of space. It may be that in the larger design of the universe this invasion from Mars is not without its ultimate benefit for men; it has robbed us of that serene confidence in the future which is the most fruitful source of decadence, the gifts to human science it has brought are enormous, and it has done much to promote the conception of the commonweal of mankind. It may be that across the immensity of space the Martians have watched the fate of these pioneers of theirs and learned their lesson, and that on the planet Venus they have found a securer settlement. Be that as it may, for many years yet there will certainly be no relaxation of the eager scrutiny of the Martian disk, and those fiery darts of the sky, the shooting stars, will bring with them as they fall an unavoidable apprehension to all the sons of men.

The broadening of men's views that has resulted can scarcely be exaggerated. Before the cylinder fell there was a general persuasion that through all the deep of space no life existed beyond the petty surface of our minute sphere. Now we see further. If the Martians can reach Venus, there is no reason to suppose that the thing is impossible for men, and when the slow cooling of the sun makes this earth uninhabitable, as at last it must do, it may be that the thread of life that has begun here will have streamed out and caught our sister planet within its toils.

Dim and wonderful is the vision I have conjured up in my mind of life spreading slowly from this little seed bed of the solar system throughout the inanimate vastness of sidereal space. But that is a remote dream. It may be, on the other hand, that the destruction of the Martians is only a reprieve. To them, and not to us, perhaps, is the future ordained.

I must confess the stress and danger of the time have left an abiding sense of doubt and insecurity in my mind. I sit in my study writing by lamplight, and suddenly I see again the healing valley below set with writhing flames, and feel the house behind and about me empty and desolate. I go out into the Byfleet Road, and vehicles pass me, a butcher boy in a cart, a cabful of visitors, a workman on a bicycle, children going to school, and suddenly they become vague and unreal, and I hurry again with the artilleryman through the hot, brooding silence. Of a night I see the black powder darkening the silent streets, and the contorted bodies shrouded in that layer; they rise upon me tattered and dog-bitten. They gibber and grow fiercer, paler, uglier, mad distortions of humanity at last, and I wake, cold and wretched, in the darkness of the night.

I go to London and see the busy multitudes in Fleet Street and the Strand, and it comes across my mind that they are but the ghosts of the past, haunting the streets that I have seen silent and wretched, going to and fro, phantasms in a dead city, the mockery of life in a galvanised body. And strange, too, it is to stand on Primrose Hill, as I did but a day before writing this last chapter, to see the great province of houses, dim and blue through the haze of the smoke and mist, vanishing at last into the vague lower sky, to see the people walking to and fro among the flower beds on the hill, to see the sight-seers about the Martian machine that stands there still, to hear the tumult of playing children, and to recall the time when I saw it all bright and clear-cut, hard and silent, under the dawn of that last great day....

And strangest of all is it to hold my wife's hand again, and to think that I have counted her, and that she has counted me, among the dead.

H.G. WELLS
A DREAM OF
ARMAGEDDON

The man with the white face entered the carriage at Rugby. He moved slowly in spite of the urgency of his porter, and even while he was still on the platform I noted how ill he seemed. He dropped into the corner over against me with a sigh, made an incomplete attempt to arrange his travelling shawl, and became motionless, with his eyes staring vacantly. Presently he was moved by a sense of my observation, looked up at me, and put out a spiritless hand for his newspaper. Then he glanced again in my direction.

I feigned to read. I feared I had unwittingly embarrassed him, and in a moment I was surprised to find him speaking.

"I beg your pardon?" said I.

"That book," he repeated, pointing a lean finger, "is about dreams."

"Obviously," I answered, for it was Fortnum-Roscoe's *Dream States*, and the title was on the cover. He hung silent for a space as if he sought words. "Yes," he said at last, "but they tell you nothing." I did not catch his meaning for a second.

"They don't know," he added.

I looked a little more attentively at his face.

"There are dreams," he said, "and dreams."

That sort of proposition I never dispute.

"I suppose—" he hesitated. "Do you ever dream? I mean vividly."

"I dream very little," I answered. "I doubt if I have three vivid dreams in a year."

"Ah!" he said, and seemed for a moment to collect his thoughts.

"Your dreams don't mix with your memories?" he asked abruptly. "You don't find yourself in doubt; did this happen or did it not?"

"Hardly ever. Except just for a momentary hesitation now and then. I suppose few people do."

"Does *he* say—" he indicated the book.

"Says it happens at times and gives the usual explanation about intensity of impression and the like to account for its not happening as a rule. I suppose you know something of these theories—"

"Very little – except that they are wrong."

His emaciated hand played with the strap of the window for a time. I prepared to resume reading, and that seemed to precipitate his next remark. He leant forward almost as though he would touch me.

"Isn't there something called consecutive dreaming – that goes on night after night?"

"I believe there is. There are cases given in most books on mental trouble."

"Mental trouble! Yes. I dare say there are. It's the right place for them. But what I mean—" He looked at his bony knuckles. "Is that sort of thing always dreaming? *Is* it dreaming? Or is it something else? Mightn't it be something else?"

I should have snubbed his persistent conversation but for the drawn anxiety of his face. I remember now the look of his faded eyes and the lids red-stained – perhaps you know that look.

"I'm not just arguing about a matter of opinion," he said. "The thing's killing me."

"Dreams?"

"If you call them dreams. Night after night. Vivid! – so vivid… this—" (he indicated the landscape that went streaming by the window) "seems unreal in comparison! I can scarcely remember who I am, what business I am on.…"

He paused. "Even now—"

"The dream is always the same – do you mean?" I asked.

"It's over."

"You mean?"

"I died."

"Died?"

"Smashed and killed, and now, so much of me as that dream was, is dead. Dead for ever. I dreamt I was another man, you know, living in a different part of the world and in a different time. I dreamt that night after night. Night after night I woke into that other life. Fresh scenes and fresh happenings – until I came upon the last—"

"When you died?"

"When I died."

"And since then—"

"No," he said. "Thank God! That was the end of the dream...."

It was clear I was in for this dream. And after all, I had an hour before me, the light was fading fast, and Fortnum-Roscoe has a dreary way with him. "Living in a different time," I said: "do you mean in some different age?"

"Yes."

"Past?"

"No, to come – to come."

"The year three thousand, for example?"

"I don't know what year it was. I did when I was asleep, when I was dreaming, that is, but not now – not now that I am awake. There's a lot of things I have forgotten since I woke out of these dreams, though I knew them at the time when I was – I suppose it was dreaming. They called the year differently from our way of calling the year.... What *did* they call it?" He put his hand to his forehead. "No," said he, "I forget."

He sat smiling weakly. For a moment I feared he did not mean to tell me his dream. As a rule I hate people who tell their dreams, but this struck me differently. I proffered assistance even. "It began—" I suggested.

"It was vivid from the first. I seemed to wake up in it suddenly. And it's curious that in these dreams I am speaking of I never remembered this life I am living now. It seemed as if the dream life was enough while it lasted. Perhaps – But I will tell you how I find myself when I do my best to recall it all. I don't remember anything dearly until I found myself sitting in a sort of loggia looking out over the sea. I had been dozing, and suddenly I woke up – fresh and vivid – not a bit dream-like – because the girl had stopped fanning me."

"The girl?"

"Yes, the girl. You must not interrupt or you will put me out."

He stopped abruptly. "You won't think I'm mad?" he said.

"No," I answered; "you've been dreaming. Tell me your dream."

"I woke up, I say, because the girl had stopped fanning me. I was not surprised to find myself there or anything of that sort, you understand. I did not feel I had fallen into it suddenly. I simply took it up at that point. Whatever memory I had of *this* life, this nineteenth-century life, faded as I woke, vanished like a dream. I knew all about myself, knew that my name was no longer Cooper but Hedon, and all about my position in the world. I've forgotten a lot since I woke – there's a want of connection – but it was all quite clear and matter of fact then."

He hesitated again, gripping the window strap, putting his face forward and looking up at me appealingly.

"This seems bosh to you?"

"No, no!" I cried. "Go on. Tell me what this loggia was like."

"It was not really a loggia – I don't know what to call it. It faced south. It was small. It was all in shadow except the semicircle above the balcony that showed the sky and sea and the corner where the girl stood. I was on a couch – it was a metal couch with light striped cushions and the girl was leaning over the balcony with her back to me. The light of the sunrise fell on her ear and cheek. Her pretty white neck and the little curls that nestled there, and her white shoulder were in the sun, and all the grace of her body was in the cool blue shadow. She was dressed – how can I describe it? It was easy and flowing. And altogether there she stood, so that it came to me how beautiful and desirable she was, as though I had never seen her before. And when at last I sighed and raised myself upon my arm she turned her face to me—"

He stopped.

"I have lived three-and-fifty years in this world. I have had mother, sisters, friends, wife, and daughters – all their faces, the play of their faces, I know. But the face of this girl – it is much more real to me. I can bring it back into memory so that I see it again – I could draw it or paint it. And after all—"

He stopped – but I said nothing.

"The face of a dream – the face of a dream. She was beautiful. Not that beauty which is terrible, cold, and worshipful, like the beauty of a saint; nor that beauty that stirs fierce passions; but a sort of radiation, sweet lips that softened into smiles, and grave grey eyes. And she moved gracefully, she seemed to have part with all pleasant and gracious things—"

He stopped, and his face was downcast and hidden. Then he looked up at me and went on, making no further attempt to disguise his absolute belief in the reality of his story.

"You see, I had thrown up my plans and ambitions, thrown up all I had ever worked for or desired for her sake. I had been a master man away there in the north, with influence and property and a great reputation, but none of it had seemed worth having beside her. I had come to the place, this city of sunny pleasures, with her, and left all those things to wreck and ruin just to save a remnant at least of my life. While I had been in love with her before I knew that she had any care for me, before I had imagined that she would dare – that we should dare, all my life had seemed vain and hollow, dust and ashes. It *was* dust and ashes. Night after night and through the long days I had longed and desired – my soul had beaten àgainst the thing forbidden!

"But it is impossible for one man to tell another just these things. It's emotion, it's a tint, a light that comes and goes. Only while it's there, everything changes, everything. The thing is I came away and left them in their Crisis to do what they could."

"Left whom?" I asked, puzzled.

"The people up in the north there. You see – in this dream, anyhow – I had been a big man, the sort of man men come to trust in, to group themselves about. Millions of men who had never seen me were ready to do things and risk things because of their confidence in me. I had been playing that game for years, that big laborious game, that vague, monstrous political game amidst intrigues and betrayals, speech and agitation. It was a vast weltering world, and at last I had a sort of leadership against the Gang – you know it was called the Gang – a sort of compromise of scoundrelly projects and base ambitions and vast public emotional stupidities and catchwords – the Gang that kept the world noisy and blind year by year, and all the while that it was drifting, drifting towards infinite disaster. But I can't expect you to understand the shades and complications of the year – the year something or other ahead. I had it all down to the smallest details – in my dream. I suppose I had been dreaming of it before I awoke, and the fading outline of some queer new development I had imagined still hung about me as I rubbed my eyes. It was some grubby affair that made me thank God for the sunlight. I sat up on the couch and remained looking at the woman and rejoicing – rejoicing that I had come away out of all that tumult and folly and violence before it was too late. After all, I thought, this is life – love and beauty, desire and delight, are they not worth all those dismal struggles for vague, gigantic ends? And I blamed myself for having ever sought to be a leader when I might have given my days to love. But then, thought I, if I had not spent my early days sternly and austerely, I might have wasted myself upon vain and worthless women, and at the thought all my being went out in love and tenderness to my dear mistress, my dear lady, who had come at last and compelled me – compelled me by her invincible charm for me – to lay that life aside.

"'You are worth it,' I said, speaking without intending her to hear; 'you are worth it, my dearest one; worth pride and praise and all things. Love! to have *you* is worth them all together.' And at the murmur of my voice she turned about.

"'Come and see,' she cried – I can hear her now—'come and see the sunrise upon Monte Solaro.'

"I remember how I sprang to my feet and joined her at the balcony. She put a white hand upon my shoulder and pointed towards great masses of limestone, flushing, as it were, into life. I looked. But first I noted the sunlight on her face caressing the lines of her cheeks and neck. How can I describe to you the scene we had before us? We were at Capri—"

"I have been there," I said. "I have clambered up Monte Solaro and drunk *vero Capri* – muddy stuff like cider – at the summit."

"Ah!" said the man with the white face; "then perhaps you can tell me – you will know if this was indeed Capri. For in this life I have never been there. Let me describe it. We were in a little room, one of a vast multitude of little rooms, very cool and sunny, hollowed out of the limestone of a sort of cape, very high above the sea. The whole island, you know, was one enormous hotel, complex beyond explaining, and on the other side there were miles of floating hotels, and huge floating stages to which the flying machines came. They called it a pleasure city. Of course, there was none of that in your time rather, I should say, *is* none of that *now*. Of course. Now! – yes.

"Well, this room of ours was at the extremity of the cape, so that one could see east and west. Eastward was a great cliff – a thousand feet high perhaps – coldly grey except for one bright edge of gold, and beyond it the Isle of the Sirens, and a falling coast that faded and passed into the hot sunrise. And when one turned to the west, distinct and near was a little bay, a little beach still in shadow. And out of that shadow rose Solaro straight and tall, flushed and golden crested, like a beauty throned, and the white moon was floating behind her in the sky. And before us from east to west stretched the many-tinted sea all dotted with little sailing boats.

"To the eastward, of course, these little boats were grey and very minute and clear, but to the westward they were little boats of gold – shining gold – almost like little flames. And just below us was a rock with an arch worn through it. The blue sea-water broke to green and foam all round the rock, and a galley came gliding out of the arch."

"I know that rock," I said. "I was nearly drowned there. It is called the Faraglioni."

"*I Faraglioni?* Yes, *she* called it that," answered the man with the white face. "There was some story – but that—"

He put his hand to his forehead again. "No," he said, "I forget that story."

"Well, that is the first thing I remember, the first dream I had, that little shaded room and the beautiful air and sky and that dear lady of mine, with her shining arms and her graceful robe, and how we sat and talked in half whispers to one another. We talked in whispers not because there was any one to hear, but because there was still such a freshness of mind between us that our thoughts were a little frightened, I think, to find themselves at last in words. And so they went softly.

"Presently we were hungry and we went from our apartment, going by a strange passage with a moving floor, until we came to the great breakfast room – there was a fountain and music. A pleasant and joyful place it was, with its sunlight and splashing, and the murmur of plucked strings. And we sat and ate and smiled at one another, and I would not heed a man who was watching me from a table near by.

"And afterwards we went on to the dancing-hall. But I cannot describe that hall. The place was enormous – larger than any building you have ever seen – and in one place there was the old gate of Capri, caught into the wall of a gallery high overhead. Light girders, stems and threads of gold, burst from the pillars like fountains, streamed like an Aurora across the roof and interlaced, like – like conjuring tricks. All about the great circle for the dancers there were beautiful figures, strange dragons, and intricate and wonderful grotesques bearing lights. The place was inundated with artificial light that shamed the newborn day. And as we went through the throng the people turned about and looked at us, for all through the world my name and face were known, and how I had suddenly thrown up pride and struggle to come to this place. And they looked also at the lady beside me, though half the story of how at last she had come to me was unknown or mistold. And few of the men who were there, I know, but judged me a happy man, in spite of all the shame and dishonour that had come upon my name.

"The air was full of music, full of harmonious scents, full of the rhythm of beautiful motions. Thousands of beautiful people swarmed about the hall, crowded the galleries, sat in a myriad recesses; they were dressed in splendid colours and crowned with flowers; thousands danced about the great circle beneath the white images of the ancient gods, and glorious processions of youths and maidens came and went. We two danced, not the dreary monotonies of your days – of this time, I mean – but dances that were beautiful, intoxicating. And even now I can see my lady dancing – dancing joyously. She danced, you know, with a serious face; she danced with a serious dignity, and yet she was smiling at me and caressing me – smiling and caressing with her eyes.

"The music was different," he murmured. "It went – I cannot describe it; but it was infinitely richer and more varied than any music that has ever come to me awake.

"And then – it was when we had done dancing – a man came to speak to me. He was a lean, resolute man, very soberly clad for that place, and already I had marked his face watching me in the breakfasting hall, and afterwards as we went along the passage I had avoided his eye. But now, as we sat in a little alcove, smiling at the pleasure of all the people who went to and fro across the shining floor, he came and touched me, and spoke to me so that I was forced to listen. And he asked that he might speak to me for a little time apart.

"'No,' I said. 'I have no secrets from this lady. What do you want to tell me?'

"He said it was a trivial matter, or at least a dry matter, for a lady to hear.

"'Perhaps for me to hear,' said I.

"He glanced at her, as though almost he would appeal to her. Then he asked me suddenly if I had heard of a great and avenging declaration that Evesham had made. Now, Evesham had always before been the man next to myself in the leadership of that great party in the north. He was a forcible, hard and tactless man, and only I had been able to control and soften him. It was on his account even more than my own, I think, that the others had been so dismayed at my retreat.

So this question about what he had done reawakened my old interest in the life I had put aside just for a moment.

"'I have taken no heed of any news for many days,' I said. 'What has Evesham been saying?'

"And with that the man began, nothing loath, and I must confess even I was struck by Evesham's reckless folly in the wild and threatening words he had used. And this messenger they had sent to me not only told me of Evesham's speech, but went on to ask counsel and to point out what need they had of me. While he talked, my lady sat a little forward and watched his face and mine.

"My old habits of scheming and organising reasserted themselves. I could even see myself suddenly returning to the north, and all the dramatic effect of it. All that this man said witnessed to the disorder of the party indeed, but not to its damage. I should go back stronger than I had come. And then I thought of my lady. You see – how can I tell you? There were certain peculiarities of our relationship – as things are I need not tell you about that – which would render her presence with me impossible. I should have had to leave her; indeed, I should have had to renounce her clearly and openly, if I was to do all that I could do in the north. And the man knew *that*, even as he talked to her and me, knew it as well as she did, that my steps to duty were – first, separation, then abandonment. At the touch of that thought my dream of a return was shattered. I turned on the man suddenly, as he was imagining his eloquence was gaining ground with me.

"'What have I to do with these things now?' I said. 'I have done with them. Do you think I am coquetting with your people in coming here?'

"'No,' he said; 'but—'

"'Why cannot you leave me alone? I have done with these things. I have ceased to be anything but a private man.'

"'Yes,' he answered. 'But have you thought? – this talk of war, these reckless challenges, these wild aggressions—'

"I stood up.

"'No,' I cried. 'I won't hear you. I took count of all those things, I weighed them – and I have come away.'

"He seemed to consider the possibility of persistence. He looked from me to where the lady sat regarding us.

"'War,' he said, as if he were speaking to himself, and then turned slowly from me and walked away. I stood, caught in the whirl of thoughts his appeal had set going.

"I heard my lady's voice.

"'Dear,' she said; 'but if they have need of you—'

"She did not finish her sentence, she let it rest there. I turned to her sweet face, and the balance of my mood swayed and reeled.

"'They want me only to do the thing they dare not do themselves,' I said. 'If they distrust Evesham they must settle with him themselves.'

"She looked at me doubtfully.

"'But war—' she said.

"I saw a doubt on her face that I had seen before, a doubt of herself and me, the first shadow of the discovery that, seen strongly and completely, must drive us apart for ever.

"Now, I was an older mind than hers, and I could sway her to this belief or that.

"'My dear one,' I said, 'you must not trouble over these things. There will be no war. Certainly there will be no war. The age of wars is past. Trust me to know the justice of this case. They have no right upon me, dearest, and no one has a right upon me. I have been free to choose my life, and I have chosen this.'

"'But *war*—' she said.

"I sat down beside her. I put an arm behind her and took her hand in mine. I set myself to drive that doubt away – I set myself to fill her mind with pleasant things again. I lied to her, and in lying to her I lied also to myself. And she was only too ready to believe me, only too ready to forget.

"Very soon the shadow had gone again, and we were hastening to our bathing-place in the Grotta del Bovo Marino, where it was our custom to bathe every day. We swam and splashed one another, and in that buoyant water I seemed to become something lighter and stronger than a man. And at last we came out dripping and rejoicing and raced among the rocks. And then I put on a dry bathing-dress, and we sat to bask in the sun, and presently I nodded, resting my head against her knee, and she put her hand upon my hair and stroked it softly and I dozed. And behold! as it were with the snapping of the string of a violin, I was awakening, and I was in my own bed in Liverpool, in the life of to-day.

"Only for a time I could not believe that all these vivid moments had been no more than the substance of a dream.

"In truth, I could not believe it a dream for all the sobering reality of things about me. I bathed and dressed as it were by habit, and as I shaved I argued why I of all men should leave the woman I loved to go back to fantastic politics in the hard and strenuous north. Even if Evesham did force the world back to war, what was that to me? I was a man, with the heart of a man, and why should I feel the responsibility of a deity for the way the world might go?

"You know that is not quite the way I think about affairs, about my real affairs. I am a solicitor, you know, with a point of view.

"The vision was so real, you must understand, so utterly unlike a dream that I kept perpetually recalling little irrelevant details; even the ornament of a book-cover that lay on my wife's sewing-machine in the breakfast-room recalled with the utmost vividness the gilt line that ran about the seat in the alcove where I had talked with the messenger from my deserted party. Have you ever heard of a dream that had a quality like that?"

"Like—?"

"So that afterwards you remembered little details you had forgotten."

I thought. I had never noticed the point before, but he was right.

"Never," I said. "That is what you never seem to do with dreams."

"No," he answered. "But that is just what I did. I am a solicitor, you must understand, in Liverpool, and I could not help wondering what the clients and business people I found myself talking to in my office would think if I told them suddenly I was in love with a girl who would be born a couple of hundred years or so hence, and worried about the politics of my great-great-great-grandchildren. I was chiefly busy that day negotiating a ninety-nine-year building lease. It was a private builder in a hurry, and we wanted to tie him in every possible way. I had an interview with him, and he showed a certain want of temper that sent me to bed still irritated. That night I had no dream. Nor did I dream the next night, at least, to remember.

"Something of that intense reality of conviction vanished. I began to feel sure it *was* a dream. And then it came again.

"When the dream came again, nearly four days later, it was very different. I think it certain that four days had also elapsed in the dream. Many things had happened in the north, and the shadow of them was back again between us, and this time it was not so easily dispelled. I began, I know, with moody musings. Why, in spite of all, should I go back, go back for all the rest of my days to toil and stress, insults and perpetual dissatisfaction, simply to save hundreds of millions of common people, whom I did not love, whom too often

I could do no other than despise, from the stress and anguish of war and infinite misrule? And after all I might fail. *They* all sought their own narrow ends, and why should not I – why should not I also live as a man? And out of such thoughts her voice summoned me, and I lifted my eyes.

"I found myself awake and walking. We had come out above the Pleasure City, we were near the summit of Monte Solaro and looking towards the bay. It was the late afternoon and very clear. Far away to the left Ischia hung in a golden haze between sea and sky, and Naples was coldly white against the hills, and before us was Vesuvius with a tall and slender streamer feathering at last towards the south, and the ruins of Torre dell' Annunziata and Castellamare glittering and near."

I interrupted suddenly: "You have been to Capri, of course?"

"Only in this dream," he said, "only in this dream. All across the bay beyond Sorrento were the floating palaces of the Pleasure City moored and chained. And northward were the broad floating stages that received the aeroplanes. Aeroplanes fell out of the sky every afternoon, each bringing its thousands of pleasure-seekers from the uttermost parts of the earth to Capri and its delights. All these things, I say, stretched below.

"But we noticed them only incidentally because of an unusual sight that evening had to show. Five war aeroplanes that had long slumbered useless in the distant arsenals of the Rhinemouth were manoeuvring now in the eastward sky. Evesham had astonished the world by producing them and others, and sending them to circle here and there. It was the threat material in the great game of bluff he was playing, and it had taken even me by surprise. He was one of those incredibly stupid energetic people who seem sent by Heaven to create disasters. His energy to the first glance seemed so wonderfully like capacity! But he had no imagination, no invention, only a stupid, vast, driving force of will, and a mad faith in his stupid idiot 'luck' to pull him through. I remember how we stood out upon the headland watching the squadron circling far away, and how I weighed the full meaning of the sight, seeing clearly the way things must go. And then even it was not too late. I might have gone back, I think, and saved the world. The people of the north would follow me, I knew, granted only that in one thing I respected their moral standards. The east and south would trust me as they would trust no other northern man. And I knew I had only to put it to her and she would have let me go.... Not because she did not love me!

"Only I did not want to go; my will was all the other way about. I had so newly thrown off the incubus of responsibility: I was still so fresh a renegade from duty that the daylight clearness of what I *ought* to do had no power at all to touch my will. My will was to live, to gather pleasures and make my dear lady happy. But though this sense of vast neglected duties had no power to draw me, it could make me silent and preoccupied, it robbed the days I had spent of half their brightness and roused me into dark meditations in the silence of the night. And as I stood and watched Evesham's aeroplanes sweep to and fro – those birds of infinite ill omen – she stood beside me watching me, perceiving the trouble indeed, but not perceiving it clearly her eyes questioning my face, her expression shaded with perplexity. Her face was grey because the sunset was fading out of the sky. It was no fault of hers that she held me. She had asked me to go from her, and again in the night time and with tears she had asked me to go.

"At last it was the sense of her that roused me from my mood. I turned upon her suddenly and challenged her to race down the mountain slopes. 'No,' she said, as if I jarred with her gravity, but I was resolved to end that gravity, and made her run – no one can be very grey and sad who is out of breath – and when she stumbled I ran with my hand beneath her arm. We ran down past a couple of men, who turned back staring in astonishment at my behaviour – they must have recognised my face. And halfway down the slope came a tumult in the air, clang-clank, clang-clank, and we stopped, and presently over the hill-crest those war things came flying one behind the other."

The man seemed hesitating on the verge of a description.

"What were they like?" I asked.

"They had never fought," he said. "They were just like our ironclads are nowadays; they had never fought. No one knew what they might do, with excited men inside them; few even cared to speculate. They were great driving things shaped like spearheads without a shaft, with a propeller in the place of the shaft."

"Steel?"

"Not steel."

"Aluminium?"

"No, no, nothing of that sort. An alloy that was very common – as common as brass, for example. It was called – let me see—." He squeezed his forehead with the fingers of one hand. "I am forgetting everything," he said.

"And they carried guns?"

"Little guns, firing high explosive shells. They fired the guns backwards, out of the base of the leaf, so to speak, and rammed with the beak. That was the theory, you know, but they had never been fought. No one could tell exactly what was going to happen. And meanwhile I suppose it was very fine to go whirling through the air like a flight of young swallows, swift and easy. I guess the captains tried not to think too clearly what the real thing would be like. And these flying war machines, you know, were only one sort of the endless war contrivances that had been invented and had fallen into abeyance during the long peace. There were all sorts of these things that people were routing out and furbishing up; infernal things, silly things; things that had never been tried; big engines, terrible explosives, great guns. You know the silly way of these ingenious sort of men who make these things; they turn 'em out as beavers build dams, and with no more sense of the rivers they're going to divert and the lands they're going to flood!

"As we went down the winding stepway to our hotel again, in the twilight, I foresaw it all: I saw how clearly and inevitably things were driving for war in Evesham's silly, violent hands, and I had some inkling of what war was bound to be under these new conditions. And even then, though I knew it was drawing near the limit of my opportunity, I could find no will to go back."

He sighed.

"That was my last chance.

"We didn't go into the city until the sky was full of stars, so we walked out upon the high terrace, to and fro, and – she counselled me to go back.

"'My dearest,' she said, and her sweet face looked up to me, 'this is Death. This life you lead is Death. Go back to them, go back to your duty—.'

"She began to weep, saying, between her sobs, and clinging to my arm as she said it, 'Go back – Go back.'

"Then suddenly she fell mute, and, glancing down at her face, I read in an instant the thing she had thought to do. It was one of those moments when one *sees*.

"'No!' I said.

"'No?' she asked, in surprise, and I think a little fearful at the answer to her thought.

"'Nothing,' I said, 'shall send me back. Nothing! I have chosen. Love, I have chosen, and the world must go. Whatever happens I will live this life – I will live for *you*! It – nothing shall turn me aside; nothing, my dear one. Even if you died – even if you died–'

"'Yes,' she murmured, softly.

"'Then – I also would die.'

"And before she could speak again I began to talk, talking eloquently – as I *could* do in that life – talking to exalt love, to make the life we were living seem heroic and glorious; and the thing I was deserting something hard and enormously ignoble that it was a fine thing to set aside. I bent all my mind to throw that glamour upon it, seeking not only to convert her but myself to that. We talked, and she clung to me, torn too between all that she deemed noble and all that she knew was sweet. And at last I did make it heroic, made all the thickening disaster of the world only a sort of glorious setting to our unparalleled love, and we two poor foolish souls strutted there at last, clad in that splendid delusion, drunken rather with that glorious delusion, under the still stars.

"And so my moment passed.

"It was my last chance. Even as we went to and fro there, the leaders of the south and east were gathering their resolve, and the hot answer that shattered Evesham's bluffing for ever, took shape and waited. And all over Asia, and the ocean, and the south, the air and the wires were throbbing with their warnings to prepare – prepare.

"No one living, you know, knew what war was; no one could imagine, with all these new inventions, what horror war might bring. I believe most people still believed it would be a matter of bright uniforms and shouting charges and triumphs and flags and bands – in a time when half the world drew its food supply from regions ten thousand miles away–."

The man with the white face paused. I glanced at him, and his face was intent on the floor of the carriage. A little railway station, a string of loaded trucks, a signal-box, and the back of a cottage, shot by the carriage window, and a bridge passed with a clap of noise, echoing the tumult of the train.

"After that," he said, "I dreamt often. For three weeks of nights that dream was my life. And the worst of it was there were nights when I could not dream, when I lay tossing on a bed in *this* accursed life; and *there* – somewhere lost to me – things were happening – momentous, terrible things.... I lived at nights – my days, my waking days, this life I am living now, became a faded, far-away dream, a drab setting, the cover of the book."

He thought.

"I could tell you all, tell you every little thing in the dream, but as to what I did in the daytime – no. I could not tell – I do not remember. My memory – my memory has gone. The business of life slips from me—"

He leant forward, and pressed his hands upon his eyes. For a long time he said nothing.

"And then?" said I.

"The war burst like a hurricane."

He stared before him at unspeakable things.

"And then?" I urged again.

"One touch of unreality," he said, in the low tone of a man who speaks to himself, "and they would have been nightmares. But they were not nightmares – they were not nightmares. *No!*"

He was silent for so long that it dawned upon me that there was a danger of losing the rest of the story. But he went on talking again in the same tone of questioning self-communion.

"What was there to do but flight? I had not thought the war would touch Capri – I had seemed to see Capri as being out of it all, as the contrast to it all; but two nights after the whole place was shouting and bawling, every woman almost and every other man wore a badge – Evesham's badge – and there was no music but a jangling war-song over and over again, and everywhere men enlisting, and in the dancing halls they were drilling. The whole island was awhirl with rumours; it was said, again and again, that fighting had begun. I had not expected this. I had seen so little of the life of pleasure that I had failed to reckon with this violence of the amateurs. And as for me, I was out of it. I was like a man who might have prevented the firing of a magazine. The time had gone. I was no one; the vainest stripling with a badge counted for more than I. The crowd jostled us and bawled in our ears; that accursed song deafened us; a woman shrieked at my lady because no badge was on her, and we two went back to our own place again, ruffled and insulted – my lady white and silent, and I aquiver with rage. So furious was I, I could have quarrelled with her if I could have found one shade of accusation in her eyes.

"All my magnificence had gone from me. I walked up and down our rock cell, and outside was the darkling sea and a light to the southward that flared and passed and came again.

"'We must get out of this place,' I said over and over. 'I have made my choice, and I will have no hand in these troubles. I will have nothing of this war. We have taken our lives out of all these things. This is no refuge for us. Let us go.'

"And the next day we were already in flight from the war that covered the world.

"And all the rest was Flight – all the rest was Flight."

He mused darkly.

"How much was there of it?"

He made no answer.

"How many days?"

His face was white and drawn and his hands were clenched. He took no heed of my curiosity.

I tried to draw him back to his story with questions.

"Where did you go?" I said.

"When?"

"When you left Capri."

"Southwest," he said, and glanced at me for a second. "We went in a boat."

"But I should have thought an aeroplane?"

"They had been seized."

I questioned him no more. Presently I thought he was beginning again. He broke out in an argumentative monotone:

"But why should it be? If, indeed, this battle, this slaughter and stress *is* life, why have we this craving for pleasure and beauty? If there *is* no refuge, if there is no place of peace, and if all our dreams of quiet places are a folly and a snare, why have we such dreams? Surely it was no ignoble cravings, no base intentions, had brought us to this; it was Love had isolated us. Love had come to me with her eyes and robed in her beauty, more glorious than all else in life, in the very shape and colour of life, and summoned me away. I had silenced all the voices, I had answered all the questions – I had come to her. And suddenly there was nothing but War and Death!"

I had an inspiration. "After all," I said, "it could have been only a dream."

"A dream!" he cried, flaming upon me, "a dream – when even now—"

For the first time he became animated. A faint flush crept into his cheek. He raised his open hand and clenched it, and dropped it to his knee. He spoke, looking away from me, and for all the rest of the time he looked away. "We are but phantoms," he said, "and the phantoms of phantoms, desires like cloud shadows and wills of straw that eddy in the wind; the days pass, use and wont carry us through as a train carries the shadow of its lights, so be it! But one thing is real and certain, one thing is no dreamstuff, but eternal and enduring. It is the centre of my life, and all other things about it are subordinate or altogether vain. I loved her, that woman of a dream. And she and I are dead together!

"A dream! How can it be a dream, when it drenched a living life with unappeasable sorrow, when it makes all that I have lived for and cared for, worthless and unmeaning?

"Until that very moment when she was killed I believed we had still a chance of getting away," he said. "All through the night and morning that we sailed across the sea from Capri to Salerno, we talked of escape. We were full of hope, and it clung about us to the end, hope for the life together we should lead, out of it all, out of the battle and struggle, the wild and empty passions, the empty arbitrary 'thou shalt' and 'thou shalt not' of the world. We were uplifted, as though our quest was a holy thing, as though love for one another was a mission....

"Even when from our boat we saw the fair face of that great rock Capri – already scarred and gashed by the gun emplacements and hiding-places that were to make it a fastness – we reckoned nothing of the imminent slaughter, though the fury of preparation hung about in puffs and clouds of dust at a hundred points amidst the grey; but, indeed, I made a text of that and talked. There, you know, was the rock, still beautiful, for all its scars, with its countless windows and arches and ways, tier upon tier, for a thousand feet, a vast carving of grey, broken by vine-clad terraces, and lemon and orange groves, and masses of agave and prickly pear, and puffs of almond blossom. And out under the archway that is built over the Piccola Marina other boats were coming; and as we came round the cape and within sight of the mainland, another little string of boats came into view, driving before the wind towards the southwest. In a little while a multitude had come out, the remoter just little specks of ultramarine in the shadow of the eastward cliff.

"'It is love and reason,' I said, 'fleeing from all this madness, of war.'

"And though we presently saw a squadron of aeroplanes flying across the southern sky we did not heed it. There it was – a line of little dots in the sky – and then more, dotting the southeastern horizon, and then still more, until all that quarter of the sky was stippled with blue specks. Now they were all thin little strokes of blue, and now one and now a multitude would heel and catch the sun and become short flashes of light. They came rising and falling and growing larger, like some huge flight of gulls or rooks, or such-like birds moving with a marvellous uniformity, and ever as they drew nearer they spread over a greater width of sky. The southward wing flung itself in an arrow-headed cloud athwart the sun. And then suddenly they swept round to the eastward and streamed eastward, growing smaller and smaller and clearer and clearer again until they vanished from the sky. And after that we noted to the northward and very high Evesham's fighting machines hanging high over Naples like an evening swarm of gnats.

"It seemed to have no more to do with us than a flight of birds.

"Even the mutter of guns far away in the southeast seemed to us to signify nothing....

"Each day, each dream after that, we were still exalted, still seeking that refuge where we might live and love. Fatigue had come upon us, pain and many distresses. For though we were dusty and stained by our toilsome tramping, and half starved and with the horror of the dead men we had seen and the flight of the peasants – for very soon a gust of fighting swept up the peninsula – with these things haunting our minds it still resulted only in a deepening resolution to escape. O, but she was brave and patient! She who had never faced hardship and exposure had courage for herself – and me. We went to and fro seeking an outlet, over a country all commandeered and ransacked by the gathering hosts of war. Always we went on foot. At first there were other fugitives, but we did not mingle with them. Some escaped northward, some were caught in the torrent of peasantry that swept along the main roads; many gave themselves into the hands of the soldiery and were sent northward. Many of the men were impressed. But we kept away from these things; we had brought no money to bribe a passage north, and I feared for my lady at the hands of these conscript crowds. We had landed at Salerno, and we had been turned back from Cava, and we had tried to cross towards Taranto by a pass over Mount Alburno, but we had been driven back for want of food, and so we had come down among the marshes by Paestum, where those great temples stand alone. I had some vague idea that by Paestum it might be possible to find a boat or something, and take once more to sea. And there it was the battle overtook us.

"A sort of soul-blindness had me. Plainly I could see that we were being hemmed in; that the great net of that giant Warfare had us in its toils. Many times we had seen the levies that had come down from the north going to and fro, and had come upon them in the distance amidst the mountains making ways for the ammunition and preparing the mounting of the guns. Once we fancied they had fired at us, taking us for spies – at any rate a shot had gone shuddering over us. Several times we had hidden in woods from hovering aeroplanes.

"But all these things do not matter now, these nights of flight and pain.... We were in an open place near those great temples at Paestum, at last, on a blank stony place dotted with spiky bushes, empty and desolate and so flat that a grove of eucalyptus far away showed to the feet of its stems. How I can see it! My lady was sitting down under a bush, resting a little, for she was very weak and weary, and I was standing up watching to see if I could tell the distance of the firing that came and went. They were still, you know, fighting far from each other, with those terrible new weapons that had never before been used: guns that would carry beyond sight, and aeroplanes that would do— What *they* would do no man could foretell.

"I knew that we were between the two armies, and that they drew together. I knew we were in danger, and that we could not stop there and rest!

"Though all these things were in my mind, they were in the background. They seemed to be affairs beyond our concern. Chiefly, I was thinking of my lady. An aching distress filled me. For the first time she had owned herself beaten and had fallen a-weeping. Behind me I could hear her sobbing, but I would not turn round to her because I knew she had need of weeping, and had held herself so far and so long for me. It was well, I thought, that she would weep and rest and then we would toil on again, for I had no inkling of the thing that hung so near. Even now I can see her as she sat there, her lovely hair upon her shoulder, can mark again the deepening hollow of her cheek.

"'If we had parted,' she said, 'if I had let you go.'

"'No,' said I. 'Even now, I do not repent. I will not repent; I made my choice, and I will hold on to the end.'

"And then—

"Overhead in the sky something flashed and burst, and all about us I heard the bullets making a noise like a handful of peas suddenly thrown. They chipped the stones about us, and whirled fragments from the bricks and passed...."

He put his hand to his mouth, and then moistened his lips.

"At the flash I had turned about....

"You know - she stood up—

"She stood up; you know, and moved a step towards me—

"As though she wanted to reach me—

"And she had been shot through the heart."

He stopped and stared at me. I felt all that foolish incapacity an Englishman feels on such occasions. I met his eyes for a moment, and then stared out of the window. For a long space we kept silence. When at last I looked at him he was sitting back in his corner, his arms folded, and his teeth gnawing at his knuckles.

He bit his nail suddenly, and stared at it.

"I carried her," he said, "towards the temples, in my arms – as though it mattered. I don't know why. They seemed a sort of sanctuary, you know, they had lasted so long, I suppose.

"She must have died almost instantly. Only – I talked to her – all the way."

Silence again.

"I have seen those temples," I said abruptly, and indeed he had brought those still, sunlit arcades of worn sandstone very vividly before me.

"It was the brown one, the big brown one. I sat down on a fallen pillar and held her in my arms.... Silent after the first babble was over. And after a little while the lizards came out and ran about again, as though nothing unusual was going on, as though nothing had changed.... It was tremendously still there, the sun high, and the shadows still; even the shadows of the weeds upon the entablature were still – in spite of the thudding and banging that went all about the sky.

"I seem to remember that the aeroplanes came up out of the south, and that the battle went away to the west. One aeroplane was struck, and overset and fell. I remember that – though it didn't interest me in the least. It didn't seem to signify. It was like a wounded gull, you know – flapping for a time in the water. I could see it down the aisle of the temple – a black thing in the bright blue water.

"Three or four times shells burst about the beach, and then that ceased. Each time that happened all the lizards scuttled in and hid for a space. That was all the mischief done, except that once a stray bullet gashed the stone hard by – made just a fresh bright surface.

"As the shadows grew longer, the stillness seemed greater.

"The curious thing," he remarked, with the manner of a man who makes a trivial conversation, "is that I didn't *think* – I didn't think at all. I sat with her in my arms amidst the stones – in a sort of lethargy – stagnant.

"And I don't remember waking up. I don't remember dressing that day. I know I found myself in my office, with my letters all slit open in front of me, and how I was struck by the absurdity of being there, seeing that in reality I was sitting, stunned, in that Paestum temple with a dead woman in my arms. I read my letters like a machine. I have forgotten what they were about."

He stopped, and there was a long silence.

Suddenly I perceived that we were running down the incline from Chalk Farm to Euston. I started at this passing of time. I turned on him with a brutal question, with the tone of Now or never.

"And did you dream again?"

"Yes."

He seemed to force himself to finish. His voice was very low.

"Once more, and as it were only for a few instants. I seemed to have suddenly awakened out of a great apathy, to have risen into a sitting position, and the body lay there on the stones beside me. A gaunt body. Not her, you know. So soon – it was not her....

"I may have heard voices. I do not know. Only I knew clearly that men were coming into the solitude and that that was a last outrage.

"I stood up and walked through the temple, and then there came into sight – first one man with a yellow face, dressed in a uniform of dirty white, trimmed with blue, and then several, climbing to the crest of the old wall of the vanished city, and crouching there. They were little bright figures in the sunlight, and there they hung, weapon in hand, peering cautiously before them.

"And further away I saw others and then more at another point in the wall. It was a long lax line of men in open order.

"Presently the man I had first seen stood up and shouted a command, and his men came tumbling down the wall and into the high weeds towards the temple. He scrambled down with them and led them. He came facing towards me, and when he saw me he stopped.

"At first I had watched these men with a mere curiosity, but when I had seen they meant to come to the temple I was moved to forbid them. I shouted to the officer.

"'You must not come here,' I cried, '*I* am here. I am here with my dead.'

"He stared, and then shouted a question back to me in some unknown tongue.

"I repeated what I had said.

"He shouted again, and I folded my arms and stood still. Presently he spoke to his men and came forward. He carried a drawn sword.

"I signed to him to keep away, but he continued to advance. I told him again very patiently and clearly: 'You must not come here. These are old temples and I am here with my dead.'

"Presently he was so close I could see his face clearly. It was a narrow face, with dull grey eyes, and a black moustache. He had a scar on his upper lip, and he was dirty and unshaven. He kept shouting unintelligible things, questions perhaps, at me.

"I know now that he was afraid of me, but at the time that did not occur to me. As I tried to explain to him he interrupted me in imperious tones, bidding me, I suppose, stand aside.

"He made to go past me, And I caught hold of him.

"I saw his face change at my grip.

"'You fool,' I cried. 'Don't you know? She is dead!'

"He started back. He looked at me with cruel eyes. I saw a sort of exultant resolve leap into them – delight. Then, suddenly, with a scowl, he swept his sword back – so – and thrust."

He stopped abruptly. I became aware of a change in the rhythm of the train. The brakes lifted their voices and the carriage jarred and jerked. This present world insisted upon itself, became clamorous. I saw through the steamy window huge electric lights glaring down from tall masts upon a fog, saw rows of stationary empty carriages passing by, and then a signal-box, hoisting its constellation of green and red into the murky London twilight marched after them. I looked again at his drawn features.

"He ran me through the heart. It was with a sort of astonishment – no fear, no pain – but just amazement, that I felt it pierce me, felt the sword drive home into my body. It didn't hurt, you know. It didn't hurt at all."

The yellow platform lights came into the field of view, passing first rapidly, then slowly, and at last stopping with a jerk. Dim shapes of men passed to and fro without.

"Euston!" cried a voice.

"Do you mean—?"

"There was no pain, no sting or smart. Amazement and then darkness sweeping over everything. The hot, brutal face before me, the face of the man who had killed me, seemed to recede. It swept out of existence—"

"Euston!" clamoured the voices outside; "Euston!"

The carriage door opened, admitting a flood of sound, and a porter stood regarding us. The sounds of doors slamming, and the hoof-clatter of cab-horses, and behind these things the featureless remote roar of the London cobble-stones, came to my ears. A truckload of lighted lamps blazed along the platform.

"A darkness, a flood of darkness that opened and spread and blotted out all things."

"Any luggage, sir?" said the porter.

"And that was the end?" I asked.

He seemed to hesitate. Then, almost inaudibly, he answered, "*No.*"

"You mean?"

"I couldn't get to her. She was there on the other side of the Temple— And then—"

"Yes," I insisted. "Yes?"

"Nightmares," he cried; "nightmares indeed! My God! Great birds that fought and tore."

H.G. WELLS
THE FIRST MEN IN THE MOON

CHAPTER 1

Mr. Bedford Meets Mr. Cavor at Lympne

As I sit down to write here amidst the shadows of vine-leaves under the blue sky of southern Italy, it comes to me with a certain quality of astonishment that my participation in these amazing adventures of Mr. Cavor was, after all, the outcome of the purest accident. It might have been any one. I fell into these things at a time when I thought myself removed from the slightest possibility of disturbing experiences. I had gone to Lympne because I had imagined it the most uneventful place in the world. "Here, at any rate," said I, "I shall find peace and a chance to work!"

And this book is the sequel. So utterly at variance is destiny with all the little plans of men. I may perhaps mention here that very recently I had come an ugly cropper in certain business enterprises. Sitting now surrounded by all the circumstances of wealth, there is a luxury in admitting my extremity. I can admit, even, that to a certain extent my disasters were conceivably of my own making. It may be there are directions in which I have some capacity, but the conduct of business operations is not among these. But in those days I was young, and my youth among other objectionable forms took that of a pride in my capacity for affairs. I am young still in years, but the things that have happened to me have rubbed something of the youth from my mind. Whether they have brought any wisdom to light below it is a more doubtful matter.

It is scarcely necessary to go into the details of the speculations that landed me at Lympne, in Kent. Nowadays even about business transactions there is a strong spice of adventure. I took risks. In these things there is invariably a certain amount of give and take, and it fell to me finally to do the giving reluctantly enough. Even when I had got out of everything, one cantankerous creditor saw fit to be malignant. Perhaps you have met that flaming sense of outraged virtue, or perhaps you have only felt it. He ran me hard. It seemed to me, at last, that there was nothing for it but to write a play, unless I wanted to drudge for my living as a clerk. I have a certain imagination, and luxurious tastes, and I meant to make a vigorous fight for it before that fate overtook me. In addition to my belief in my powers as a business man, I had always in those days had an idea that I was equal to writing a very good play. It is not, I believe, a very uncommon persuasion. I knew there is nothing a man can do outside legitimate business transactions that has such opulent possibilities, and very probably that biased my opinion. I had, indeed, got into the habit of regarding this unwritten drama as a convenient little reserve put by for a rainy day. That rainy day had come, and I set to work.

I soon discovered that writing a play was a longer business than I had supposed; at first I had reckoned ten days for it, and it was to have a *pied-a-terre* while it was in hand that I came to Lympne. I reckoned myself lucky in getting that little bungalow. I got it on a three years' agreement. I put in a few sticks of furniture, and while the play was in hand I did my own cooking. My cooking would have shocked Mrs. Bond. And yet, you know, it had flavour. I had a coffee-pot, a sauce-pan for eggs, and one for potatoes, and a frying-pan for sausages and bacon – such was the simple apparatus of my comfort. One cannot always be magnificent, but simplicity is always a possible alternative. For the rest I laid in an eighteen-gallon cask of beer on credit, and a trustful baker came each day. It was not, perhaps, in the style of Sybaris, but I have had worse times. I was a little sorry for the baker, who was a very decent man indeed, but even for him I hoped.

Certainly if any one wants solitude, the place is Lympne. It is in the clay part of Kent, and my bungalow stood on the edge of an old sea cliff and stared across the flats of Romney Marsh at the sea. In very wet weather the place is almost inaccessible, and I have heard that at times the postman used to traverse the more succulent portions of his route with boards upon his feet. I never saw him doing so, but I can quite imagine it. Outside the doors of the few cottages and houses that make up the present village big birch besoms are stuck, to wipe off the worst of the clay, which will give some idea of the texture of the district. I doubt if the place would be there at all, if it were not a fading memory of things gone for ever. It was the big port of England in Roman times, Portus Lemanis, and now the sea is four miles away. All down the steep hill are boulders and masses of Roman brickwork, and from it old Watling Street, still paved in places, starts like an arrow to the north. I used to stand on the hill and think of it all, the galleys and legions, the captives and officials, the women and traders, the speculators like myself, all the swarm and tumult that came clanking in and out of the harbour. And now just a few lumps of rubble on a grassy slope, and a sheep or two – and I. And where the port had been were the levels of the marsh, sweeping round in a broad curve to distant Dungeness, and dotted here and there with tree clumps and the church towers of old medieval towns that are following Lemanis now towards extinction.

That outlook on the marsh was, indeed, one of the finest views I have ever seen. I suppose Dungeness was fifteen miles away; it lay like a raft on the sea, and farther westward were the hills by Hastings under the setting sun. Sometimes they hung close and clear, sometimes they were faded and low, and often the drift of the weather took them clean out of sight. And all the nearer parts of the marsh were laced and lit by ditches and canals.

The window at which I worked looked over the skyline of this crest, and it was from this window that I first set eyes on Cavor. It was just as I was struggling with my scenario, holding down my mind to the sheer hard work of it, and naturally enough he arrested my attention.

The sun had set, the sky was a vivid tranquillity of green and yellow, and against that he came out black – the oddest little figure.

He was a short, round-bodied, thin-legged little man, with a jerky quality in his motions; he had seen fit to clothe his extraordinary mind in a cricket cap, an overcoat, and cycling knickerbockers and stockings. Why he did so I do not know, for he never cycled and he never played cricket. It was a fortuitous concurrence of garments, arising I know not how. He gesticulated with his hands and arms, and jerked his head about and *buzzed*. He buzzed like something electric. You never heard such buzzing. And ever and again he cleared his throat with a most extraordinary noise.

There had been rain, and that spasmodic walk of his was enhanced by the extreme slipperiness of the footpath. Exactly as he came against the sun he stopped, pulled out a watch, hesitated. Then with a sort of convulsive gesture he turned and retreated with every manifestation of haste, no longer gesticulating, but going with ample strides that showed the relatively large size of his feet – they were, I remember, grotesquely exaggerated in size by adhesive clay – to the best possible advantage.

This occurred on the first day of my sojourn, when my playwriting energy was at its height and I regarded the incident simply as an annoying distraction – the waste of five minutes. I returned to my scenario. But when next evening the apparition was repeated with remarkable precision, and again the next evening, and indeed every evening when rain was not falling, concentration upon the scenario became a considerable effort. "Confound the man," I said, "one would think he was learning to be a marionette!" and for several evenings I cursed him pretty heartily. Then my annoyance gave way to amazement and curiosity. Why on earth should a man do this thing? On the fourteenth evening I could stand it no longer, and so soon as he appeared I opened the french window, crossed the verandah, and directed myself to the point where he invariably stopped.

He had his watch out as I came up to him. He had a chubby, rubicund face with reddish brown eyes – previously I had seen him only against the light. "One moment, sir," said I as he turned. He stared. "One moment," he said, "certainly. Or if you wish to speak to me for longer, and it is not asking too much – your moment is up – would it trouble you to accompany me?"

"Not in the least," said I, placing myself beside him.

"My habits are regular. My time for intercourse – limited."

"This, I presume, is your time for exercise?"

"It is. I come here to enjoy the sunset."

"You don't."

"Sir?"

"You never look at it."

"Never look at it?"

"No. I've watched you thirteen nights, and not once have you looked at the sunset – not once."

He knitted his brows like one who encounters a problem.

"Well, I enjoy the sunlight – the atmosphere – I go along this path, through that gate" – he jerked his head over his shoulder – "and round—"

"You don't. You never have been. It's all nonsense. There isn't a way. To-night for instance—"

"Oh! to-night! Let me see. Ah! I just glanced at my watch, saw that I had already been out just three minutes over the precise half-hour, decided there was not time to go round, turned—"

"You always do."

He looked at me – reflected. "Perhaps I do, now I come to think of it. But what was it you wanted to speak to me about?"

"Why, this!"

"This?"

"Yes. Why do you do it? Every night you come making a noise—"

"Making a noise?"

"Like this." I imitated his buzzing noise. He looked at me, and it was evident the buzzing awakened distaste. "Do I do *that*?" he asked.

"Every blessed evening."

"I had no idea."

He stopped dead. He regarded me gravely. "Can it be," he said, "that I have formed a Habit?"

"Well, it looks like it. Doesn't it?"

He pulled down his lower lip between finger and thumb. He regarded a puddle at his feet.

"My mind is much occupied," he said. "And you want to know *why*! Well, sir, I can assure you that not only do I not know why I do these things, but I did not even know I did them. Come to think, it is just as you say; I never *have* been beyond that field.... And these things annoy you?"

For some reason I was beginning to relent towards him. "Not *annoy*," I said. "But - imagine yourself writing a play!"

"I couldn't."

"Well, anything that needs concentration."

"Ah!" he said, "of course," and meditated. His expression became so eloquent of distress, that I relented still more. After all, there *is* a touch of aggression in demanding of a man you don't know why he hums on a public footpath.

"You see," he said weakly, "it's a habit."

"Oh, I recognise that."

"I must stop it."

"But not if it puts you out. After all, I had no business – it's something of a liberty."

"Not at all, sir," he said, "not at all. I am greatly indebted to you. I should guard myself against these things. In future I will. Could I trouble you – once again? That noise?"

"Something like this," I said. "Zuzzoo, zuzzoo. But really, you know—"

"I am greatly obliged to you. In fact, I know I am getting absurdly absent-minded. You are quite justified, sir – perfectly justified. Indeed, I am indebted to you. The thing shall end. And now, sir, I have already brought you farther than I should have done."

"I do hope my impertinence—"

"Not at all, sir, not at all."

We regarded each other for a moment. I raised my hat and wished him a good evening. He responded convulsively, and so we went our ways.

At the stile I looked back at his receding figure. His bearing had changed remarkably, he seemed limp, shrunken. The contrast with his former gesticulating, zuzzoing self took me in some absurd way as pathetic. I watched him out of sight. Then wishing very heartily I had kept to my own business, I returned to my bungalow and my play.

The next evening I saw nothing of him, nor the next. But he was very much in my mind, and it had occurred to me that as a sentimental comic character he might serve a useful purpose in the development of my plot. The third day he called upon me.

For a time I was puzzled to think what had brought him. He made indifferent conversation in the most formal way, then abruptly he came to business. He wanted to buy me out of my bungalow.

"You see," he said, "I don't blame you in the least, but you've destroyed a habit, and it disorganises my day. I've walked past here for years – years. No doubt I've hummed.... You've made all that impossible!"

I suggested he might try some other direction.

"No. There is no other direction. This is the only one. I've inquired. And now – every afternoon at four – I come to a dead wall."

"But, my dear sir, if the thing is so important to you—"

"It's vital. You see, I'm – I'm an investigator – I am engaged in a scientific research. I live—" he paused and seemed to think. "Just over there," he said, and pointed suddenly dangerously near my eye. "The house with white chimneys you see just over the trees. And my circumstances are abnormal – abnormal. I am on the point of completing one of the most important demonstrations – I can assure you one of *the most important* demonstrations that have ever been made. It requires constant thought, constant mental ease and activity. And the afternoon was my brightest time! – effervescing with new ideas – new points of view."

"But why not come by still?"

"It would be all different. I should be self-conscious. I should think of you at your play – watching me irritated – instead of thinking of my work. No! I must have the bungalow."

I meditated. Naturally, I wanted to think the matter over thoroughly before anything decisive was said. I was generally ready enough for business in those days, and selling always attracted me; but in the first place it was not my bungalow, and even if I sold it to him at a good price I might get inconvenienced in the delivery of goods if the current owner got wind of the transaction, and in the second I was, well – undischarged. It was clearly a business that required delicate handling. Moreover, the possibility of his being in pursuit of some valuable invention also interested me. It occurred to me that I would like to know more of this research, not with any dishonest intention, but simply with an idea that to know what it was would be a relief from play-writing. I threw out feelers.

He was quite willing to supply information. Indeed, once he was fairly under way the conversation became a monologue. He talked like a man long pent up, who has had it over with himself again and again. He talked for nearly an hour, and I must confess I found it a pretty stiff bit of listening. But through it all there was the undertone of satisfaction one feels when one is neglecting work one has set oneself. During that first interview I gathered very little of the drift of his work. Half his words were technicalities entirely strange to me, and he illustrated one or two points with what he was pleased to call elementary mathematics, computing on an envelope with a copying-ink pencil, in a manner that made it hard even to seem to understand. "Yes," I said, "yes. Go on!" Nevertheless I made out enough to convince me that he was no mere crank playing at discoveries. In spite of his crank-like appearance there was a force about him that made that impossible. Whatever it was, it was a thing with mechanical possibilities. He told me of a work-shed he had, and of three assistants – originally jobbing carpenters – whom he had trained. Now, from the work-shed to the patent office is clearly only one step. He invited me to see those things. I accepted readily, and took care, by a remark or so, to underline that. The proposed transfer of the bungalow remained very conveniently in suspense.

At last he rose to depart, with an apology for the length of his call. Talking over his work was, he said, a pleasure enjoyed only too rarely. It was not often he found such an intelligent listener as myself, he mingled very little with professional scientific men.

"So much pettiness," he explained; "so much intrigue! And really, when one has an idea – a novel, fertilising idea – I don't want to be uncharitable, but—"

I am a man who believes in impulses. I made what was perhaps a rash proposition. But you must remember, that I had been alone, play-writing in Lympne, for fourteen days, and my compunction for his ruined walk still hung about me. "Why not," said I, "make this your new habit? In the place of the one I spoilt? At least, until we can settle about the bungalow. What you want is to turn over your work in your mind. That you have always done during your afternoon walk. Unfortunately that's over – you can't get things back as they were. But why not come and talk about your work to me; use me as a sort of wall against which you may throw your thoughts and catch them again? It's certain I don't know enough to steal your ideas myself – and I know no scientific men—"

I stopped. He was considering. Evidently the thing, attracted him. "But I'm afraid I should bore you," he said.

"You think I'm too dull?"

"Oh, no; but technicalities—"

"Anyhow, you've interested me immensely this afternoon."

"Of course it *would* be a great help to me. Nothing clears up one's ideas so much as explaining them. Hitherto—"

"My dear sir, say no more."

"But really can you spare the time?"

"There is no rest like change of occupation," I said, with profound conviction.

The affair was over. On my verandah steps he turned. "I am already greatly indebted to you," he said.

I made an interrogative noise.

"You have completely cured me of that ridiculous habit of humming," he explained.

I think I said I was glad to be of any service to him, and he turned away.

Immediately the train of thought that our conversation had suggested must have resumed its sway. His arms began to wave in their former fashion. The faint echo of "zuzzoo" came back to me on the breeze....

Well, after all, that was not my affair....

He came the next day, and again the next day after that, and delivered two lectures on physics to our mutual satisfaction. He talked with an air of being extremely lucid about the "ether" and "tubes of force," and "gravitational potential," and things like that, and I sat in my other folding-chair and said, "Yes," "Go on," "I follow you," to keep him going. It was tremendously difficult stuff, but I do not think he ever suspected how much I did not understand him. There were moments when I doubted whether I was well employed, but at any rate I was resting from that confounded play. Now and then things gleamed on me clearly for a space, only to vanish just when I thought I had hold of them. Sometimes my attention failed altogether, and I would give it up and sit and stare at him, wondering whether, after all, it would not be better to use him as a central figure in a good farce and let all this other stuff slide. And then, perhaps, I would catch on again for a bit.

At the earliest opportunity I went to see his house. It was large and carelessly furnished; there were no servants other than his three assistants, and his dietary and private life were characterised by a philosophical simplicity. He was a water-drinker, a vegetarian, and all those logical disciplinary things. But the sight of his equipment settled many doubts. It looked like business from cellar to attic – an amazing little place to find in an out-of-the-way village. The ground-floor rooms contained benches and apparatus, the bakehouse and scullery boiler had developed into respectable furnaces, dynamos occupied the cellar, and there was a gasometer in the garden. He showed it to me with all the confiding zest of a man who has been living too much alone. His seclusion was overflowing now in an excess of confidence, and I had the good luck to be the recipient.

The three assistants were creditable specimens of the class of "handy-men" from which they came. Conscientious if unintelligent, strong, civil, and willing. One, Spargus, who did the cooking and all the metal work, had been a sailor; a second, Gibbs, was a joiner; and the third was an ex-jobbing gardener, and now general assistant. They were the merest labourers. All the intelligent work was done by Cavor. Theirs was the darkest ignorance compared even with my muddled impression.

And now, as to the nature of these inquiries. Here, unhappily, comes a grave difficulty. I am no scientific expert, and if I were to attempt to set forth in the highly scientific language of Mr. Cavor the aim to which his experiments tended, I am afraid I should confuse not only the reader but myself, and almost certainly I should make some blunder that would bring upon me the mockery of every up-to-date student of mathematical physics in the country. The best thing I can do therefore is, I think to give my impressions in my own inexact language, without any attempt to wear a garment of knowledge to which I have no claim.

The object of Mr. Cavor's search was a substance that should be "opaque" – he used some other word I have forgotten, but "opaque" conveys the idea – to "all forms of radiant energy." "Radiant energy," he made me understand, was anything like light or heat, or those Rontgen Rays there was so much talk about a year or so ago, or the electric waves of Marconi, or gravitation. All these things, he said, *radiate* out from centres, and act on bodies at a distance, whence comes the term "radiant energy." Now almost all substances are opaque to some form or other of radiant energy. Glass, for example, is transparent to light, but much less so to heat, so that it is useful as a fire-screen; and alum is transparent to light, but blocks heat completely. A solution of iodine in carbon bisulphide, on the other hand, completely blocks light, but is quite transparent to heat. It will hide a fire from you, but permit all its warmth to reach you. Metals are not only opaque to light and heat, but also to electrical energy, which passes through both iodine solution and glass almost as though they were not interposed. And so on.

Now all known substances are "transparent" to gravitation. You can use screens of various sorts to cut off the light or heat, or electrical influence of the sun, or the warmth of the earth from anything; you can screen things by sheets of metal from Marconi's rays, but nothing will cut off the gravitational attraction of the sun or the gravitational attraction of the earth. Yet why there should be nothing is hard to say. Cavor did not see why such a substance should not exist, and certainly I could not tell him. I had never thought of such a possibility before. He showed me by calculations on paper, which Lord Kelvin, no doubt, or Professor Lodge, or Professor Karl Pearson, or any of those great scientific people might have understood, but which simply reduced me to a hopeless muddle, that not only was such a substance possible, but that it must satisfy certain conditions. It was an amazing piece of reasoning. Much as it amazed and exercised me at the time, it would be impossible to reproduce it here. "Yes," I said to it all, "yes;

go on!" Suffice it for this story that he believed he might be able to manufacture this possible substance opaque to gravitation out of a complicated alloy of metals and something new – a new element, I fancy – called, I believe, *helium*, which was sent to him from London in sealed stone jars. Doubt has been thrown upon this detail, but I am almost certain it was *helium* he had sent him in sealed stone jars. It was certainly something very gaseous and thin. If only I had taken notes...

But then, how was I to foresee the necessity of taking notes?

Any one with the merest germ of an imagination will understand the extraordinary possibilities of such a substance, and will sympathise a little with the emotion I felt as this understanding emerged from the haze of abstruse phrases in which Cavor expressed himself. Comic relief in a play indeed! It was some time before I would believe that I had interpreted him aright, and I was very careful not to ask questions that would have enabled him to gauge the profundity of misunderstanding into which he dropped his daily exposition. But no one reading the story of it here will sympathise fully, because from my barren narrative it will be impossible to gather the strength of my conviction that this astonishing substance was positively going to be made.

I do not recall that I gave my play an hour's consecutive work at any time after my visit to his house. My imagination had other things to do. There seemed no limit to the possibilities of the stuff; whichever way I tried I came on miracles and revolutions. For example, if one wanted to lift a weight, however enormous, one had only to get a sheet of this substance beneath it, and one might lift it with a straw. My first natural impulse was to apply this principle to guns and ironclads, and all the material and methods of war, and from that to shipping, locomotion, building, every conceivable form of human industry. The chance that had brought me into the very birth-chamber of this new time – it was an epoch, no less – was one of those chances that come once in a thousand years. The thing unrolled, it expanded and expanded. Among other things I saw in it my redemption as a business man. I saw a parent company, and daughter companies, applications to right of us, applications to left, rings and trusts, privileges, and concessions spreading and spreading, until one vast, stupendous Cavorite company ran and ruled the world.

And I was in it!

I took my line straight away. I knew I was staking everything, but I jumped there and then.

"We're on absolutely the biggest thing that has ever been invented," I said, and put the accent on "we." "If you want to keep me out of this, you'll have to do it with a gun. I'm coming down to be your fourth labourer to-morrow."

He seemed surprised at my enthusiasm, but not a bit suspicious or hostile. Rather, he was self-depreciatory. He looked at me doubtfully. "But do you really think—?" he said. "And your play! How about that play?"

"It's vanished!" I cried. "My dear sir, don't you see what you've got? Don't you see what you're going to do?"

That was merely a rhetorical turn, but positively, he didn't. At first I could not believe it. He had not had the beginning of the inkling of an idea. This astonishing little man had been working on purely theoretical grounds the whole time! When he said it was "the most important" research the world had ever seen, he simply meant it squared up so many theories, settled so much that was in doubt; he had troubled no more about the application of the stuff he was going to turn out than if he had been a machine that makes guns. This was a possible substance, and he was going to make it! *V'la tout*, as the Frenchman says.

Beyond that, he was childish! If he made it, it would go down to posterity as Cavorite or Cavorine, and he would be made an F.R.S., and his portrait given away as a scientific worthy with *Nature*, and things like that. And that was all he saw! He would have dropped this bombshell into the world as though he had discovered a new species of gnat, if it had not happened that I had come along. And there it would have lain and fizzled, like one or two other little things these scientific people have lit and dropped about us.

When I realised this, it was I did the talking, and Cavor who said, "Go on!" I jumped up. I paced the room, gesticulating like a boy of twenty. I tried to make him understand his duties and responsibilities in the matter – *our* duties and responsibilities in the matter. I assured him we might make wealth enough to work any sort of social revolution we fancied, we might own and order the whole world. I told him of companies and patents, and the case for secret processes. All these things seemed to take him much as his mathematics had taken me. A look of perplexity came into his ruddy little face. He stammered something about indifference to wealth, but I brushed all that aside. He had got to be rich, and it was no good his stammering. I gave him to understand the sort of man I was, and that I had had very considerable business experience. I did not tell him I was an undischarged bankrupt at the time, because that was temporary, but I think I reconciled my evident poverty with my financial claims. And quite insensibly, in the way such projects grow, the understanding of a Cavorite monopoly grew up between us. He was to make the stuff, and I was to make the boom.

I stuck like a leech to the "we" – "you" and "I" didn't exist for me.

His idea was that the profits I spoke of might go to endow research, but that, of course, was a matter we had to settle later. "That's all right," I shouted, "that's all right." The great point, as I insisted, was to get the thing done.

"Here is a substance," I cried, "no home, no factory, no fortress, no ship can dare to be without – more universally applicable even than a patent medicine. There isn't a solitary aspect of it, not one of its ten thousand possible uses that will not make us rich, Cavor, beyond the dreams of avarice!"

"No!" he said. "I begin to see. It's extraordinary how one gets new points of view by talking over things!"

"And as it happens you have just talked to the right man!"

"I suppose no one," he said, "is absolutely *averse* to enormous wealth. Of course there is one thing—"

He paused. I stood still.

"It is just possible, you know, that we may not be able to make it after all! It may be one of those things that are a theoretical possibility, but a practical absurdity. Or when we make it, there may be some little hitch!"

"We'll tackle the hitch when it comes." said I.

CHAPTER 2

The First Making of Cavorite

But **Cavor's fears** were groundless, so far as the actual making was concerned. On the 14th of October, 1899, this incredible substance was made!

Oddly enough, it was made at last by accident, when Mr. Cavor least expected it. He had fused together a number of metals and certain other things – I wish I knew the particulars now! – and he intended to leave the mixture a week and then allow it to cool slowly. Unless he had miscalculated, the last stage in the combination would occur when the stuff sank to a temperature of 60 degrees Fahrenheit. But it chanced that, unknown to Cavor, dissension had arisen about the furnace tending. Gibbs, who had previously seen to this, had suddenly attempted to shift it to the man who had been a gardener, on the score that coal was soil, being dug, and therefore could not possibly fall within the province of a joiner; the man who had been a jobbing gardener alleged, however, that coal was a metallic or ore-like substance, let alone that he was cook. But Spargus insisted on Gibbs doing the coaling, seeing that he was a joiner and that coal is notoriously fossil wood. Consequently Gibbs ceased to replenish the furnace, and no one else did so, and Cavor was too much immersed in certain interesting problems concerning a Cavorite flying machine (neglecting the resistance of the air and one or two other points) to perceive that anything was wrong. And the premature birth of his invention took place just as he was coming across the field to my bungalow for our afternoon talk and tea.

I remember the occasion with extreme vividness. The water was boiling, and everything was prepared, and the sound of his "zuzzoo" had brought me out upon the verandah. His active little figure was black against the autumnal sunset, and to the right the chimneys of his house just rose above a gloriously tinted group of trees. Remoter rose the Wealden Hills, faint and blue, while to the left the hazy marsh spread out spacious and serene. And then—

The chimneys jerked heavenward, smashing into a string of bricks as they rose, and the roof and a miscellany of furniture followed. Then overtaking them came a huge white flame. The trees about the building swayed and whirled and tore themselves to pieces, that sprang towards the flare. My ears were smitten with a clap of thunder that left me deaf on one side for life, and all about me windows smashed, unheeded.

I took three steps from the verandah towards Cavor's house, and even as I did so came the wind.

Instantly my coat tails were over my head, and I was progressing in great leaps and bounds, and quite against my will, towards him. In the same moment the discoverer was seized, whirled about, and flew through the screaming air. I saw one of my chimney pots hit the ground within six yards of me, leap a score of feet, and so hurry in great strides towards the focus of the disturbance. Cavor, kicking and flapping, came down again, rolled over and over on the ground for a space, struggled up and was lifted and borne forward at an enormous velocity, vanishing at last among the labouring, lashing trees that writhed about his house.

A mass of smoke and ashes, and a square of bluish shining substance rushed up towards the zenith. A large fragment of fencing came sailing past me, dropped edgeways, hit the ground and fell flat, and then the worst was over. The aerial commotion fell swiftly until it was a mere strong gale, and I became once more aware that I had breath and feet. By leaning back against the wind I managed to stop, and could collect such wits as still remained to me.

In that instant the whole face of the world had changed. The tranquil sunset had vanished, the sky was dark with scurrying clouds, everything was flattened and swaying with the gale. I glanced back to see if my bungalow was still in a general way standing, then staggered forwards towards the trees amongst which Cavor had vanished, and through whose tall and leaf-denuded branches shone the flames of his burning house.

I entered the copse, dashing from one tree to another and clinging to them, and for a space I sought him in vain. Then amidst a heap of smashed branches and fencing that had banked itself against a portion of his garden wall I perceived something stir. I made a run for this, but before I reached it a brown object separated itself, rose on two muddy legs, and protruded two drooping, bleeding hands. Some tattered ends of garment fluttered out from its middle portion and streamed before the wind.

For a moment I did not recognise this earthy lump, and then I saw that it was Cavor, caked in the mud in which he had rolled. He leant forward against the wind, rubbing the dirt from his eyes and mouth.

He extended a muddy lump of hand, and staggered a pace towards me. His face worked with emotion, little lumps of mud kept falling from it. He looked as damaged and pitiful as any living creature I have ever seen, and his remark therefore amazed me exceedingly.

"Gratulate me," he gasped; "gratulate me!"

"Congratulate you!" said I. "Good heavens! What for?"

"I've done it."

"You *have*. What on earth caused that explosion?"

A gust of wind blew his words away. I understood him to say that it wasn't an explosion at all. The wind hurled me into collision with him, and we stood clinging to one another.

"Try and get back – to my bungalow," I bawled in his ear. He did not hear me, and shouted something about "three martyrs – science," and also something about "not much good." At the time he laboured under the impression that his three attendants had perished in the whirlwind. Happily this was incorrect. Directly he had left for my bungalow they had gone off to the public-house in Lympne to discuss the question of the furnaces over some trivial refreshment.

I repeated my suggestion of getting back to my bungalow, and this time he understood. We clung arm-in-arm and started, and managed at last to reach the shelter of as much roof as was left to me. For a space we sat in arm-chairs and panted. All the windows were broken, and the lighter articles of furniture were in great disorder, but no irrevocable damage was done. Happily the kitchen door had stood the pressure upon it, so that all my crockery and cooking materials had survived. The oil stove was still burning, and I put on the water to boil again for tea. And that prepared, I could turn on Cavor for his explanation.

"Quite correct," he insisted; "quite correct. I've done it, and it's all right."

"But," I protested. "All right! Why, there can't be a rick standing, or a fence or a thatched roof undamaged for twenty miles round...."

"It's all right – *really*. I didn't, of course, foresee this little upset. My mind was preoccupied with another problem, and I'm apt to disregard these practical side issues. But it's all right—"

"My dear sir," I cried, "don't you see you've done thousands of pounds' worth of damage?"

"There, I throw myself on your discretion. I'm not a practical man, of course, but don't you think they will regard it as a cyclone?"

"But the explosion—"

"It was *not* an explosion. It's perfectly simple. Only, as I say, I'm apt to overlook these little things. It's that zuzzoo business on a larger scale. Inadvertently I made this substance of mine, this Cavorite, in a thin, wide sheet...."

He paused. "You are quite clear that the stuff is opaque to gravitation, that it cuts off things from gravitating towards each other?"

"Yes," said I. "Yes."

"Well, so soon as it reached a temperature of 60 degrees Fahrenheit, and the process of its manufacture was complete, the air above it, the portions of roof and ceiling and floor above it ceased to have weight. I suppose you know – everybody knows nowadays – that, as a usual thing, the air *has* weight, that it presses on everything at the surface of the earth, presses in all directions, with a pressure of fourteen and a half pounds to the square inch?"

"I know that," said I. "Go on."

"I know that too," he remarked. "Only this shows you how useless knowledge is unless you apply it. You see, over our Cavorite this ceased to be the case, the air there ceased to exert any pressure, and the air round it and not over the Cavorite was exerting a pressure of fourteen pounds and a half to the square in upon this suddenly weightless air. Ah! you begin to see! The air all about the Cavorite crushed in upon the air above it with irresistible force. The air above the Cavorite was forced upward violently, the air that rushed in to replace it immediately lost weight, ceased to exert any pressure, followed suit, blew the ceiling through and the roof off...."

"You perceive," he said, "it formed a sort of atmospheric fountain, a kind of chimney in the atmosphere. And if the Cavorite itself hadn't been loose and so got sucked up the chimney, does it occur to you what would have happened?"

I thought. "I suppose," I said, "the air would be rushing up and up over that infernal piece of stuff now."

"Precisely," he said. "A huge fountain—"

"Spouting into space! Good heavens! Why, it would have squirted all the atmosphere of the earth away! It would have robbed the world of air! It would have been the death of all mankind! That little lump of stuff!"

"Not exactly into space," said Cavor, "but as bad – practically. It would have whipped the air off the world as one peels a banana, and flung it thousands of miles. It would have dropped back again, of course – but on an asphyxiated world! From our point of view very little better than if it never came back!"

I stared. As yet I was too amazed to realise how all my expectations had been upset. "What do you mean to do now?" I asked.

"In the first place if I may borrow a garden trowel I will remove some of this earth with which I am encased, and then if I may avail myself of your domestic conveniences I will have a bath. This done, we will converse more at leisure. It will be wise, I think" – he laid a muddy hand on my arm – "if nothing were said of this affair beyond ourselves. I know I have caused great damage – probably even dwelling-houses may be ruined here and there upon the country-side. But on the other hand, I cannot possibly pay for the damage I have done, and if the real cause of this is published, it will lead only to heartburning and the obstruction of my work. One cannot foresee *everything*, you know, and I cannot consent for one moment to add the burthen of practical considerations to my theorising. Later on, when you have come in with your practical mind, and Cavorite is floated – floated *is* the word, isn't it? – and it has realised all you anticipate for it, we may set matters right with these persons. But not now – not now. If no other explanation is offered, people, in the present unsatisfactory state of meteorological science, will ascribe all this to a cyclone; there might be a public subscription, and as my house has collapsed and been burnt, I should in that case receive a considerable share in the compensation, which would be extremely helpful to the prosecution of our researches. But if it is known that I caused this, there will be no public subscription, and everybody will be put out. Practically I should never get a chance of working in peace again. My three assistants may or may not have perished. That is a detail. If they have, it is no great loss; they were more zealous than able, and this premature event must be largely due to their joint neglect of the furnace. If they have not perished, I doubt if they have the intelligence to explain the affair. They will accept the cyclone story. And if during the temporary unfitness of my house for occupation, I may lodge in one of the untenanted rooms of this bungalow of yours—"

He paused and regarded me.

A man of such possibilities, I reflected, is no ordinary guest to entertain.

"Perhaps," said I, rising to my feet, "we had better begin by looking for a trowel," and I led the way to the scattered vestiges of the greenhouse.

And while he was having his bath I considered the entire question alone. It was clear there were drawbacks to Mr. Cavor's society I had not foreseen. The absentmindedness that had just escaped depopulating the terrestrial globe, might at any moment result in some other grave inconvenience. On the other hand I was young, my affairs were in a mess, and I was in just the mood for reckless adventure – with a chance of something good at the end of it. I had quite settled in my mind that I was to have half at least in that aspect of the affair. Fortunately I held my bungalow, as I have already explained, on a three-year agreement, without being responsible for repairs; and my furniture, such as there was of it, had been hastily purchased, was unpaid for, insured, and altogether devoid of associations. In the end I decided to keep on with him, and see the business through.

Certainly the aspect of things had changed very greatly. I no longer doubted at all the enormous possibilities of the substance, but I began to have doubts about the gun-carriage and the patent boots. We set to work at once to reconstruct his laboratory and proceed with our experiments. Cavor talked more on my level than he had ever done before, when it came to the question of how we should make the stuff next.

"Of course we must make it again," he said, with a sort of glee I had not expected in him, "of course we must make it again. We have caught a Tartar, perhaps, but we have left the theoretical behind us for good and all. If we can possibly avoid wrecking this little planet of ours, we will. But – there *must* be risks! There must be. In experimental work there always are. And here, as a practical man, *you* must come in. For my own part it seems to me we might make it edgeways, perhaps, and very thin. Yet I don't know. I have a certain dim perception of another method. I can hardly explain it yet. But curiously enough it came into my mind, while I was rolling over and over in the mud before the wind, and very doubtful how the whole adventure was to end, as being absolutely the thing I ought to have done."

Even with my aid we found some little difficulty, and meanwhile we kept at work restoring the laboratory. There was plenty to do before it became absolutely necessary to decide upon the precise form and method of our second attempt. Our only hitch was the strike of the three labourers, who objected to my activity as a foreman. But that matter we compromised after two days' delay.

CHAPTER 3

The Building of the Sphere

I remember the occasion very distinctly when Cavor told me of his idea of the sphere. He had had intimations of it before, but at the time it seemed to come to him in a rush. We were returning to the bungalow for tea, and on the way he fell humming. Suddenly he shouted, "That's it! That finishes it! A sort of roller blind!"

"Finishes what?" I asked.

"Space – anywhere! The moon."

"What do you mean?"

"Mean? Why – it must be a sphere! That's what I mean!"

I saw I was out of it, and for a time I let him talk in his own fashion. I hadn't the ghost of an idea then of his drift. But after he had taken tea he made it clear to me.

"It's like this," he said. "Last time I ran this stuff that cuts things off from gravitation into a flat tank with an overlap that held it down. And directly it had cooled and the manufacture was completed all that uproar happened, nothing above it weighed anything, the air went squirting up, the house squirted up, and if the stuff itself hadn't squirted up too, I don't know what would have happened! But suppose the substance is loose, and quite free to go up?"

"It will go up at once!"

"Exactly. With no more disturbance than firing a big gun."

"But what good will that do?"

"I'm going up with it!"

I put down my teacup and stared at him.

"Imagine a sphere," he explained, "large enough to hold two people and their luggage. It will be made of steel lined with thick glass; it will contain a proper store of solidified air, concentrated food, water distilling apparatus, and so forth. And enamelled, as it were, on the outer steel—"

"Cavorite?"

"Yes."

"But how will you get inside?"

"There was a similar problem about a dumpling."

"Yes, I know. But how?"

"That's perfectly easy. An air-tight manhole is all that is needed. That, of course, will have to be a little complicated; there will have to be a valve, so that things may be thrown out, if necessary, without much loss of air."

"Like Jules Verne's thing in *A Trip to the Moon*."

But Cavor was not a reader of fiction.

"I begin to see," I said slowly. "And you could get in and screw yourself up while the Cavorite was warm, and as soon as it cooled it would become impervious to gravitation, and off you would fly—"

"At a tangent."

"You would go off in a straight line—" I stopped abruptly. "What is to prevent the thing travelling in a straight line into space for ever?" I asked. "You're not safe to get anywhere, and if you do – how will you get back?"

"I've just thought of that," said Cavor. "That's what I meant when I said the thing is finished. The inner glass sphere can be air-tight, and, except for the manhole, continuous, and the steel sphere can be made in sections, each section capable of rolling up after the fashion of a roller blind. These can easily be worked by springs, and released and checked by electricity conveyed by platinum wires fused through the glass. All that is merely a question of detail. So you see, that except for the thickness of the blind rollers, the Cavorite exterior of the sphere will consist of windows or blinds, whichever you like to call them. Well, when all these windows or blinds are shut, no light, no heat, no gravitation, no radiant energy of any sort will get at the inside of the sphere, it will fly on through space in a straight line, as you say. But open a window, imagine one of the windows open. Then at once any heavy body that chances to be in that direction will attract us—"

I sat taking it in.

"You see?" he said.

"Oh, I *see*."

"Practically we shall be able to tack about in space just as we wish. Get attracted by this and that."

"Oh, yes. *That's* clear enough. Only—"

"Well?"

"I don't quite see what we shall do it for! It's really only jumping off the world and back again."

"Surely! For example, one might go to the moon."

"And when one got there? What would you find?"

"We should see— Oh! consider the new knowledge."

"Is there air there?"

"There may be."

"It's a fine idea," I said, "but it strikes me as a large order all the same. The moon! I'd much rather try some smaller things first."

"They're out of the question, because of the air difficulty."

"Why not apply that idea of spring blinds – Cavorite blinds in strong steel cases – to lifting weights?"

"It wouldn't work," he insisted. "After all, to go into outer space is not so much worse, if at all, than a polar expedition. Men go on polar expeditions."

"Not business men. And besides, they get paid for polar expeditions. And if anything goes wrong there are relief parties. But this – it's just firing ourselves off the world for nothing."

"Call it prospecting."

"You'll have to call it that.... One might make a book of it perhaps," I said.

"I have no doubt there will be minerals," said Cavor.

"For example?"

"Oh! sulphur, ores, gold perhaps, possibly new elements."

"Cost of carriage," I said. "You know you're *not* a practical man. The moon's a quarter of a million miles away."

"It seems to me it wouldn't cost much to cart any weight anywhere if you packed it in a Cavorite case."

I had not thought of that. "Delivered free on head of purchaser, eh?"

"It isn't as though we were confined to the moon."

"You mean?"

"There's Mars – clear atmosphere, novel surroundings, exhilarating sense of lightness. It might be pleasant to go there."

"Is there air on Mars?"

"Oh, yes!"

"Seems as though you might run it as a sanatorium. By the way, how far is Mars?"

"Two hundred million miles at present," said Cavor airily; "and you go close by the sun."

My imagination was picking itself up again. "After all," I said, "there's something in these things. There's travel—"

An extraordinary possibility came rushing into my mind. Suddenly I saw, as in a vision, the whole solar system threaded with Cavorite liners and spheres *de luxe*. "Rights of pre-emption," came floating into my head – planetary rights of pre-emption. I recalled the old Spanish monopoly in American gold. It wasn't as though it was just this planet or that – it was all of them. I stared at Cavor's rubicund face, and suddenly my imagination was leaping and dancing. I stood up, I walked up and down; my tongue was unloosened.

"I'm beginning to take it in," I said; "I'm beginning to take it in." The transition from doubt to enthusiasm seemed to take scarcely any time at all. "But this is tremendous!" I cried. "This is Imperial! I haven't been dreaming of this sort of thing."

Once the chill of my opposition was removed, his own pent-up excitement had play. He too got up and paced. He too gesticulated and shouted. We behaved like men inspired. We *were* men inspired.

"We'll settle all that!" he said in answer to some incidental difficulty that had pulled me up. "We'll soon settle that! We'll start the drawings for mouldings this very night."

"We'll start them now," I responded, and we hurried off to the laboratory to begin upon this work forthwith.

I was like a child in Wonderland all that night. The dawn found us both still at work – we kept our electric light going heedless of the day. I remember now exactly how these drawings looked. I shaded and tinted while Cavor drew – smudged and haste-marked they were in every line, but wonderfully correct. We got out the orders for the steel blinds and frames we needed from that night's work, and the glass sphere was designed within a week. We gave up our afternoon conversations and our old routine altogether. We worked, and we slept and ate when we could work no longer for hunger and fatigue. Our enthusiasm infected even our three men, though they had no idea what the sphere was for. Through those days the man Gibbs gave up walking, and went everywhere, even across the room, at a sort of fussy run.

And it grew – the sphere. December passed, January – I spent a day with a broom sweeping a path through the snow from bungalow to laboratory – February, March. By the end of March the completion was in sight. In January had come a team of horses, a huge packing-case; we had our thick glass sphere now ready, and in position under the crane we had rigged to sling it into the steel shell. All the bars and blinds of the steel shell – it was not really a spherical shell, but polyhedral, with a roller blind to each facet – had arrived by February, and the lower half was bolted together. The Cavorite was half made by March, the metallic paste had gone through two of the stages in its manufacture, and we had plastered quite half of it on to the steel bars and blinds. It was astonishing how closely we kept to the lines of Cavor's first inspiration in working out the scheme. When the bolting together of the sphere was finished, he proposed to remove the rough roof of the temporary laboratory in which the work was done, and build a furnace about it. So the last stage of Cavorite making, in which the paste is heated to a dull red glow in a stream of helium, would be accomplished when it was already on the sphere.

And then we had to discuss and decide what provisions we were to take – compressed foods, concentrated essences, steel cylinders containing reserve oxygen, an arrangement for removing carbonic acid and waste from the air and restoring oxygen by means of sodium peroxide, water condensers, and so forth. I remember the little heap they made in the corner – tins, and rolls, and boxes – convincingly matter-of-fact.

It was a strenuous time, with little chance of thinking. But one day, when we were drawing near the end, an odd mood came over me.

I had been bricking up the furnace all the morning, and I sat down by these possessions dead beat. Everything seemed dull and incredible.

"But look here, Cavor," I said. "After all! What's it all for?"

He smiled. "The thing now is to go."

"The moon," I reflected. "But what do you expect? I thought the moon was a dead world."

He shrugged his shoulders.

"We're going to see."

"*Are* we?" I said, and stared before me.

"You are tired," he remarked. "You'd better take a walk this afternoon."

"No," I said obstinately; "I'm going to finish this brickwork."

And I did, and insured myself a night of insomnia. I don't think I have ever had such a night. I had some bad times before my business collapse, but the very worst of those was sweet slumber compared to this infinity of aching wakefulness. I was suddenly in the most enormous funk at the thing we were going to do.

I do not remember before that night thinking at all of the risks we were running. Now they came like that array of spectres that once beleaguered Prague, and camped around me. The strangeness of what we were about to do, the unearthliness of it, overwhelmed me. I was like a man awakened out of pleasant dreams to the most horrible surroundings. I lay, eyes wide open, and the sphere seemed to get more flimsy and feeble, and Cavor more unreal and fantastic, and the whole enterprise madder and madder every moment.

I got out of bed and wandered about. I sat at the window and stared at the immensity of space. Between the stars was the void, the unfathomable darkness! I tried to recall the fragmentary knowledge of astronomy I had gained in my irregular reading, but it was all too vague to furnish any idea of the things we might expect. At last I got back to bed and snatched some moments of sleep – moments of nightmare rather – in which I fell and fell and fell for evermore into the abyss of the sky.

I astonished Cavor at breakfast. I told him shortly, "I'm not coming with you in the sphere."

I met all his protests with a sullen persistence. "The thing's too mad," I said, "and I won't come. The thing's too mad."

I would not go with him to the laboratory. I fretted about my bungalow for a time, and then took hat and stick and set out alone, I knew not whither. It chanced to be a glorious morning: a warm wind and deep blue sky, the first green of spring abroad, and multitudes of birds singing. I lunched on beef and beer in a little public-house near Elham, and startled the landlord by remarking *apropos* of the weather, "A man who leaves the world when days of this sort are about is a fool!"

"That's what I says when I heerd on it!" said the landlord, and I found that for one poor soul at least this world had proved excessive, and there had been a throat-cutting. I went on with a new twist to my thoughts.

In the afternoon I had a pleasant sleep in a sunny place, and went on my way refreshed. I came to a comfortable-looking inn near Canterbury. It was bright with creepers, and the landlady was a clean old woman and took my eye. I found I had just enough money to pay for my lodging with her. I decided to stop the night there. She was a talkative body, and among many other particulars learnt she had never been to London. "Canterbury's as far as ever I been," she said. "I'm not one of your gad-about sort."

"How would you like a trip to the moon?" I cried.

"I never did hold with them ballooneys," she said evidently under the impression that this was a common excursion enough. "I wouldn't go up in one – not for ever so."

This struck me as being funny. After I had supped I sat on a bench by the door of the inn and gossiped with two labourers about brickmaking, and motor cars, and the cricket of last year. And in the sky a faint new crescent, blue and vague as a distant Alp, sank westward over the sun.

The next day I returned to Cavor. "I am coming," I said. "I've been a little out of order, that's all."

That was the only time I felt any serious doubt our enterprise. Nerves purely! After that I worked a little more carefully, and took a trudge for an hour every day. And at last, save for the heating in the furnace, our labours were at an end.

CHAPTER 4

Inside the Sphere

"**G**o on," said Cavor, as I sat across the edge of the manhole, and looked down into the black interior of the sphere. We two were alone. It was evening, the sun had set, and the stillness of the twilight was upon everything.

I drew my other leg inside and slid down the smooth glass to the bottom of the sphere, then turned to take the cans of food and other impedimenta from Cavor. The interior was warm, the thermometer stood at eighty, and as we should lose little or none of this by radiation, we were dressed in shoes and thin flannels. We had, however, a bundle of thick woollen clothing and several thick blankets to guard against mischance.

By Cavor's direction I placed the packages, the cylinders of oxygen, and so forth, loosely about my feet, and soon we had everything in. He walked about the roofless shed for a time seeking anything we had overlooked, and then crawled in after me. I noted something in his hand.

"What have you got there?" I asked.

"Haven't you brought anything to read?"

"Good Lord! No."

"I forgot to tell you. There are uncertainties— The voyage may last— We may be weeks!"

"But—"

"We shall be floating in this sphere with absolutely no occupation."

"I wish I'd known—"

He peered out of the manhole. "Look!" he said. "There's something there!"

"Is there time?"

"We shall be an hour."

I looked out. It was an old number of *Tit-Bits* that one of the men must have brought. Farther away in the corner I saw a torn *Lloyd's News*. I scrambled back into the sphere with these things. "What have you got?" I said.

I took the book from his hand and read, "The Works of William Shakespeare".

He coloured slightly. "My education has been so purely scientific—" he said apologetically.

"Never read him?"

"Never."

"He knew a little, you know – in an irregular sort of way."

"Precisely what I am told," said Cavor.

I assisted him to screw in the glass cover of the manhole, and then he pressed a stud to close the corresponding blind in the outer case. The little oblong of twilight vanished. We were in darkness. For a time neither of us spoke. Although our case would not be impervious to sound, everything was very still. I perceived there was nothing to grip when the shock of our start should come, and I realised that I should be uncomfortable for want of a chair.

"Why have we no chairs?" I asked.

"I've settled all that," said Cavor. "We won't need them."

"Why not?"

"You will see," he said, in the tone of a man who refuses to talk.

I became silent. Suddenly it had come to me clear and vivid that I was a fool to be inside that sphere. Even now, I asked myself, is to too late to withdraw? The world outside the sphere, I knew, would be cold and inhospitable enough for me – for weeks I had been living on subsidies from Cavor – but after all, would it be as cold as the infinite zero, as inhospitable as empty space? If it had not been for the appearance of cowardice, I believe that even then I should have made him let me out. But I hesitated on that score, and hesitated, and grew fretful and angry, and the time passed.

There came a little jerk, a noise like champagne being uncorked in another room, and a faint whistling sound. For just one instant I had a sense of enormous tension, a transient conviction that my feet were pressing downward with a force of countless tons. It lasted for an infinitesimal time.

But it stirred me to action. "Cavor!" I said into the darkness, "my nerve's in rags. I don't think—"

I stopped. He made no answer.

"Confound it!" I cried; "I'm a fool! What business have I here? I'm not coming, Cavor. The thing's too risky. I'm getting out."

"You can't," he said.

"Can't! We'll soon see about that!"

He made no answer for ten seconds. "It's too late for us to quarrel now, Bedford," he said. "That little jerk was the start. Already we are flying as swiftly as a bullet up into the gulf of space."

"I—" I said, and then it didn't seem to matter what happened. For a time I was, as it were, stunned; I had nothing to say. It was just as if I had never heard of this idea of leaving the world before. Then I perceived an unaccountable change in my bodily sensations. It was a feeling of lightness, of unreality. Coupled with that was a queer sensation in the head, an apoplectic effect almost, and a thumping of blood vessels at the ears. Neither of these feelings diminished as time went on, but at last I got so used to them that I experienced no inconvenience.

I heard a click, and a little glow lamp came into being.

I saw Cavor's face, as white as I felt my own to be. We regarded one another in silence. The transparent blackness of the glass behind him made him seem as though he floated in a void.

"Well, we're committed," I said at last.

"Yes," he said, "we're committed."

"Don't move," he exclaimed, at some suggestion of a gesture. "Let your muscles keep quite lax – as if you were in bed. We are in a little universe of our own. Look at those things!"

He pointed to the loose cases and bundles that had been lying on the blankets in the bottom of the sphere. I was astonished to see that they were floating now nearly a foot from the spherical wall. Then I saw from his shadow that Cavor was no longer leaning against the glass. I thrust out my hand behind me, and found that I too was suspended in space, clear of the glass.

I did not cry out nor gesticulate, but fear came upon me. It was like being held and lifted by something – you know not what. The mere touch of my hand against the glass moved me rapidly. I understood what had happened, but that did not prevent my being afraid. We were cut off from all exterior gravitation, only the attraction of objects within our sphere had effect. Consequently everything that was not fixed to the glass was falling – slowly because of the slightness of our masses – towards the centre of gravity of our little world, which seemed to be somewhere about the middle of the sphere, but rather nearer to myself than Cavor, on account of my greater weight.

"We must turn round," said Cavor, "and float back to back, with the things between us."

It was the strangest sensation conceivable, floating thus loosely in space, at first indeed horribly strange, and when the horror passed, not disagreeable at all, exceeding restful; indeed, the nearest thing in earthly experience to it that I know is lying on a very thick, soft feather bed. But the quality of utter detachment and independence! I had not reckoned on things like this. I had expected a violent jerk at starting, a giddy sense of speed. Instead I felt – as if I were disembodied. It was not like the beginning of a journey; it was like the beginning of a dream.

CHAPTER 5

The Journey to the Moon

Presently Cavor extinguished the light. He said we had not overmuch energy stored, and that what we had we must economise for reading. For a time, whether it was long or short I do not know, there was nothing but blank darkness.

A question floated up out of the void. "How are we pointing?" I said. "What is our direction?"

"We are flying away from the earth at a tangent, and as the moon is near her third quarter we are going somewhere towards her. I will open a blind—"

Came a click, and then a window in the outer case yawned open. The sky outside was as black as the darkness within the sphere, but the shape of the open window was marked by an infinite number of stars.

Those who have only seen the starry sky from the earth cannot imagine its appearance when the vague, half luminous veil of our air has been withdrawn. The stars we see on earth are the mere scattered survivors that penetrate our misty atmosphere. But now at last I could realise the meaning of the hosts of heaven!

Stranger things we were presently to see, but that airless, star-dusted sky! Of all things, I think that will be one of the last I shall forget.

The little window vanished with a click, another beside it snapped open and instantly closed, and then a third, and for a moment I had to close my eyes because of the blinding splendour of the waning moon.

For a space I had to stare at Cavor and the white-lit things about me to season my eyes to light again, before I could turn them towards that pallid glare.

Four windows were open in order that the gravitation of the moon might act upon all the substances in our sphere. I found I was no longer floating freely in space, but that my feet were resting on the glass in the direction of the moon. The blankets and cases of provisions were also creeping slowly down the glass, and presently came to rest so as to block out a portion of the view. It seemed to me, of course, that I looked "down" when I looked at the moon. On earth "down" means earthward, the way things fall, and "up" the reverse direction. Now the pull of gravitation was towards the moon, and for all I knew to the contrary our earth was overhead. And, of course, when all the Cavorite blinds were closed, "down" was towards the centre of our sphere, and "up" towards its outer wall.

It was curiously unlike earthly experience, too, to have the light coming *up* to one. On earth light falls from above, or comes slanting down sideways, but here it came from beneath our feet, and to see our shadows we had to look up.

At first it gave me a sort of vertigo to stand only on thick glass and look down upon the moon through hundreds of thousands of miles of vacant space; but this sickness passed very speedily. And then – the splendour of the sight!

The reader may imagine it best if he will lie on the ground some warm summer's night and look between his upraised feet at the moon, but for some reason, probably because the absence of air made it so much more luminous, the moon seemed already considerably larger than it does from earth. The minutest details of its surface were acutely clear. And since we did not see it through air, its outline was bright and sharp, there was no glow or halo about it, and the star-dust that covered the sky came right to its very margin, and marked the outline of its unilluminated part. And as I stood and stared at the moon between my feet, that perception of the impossible that had been with me off and on ever since our start, returned again with tenfold conviction.

"Cavor," I said, "this takes me queerly. Those companies we were going to run, and all that about minerals?"

"Well?"

"I don't see 'em here."

"No," said Cavor; "but you'll get over all that."

"I suppose I'm made to turn right side up again. Still, *this*— For a moment I could half believe there never was a world."

"That copy of *Lloyd's News* might help you."

I stared at the paper for a moment, then held it above the level of my face, and found I could read it quite easily. I struck a column of mean little advertisements. "A gentleman of private means is willing to lend money," I read. I knew that gentleman. Then somebody eccentric wanted to sell a Cutaway bicycle, "quite new and cost 15 pounds," for five pounds; and a lady in distress wished to dispose of some fish knives and forks, "a wedding present," at a great sacrifice. No doubt some simple soul was sagely examining these knives and forks, and another triumphantly riding off on that bicycle, and a third trustfully consulting that benevolent gentleman of means even as I read. I laughed, and let the paper drift from my hand.

"Are we visible from the earth?" I asked.

"Why?"

"I knew some one who was rather interested in astronomy. It occurred to me that it would be rather odd if – my friend – chanced to be looking through some telescope."

"It would need the most powerful telescope on earth even now to see us as the minutest speck."

For a time I stared in silence at the moon.

"It's a world," I said; "one feels that infinitely more than one ever did on earth. People perhaps—"

"People!" he exclaimed. "*No!* Banish all that! Think yourself a sort of ultra-arctic voyager exploring the desolate places of space. Look at it!"

He waved his hand at the shining whiteness below. "It's dead – dead! Vast extinct volcanoes, lava wildernesses, tumbled wastes of snow, or frozen carbonic acid, or frozen air, and everywhere landslip seams and cracks and gulfs. Nothing happens. Men have watched this planet systematically with telescopes for over two hundred years. How much change do you think they have seen?"

"None."

"They have traced two indisputable landslips, a doubtful crack, and one slight periodic change of colour, and that's all."

"I didn't know they'd traced even that."

"Oh, yes. But as for people—!"

"By the way," I asked, "how small a thing will the biggest telescopes show upon the moon?"

"One could see a fair-sized church. One could certainly see any towns or buildings, or anything like the handiwork of men. There might perhaps be insects, something in the way of ants, for example, so that they could hide in deep burrows from the lunar light, or some new sort of creatures having no earthly parallel. That is the most probable thing, if we are to find life there at all. Think of the difference in conditions! Life must fit itself to a day as long as fourteen earthly days, a cloudless sun-blaze of fourteen days, and then a night of equal length, growing ever colder and colder under these cold, sharp stars.

In that night there must be cold, the ultimate cold, absolute zero, 273 degrees Centigrade, below the earthly freezing point. Whatever life there is must hibernate through *that*, and rise again each day."

He mused. "One can imagine something worm-like," he said, "taking its air solid as an earth-worm swallows earth, or thick-skinned monsters—"

"By the bye," I said, "why didn't we bring a gun?"

He did not answer that question. "No," he concluded, "we just have to go. We shall see when we get there."

I remembered something. "Of course, there's my minerals, anyhow," I said; "whatever the conditions may be."

Presently he told me he wished to alter our course a little by letting the earth tug at us for a moment. He was going to open one earthward blind for thirty seconds. He warned me that it would make my head swim, and advised me to extend my hands against the glass to break my fall. I did as he directed, and thrust my feet against the bales of food cases and air cylinders to prevent their falling upon me. Then with a click the window flew open. I fell clumsily upon hands and face, and saw for a moment between my black extended fingers our mother earth – a planet in a downward sky.

We were still very near – Cavor told me the distance was perhaps eight hundred miles and the huge terrestrial disc filled all heaven. But already it was plain to see that the world was a globe. The land below us was in twilight and vague, but westward the vast gray stretches of the Atlantic shone like molten silver under the receding day. I think I recognised the cloud-dimmed coast-lines of France and Spain and the south of England, and then, with a click, the shutter closed again, and I found myself in a state of extraordinary confusion sliding slowly over the smooth glass.

When at last things settled themselves in my mind again, it seemed quite beyond question that the moon was "down" and under my feet, and that the earth was somewhere away on the level of the horizon – the earth that had been "down" to me and my kindred since the beginning of things.

So slight were the exertions required of us, so easy did the practical annihilation of our weight make all we had to do, that the necessity for taking refreshment did not occur to us for nearly six hours (by Cavor's chronometer) after our start. I was amazed at that lapse of time. Even then I was satisfied with very little. Cavor examined the apparatus for absorbing carbonic acid and water, and pronounced it to be in satisfactory order, our consumption of oxygen having been extraordinarily slight. And our talk being exhausted for the time, and there being nothing further for us to do, we gave way to a curious drowsiness that had come upon us, and spreading our blankets on the bottom of the sphere in such a manner as to shut out most of the moonlight, wished each other good-night, and almost immediately fell asleep.

And so, sleeping, and sometimes talking and reading a little, and at times eating, although without any keenness of appetite,* but for the most part in a sort of quiescence that was neither waking nor slumber, we fell through a space of time that had neither night nor day in it, silently, softly, and swiftly down towards the moon.

[* Footnote: It is a curious thing, that while we were in the sphere we felt not the slightest desire for food, nor did we feel the want of it when we abstained. At first we forced our appetites, but afterwards we fasted completely. Altogether we did not consume one-hundredth part of the compressed provisions we had brought with us. The amount of carbonic acid we breathed was also unnaturally low, but why this was, I am quite unable to explain.]

CHAPTER 6

The Landing on the Moon

I remember how one day Cavor suddenly opened six of our shutters and blinded me so that I cried aloud at him. The whole area was moon, a stupendous scimitar of white dawn with its edge hacked out by notches of darkness, the crescent shore of an ebbing tide of darkness, out of which peaks and pinnacles came glittering into the blaze of the sun. I take it the reader has seen pictures or photographs of the moon and that I need not describe the broader features of that landscape, those spacious ring-like ranges vaster than any terrestrial mountains, their summits shining in the day, their shadows harsh and deep, the gray disordered plains, the ridges, hills, and craterlets, all passing at last from a blazing illumination into a common mystery of black. Athwart this world we were flying scarcely a hundred miles above its crests and pinnacles. And now we could see, what no eye on earth will ever see, that under the blaze of the day the harsh outlines of the rocks and ravines of the plains and crater floor grew gray and indistinct under a thickening haze, that the white of their lit surfaces broke into lumps and patches, and broke again and shrank and vanished, and that here and there strange tints of brown and olive grew and spread.

But little time we had for watching then. For now we had come to the real danger of our journey. We had to drop ever closer to the moon as we spun about it, to slacken our pace and watch our chance, until at last we could dare to drop upon its surface.

For Cavor that was a time of intense exertion; for me it was an anxious inactivity. I seemed perpetually to be getting out of his way. He leapt about the sphere from point to point with an agility that would have been impossible on earth. He was perpetually opening and closing the Cavorite windows, making calculations, consulting his chronometer by means of the glow lamp during those last eventful hours. For a long time we had all our windows closed and hung silently in darkness hurling through space.

Then he was feeling for the shutter studs, and suddenly four windows were open. I staggered and covered my eyes, drenched and scorched and blinded by the unaccustomed splendour of the sun beneath my feet. Then again the shutters snapped, leaving my brain spinning in a darkness that pressed against the eyes. And after that I floated in another vast, black silence.

Then Cavor switched on the electric light, and told me he proposed to bind all our luggage together with the blankets about it, against the concussion of our descent. We did this with our windows closed, because in that way our goods arranged themselves naturally at the centre of the sphere. That too was a strange business; we two men floating loose in that spherical space, and packing and pulling ropes. Imagine it if you can! No up nor down, and every effort resulting in unexpected movements. Now I would be pressed against the glass with the full force of Cavor's thrust, now I would be kicking helplessly in a void. Now the star of the electric light would be overhead, now under foot. Now Cavor's feet would float up before my eyes, and now we would be crossways to each other. But at last our goods were safely bound together in a big soft bale, all except two blankets with head holes that we were to wrap about ourselves.

Then for a flash Cavor opened a window moonward, and we saw that we were dropping towards a huge central crater with a number of minor craters grouped in a sort of cross about it. And then again Cavor flung our little sphere open to the scorching, blinding sun. I think he was using the sun's attraction as a brake. "Cover yourself with a blanket," he cried, thrusting himself from me, and for a moment I did not understand.

Then I hauled the blanket from beneath my feet and got it about me and over my head and eyes. Abruptly he closed the shutters again, snapped one open again and closed it, then suddenly began snapping them all open, each safely into its steel roller. There came a jar, and then we were rolling over and over, bumping against the glass and against the big bale of our luggage, and clutching at each other, and outside some white substance splashed as if we were rolling down a slope of snow....

Over, clutch, bump, clutch, bump, over....

Came a thud, and I was half buried under the bale of our possessions, and for a space everything was still. Then I could hear Cavor puffing and grunting, and the snapping of a shutter in its sash. I made an effort, thrust back our blanket-wrapped luggage, and emerged from beneath it. Our open windows were just visible as a deeper black set with stars.

We were still alive, and we were lying in the darkness of the shadow of the wall of the great crater into which we had fallen.

We sat getting our breath again, and feeling the bruises on our limbs. I don't think either of us had had a very clear expectation of such rough handling as we had received. I struggled painfully to my feet. "And now," said I, "to look at the landscape of the moon! But—! It's tremendously dark, Cavor!"

The glass was dewy, and as I spoke I wiped at it with my blanket. "We're half an hour or so beyond the day," he said. "We must wait."

It was impossible to distinguish anything. We might have been in a sphere of steel for all that we could see. My rubbing with the blanket simply smeared the glass, and as fast as I wiped it, it became opaque again with freshly condensed moisture mixed with an increasing quantity of blanket hairs. Of course I ought not to have used the blanket. In my efforts to clear the glass I slipped upon the damp surface, and hurt my shin against one of the oxygen cylinders that protruded from our bale.

The thing was exasperating – it was absurd. Here we were just arrived upon the moon, amidst we knew not what wonders, and all we could see was the gray and streaming wall of the bubble in which we had come.

"Confound it!" I said, "but at this rate we might have stopped at home;" and I squatted on the bale and shivered, and drew my blanket closer about me.

Abruptly the moisture turned to spangles and fronds of frost. "Can you reach the electric heater," said Cavor. "Yes – that black knob. Or we shall freeze."

I did not wait to be told twice. "And now," said I, "what are we to do?"

"Wait," he said.

"Wait?"

"Of course. We shall have to wait until our air gets warm again, and then this glass will clear. We can't do anything till then. It's night here yet; we must wait for the day to overtake us. Meanwhile, don't you feel hungry?"

For a space I did not answer him, but sat fretting. I turned reluctantly from the smeared puzzle of the glass and stared at his face. "Yes," I said, "I am hungry. I feel somehow enormously disappointed. I had expected – I don't know what I had expected, but not this."

I summoned my philosophy, and rearranging my blanket about me sat down on the bale again and began my first meal on the moon. I don't think I finished it – I forget. Presently, first in patches, then running rapidly together into wider spaces, came the clearing of the glass, came the drawing of the misty veil that hid the moon world from our eyes.

We peered out upon the landscape of the moon.

CHAPTER 7

Sunrise on the Moon

As we saw it first it was the wildest and most desolate of scenes. We were in an enormous amphitheatre, a vast circular plain, the floor of the giant crater. Its cliff-like walls closed us in on every side. From the westward the light of the unseen sun fell upon them, reaching to the very foot of the cliff, and showed a disordered escarpment of drab and grayish rock, lined here and there with banks and crevices of snow. This was perhaps a dozen miles away, but at first no intervening atmosphere diminished in the slightest the minutely detailed brilliancy with which these things glared at us. They stood out clear and dazzling against a background of starry blackness that seemed to our earthly eyes rather a gloriously spangled velvet curtain than the spaciousness of the sky.

The eastward cliff was at first merely a starless selvedge to the starry dome. No rosy flush, no creeping pallor, announced the commencing day. Only the Corona, the Zodiacal light, a huge cone-shaped, luminous haze, pointing up towards the splendour of the morning star, warned us of the imminent nearness of the sun.

Whatever light was about us was reflected by the westward cliffs. It showed a huge undulating plain, cold and gray, a gray that deepened eastward into the absolute raven darkness of the cliff shadow. Innumerable rounded gray summits, ghostly hummocks, billows of snowy substance, stretching crest beyond crest into the remote obscurity, gave us our first inkling of the distance of the crater wall. These hummocks looked like snow. At the time I thought they were snow. But they were not – they were mounds and masses of frozen air.

So it was at first; and then, sudden, swift, and amazing, came the lunar day.

The sunlight had crept down the cliff, it touched the drifted masses at its base and incontinently came striding with seven-leagued boots towards us. The distant cliff seemed to shift and quiver, and at the touch of the dawn a reek of gray vapour poured upward from the crater floor, whirls and puffs and drifting wraiths of gray, thicker and broader and denser, until at last the whole westward plain was steaming like a wet handkerchief held before the fire, and the westward cliffs were no more than refracted glare beyond.

"It is air," said Cavor. "It must be air – or it would not rise like this – at the mere touch of a sun-beam. And at this pace...."

He peered upwards. "Look!" he said.

"What?" I asked.

"In the sky. Already. On the blackness – a little touch of blue. See! The stars seem larger. And the little ones and all those dim nebulosities we saw in empty space – they are hidden!"

Swiftly, steadily, the day approached us. Gray summit after gray summit was overtaken by the blaze, and turned to a smoking white intensity. At last there was nothing to the west of us but a bank of surging fog, the tumultuous advance and ascent of cloudy haze. The distant cliff had receded farther and farther, had loomed and changed through the whirl, and foundered and vanished at last in its confusion.

Nearer came that steaming advance, nearer and nearer, coming as fast as the shadow of a cloud before the south-west wind. About us rose a thin anticipatory haze.

Cavor gripped my arm. "What?" I said.

"Look! The sunrise! The sun!"

He turned me about and pointed to the brow of the eastward cliff, looming above the haze about us, scarce lighter than the darkness of the sky. But now its line was marked by strange reddish shapes, tongues of vermilion flame that writhed and danced. I fancied it must be spirals of vapour that had caught the light and made this crest of fiery tongues against the sky, but indeed it was the solar prominences I saw, a crown of fire about the sun that is forever hidden from earthly eyes by our atmospheric veil.

And then – the sun!

Steadily, inevitably came a brilliant line, came a thin edge of intolerable effulgence that took a circular shape, became a bow, became a blazing sceptre, and hurled a shaft of heat at us as though it was a spear.

It seemed verily to stab my eyes! I cried aloud and turned about blinded, groping for my blanket beneath the bale.

And with that incandescence came a sound, the first sound that had reached us from without since we left the earth, a hissing and rustling, the stormy trailing of the aerial garment of the advancing day. And with the coming of the sound and the light the sphere lurched, and blinded and dazzled we staggered helplessly against each other. It lurched again, and the hissing grew louder. I had shut my eyes perforce, I was making clumsy efforts to cover my head with my blanket, and this second lurch sent me helplessly off my feet. I fell against the bale, and opening my eyes had a momentary glimpse of the air just outside our glass. It was running – it was boiling – like snow into which a white-hot rod is thrust. What had been solid air had suddenly at the touch of the sun become a paste, a mud, a slushy liquefaction, that hissed and bubbled into gas.

There came a still more violent whirl of the sphere and we had clutched one another. In another moment we were spun about again.

Round we went and over, and then I was on all fours. The lunar dawn had hold of us. It meant to show us little men what the moon could do with us.

I caught a second glimpse of things without, puffs of vapour, half liquid slush, excavated, sliding, falling, sliding. We dropped into darkness. I went down with Cavor's knees in my chest. Then he seemed to fly away from me, and for a moment I lay with all the breath out of my body staring upward. A toppling crag of the melting stuff had splashed over us, buried us, and now it thinned and boiled off us. I saw the bubbles dancing on the glass above. I heard Cavor exclaiming feebly.

Then some huge landslip in the thawing air had caught us, and spluttering expostulation, we began to roll down a slope, rolling faster and faster, leaping crevasses and rebounding from banks, faster and faster, westward into the white-hot boiling tumult of the lunar day.

Clutching at one another we spun about, pitched this way and that, our bale of packages leaping at us, pounding at us. We collided, we gripped, we were torn asunder – our heads met, and the whole universe burst into fiery darts and stars! On the earth we should have smashed one another a dozen times, but on the moon, luckily for us, our weight was only one-sixth of what it is terrestrially, and we fell very mercifully. I recall a sensation of utter sickness, a feeling as if my brain were upside down within my skull, and then—

Something was at work upon my face, some thin feelers worried my ears. Then I discovered the brilliance of the landscape around was mitigated by blue spectacles. Cavor bent over me, and I saw his face upside down, his eyes also protected by tinted goggles. His breath came irregularly, and his lip was bleeding from a bruise. "Better?" he said, wiping the blood with the back of his hand.

Everything seemed swaying for a space, but that was simply my giddiness. I perceived that he had closed some of the shutters in the outer sphere to save me – from the direct blaze of the sun. I was aware that everything about us was very brilliant.

"Lord!" I gasped. "But this—"

I craned my neck to see. I perceived there was a blinding glare outside, an utter change from the gloomy darkness of our first impressions. "Have I been insensible long?" I asked.

"I don't know – the chronometer is broken. Some little time…. My dear chap! I have been afraid…"

I lay for a space taking this in. I saw his face still bore evidences of emotion. For a while I said nothing. I passed an inquisitive hand over my contusions, and surveyed his face for similar damages. The back of my right hand had suffered most, and was skinless and raw. My forehead was bruised and had bled. He handed me a little measure with some of the restorative – I forget the name of it – he had brought with us. After a time I felt a little better. I began to stretch my limbs carefully. Soon I could talk.

"It wouldn't have done," I said, as though there had been no interval.

"No! it *wouldn't*."

He thought, his hands hanging over his knees. He peered through the glass and then stared at me.

"Good Lord!" he said. "*No!*"

"What has happened?" I asked after a pause. "Have we jumped to the tropics?"

"It was as I expected. This air has evaporated – if it is air. At any rate, it has evaporated, and the surface of the moon is showing. We are lying on a bank of earthy rock. Here and there bare soil is exposed. A queer sort of soil!"

It occurred to him that it was unnecessary to explain. He assisted me into a sitting position, and I could see with my own eyes.

CHAPTER 8

A Lunar Morning

The harsh emphasis, the pitiless black and white of scenery had altogether disappeared. The glare of the sun had taken upon itself a faint tinge of amber; the shadows upon the cliff of the crater wall were deeply purple. To the eastward a dark bank of fog still crouched and sheltered from the sunrise, but to the westward the sky was blue and clear. I began to realise the length of my insensibility.

We were no longer in a void. An atmosphere had arisen about us. The outline of things had gained in character, had grown acute and varied; save for a shadowed space of white substance here and there, white substance that was no longer air but snow, the arctic appearance had gone altogether. Everywhere broad rusty brown spaces of bare and tumbled earth spread to the blaze of the sun. Here and there at the edge of the snowdrifts were transient little pools and eddies of water, the only things stirring in that expanse of barrenness. The sunlight inundated the upper two blinds of our sphere and turned our climate to high summer, but our feet were still in shadow, and the sphere was lying upon a drift of snow.

And scattered here and there upon the slope, and emphasised by little white threads of unthawed snow upon their shady sides, were shapes like sticks, dry twisted sticks of the same rusty hue as the rock upon which they lay. That caught one's thoughts sharply. Sticks! On a lifeless world? Then as my eye grew more accustomed to the texture of their substance, I perceived that almost all this surface had a fibrous texture, like the carpet of brown needles one finds beneath the shade of pine trees.

"Cavor!" I said.

"Yes."

"It may be a dead world now – but once–"

Something arrested my attention. I had discovered among these needles a number of little round objects. And it seemed to me that one of these had moved. "Cavor," I whispered.

"What?"

But I did not answer at once. I stared incredulous. For an instant I could not believe my eyes. I gave an inarticulate cry. I gripped his arm. I pointed. "Look!" I cried, finding my tongue. "There! Yes! And there!"

His eyes followed my pointing finger. "Eh?" he said.

How can I describe the thing I saw? It is so petty a thing to state, and yet it seemed so wonderful, so pregnant with emotion. I have said that amidst the stick-like litter were these rounded bodies, these little oval bodies that might have passed as very small pebbles. And now first one and then another had stirred, had rolled over and cracked, and down the crack of each of them showed a minute line of yellowish green, thrusting outward to meet the hot encouragement of the newly-risen sun. For a moment that was all, and then there stirred, and burst a third!

"It is a seed," said Cavor. And then I heard him whisper very softly, "*Life*!"

"Life!" And immediately it poured upon us that our vast journey had not been made in vain, that we had come to no arid waste of minerals, but to a world that lived and moved! We watched intensely.

I remember I kept rubbing the glass before me with my sleeve, jealous of the faintest suspicion of mist.

The picture was clear and vivid only in the middle of the field. All about that centre the dead fibres and seeds were magnified and distorted by the curvature of the glass. But we could see enough! One after another all down the sunlit slope these miraculous little brown bodies burst and gaped apart, like seed-pods, like the husks of fruits; opened eager mouths. that drank in the heat and light pouring in a cascade from the newly-risen sun.

Every moment more of these seed coats ruptured, and even as they did so the swelling pioneers overflowed their rent-distended seed-cases, and passed into the second stage of growth. With a steady assurance, a swift deliberation, these amazing seeds thrust a rootlet downward to the earth and a queer little bundle-like bud into the air. In a little while the whole slope was dotted with minute plantlets standing at attention in the blaze of the sun.

They did not stand for long. The bundle-like buds swelled and strained and opened with a jerk, thrusting out a coronet of little sharp tips, spreading a whorl of tiny, spiky, brownish leaves, that lengthened rapidly, lengthened visibly even as we watched. The movement was slower than any animal's, swifter than any plant's I have ever seen before. How can I suggest it to you – the way that growth went on? The leaf tips grew so that they moved onward even while we looked at them. The brown seed-case shrivelled and was absorbed with an equal rapidity. Have you ever on a cold day taken a thermometer into your warm hand and watched the little thread of mercury creep up the tube? These moon plants grew like that.

In a few minutes, as it seemed, the buds of the more forward of these plants had lengthened into a stem and were even putting forth a second whorl of leaves, and all the slope that had seemed so recently a lifeless stretch of litter was now dark with the stunted olive-green herbage of bristling spikes that swayed with the vigour of their growing.

I turned about, and behold! along the upper edge of a rock to the eastward a similar fringe in a scarcely less forward condition swayed and bent, dark against the blinding glare of the sun. And beyond this fringe was the silhouette of a plant mass, branching clumsily like a cactus, and swelling visibly, swelling like a bladder that fills with air.

Then to the westward also I discovered that another such distended form was rising over the scrub. But here the light fell upon its sleek sides, and I could see that its colour was a vivid orange hue. It rose as one watched it; if one looked away from it for a minute and then back, its outline had changed; it thrust out blunt congested branches until in a little time it rose a coralline shape of many feet in height. Compared with such a growth the terrestrial puff-ball, which will sometimes swell a foot in diameter in a single night, would be a hopeless laggard. But then the puff-ball grows against a gravitational pull six times that of the moon. Beyond, out of gullies and flats that had been hidden from us, but not from the quickening sun, over reefs and banks of shining rock, a bristling beard of spiky and fleshy vegetation was straining into view, hurrying tumultuously to take advantage of the brief day in which it must flower and fruit and seed again and die. It was like a miracle, that growth. So, one must imagine, the trees and plants arose at the Creation and covered the desolation of the new-made earth.

Imagine it! Imagine that dawn! The resurrection of the frozen air, the stirring and quickening of the soil, and then this silent uprising of vegetation, this unearthly ascent of fleshiness and spikes. Conceive it all lit by a blaze that would make the intensest sunlight of earth seem watery and weak. And still around this stirring jungle, wherever there was shadow, lingered banks of bluish snow. And to have the picture of our impression complete, you must bear in mind that we saw it all through a thick bent glass, distorting it as things are distorted by a lens, acute only in the centre of the picture, and very bright there, and towards the edges magnified and unreal.

CHAPTER 9

Prospecting Begins

We ceased to gaze. We turned to each other, the same thought, the same question in our eyes. For these plants to grow, there must be some air, however attenuated, air that we also should be able to breathe.

"The manhole?" I said.

"Yes!" said Cavor, "if it is air we see!"

"In a little while," I said, "these plants will be as high as we are. Suppose – suppose after all– Is it certain? How do you know that stuff *is* air? It may be nitrogen – it may be carbonic acid even!"

"That's easy," he said, and set about proving it. He produced a big piece of crumpled paper from the bale, lit it, and thrust it hastily through the man-hole valve. I bent forward and peered down through the thick glass for its appearance outside, that little flame on whose evidence depended so much!

I saw the paper drop out and lie lightly upon the snow. The pink flame of its burning vanished. For an instant it seemed to be extinguished. And then I saw a little blue tongue upon the edge of it that trembled, and crept, and spread!

Quietly the whole sheet, save where it lay in immediate contact with the snow, charred and shrivelled and sent up a quivering thread of smoke. There was no doubt left to me; the atmosphere of the moon was either pure oxygen or air, and capable therefore – unless its tenuity was excessive – of supporting our alien life. We might emerge – and live!

I sat down with my legs on either side of the manhole and prepared to unscrew it, but Cavor stopped me. "There is first a little precaution," he said. He pointed out that although it was certainly an oxygenated atmosphere outside, it might still be so rarefied as to cause us grave injury. He reminded me of mountain sickness, and of the bleeding that often afflicts aeronauts who have ascended too swiftly, and he spent some time in the preparation of a sickly-tasting drink which he insisted on my sharing. It made me feel a little numb, but otherwise had no effect on me. Then he permitted me to begin unscrewing.

Presently the glass stopper of the manhole was so far undone that the denser air within our sphere began to escape along the thread of the screw, singing as a kettle sings before it boils. Thereupon he made me desist. It speedily became evident that the pressure outside was very much less than it was within. How much less it was we had no means of telling.

I sat grasping the stopper with both hands, ready to close it again if, in spite of our intense hope, the lunar atmosphere should after all prove too rarefied for us, and Cavor sat with a cylinder of compressed oxygen at hand to restore our pressure. We looked at one another in silence, and then at the fantastic vegetation that swayed and grew visibly and noiselessly without. And ever that shrill piping continued.

My blood-vessels began to throb in my ears, and the sound of Cavor's movements diminished. I noted how still everything had become, because of the thinning of the air.

As our air sizzled out from the screw the moisture of it condensed in little puffs.

Presently I experienced a peculiar shortness of breath that lasted indeed during the whole of the time of our exposure to the moon's exterior atmosphere, and a rather unpleasant sensation about the ears and finger-nails and the back of the throat grew upon my attention, and presently passed off again.

But then came vertigo and nausea that abruptly changed the quality of my courage. I gave the lid of the manhole half a turn and made a hasty explanation to Cavor; but now he was the more sanguine. He answered me in a voice that seemed extraordinarily small and remote, because of the thinness of the air that carried the sound. He recommended a nip of brandy, and set me the example, and presently I felt better. I turned the manhole stopper back again. The throbbing in my ears grew louder, and then I remarked that the piping note of the outrush had ceased. For a time I could not be sure that it had ceased.

"Well?" said Cavor, in the ghost of a voice.

"Well?" said I.

"Shall we go on?"

I thought. "Is this all?"

"If you can stand it."

By way of answer I went on unscrewing. I lifted the circular operculum from its place and laid it carefully on the bale. A flake or so of snow whirled and vanished as that thin and unfamiliar air took possession of our sphere. I knelt, and then seated myself at the edge of the manhole, peering over it. Beneath, within a yard of my face, lay the untrodden snow of the moon.

There came a little pause. Our eyes met.

"It doesn't distress your lungs too much?" said Cavor.

"No," I said. "I can stand this."

He stretched out his hand for his blanket, thrust his head through its central hole, and wrapped it about him. He sat down on the edge of the manhole, he let his feet drop until they were within six inches of the lunar ground. He hesitated for a moment, then thrust himself forward, dropped these intervening inches, and stood upon the untrodden soil of the moon.

As he stepped forward he was refracted grotesquely by the edge of the glass. He stood for a moment looking this way and that. Then he drew himself together and leapt.

The glass distorted everything, but it seemed to me even then to be an extremely big leap. He had at one bound become remote. He seemed twenty or thirty feet off. He was standing high upon a rocky mass and gesticulating back to me. Perhaps he was shouting – but the sound did not reach me. But how the deuce had he done this? I felt like a man who has just seen a new conjuring trick.

In a puzzled state of mind I too dropped through the manhole. I stood up. Just in front of me the snowdrift had fallen away and made a sort of ditch. I made a step and jumped.

I found myself flying through the air, saw the rock on which he stood coming to meet me, clutched it and clung in a state of infinite amazement.

I gasped a painful laugh. I was tremendously confused. Cavor bent down and shouted in piping tones for me to be careful.

I had forgotten that on the moon, with only an eighth part of the earth's mass and a quarter of its diameter, my weight was barely a sixth what it was on earth. But now that fact insisted on being remembered.

"We are out of Mother Earth's leading-strings now," he said.

With a guarded effort I raised myself to the top, and moving as cautiously as a rheumatic patient, stood up beside him under the blaze of the sun. The sphere lay behind us on its dwindling snowdrift thirty feet away.

As far as the eye could see over the enormous disorder of rocks that formed the crater floor, the same bristling scrub that surrounded us was starting into life, diversified here and there by bulging masses of a cactus form, and scarlet and purple lichens that grew so fast they seemed to crawl over the rocks. The whole area of the crater seemed to me then to be one similar wilderness up to the very foot of the surrounding cliff.

This cliff was apparently bare of vegetation save at its base, and with buttresses and terraces and platforms that did not very greatly attract our attention at the time. It was many miles away from us in every direction; we seemed to be almost at the centre of the crater, and we saw it through a certain haziness that drove before the wind. For there was even a wind now in the thin air, a swift yet weak wind that chilled exceedingly but exerted little pressure. It was blowing round the crater, as it seemed, to the hot illuminated side from the foggy darkness under the sunward wall. It was difficult to look into this eastward fog; we had to peer with half-closed eyes beneath the shade of our hands, because of the fierce intensity of the motionless sun.

"It seems to be deserted," said Cavor, "absolutely desolate."

I looked about me again. I retained even then a clinging hope of some quasi-human evidence, some pinnacle of building, some house or engine, but everywhere one looked spread the tumbled rocks in peaks and crests, and the darting scrub and those bulging cacti that swelled and swelled, a flat negation as it seemed of all such hope.

"It looks as though these plants had it to themselves," I said. "I see no trace of any other creature."

"No insects – no birds, no! Not a trace, not a scrap nor particle of animal life. If there was – what would they do in the night? ... No; there's just these plants alone."

I shaded my eyes with my hand. "It's like the landscape of a dream. These things are less like earthly land plants than the things one imagines among the rocks at the bottom of the sea. Look at that yonder! One might imagine it a lizard changed into a plant. And the glare!"

"This is only the fresh morning," said Cavor.

He sighed and looked about him. "This is no world for men," he said. "And yet in a way – it appeals."

He became silent for a time, then commenced his meditative humming.

I started at a gentle touch, and found a thin sheet of livid lichen lapping over my shoe. I kicked at it and it fell to powder, and each speck began to grow.

I heard Cavor exclaim sharply, and perceived that one of the fixed bayonets of the scrub had pricked him. He hesitated, his eyes sought among the rocks about us. A sudden blaze of pink had crept up a ragged pillar of crag. It was a most extraordinary pink, a livid magenta.

"Look!" said I, turning, and behold Cavor had vanished.

For an instant I stood transfixed. Then I made a hasty step to look over the verge of the rock. But in my surprise at his disappearance I forgot once more that we were on the moon. The thrust of my foot that I made in striding would have carried me a yard on earth; on the moon it carried me six – a good five yards over the edge. For the moment the thing had something of the effect of those nightmares when one falls and falls. For while one falls sixteen feet in the first second of a fall on earth, on the moon one falls two, and with only a sixth of one's weight. I fell, or rather I jumped down, about ten yards I suppose. It seemed to take quite a long time, five or six seconds, I should think. I floated through the air and fell like a feather, knee-deep in a snow-drift in the bottom of a gully of blue-gray, white-veined rock.

I looked about me. "Cavor!" I cried; but no Cavor was visible.

"Cavor!" I cried louder, and the rocks echoed me.

I turned fiercely to the rocks and clambered to the summit of them. "Cavor!" I cried. My voice sounded like the voice of a lost lamb.

The sphere, too, was not in sight, and for a moment a horrible feeling of desolation pinched my heart.

Then I saw him. He was laughing and gesticulating to attract my attention. He was on a bare patch of rock twenty or thirty yards away. I could not hear his voice, but "jump" said his gestures. I hesitated, the distance seemed enormous. Yet I reflected that surely I must be able to clear a greater distance than Cavor.

I made a step back, gathered myself together, and leapt with all my might. I seemed to shoot right up in the air as though I should never come down.

It was horrible and delightful, and as wild as a nightmare, to go flying off in this fashion. I realised my leap had been altogether too violent. I flew clean over Cavor's head and beheld a spiky confusion in a gully spreading to meet my fall. I gave a yelp of alarm. I put out my hands and straightened my legs.

I hit a huge fungoid bulk that burst all about me, scattering a mass of orange spores in every direction, and covering me with orange powder. I rolled over spluttering, and came to rest convulsed with breathless laughter.

I became aware of Cavor's little round face peering over a bristling hedge. He shouted some faded inquiry. "Eh?" I tried to shout, but could not do so for want of breath. He made his way towards me, coming gingerly among the bushes.

"We've got to be careful," he said. "This moon has no discipline. She'll let us smash ourselves."

He helped me to my feet. "You exerted yourself too much," he said, dabbing at the yellow stuff with his hand to remove it from my garments.

I stood passive and panting, allowing him to beat off the jelly from my knees and elbows and lecture me upon my misfortunes. "We don't quite allow for the gravitation. Our muscles are scarcely educated yet. We must practise a little, when you have got your breath."

I pulled two or three little thorns out of my hand, and sat for a time on a boulder of rock. My muscles were quivering, and I had that feeling of personal disillusionment that comes at the first fall to the learner of cycling on earth.

It suddenly occurred to Cavor that the cold air in the gully, after the brightness of the sun, might give me a fever. So we clambered back into the sunlight. We found that beyond a few abrasions I had received no serious injuries from my tumble, and at Cavor's suggestion we were presently looking round for some safe and easy landing-place for my next leap. We chose a rocky slab some ten yards off, separated from us by a little thicket of olive-green spikes.

"Imagine it there!" said Cavor, who was assuming the airs of a trainer, and he pointed to a spot about four feet from my toes. This leap I managed without difficulty, and I must confess I found a certain satisfaction in Cavor's falling short by a foot or so and tasting the spikes of the scrub. "One has to be careful you see," he said, pulling out his thorns, and with that he ceased to be my mentor and became my fellow-learner in the art of lunar locomotion.

We chose a still easier jump and did it without difficulty, and then leapt back again, and to and fro several times, accustoming our muscles to the new standard. I could never have believed had I not experienced it, how rapid that adaptation would be. In a very little time indeed, certainly after fewer than thirty leaps, we could judge the effort necessary for a distance with almost terrestrial assurance.

And all this time the lunar plants were growing around us, higher and denser and more entangled, every moment thicker and taller, spiked plants, green cactus masses, fungi, fleshy and lichenous things, strangest radiate and sinuous shapes. But we were so intent upon our leaping, that for a time we gave no heed to their unfaltering expansion.

An extraordinary elation had taken possession of us. Partly, I think, it was our sense of release from the confinement of the sphere. Mainly, however, the thin sweetness of the air, which I am certain contained a much larger proportion of oxygen than our terrestrial atmosphere. In spite of the strange quality of all about us, I felt as adventurous and experimental as a cockney would do placed for the first time among mountains and I do not think it occurred to either of us, face to face though we were with the unknown, to be very greatly afraid.

We were bitten by a spirit of enterprise. We selected a lichenous kopje perhaps fifteen yards away, and landed neatly on its summit one after the other. "Good!" we cried to each other; "good!" and Cavor made three steps and went off to a tempting slope of snow a good twenty yards and more beyond. I stood for a moment struck by the grotesque effect of his soaring figure – his dirty cricket cap, and spiky hair, his little round body, his arms and his knicker-bockered legs tucked up tightly – against the weird spaciousness of the lunar scene. A gust of laughter seized me, and then I stepped off to follow. Plump! I dropped beside him.

We made a few gargantuan strides, leapt three or four times more, and sat down at last in a lichenous hollow. Our lungs were painful. We sat holding our sides and recovering our breath, looking appreciation to one another. Cavor panted something about "amazing sensations." And then came a thought into my head. For the moment it did not seem a particularly appalling thought, simply a natural question arising out of the situation.

"By the way," I said, "where exactly is the sphere?"

Cavor looked at me. "Eh?"

The full meaning of what we were saying struck me sharply.

"Cavor!" I cried, laying a hand on his arm, "where is the sphere?"

CHAPTER 10

Lost Men in the Moon

His face caught something of my dismay. He stood up and stared about him at the scrub that fenced us in and rose about us, straining upward in a passion of growth. He put a dubious hand to his lips. He spoke with a sudden lack of assurance. "I think," he said slowly, "we left it ... somewhere ... about *there*."

He pointed a hesitating finger that wavered in an arc.

"I'm not sure." His look of consternation deepened. "Anyhow," he said, with his eyes on me, "it can't be far."

We had both stood up. We made unmeaning ejaculations, our eyes sought in the twining, thickening jungle round about us.

All about us on the sunlit slopes frothed and swayed the darting shrubs, the swelling cactus, the creeping lichens, and wherever the shade remained the snow-drifts lingered. North, south, east, and west spread an identical monotony of unfamiliar forms. And somewhere, buried already among this tangled confusion, was our sphere, our home, our only provision, our only hope of escape from this fantastic wilderness of ephemeral growths into which we had come.

"I think after all," he said, pointing suddenly, "it might be over there."

"No," I said. "We have turned in a curve. See! here is the mark of my heels. It's clear the thing must be more to the eastward, much more. No – the sphere must be over there."

"I *think*," said Cavor, "I kept the sun upon my right all the time."

"Every leap, it seems to *me*," I said, "my shadow flew before me."

We stared into one another's eyes. The area of the crater had become enormously vast to our imaginations, the growing thickets already impenetrably dense.

"Good heavens! What fools we have been!"

"It's evident that we must find it again," said Cavor, "and that soon. The sun grows stronger. We should be fainting with the heat already if it wasn't so dry. And ... I'm hungry."

I stared at him. I had not suspected this aspect of the matter before. But it came to me at once – a positive craving. "Yes," I said with emphasis. "I am hungry too."

He stood up with a look of active resolution. "Certainly we must find the sphere."

As calmly as possible we surveyed the interminable reefs and thickets that formed the floor of the crater, each of us weighing in silence the chances of our finding the sphere before we were overtaken by heat and hunger.

"It can't be fifty yards from here," said Cavor, with indecisive gestures. "The only thing is to beat round about until we come upon it."

"That is all we can do," I said, without any alacrity to begin our hunt. "I wish this confounded spike bush did not grow so fast!"

"That's just it," said Cavor. "But it *was* lying on a bank of snow."

I stared about me in the vain hope of recognising some knoll or shrub that had been near the sphere. But everywhere was a confusing sameness, everywhere the aspiring bushes, the distending fungi, the dwindling snow banks, steadily and inevitably changed. The sun scorched and stung, the faintness of an unaccountable hunger mingled with our infinite perplexity. And even as we stood there, confused and lost amidst unprecedented things, we became aware for the first time of a sound upon the moon other than the air of the growing plants, the faint sighing of the wind, or those that we ourselves had made.

Boom.... Boom.... Boom.

It came from beneath our feet, a sound in the earth. We seemed to hear it with our feet as much as with our ears. Its dull resonance was muffled by distance, thick with the quality of intervening substance. No sound that I can imagine could have astonished us more, or have changed more completely the quality of things about us. For this sound, rich, slow, and deliberate, seemed to us as though it could be nothing but the striking of some gigantic buried clock.

Boom.... Boom.... Boom.

Sound suggestive of still cloisters, of sleepless nights in crowded cities, of vigils and the awaited hour, of all that is orderly and methodical in life, booming out pregnant and mysterious in this fantastic desert! To the eye everything was unchanged: the desolation of bushes and cacti waving silently in the wind, stretched unbroken to the distant cliffs, the still dark sky was empty overhead, and the hot sun hung and burned. And through it all, a warning, a threat, throbbed this enigma of sound.

Boom.... Boom.... Boom....

We questioned one another in faint and faded voices.

"A clock?"

"Like a clock!"

"What is it?"

"What can it be?"

"Count," was Cavor's belated suggestion, and at that word the striking ceased.

The silence, the rhythmic disappointment of the silence, came as a fresh shock. For a moment one could doubt whether one had ever heard a sound. Or whether it might not still be going on. Had I indeed heard a sound?

I felt the pressure of Cavor's hand upon my arm. He spoke in an undertone, as though he feared to wake some sleeping thing. "Let us keep together," he whispered, "and look for the sphere. We must get back to the sphere. This is beyond our understanding."

"Which way shall we go?"

He hesitated. An intense persuasion of presences, of unseen things about us and near us, dominated our minds. What could they be? Where could they be? Was this arid desolation, alternately frozen and scorched, only the outer rind and mask of some subterranean world? And if so, what sort of world? What sort of inhabitants might it not presently disgorge upon us?

And then, stabbing the aching stillness as vivid and sudden as an unexpected thunderclap, came a clang and rattle as though great gates of metal had suddenly been flung apart.

It arrested our steps. We stood gaping helplessly. Then Cavor stole towards me.

"I do not understand!" he whispered close to my face. He waved his hand vaguely skyward, the vague suggestion of still vaguer thoughts.

"A hiding-place! If anything came…"

I looked about us. I nodded my head in assent to him.

We started off, moving stealthily with the most exaggerated precautions against noise. We went towards a thicket of scrub. A clangour like hammers flung about a boiler hastened our steps. "We must crawl," whispered Cavor.

The lower leaves of the bayonet plants, already overshadowed by the newer ones above, were beginning to wilt and shrivel so that we could thrust our way in among the thickening stems without serious injury. A stab in the face or arm we did not heed. At the heart of the thicket I stopped, and stared panting into Cavor's face.

"Subterranean," he whispered. "Below."

"They may come out."

"We must find the sphere!"

"Yes," I said; "but how?"

"Crawl till we come to it."

"But if we don't?"

"Keep hidden. See what they are like."

"We will keep together," said I.

He thought. "Which way shall we go?"

"We must take our chance."

We peered this way and that. Then very circumspectly, we began to crawl through the lower jungle, making, so far as we could judge, a circuit, halting now at every waving fungus, at every sound, intent only on the sphere from which we had so foolishly emerged. Ever and again from out of the earth beneath us came concussions, beatings, strange, inexplicable, mechanical sounds; and once, and then again, we thought we heard something, a faint rattle and tumult, borne to us through the air. But fearful as we were we dared essay no vantage-point to survey the crater. For long we saw nothing of the beings whose sounds were so abundant and insistent. But for the faintness of our hunger and the drying of our throats that crawling would have had the quality of a very vivid dream. It was so absolutely unreal. The only element with any touch of reality was these sounds.

Picture it to yourself! About us the dream-like jungle, with the silent bayonet leaves darting overhead, and the silent, vivid, sun-splashed lichens under our hands and knees, waving with the vigour of their growth as a carpet waves when the wind gets beneath it. Ever and again one of the bladder fungi, bulging and distending under the sun, loomed upon us. Ever and again some novel shape in vivid colour obtruded. The very cells that built up these plants were as large as my thumb, like beads of coloured glass. And all these things were saturated in the unmitigated glare of the sun, were seen against a sky that was bluish black and spangled still, in spite of the sunlight, with a few surviving stars. Strange! the very forms and texture of the stones were strange. It was all strange, the feeling of one's body was unprecedented, every other movement ended in a surprise. The breath sucked thin in one's throat, the blood flowed through one's ears in a throbbing tide – thud, thud, thud, thud....

And ever and again came gusts of turmoil, hammering, the clanging and throb of machinery, and presently – the bellowing of great beasts!

CHAPTER 11

The Mooncalf Pastures

So we two poor terrestrial castaways, lost in that wild-growing moon jungle, crawled in terror before the sounds that had come upon us. We crawled, as it seemed, a long time before we saw either Selenite or mooncalf, though we heard the bellowing and gruntulous noises of these latter continually drawing nearer to us. We crawled through stony ravines, over snow slopes, amidst fungi that ripped like thin bladders at our thrust, emitting a watery humour, over a perfect pavement of things like puff-balls, and beneath interminable thickets of scrub. And ever more helplessly our eyes sought for our abandoned sphere. The noise of the mooncalves would at times be a vast flat calf-like sound, at times it rose to an amazed and wrathy bellowing, and again it would become a clogged bestial sound, as though these unseen creatures had sought to eat and bellow at the same time.

Our first view was but an inadequate transitory glimpse, yet none the less disturbing because it was incomplete. Cavor was crawling in front at the time, and he first was aware of their proximity. He stopped dead, arresting me with a single gesture.

A crackling and smashing of the scrub appeared to be advancing directly upon us, and then, as we squatted close and endeavoured to judge of the nearness and direction of this noise, there came a terrific bellow behind us, so close and vehement that the tops of the bayonet scrub bent before it, and one felt the breath of it hot and moist. And, turning about, we saw indistinctly through a crowd of swaying stems the mooncalf's shining sides, and the long line of its back loomed out against the sky.

Of course it is hard for me now to say how much I saw at that time, because my impressions were corrected by subsequent observation. First of all impressions was its enormous size; the girth of its body was some fourscore feet, its length perhaps two hundred. Its sides rose and fell with its laboured breathing. I perceived that its gigantic, flabby body lay along the ground, and that its skin was of a corrugated white, dappling into blackness along the backbone. But of its feet we saw nothing. I think also that we saw then the profile at least of the almost brainless head, with its fat-encumbered neck, its slobbering omnivorous mouth, its little nostrils, and tight shut eyes. (For the mooncalf invariably shuts its eyes in the presence of the sun.) We had a glimpse of a vast red pit as it opened its mouth to bleat and bellow again; we had a breath from the pit, and then the monster heeled over like a ship, dragged forward along the ground, creasing all its leathery skin, rolled again, and so wallowed past us, smashing a path amidst the scrub, and was speedily hidden from our eyes by the dense interlacings beyond. Another appeared more distantly, and then another, and then, as though he was guiding these animated lumps of provender to their pasture, a Selenite came momentarily into ken. My grip upon Cavor's foot became convulsive at the sight of him, and we remained motionless and peering long after he had passed out of our range.

By contrast with the mooncalves he seemed a trivial being, a mere ant, scarcely five feet high. He was wearing garments of some leathery substance, so that no portion of his actual body appeared, but of this, of course, we were entirely ignorant. He presented himself, therefore, as a compact, bristling creature, having much of the quality of a complicated insect, with whip-like tentacles and a clanging arm projecting from his shining cylindrical body case. The form of his head was hidden by his enormous many-spiked helmet – we discovered afterwards that he used the spikes for prodding refractory mooncalves – and a pair of goggles of darkened glass, set very much at the side, gave a bird-like quality to the metallic apparatus that covered his face. His arms did not project beyond his body case, and he carried himself upon short legs that, wrapped though they were in warm coverings, seemed to our terrestrial eyes inordinately flimsy. They had very short thighs, very long shanks, and little feet.

In spite of his heavy-looking clothing, he was progressing with what would be, from the terrestrial point of view, very considerable strides, and his clanging arm was busy. The quality of his motion during the instant of his passing suggested haste and a certain anger, and soon after we had lost sight of him we heard the bellow of a mooncalf change abruptly into a short, sharp squeal followed by the scuffle of its acceleration. And gradually that bellowing receded, and then came to an end, as if the pastures sought had been attained.

We listened. For a space the moon world was still. But it was some time before we resumed our crawling search for the vanished sphere.

When next we saw mooncalves they were some little distance away from us in a place of tumbled rocks. The less vertical surfaces of the rocks were thick with a speckled green plant growing in dense mossy clumps, upon which these creatures were browsing. We stopped at the edge of the reeds amidst which we were crawling at the sight of them, peering out at then and looking round for a second glimpse of a Selenite. They lay against their food like stupendous slugs, huge, greasy hulls, eating greedily and noisily, with a sort of sobbing avidity. They seemed monsters of mere fatness, clumsy and overwhelmed to a degree that would make a Smithfield ox seem a model of agility. Their busy, writhing, chewing mouths, and eyes closed, together with the appetising sound of their munching, made up an effect of animal enjoyment that was singularly stimulating to our empty frames.

"Hogs!" said Cavor, with unusual passion. "Disgusting hogs!" and after one glare of angry envy crawled off through the bushes to our right. I stayed long enough to see that the speckled plant was quite hopeless for human nourishment, then crawled after him, nibbling a quill of it between my teeth.

Presently we were arrested again by the proximity of a Selenite, and this time we were able to observe him more exactly. Now we could see that the Selenite covering was indeed clothing, and not a sort of crustacean integument. He was quite similar in his costume to the former one we had glimpsed, except that ends of something like wadding were protruding from his neck, and he stood on a promontory of rock and moved his head this way and that, as though he was surveying the crater. We lay quite still, fearing to attract his attention if we moved, and after a time he turned about and disappeared.

We came upon another drove of mooncalves bellowing up a ravine, and then we passed over a place of sounds, sounds of beating machinery as if some huge hall of industry came near the surface there. And while these sounds were still about us we came to the edge of a great open space, perhaps two hundred yards in diameter, and perfectly level. Save for a few lichens that advanced from its margin this space was bare, and presented a powdery surface of a dusty yellow colour. We were afraid to strike out across this space, but as it presented less obstruction to our crawling than the scrub, we went down upon it and began very circumspectly to skirt its edge.

For a little while the noises from below ceased and everything, save for the faint stir of the growing vegetation, was very still. Then abruptly there began an uproar, louder, more vehement, and nearer than any we had so far heard. Of a certainty it came from below. Instinctively we crouched as flat as we could, ready for a prompt plunge into the thicket beside us. Each knock and throb seemed to vibrate through our bodies. Louder grew this throbbing and beating, and that irregular vibration increased until the whole moon world seemed to be jerking and pulsing.

"Cover," whispered Cavor, and I turned towards the bushes.

At that instant came a thud like the thud of a gun, and then a thing happened – it still haunts me in my dreams. I had turned my head to look at Cavor's face, and thrust out my hand in front of me as I did so. And my hand met nothing! I plunged suddenly into a bottomless hole!

My chest hit something hard, and I found myself with my chin on the edge of an unfathomable abyss that had suddenly opened beneath me, my hand extended stiffly into the void. The whole of that flat circular area was no more than a gigantic lid, that was now sliding sideways from off the pit it had covered into a slot prepared for it.

Had it not been for Cavor I think I should have remained rigid, hanging over this margin and staring into the enormous gulf below, until at last the edges of the slot scraped me off and hurled me into its depths. But Cavor had not received the shock that had paralysed me. He had been a little distance from the edge when the lid had first opened, and perceiving the peril that held me helpless, gripped my legs and pulled me backward. I came into a sitting position, crawled away from the edge for a space on all fours, then staggered up and ran after him across the thundering, quivering sheet of metal. It seemed to be swinging open with a steadily accelerated velocity, and the bushes in front of me shifted sideways as I ran.

I was none too soon. Cavor's back vanished amidst the bristling thicket, and as I scrambled up after him, the monstrous valve came into its position with a clang. For a long time we lay panting, not daring to approach the pit.

But at last very cautiously and bit by bit we crept into a position from which we could peer down. The bushes about us creaked and waved with the force of a breeze that was blowing down the shaft. We could see nothing at first except smooth vertical walls descending at last into an impenetrable black. And then very gradually we became aware of a number of very faint and little lights going to and fro.

For a time that stupendous gulf of mystery held us so that we forgot even our sphere. In time, as we grew more accustomed to the darkness, we could make out very small, dim, elusive shapes moving about among those needle-point illuminations. We peered amazed and incredulous, understanding so little that we could find no words to say. We could distinguish nothing that would give us a clue to the meaning of the faint shapes we saw.

"What can it be?" I asked; "what can it be?"

"The engineering!... They must live in these caverns during the night, and come out during the day."

"Cavor!" I said. "Can they be – *that* – it was something like – men?"

"*That* was not a man."

"We dare risk nothing!"

"We dare do nothing until we find the sphere!"

"We *can* do nothing until we find the sphere."

He assented with a groan and stirred himself to move. He stared about him for a space, sighed, and indicated a direction. We struck out through the jungle. For a time we crawled resolutely, then with diminishing vigour. Presently among great shapes of flabby purple there came a noise of trampling and cries about us. We lay close, and for a long time the sounds went to and fro and very near. But this time we saw nothing. I tried to whisper to Cavor that I could hardly go without food much longer, but my mouth had become too dry for whispering.

"Cavor," I said, "I must have food."

He turned a face full of dismay towards me. "It's a case for holding out," he said.

"But I *must*," I said, "and look at my lips!"

"I've been thirsty some time."

"If only some of that snow had remained!"

"It's clean gone! We're driving from arctic to tropical at the rate of a degree a minute...."

I gnawed my hand.

"The sphere!" he said. "There is nothing for it but the sphere."

We roused ourselves to another spurt of crawling. My mind ran entirely on edible things, on the hissing profundity of summer drinks, more particularly I craved for beer. I was haunted by the memory of a sixteen gallon cask that had swaggered in my Lympne cellar. I thought of the adjacent larder, and especially of steak and kidney pie – tender steak and plenty of kidney, and rich, thick gravy between. Ever and again I was seized with fits of hungry yawning. We came to flat places overgrown with fleshy red things, monstrous coralline growths; as we pushed against them they snapped and broke. I noted the quality of the broken surfaces. The confounded stuff certainly looked of a biteable texture. Then it seemed to me that it smelt rather well.

I picked up a fragment and sniffed at it.

"Cavor," I said in a hoarse undertone.

He glanced at me with his face screwed up. "Don't," he said. I put down the fragment, and we crawled on through this tempting fleshiness for a space.

"Cavor," I asked, "*why not?*"

"Poison," I heard him say, but he did not look round.

We crawled some way before I decided.

"I'll chance it," said I.

He made a belated gesture to prevent me. I stuffed my mouth full. He crouched watching my face, his own twisted into the oddest expression. "It's good," I said.

"O Lord!" he cried.

He watched me munch, his face wrinkled between desire and disapproval, then suddenly succumbed to appetite and began to tear off huge mouthfuls. For a time we did nothing but eat.

The stuff was not unlike a terrestrial mushroom, only it was much laxer in texture, and, as one swallowed it, it warmed the throat. At first we experienced a mere mechanical satisfaction in eating; then our blood began to run warmer, and we tingled at the lips and fingers, and then new and slightly irrelevant ideas came bubbling up in our minds.

"Its good," said I. "Infernally good! What a home for our surplus population! Our poor surplus population," and I broke off another large portion. It filled me with a curiously benevolent satisfaction that there was such good food in the moon. The depression of my hunger gave way to an irrational exhilaration. The dread and discomfort in which I had been living vanished entirely. I perceived the moon no longer as a planet from which I most earnestly desired the means of escape, but as a possible refuge from human destitution. I think I forgot the Selenites, the mooncalves, the lid, and the noises completely so soon as I had eaten that fungus.

Cavor replied to my third repetition of my "surplus population" remark with similar words of approval. I felt that my head swam, but I put this down to the stimulating effect of food after a long fast. "Ess'lent discov'ry yours, Cavor," said I. "Se'nd on'y to the 'tato."

"Whajer mean?" asked Cavor. "'Scovery of the moon - se'nd on'y to the tato?"

I looked at him, shocked at his suddenly hoarse voice, and by the badness of his articulation. It occurred to me in a flash that he was intoxicated, possibly by the fungus. It also occurred to me that he erred in imagining that he had discovered the moon; he had not discovered it, he had only reached it. I tried to lay my hand on his arm and explain this to him, but the issue was too subtle for his brain. It was also unexpectedly difficult to express. After a momentary attempt to understand me - I remember wondering if the fungus had made my eyes as fishy as his - he set off upon some observations on his own account.

"We are," he announced with a solemn hiccup, "the creashurs o' what we eat and drink."

He repeated this, and as I was now in one of my subtle moods, I determined to dispute it. Possibly I wandered a little from the point. But Cavor certainly did not attend at all properly. He stood up as well as he could, putting a hand on my head to steady himself, which was disrespectful, and stood staring about him, quite devoid now of any fear of the moon beings.

I tried to point out that this was dangerous for some reason that was not perfectly clear to me, but the word "dangerous" had somehow got mixed with "indiscreet," and came out rather more like "injurious" than either; and after an attempt to disentangle them, I resumed my argument, addressing myself principally to the unfamiliar but attentive coralline growths on either side. I felt that it was necessary to clear up this confusion between the moon and a potato at once – I wandered into a long parenthesis on the importance of precision of definition in argument. I did my best to ignore the fact that my bodily sensations were no longer agreeable.

In some way that I have now forgotten, my mind was led back to projects of colonisation. "We must annex this moon," I said. "There must be no shilly-shally. This is part of the White Man's Burthen. Cavor – we are – *hic* – Satap – mean Satraps! Nempire Caesar never dreamt. B'in all the newspapers. Cavorecia. Bedfordecia. Bedfordecia – *hic* – Limited. Mean – unlimited! Practically."

Certainly I was intoxicated.

I embarked upon an argument to show the infinite benefits our arrival would confer on the moon. I involved myself in a rather difficult proof that the arrival of Columbus was, on the whole, beneficial to America. I found I had forgotten the line of argument I had intended to pursue, and continued to repeat "sim'lar to C'lumbus," to fill up time.

From that point my memory of the action of that abominable fungus becomes confused. I remember vaguely that we declared our intention of standing no nonsense from any confounded insects, that we decided it ill became men to hide shamefully upon a mere satellite, that we equipped ourselves with huge armfuls of the fungus – whether for missile purposes or not I do not know – and, heedless of the stabs of the bayonet scrub, we started forth into the sunshine.

Almost immediately we must have come upon the Selenites. There were six of them, and they were marching in single file over a rocky place, making the most remarkable piping and whining sounds. They all seemed to become aware of us at once, all instantly became silent and motionless, like animals, with their faces turned towards us.

For a moment I was sobered.

"Insects," murmured Cavor, "insects! And they think I'm going to crawl about on my stomach – on my vertebrated stomach!

"Stomach," he repeated slowly, as though he chewed the indignity.

Then suddenly, with a sort of fury, he made three vast strides and leapt towards them. He leapt badly; he made a series of somersaults in the air, whirled right over them, and vanished with an enormous splash amidst the cactus bladders. What the Selenites made of this amazing, and to my mind undignified irruption from another planet, I have no means of guessing. I seem to remember the sight of their backs as they ran in all directions, but I am not sure. All these last incidents before oblivion came are vague and faint in my mind. I know I made a step to follow Cavor, and tripped and fell headlong among the rocks. I was, I am certain, suddenly and vehemently ill. I seem to remember, a violent struggle and being gripped by metallic clasps....

My next clear recollection is that we were prisoners at we knew not what depths beneath the moon's surface; we were in darkness amidst strange distracting noises; our bodies were covered with scratches and bruises, and our heads racked with pain.

CHAPTER 12

The Selenite's Face

I found myself sitting crouched together in a tumultuous darkness. For a long time I could not understand where I was, nor how I had come to this perplexity. I thought of the cupboard into which I had been thrust at times when I was a child, and then of a very dark and noisy bedroom in which I had slept during an illness. But these sounds about me were not the noises I had known, and there was a thin flavour in the air like the wind of a stable. Then I supposed we must still be at work upon the sphere, and that somehow I had got into the cellar of Cavor's house. I remembered we had finished the sphere, and fancied I must still be in it and travelling through space.

"Cavor," I said, "cannot we have some light?"

There came no answer.

"Cavor!" I insisted.

I was answered by a groan. "My head!" I heard him say; "my head!"

I attempted to press my hands to my brow, which ached, and discovered they were tied together. This startled me very much. I brought them up to my mouth and felt the cold smoothness of metal. They were chained together. I tried to separate my legs and made out they were similarly fastened, and also that I was fastened to the ground by a much thicker chain about the middle of my body.

I was more frightened than I had yet been by anything in all our strange experiences. For a time I tugged silently at my bonds. "Cavor!" I cried out sharply. "Why am I tied? Why have you tied me hand and foot?"

"I haven't tied you," he answered. "It's the Selenites."

The Selenites! My mind hung on that for a space. Then my memories came back to me: the snowy desolation, the thawing of the air, the growth of the plants, our strange hopping and crawling among the rocks and vegetation of the crater. All the distress of our frantic search for the sphere returned to me.... Finally the opening of the great lid that covered the pit!

Then as I strained to trace our later movements down to our present plight, the pain in my head became intolerable. I came to an insurmountable barrier, an obstinate blank.

"Cavor!"

"Yes?"

"Where are we?"

"How should I know?"

"Are we dead?"

"What nonsense!"

"They've got us, then!"

He made no answer but a grunt. The lingering traces of the poison seemed to make him oddly irritable.

"What do you mean to do?"

"How should I know what to do?"

"Oh, very well!" said I, and became silent. Presently, I was roused from a stupor. "O *Lord!*" I cried; "I wish you'd stop that buzzing!"

We lapsed into silence again, listening to the dull confusion of noises like the muffled sounds of a street or factory that filled our ears. I could make nothing of it, my mind pursued first one rhythm and then another, and questioned it in vain. But after a long time I became aware of a new and sharper element, not mingling with the rest but standing out, as it were, against that cloudy background of sound. It was a series of relatively very little definite sounds, tappings and rubbings, like a loose spray of ivy against a window or a bird moving about upon a box. We listened and peered about us, but the darkness was a velvet pall. There followed a noise like the subtle movement of the wards of a well-oiled lock. And then there appeared before me, hanging as it seemed in an immensity of black, a thin bright line.

"Look!" whispered Cavor very softly.

"What is it?"

"I don't know."

We stared.

The thin bright line became a band, and broader and paler. It took upon itself the quality of a bluish light falling upon a white-washed wall. It ceased to be parallel-sided; it developed a deep indentation on one side. I turned to remark this to Cavor, and was amazed to see his ear in a brilliant illumination – all the rest of him in shadow. I twisted my head round as well as my bonds would permit. "Cavor," I said, "it's behind!"

His ear vanished – gave place to an eye!

Suddenly the crack that had been admitting the light broadened out, and revealed itself as the space of an opening door. Beyond was a sapphire vista, and in the doorway stood a grotesque outline silhouetted against the glare.

We both made convulsive efforts to turn, and failing, sat staring over our shoulders at this. My first impression was of some clumsy quadruped with lowered head. Then I perceived it was the slender pinched body and short and extremely attenuated bandy legs of a Selenite, with his head depressed between his shoulders. He was without the helmet and body covering they wear upon the exterior.

He was a blank, black figure to us, but instinctively our imaginations supplied features to his very human outline. I, at least, took it instantly that he was somewhat hunchbacked, with a high forehead and long features.

He came forward three steps and paused for a time. His movements seemed absolutely noiseless. Then he came forward again. He walked like a bird, his feet fell one in front of the other. He stepped out of the ray of light that came through the doorway, and it seemed as though he vanished altogether in the shadow.

For a moment my eyes sought him in the wrong place, and then I perceived him standing facing us both in the full light. Only the human features I had attributed to him were not there at all!

Of course I ought to have expected that, only I didn't. It came to me as an absolute, for a moment an overwhelming shock. It seemed as though it wasn't a face, as though it must needs be a mask, a horror, a deformity, that would presently be disavowed or explained. There was no nose, and the thing had dull bulging eyes at the side – in the silhouette I had supposed they were ears. There were no ears.... I have tried to draw one of these heads, but I cannot. There was a mouth, downwardly curved, like a human mouth in a face that stares ferociously....

The neck on which the head was poised was jointed in three places, almost like the short joints in the leg of a crab. The joints of the limbs I could not see, because of the puttee-like straps in which they were swathed, and which formed the only clothing the being wore.

There the thing was, looking at us!

At the time my mind was taken up by the mad impossibility of the creature. I suppose he also was amazed, and with more reason, perhaps, for amazement than we. Only, confound him! he did not show it. We did at least know what had brought about this meeting of incompatible creatures. But conceive how it would seem to decent Londoners, for example, to come upon a couple of living things, as big as men and absolutely unlike any other earthly animals, careering about among the sheep in Hyde Park! It must have taken him like that.

Figure us! We were bound hand and foot, fagged and filthy; our beards two inches long, our faces scratched and bloody. Cavor you must imagine in his knickerbockers (torn in several places by the bayonet scrub) his Jaegar shirt and old cricket cap, his wiry hair wildly disordered, a tail to every quarter of the heavens. In that blue light his face did not look red but very dark, his lips and the drying blood upon my hands seemed black. If possible I was in a worse plight than he, on account of the yellow fungus into which I had jumped. Our jackets were unbuttoned, and our shoes had been taken off and lay at our feet. And we were sitting with our backs to this queer bluish light, peering at such a monster as Durer might have invented.

Cavor broke the silence; started to speak, went hoarse, and cleared his throat. Outside began a terrific bellowing, as if a mooncalf were in trouble. It ended in a shriek, and everything was still again.

Presently the Selenite turned about, flickered into the shadow, stood for a moment retrospective at the door, and then closed it on us; and once more we were in that murmurous mystery of darkness into which we had awakened.

CHAPTER 13

Mr. Cavor Makes Some Suggestions

For a time neither of us spoke. To focus together all the things we had brought upon ourselves seemed beyond my mental powers.

"They've got us," I said at last.

"It was that fungus."

"Well – if I hadn't taken it we should have fainted and starved."

"We might have found the sphere."

I lost my temper at his persistence, and swore to myself. For a time we hated one another in silence. I drummed with my fingers on the floor between my knees, and gritted the links of my fetters together. Presently I was forced to talk again.

"What do you make of it, anyhow?" I asked humbly.

"They are reasonable creatures – they can make things and do things. Those lights we saw…"

He stopped. It was clear he could make nothing of it.

When he spoke again it was to confess, "After all, they are more human than we had a right to expect. I suppose—"

He stopped irritatingly.

"Yes?"

"I suppose, anyhow – on any planet where there is an intelligent animal – it will carry its brain case upward, and have hands, and walk erect."

Presently he broke away in another direction.

"We are some way in," he said. "I mean – perhaps a couple of thousand feet or more."

"Why?"

"It's cooler. And our voices are so much louder. That faded quality – it has altogether gone. And the feeling in one's ears and throat."

I had not noted that, but I did now.

"The air is denser. We must be some depths – a mile even, we may be – inside the moon."

"We never thought of a world inside the moon."

"No."

"How could we?"

"We might have done. Only one gets into habits of mind."

He thought for a time.

"*Now*," he said, "it seems such an obvious thing."

"Of course! The moon must be enormously cavernous, with an atmosphere within, and at the centre of its caverns a sea.

"One knew that the moon had a lower specific gravity than the earth, one knew that it had little air or water outside, one knew, too, that it was sister planet to the earth, and that it was unaccountable that it should be different in composition. The inference that it was hollowed out was as clear as day. And yet one never saw it as a fact. Kepler, of course—"

His voice had the interest now of a man who has discerned a pretty sequence of reasoning.

"Yes," he said, "Kepler with his *sub-volvani* was right after all."

"I wish you had taken the trouble to find that out before we came," I said.

He answered nothing, buzzing to himself softly, as he pursued his thoughts. My temper was going.

"What do you think has become of the sphere, anyhow?" I asked.

"Lost," he said, like a man who answers an uninteresting question.

"Among those plants?"

"Unless they find it."

"And then?"

"How can I tell?"

"Cavor," I said, with a sort of hysterical bitterness, "things look bright for my Company..."

He made no answer.

"Good Lord!" I exclaimed. "Just think of all the trouble we took to get into this pickle! What did we come for? What are we after? What was the moon to us or we to the moon? We wanted too much, we tried too much. We ought to have started the little things first. It was you proposed the moon! Those Cavorite spring blinds! I am certain we could have worked them for terrestrial purposes. Certain! Did you really understand what I proposed? A steel cylinder—"

"Rubbish!" said Cavor.

We ceased to converse.

For a time Cavor kept up a broken monologue without much help from me.

"If they find it," he began, "if they find it ... what will they do with it? Well, that's a question. It may be that's *the* question. They won't understand it, anyhow. If they understood that sort of thing they would have come long since to the earth. Would they? Why shouldn't they? But they would have sent something – they couldn't keep their hands off such a possibility. No! But they will examine it. Clearly they are intelligent and inquisitive. They will examine it – get inside it – trifle with the studs. Off! ... That would mean the moon for us for all the rest of our lives. Strange creatures, strange knowledge...."

"As for strange knowledge—" said I, and language failed me.

"Look here, Bedford," said Cavor, "you came on this expedition of your own free will."

"You said to me, 'Call it prospecting'."

"There's always risks in prospecting."

"Especially when you do it unarmed and without thinking out every possibility."

"I was so taken up with the sphere. The thing rushed on us, and carried us away."

"Rushed on *me*, you mean."

"Rushed on me just as much. How was *I* to know when I set to work on molecular physics that the business would bring me here – of all places?"

"It's this accursed science," I cried. "It's the very Devil. The medieval priests and persecutors were right and the Moderns are all wrong. You tamper with it – and it offers you gifts. And directly you take them it knocks you to pieces in some unexpected way. Old passions and new weapons – now it upsets your religion, now it upsets your social ideas, now it whirls you off to desolation and misery!"

"Anyhow, it's no use your quarrelling with me *now*. These creatures – these Selenites, or whatever we choose to call them – have got us tied hand and foot. Whatever temper you choose to go through with it in, you will have to go through with it…. We have experiences before us that will need all our coolness."

He paused as if he required my assent. But I sat sulking. "Confound your science!" I said.

"The problem is communication. Gestures, I fear, will be different. Pointing, for example. No creatures but men and monkeys point."

That was too obviously wrong for me. "Pretty nearly every animal," I cried, "points with its eyes or nose."

Cavor meditated over that. "Yes," he said at last, "and we don't. There's such differences – such differences!"

"One might.... But how can I tell? There is speech. The sounds they make, a sort of fluting and piping. I don't see how we are to imitate that. Is it their speech, that sort of thing? They may have different senses, different means of communication. Of course they are minds and we are minds; there must be something in common. Who knows how far we may not get to an understanding?"

"The things are outside us," I said. "They're more different from us than the strangest animals on earth. They are a different clay. What is the good of talking like this?"

Cavor thought. "I don't see that. Where there are minds they will have something *similar* – even though they have been evolved on different planets. Of course if it was a question of instincts, if we or they are no more than animals—"

"Well, *are* they? They're much more like ants on their hind legs than human beings, and who ever got to any sort of understanding with ants?"

"But these machines and clothing! No, I don't hold with you, Bedford. The difference is wide—"

"It's insurmountable."

"The resemblance must bridge it. I remember reading once a paper by the late Professor Galton on the possibility of communication between the planets. Unhappily, at that time it did not seem probable that that would be of any material benefit to me, and I fear I did not give it the attention I should have done – in view of this state of affairs. Yet.... Now, let me see!

"His idea was to begin with those broad truths that must underlie all conceivable mental existences and establish a basis on those. The great principles of geometry, to begin with. He proposed to take some leading proposition of Euclid's, and show by construction that its truth was known to us, to demonstrate, for example, that the angles at the base of an isosceles triangle are equal, and that if the equal sides be produced the angles on the other side of the base are equal also, or that the square on the hypotenuse of a right-angled triangle is equal to the sum of the squares on the two other sides. By demonstrating our knowledge of these things we should demonstrate our possession of a reasonable intelligence…. Now, suppose I … I might draw the geometrical figure with a wet finger, or even trace it in the air…."

He fell silent. I sat meditating his words. For a time his wild hope of communication, of interpretation, with these weird beings held me. Then that angry despair that was a part of my exhaustion and physical misery resumed its sway. I perceived with a sudden novel vividness the extraordinary folly of everything I had ever done. "Ass!" I said; "oh, ass, unutterable ass…. I seem to exist only to go about doing preposterous things. Why did we ever leave the thing? … Hopping about looking for patents and concessions in the craters of the moon!… If only we had had the sense to fasten a handkerchief to a stick to show where we had left the sphere!"

I subsided, fuming.

"It is clear," meditated Cavor, "they are intelligent. One can hypothecate certain things. As they have not killed us at once, they must have ideas of mercy. Mercy! at any rate of restraint. Possibly of intercourse. They may meet us. And this apartment and the glimpses we had of its guardian. These fetters! A high degree of intelligence…"

"I wish to heaven," cried I, "I'd thought even twice! Plunge after plunge. First one fluky start and then another. It was my confidence in you! *Why* didn't I stick to my play? That was what I was equal to. That was my world and the life I was made for. I could have finished that play. I'm certain … it was a good play. I had the scenario as good as done. Then…. Conceive it! leaping to the moon! Practically – I've thrown my life away! That old woman in the inn near Canterbury had better sense."

I looked up, and stopped in mid-sentence. The darkness had given place to that bluish light again. The door was opening, and several noiseless Selenites were coming into the chamber. I became quite still, staring at their grotesque faces.

Then suddenly my sense of disagreeable strangeness changed to interest. I perceived that the foremost and second carried bowls. One elemental need at least our minds could understand in common. They were bowls of some metal that, like our fetters, looked dark in that bluish light; and each contained a number of whitish fragments. All the cloudy pain and misery that oppressed me rushed together and took the shape of hunger. I eyed these bowls wolfishly, and, though it returned to me in dreams, at that time it seemed a small matter that at the end of the arms that lowered one towards me were not hands, but a sort of flap and thumb, like the end of an elephant's trunk. The stuff in the bowl was loose in texture, and whitish brown in colour – rather like lumps of some cold souffle, and it smelt faintly like mushrooms. From a partially divided carcass of a mooncalf that we presently saw, I am inclined to believe it must have been mooncalf flesh.

My hands were so tightly chained that I could barely contrive to reach the bowl; but when they saw the effort I made, two of them dexterously released one of the turns about my wrist. Their tentacle hands were soft and cold to my skin. I immediately seized a mouthful of the food. It had the same laxness in texture that all organic structures seem to have upon the moon; it tasted rather like a gauffre or a damp meringue, but in no way was it disagreeable. I took two other mouthfuls. "I *wanted* – foo'!" said I, tearing off a still larger piece….

For a time we ate with an utter absence of self-consciousness. We ate and presently drank like tramps in a soup kitchen. Never before nor since have I been hungry to the ravenous pitch, and save that I have had this very experience I could never have believed that, a quarter of a million of miles out of our proper world, in utter perplexity of soul, surrounded, watched, touched by beings more grotesque and inhuman than the worst creations of a nightmare, it would be possible for me to eat in utter forgetfulness of all these things. They stood about us watching us, and ever and again making a slight elusive twittering that stood, I suppose, in the stead of speech. I did not even shiver at their touch. And when the first zeal of my feeding was over, I could note that Cavor, too, had been eating with the same shameless abandon.

CHAPTER 14

Experiments in Intercourse

When at last we had made an end of eating, the Selenites linked our hands closely together again, and then untwisted the chains about our feet and rebound them, so as to give us a limited freedom of movement. Then they unfastened the chains about our waists. To do all this they had to handle us freely, and ever and again one of their queer heads came down close to my face, or a soft tentacle-hand touched my head or neck. I don't remember that I was afraid then or repelled by their proximity. I think that our incurable anthropomorphism made us imagine there were human heads inside their masks. The skin, like everything else, looked bluish, but that was on account of the light; and it was hard and shiny, quite in the beetle-wing fashion, not soft, or moist, or hairy, as a vertebrated animal's would be. Along the crest of the head was a low ridge of whitish spines running from back to front, and a much larger ridge curved on either side over the eyes. The Selenite who untied me used his mouth to help his hands.

"They seem to be releasing us," said Cavor. "Remember we are on the moon! Make no sudden movements!"

"Are you going to try that geometry?"

"If I get a chance. But, of course, they may make an advance first."

We remained passive, and the Selenites, having finished their arrangements, stood back from us, and seemed to be looking at us.

I say seemed to be, because as their eyes were at the side and not in front, one had the same difficulty in determining the direction in which they were looking as one has in the case of a hen or a fish. They conversed with one another in their reedy tones, that seemed to me impossible to imitate or define. The door behind us opened wider, and, glancing over my shoulder, I saw a vague large space beyond, in which quite a little crowd of Selenites were standing. They seemed a curiously miscellaneous rabble.

"Do they want us to imitate those sounds?" I asked Cavor.

"I don't think so," he said.

"It seems to me that they are trying to make us understand something."

"I can't make anything of their gestures. Do you notice this one, who is worrying with his head like a man with an uncomfortable collar?"

"Let us shake our heads at him."

We did that, and finding it ineffectual, attempted an imitation of the Selenites' movements. That seemed to interest them. At any rate they all set up the same movement. But as that seemed to lead to nothing, we desisted at last and so did they, and fell into a piping argument among themselves. Then one of them, shorter and very much thicker than the others, and with a particularly wide mouth, squatted down suddenly beside Cavor, and put his hands and feet in the same posture as Cavor's were bound, and then by a dexterous movement stood up.

"Cavor," I shouted, "they want us to get up!"

He stared open-mouthed. "That's it!" he said.

And with much heaving and grunting, because our hands were tied together, we contrived to struggle to our feet. The Selenites made way for our elephantine heavings, and seemed to twitter more volubly. As soon as we were on our feet the thick-set Selenite came and patted each of our faces with his tentacles, and walked towards the open doorway. That also was plain enough, and we followed him. We saw that four of the Selenites standing in the doorway were much taller than the others, and clothed in the same manner as those we had seen in the crater, namely, with spiked round helmets and cylindrical body-cases, and that each of the four carried a goad with spike and guard made of that same dull-looking metal as the bowls. These four closed about us, one on either side of each of us, as we emerged from our chamber into the cavern from which the light had come.

We did not get our impression of that cavern all at once. Our attention was taken up by the movements and attitudes of the Selenites immediately about us, and by the necessity of controlling our motion, lest we should startle and alarm them and ourselves by some excessive stride. In front of us was the short, thick-set being who had solved the problem of asking us to get up, moving with gestures that seemed, almost all of them, intelligible to us, inviting us to follow him. His spout-like face turned from one of us to the other with a quickness that was clearly interrogative. For a time, I say, we were taken up with these things.

But at last the great place that formed a background to our movements asserted itself. It became apparent that the source of much, at least, of the tumult of sounds which had filled our ears ever since we had recovered from the stupefaction of the fungus was a vast mass of machinery in active movement, whose flying and whirling parts were visible indistinctly over the heads and between the bodies of the Selenites who walked about us. And not only did the web of sounds that filled the air proceed from this mechanism, but also the peculiar blue light that irradiated the whole place. We had taken it as a natural thing that a subterranean cavern should be artificially lit, and even now, though the fact was patent to my eyes, I did not really grasp its import until presently the darkness came. The meaning and structure of this huge apparatus we saw I cannot explain, because we neither of us learnt what it was for or how it worked. One after another, big shafts of metal flung out and up from its centre, their heads travelling in what seemed to me to be a parabolic path; each dropped a sort of dangling arm as it rose towards the apex of its flight and plunged down into a vertical cylinder, forcing this down before it. About it moved the shapes of tenders, little figures that seemed vaguely different from the beings about us. As each of the three dangling arms of the machine plunged down, there was a clank and then a roaring, and out of the top of the vertical cylinder came pouring this incandescent substance that lit the place, and ran over as milk runs over a boiling pot, and dripped luminously into a tank of light below. It was a cold blue light, a sort of phosphorescent glow but infinitely brighter, and from the tanks into which it fell it ran in conduits athwart the cavern.

Thud, thud, thud, thud, came the sweeping arms of this unintelligible apparatus, and the light substance hissed and poured. At first the thing seemed only reasonably large and near to us, and then I saw how exceedingly little the Selenites upon it seemed, and I realised the full immensity of cavern and machine. I looked from this tremendous affair to the faces of the Selenites with a new respect. I stopped, and Cavor stopped, and stared at this thunderous engine.

"But this is stupendous!" I said. "What can it be for?"

Cavor's blue-lit face was full of an intelligent respect. "I can't dream! Surely these beings— Men could not make a thing like that! Look at those arms, are they on connecting rods?"

The thick-set Selenite had gone some paces unheeded. He came back and stood between us and the great machine. I avoided seeing him, because I guessed somehow that his idea was to beckon us onward. He walked away in the direction he wished us to go, and turned and came back, and flicked our faces to attract our attention.

Cavor and I looked at one another.

"Cannot we show him we are interested in the machine?" I said.

"Yes," said Cavor. "We'll try that." He turned to our guide and smiled, and pointed to the machine, and pointed again, and then to his head, and then to the machine. By some defect of reasoning he seemed to imagine that broken English might help these gestures. "Me look 'im," he said, "me think 'im very much. Yes."

His behaviour seemed to check the Selenites in their desire for our progress for a moment. They faced one another, their queer heads moved, the twittering voices came quick and liquid. Then one of them, a lean, tall creature, with a sort of mantle added to the puttee in which the others were dressed, twisted his elephant trunk of a hand about Cavor's waist, and pulled him gently to follow our guide, who again went on ahead. Cavor resisted. "We may just as well begin explaining ourselves now. They may think we are new animals, a new sort of mooncalf perhaps! It is most important that we should show an intelligent interest from the outset."

He began to shake his head violently. "No, no," he said, "me not come on one minute. Me look at 'im."

"Isn't there some geometrical point you might bring in *apropos* of that affair?" I suggested, as the Selenites conferred again.

"Possibly a parabolic—" he began.

He yelled loudly, and leaped six feet or more!

One of the four armed moon-men had pricked him with a goad!

I turned on the goad-bearer behind me with a swift threatening gesture, and he started back. This and Cavor's sudden shout and leap clearly astonished all the Selenites. They receded hastily, facing us. For one of those moments that seem to last for ever, we stood in angry protest, with a scattered semicircle of these inhuman beings about us.

"He pricked me!" said Cavor, with a catching of the voice.

"I saw him," I answered.

"Confound it!" I said to the Selenites; "we're not going to stand that! What on earth do you take us for?"

I glanced quickly right and left. Far away across the blue wilderness of cavern I saw a number of other Selenites running towards us; broad and slender they were, and one with a larger head than the others. The cavern spread wide and low, and receded in every direction into darkness. Its roof, I remember, seemed to bulge down as if with the weight of the vast thickness of rocks that prisoned us. There was no way out of it – no way out of it. Above, below, in every direction, was the unknown, and these inhuman creatures, with goads and gestures, confronting us, and we two unsupported men!

CHAPTER 15

The Giddy Bridge

Just for a moment that hostile pause endured. I suppose that both we and the Selenites did some very rapid thinking. My clearest impression was that there was nothing to put my back against, and that we were bound to be surrounded and killed. The overwhelming folly of our presence there loomed over me in black, enormous reproach. Why had I ever launched myself on this mad, inhuman expedition?

Cavor came to my side and laid his hand on my arm. His pale and terrified face was ghastly in the blue light.

"We can't do anything," he said. "It's a mistake. They don't understand. We must go. As they want us to go."

I looked down at him, and then at the fresh Selenites who were coming to help their fellows. "If I had my hands free—"

"It's no use," he panted.

"No."

"We'll go."

And he turned about and led the way in the direction that had been indicated for us.

I followed, trying to look as subdued as possible, and feeling at the chains about my wrists. My blood was boiling. I noted nothing more of that cavern, though it seemed to take a long time before we had marched across it, or if I noted anything I forgot it as I saw it. My thoughts were concentrated, I think, upon my chains and the Selenites, and particularly upon the helmeted ones with the goads. At first they marched parallel with us, and at a respectful distance, but presently they were overtaken by three others, and then they drew nearer, until they were within arms length again. I winced like a beaten horse as they came near to us. The shorter, thicker Selenite marched at first on our right flank, but presently came in front of us again.

How well the picture of that grouping has bitten into my brain; the back of Cavor's downcast head just in front of me, and the dejected droop of his shoulders, and our guide's gaping visage, perpetually jerking about him, and the goad-bearers on either side, watchful, yet open-mouthed – a blue monochrome. And after all, I *do* remember one other thing besides the purely personal affair, which is, that a sort of gutter came presently across the floor of the cavern, and then ran along by the side of the path of rock we followed. And it was full of that same bright blue luminous stuff that flowed out of the great machine. I walked close beside it, and I can testify it radiated not a particle of heat. It was brightly shining, and yet it was neither warmer nor colder than anything else in the cavern.

Clang, clang, clang, we passed right under the thumping levers of another vast machine, and so came at last to a wide tunnel, in which we could even hear the pad, pad, of our shoeless feet, and which, save for the trickling thread of blue to the right of us, was quite unlit. The shadows made gigantic travesties of our shapes and those of the Selenites on the irregular wall and roof of the tunnel. Ever and again crystals in the walls of the tunnel scintillated like gems, ever and again the tunnel expanded into a stalactitic cavern, or gave off branches that vanished into darkness.

We seemed to be marching down that tunnel for a long time. "Trickle, trickle," went the flowing light very softly, and our footfalls and their echoes made an irregular paddle, paddle. My mind settled down to the question of my chains. If I were to slip off one turn *so*, and then to twist it *so* ...

If I tried to do it very gradually, would they see I was slipping my wrist out of the looser turn? If they did, what would they do?

"Bedford," said Cavor, "it goes down. It keeps on going down."

His remark roused me from my sullen pre-occupation.

"If they wanted to kill us," he said, dropping back to come level with me, "there is no reason why they should not have done it."

"No," I admitted, "that's true."

"They don't understand us," he said, "they think we are merely strange animals, some wild sort of mooncalf birth, perhaps. It will be only when they have observed us better that they will begin to think we have minds—"

"When you trace those geometrical problems," said I.

"It may be that."

We tramped on for a space.

"You see," said Cavor, "these may be Selenites of a lower class."

"The infernal fools!" said I viciously, glancing at their exasperating faces.

"If we endure what they do to us—"

"We've got to endure it," said I.

"There may be others less stupid. This is the mere outer fringe of their world. It must go down and down, cavern, passage, tunnel, down at last to the sea – hundreds of miles below."

His words made me think of the mile or so of rock and tunnel that might be over our heads already. It was like a weight dropping, on my shoulders. "Away from the sun and air," I said. "Even a mine half a mile deep is stuffy."

"This is not, anyhow. It's probable— Ventilation! The air would blow from the dark side of the moon to the sunlit, and all the carbonic acid would well out there and feed those plants. Up this tunnel, for example, there is quite a breeze. And what a world it must be. The earnest we have in that shaft, and those machines—"

"And the goad," I said. "Don't forget the goad!"

He walked a little in front of me for a time.

"Even that goad—" he said.

"Well?"

"I was angry at the time. But – it was perhaps necessary we should get on. They have different skins, and probably different nerves. They may not understand our objection – just as a being from Mars might not like our earthly habit of nudging."

"They'd better be careful how they nudge *me*."

"And about that geometry. After all, their way is a way of understanding, too. They begin with the elements of life and not of thought. Food. Compulsion. Pain. They strike at fundamentals."

"There's no doubt about *that*," I said.

He went on to talk of the enormous and wonderful world into which we were being taken. I realised slowly from his tone, that even now he was not absolutely in despair at the prospect of going ever deeper into this inhuman planet-burrow. His mind ran on machines and invention, to the exclusion of a thousand dark things that beset me. It wasn't that he intended to make any use of these things, he simply wanted to know them.

"After all," he said, "this is a tremendous occasion. It is the meeting of two worlds! What are we going to see? Think of what is below us here."

"We shan't see much if the light isn't better," I remarked.

"This is only the outer crust. Down below— On this scale— There will be everything. Do you notice how different they seem one from another? The story we shall take back!"

"Some rare sort of animal," I said, "might comfort himself in that way while they were bringing him to the Zoo.... It doesn't follow that we are going to be shown all these things."

"When they find we have reasonable minds," said Cavor, "they will want to learn about the earth. Even if they have no generous emotions, they will teach in order to learn.... And the things they must know! The unanticipated things!"

He went on to speculate on the possibility of their knowing things he had never hoped to learn on earth, speculating in that way, with a raw wound from that goad already in his skin! Much that he said I forget, for my attention was drawn to the fact that the tunnel along which we had been marching was opening out wider and wider. We seemed, from the feeling of the air, to be going out into a huge space. But how big the space might really be we could not tell, because it was unlit. Our little stream of light ran in a dwindling thread and vanished far ahead. Presently the rocky walls had vanished altogether on either hand. There was nothing to be seen but the path in front of us and the trickling hurrying rivulet of blue phosphorescence. The figures of Cavor and the guiding Selenite marched before me, the sides of their legs and heads that were towards the rivulet were clear and bright blue, their darkened sides, now that the reflection of the tunnel wall no longer lit them, merged indistinguishably in the darkness beyond.

And soon I perceived that we were approaching a declivity of some sort, because the little blue stream dipped suddenly out of sight.

In another moment, as it seemed, we had reached the edge. The shining stream gave one meander of hesitation and then rushed over. It fell to a depth at which the sound of its descent was absolutely lost to us. Far below was a bluish glow, a sort of blue mist – at an infinite distance below. And the darkness the stream dropped out of became utterly void and black, save that a thing like a plank projected from the edge of the cliff and stretched out and faded and vanished altogether. There was a warm air blowing up out of the gulf.

For a moment I and Cavor stood as near the edge as we dared, peering into a blue-tinged profundity. And then our guide was pulling at my arm.

Then he left me, and walked to the end of that plank and stepped upon it, looking back. Then when he perceived we watched him, he turned about and went on along it, walking as surely as though he was on firm earth. For a moment his form was distinct, then he became a blue blur, and then vanished into the obscurity. I became aware of some vague shape looming darkly out of the black.

There was a pause. "Surely!—" said Cavor.

One of the other Selenites walked a few paces out upon the plank, and turned and looked back at us unconcernedly. The others stood ready to follow after us. Our guide's expectant figure reappeared. He was returning to see why we had not advanced.

"What is that beyond there?" I asked.

"I can't see."

"We can't cross this at any price," said I.

"I could not go three steps on it," said Cavor, "even with my hands free."

We looked at each other's drawn faces in blank consternation.

"They can't know what it is to be giddy!" said Cavor.

"It's quite impossible for us to walk that plank."

"I don't believe they see as we do. I've been watching them. I wonder if they know this is simply blackness for us. How can we make them understand?"

"Anyhow, we must make them understand."

I think we said these things with a vague half hope the Selenites might somehow understand. I knew quite clearly that all that was needed was an explanation. Then as I saw their faces, I realised that an explanation was impossible. Just here it was that our resemblances were not going to bridge our differences. Well, I wasn't going to walk the plank, anyhow. I slipped my wrist very quickly out of the coil of chain that was loose, and then began to twist my wrists in opposite directions. I was standing nearest to the bridge, and as I did this two of the Selenites laid hold of me, and pulled me gently towards it.

I shook my head violently. "No go," I said, "no use. You don't understand."

Another Selenite added his compulsion. I was forced to step forward.

"I've got an idea," said Cavor; but I knew his ideas.

"Look here!" I exclaimed to the Selenites. "Steady on! It's all very well for you—"

I sprang round upon my heel. I burst out into curses. For one of the armed Selenites had stabbed me behind with his goad.

I wrenched my wrists free from the little tentacles that held them. I turned on the goad-bearer. "Confound you!" I cried. "I've warned you of that. What on earth do you think I'm made of, to stick that into me? If you touch me again—"

By way of answer he pricked me forthwith.

I heard Cavor's voice in alarm and entreaty. Even then I think he wanted to compromise with these creatures. "I say, Bedford," he cried, "I know a way!" But the sting of that second stab seemed to set free some pent-up reserve of energy in my being. Instantly the link of the wrist-chain snapped, and with it snapped all considerations that had held us unresisting in the hands of these moon creatures. For that second, at least, I was mad with fear and anger. I took no thought of consequences. I hit straight out at the face of the thing with the goad. The chain was twisted round my fist.

There came another of these beastly surprises of which the moon world is full.

My mailed hand seemed to go clean through him. He smashed like – like some softish sort of sweet with liquid in it! He broke right in! He squelched and splashed. It was like hitting a damp toadstool. The flimsy body went spinning a dozen yards, and fell with a flabby impact. I was astonished. I was incredulous that any living thing could be so flimsy. For an instant I could have believed the whole thing a dream.

Then it had become real and imminent again. Neither Cavor nor the other Selenites seemed to have done anything from the time when I had turned about to the time when the dead Selenite hit the ground. Every one stood back from us two, every one alert. That arrest seemed to last at least a second after the Selenite was down. Every one must have been taking the thing in. I seem to remember myself standing with my arm half retracted, trying also to take it in. "What next?" clamoured my brain; "what next?" Then in a moment every one was moving!

I perceived we must get our chains loose, and that before we could do this these Selenites had to be beaten off. I faced towards the group of the three goad-bearers. Instantly one threw his goad at me. It swished over my head, and I suppose went flying into the abyss behind.

I leaped right at him with all my might as the goad flew over me. He turned to run as I jumped, and I bore him to the ground, came down right upon him, and slipped upon his smashed body and fell. He seemed to wriggle under my foot.

I came into a sitting position, and on every hand the blue backs of the Selenites were receding into the darkness. I bent a link by main force and untwisted the chain that had hampered me about the ankles, and sprang to my feet, with the chain in my hand. Another goad, flung javelin-wise, whistled by me, and I made a rush towards the darkness out of which it had come. Then I turned back towards Cavor, who was still standing in the light of the rivulet near the gulf convulsively busy with his wrists, and at the same time jabbering nonsense about his idea.

"Come on!" I cried.

"My hands!" he answered.

Then, realising that I dared not run back to him, because my ill-calculated steps might carry me over the edge, he came shuffling towards me, with his hands held out before him.

I gripped his chains at once to unfasten them.

"Where are they?" he panted.

"Run away. They'll come back. They're throwing things! Which way shall we go?"

"By the light. To that tunnel. Eh?"

"Yes," said I, and his hands were free.

I dropped on my knees and fell to work on his ankle bonds. Whack came something – I know not what – and splashed the livid streamlet into drops about us. Far away on our right a piping and whistling began.

I whipped the chain off his feet, and put it in his hand. "Hit with that!" I said, and without waiting for an answer, set off in big bounds along the path by which we had come. I had a nasty sort of feeling that these things could jump out of the darkness on to my back. I heard the impact of his leaps come following after me.

We ran in vast strides. But that running, you must understand, was an altogether different thing from any running on earth. On earth one leaps and almost instantly hits the ground again, but on the moon, because of its weaker pull, one shot through the air for several seconds before one came to earth. In spite of our violent hurry this gave an effect of long pauses, pauses in which one might have counted seven or eight. "Step," and one soared off! All sorts of questions ran through my mind: "Where are the Selenites? What will they do? Shall we ever get to that tunnel? Is Cavor far behind? Are they likely to cut him off?" Then whack, stride, and off again for another step.

I saw a Selenite running in front of me, his legs going exactly as a man's would go on earth, saw him glance over his shoulder, and heard him shriek as he ran aside out of my way into the darkness. He was, I think, our guide, but I am not sure. Then in another vast stride the walls of rock had come into view on either hand, and in two more strides I was in the tunnel, and tempering my pace to its low roof. I went on to a bend, then stopped and turned back, and plug, plug, plug, Cavor came into view, splashing into the stream of blue light at every stride, and grew larger and blundered into me. We stood clutching each other. For a moment, at least, we had shaken off our captors and were alone.

We were both very much out of breath. We spoke in panting, broken sentences.

"You've spoilt it all!" panted Cavor. "Nonsense," I cried. "It was that or death!"

"What are we to do?"

"Hide."

"How can we?"

"It's dark enough."

"But where?"

"Up one of these side caverns."

"And then?"

"Think."

"Right – come on."

We strode on, and presently came to a radiating dark cavern. Cavor was in front. He hesitated, and chose a black mouth that seemed to promise good hiding. He went towards it and turned.

"It's dark," he said.

"Your legs and feet will light us. You're wet with that luminous stuff."

"But—"

A tumult of sounds, and in particular a sound like a clanging gong, advancing up the main tunnel, became audible. It was horribly suggestive of a tumultuous pursuit. We made a bolt for the unlit side cavern forthwith. As we ran along it our way was lit by the irradiation of Cavor's legs. "It's lucky," I panted, "they took off our boots, or we should fill this place with clatter." On we rushed, taking as small steps as we could to avoid striking the roof of the cavern. After a time we seemed to be gaining on the uproar. It became muffled, it dwindled, it died away.

I stopped and looked back, and I heard the pad, pad of Cavor's feet receding. Then he stopped also. "Bedford," he whispered; "there's a sort of light in front of us."

I looked, and at first could see nothing. Then I perceived his head and shoulders dimly outlined against a fainter darkness. I saw, also, that this mitigation of the darkness was not blue, as all the other light within the moon had been, but a pallid gray, a very vague, faint white, the daylight colour. Cavor noted this difference as soon, or sooner, than I did, and I think, too, that it filled him with much the same wild hope.

"Bedford," he whispered, and his voice trembled. "That light – it is possible—"

He did not dare to say the thing he hoped. Then came a pause. Suddenly I knew by the sound of his feet that he was striding towards that pallor. I followed him with a beating heart.

CHAPTER 16

Points of View

The light grew stronger as we advanced. In a little time it was nearly as strong as the phosphorescence on Cavor's legs. Our tunnel was expanding into a cavern, and this new light was at the farther end of it. I perceived something that set my hopes leaping and bounding.

"Cavor," I said, "it comes from above! I am certain it comes from above!"

He made no answer, but hurried on.

Indisputably it was a gray light, a silvery light.

In another moment we were beneath it. It filtered down through a chink in the walls of the cavern, and as I stared up, drip, came a drop of water upon my face. I started and stood aside – drip, fell another drop quite audibly on the rocky floor.

"Cavor," I said, "if one of us lifts the other, he can reach that crack!"

"I'll lift you," he said, and incontinently hoisted me as though I was a baby.

I thrust an arm into the crack, and just at my finger tips found a little ledge by which I could hold. I could see the white light was very much brighter now. I pulled myself up by two fingers with scarcely an effort, though on earth I weigh twelve stone, reached to a still higher corner of rock, and so got my feet on the narrow ledge. I stood up and searched up the rocks with my fingers; the cleft broadened out upwardly. "It's climbable," I said to Cavor. "Can you jump up to my hand if I hold it down to you?"

I wedged myself between the sides of the cleft, rested knee and foot on the ledge, and extended a hand. I could not see Cavor, but I could hear the rustle of his movements as he crouched to spring. Then whack and he was hanging to my arm – and no heavier than a kitten! I lugged him up until he had a hand on my ledge, and could release me.

"Confound it!" I said, "any one could be a mountaineer on the moon;" and so set myself in earnest to the climbing. For a few minutes I clambered steadily, and then I looked up again. The cleft opened out steadily, and the light was brighter. Only—

It was not daylight after all.

In another moment I could see what it was, and at the sight I could have beaten my head against the rocks with disappointment. For I beheld simply an irregularly sloping open space, and all over its slanting floor stood a forest of little club-shaped fungi, each shining gloriously with that pinkish silvery light. For a moment I stared at their soft radiance, then sprang forward and upward among them. I plucked up half a dozen and flung them against the rocks, and then sat down, laughing bitterly, as Cavor's ruddy face came into view.

"It's phosphorescence again!" I said. "No need to hurry. Sit down and make yourself at home." And as he spluttered over our disappointment, I began to lob more of these growths into the cleft.

"I thought it was daylight," he said.

"Daylight!" cried I. "Daybreak, sunset, clouds, and windy skies! Shall we ever see such things again?"

As I spoke, a little picture of our world seemed to rise before me, bright and little and clear, like the background of some old Italian picture. "The sky that changes, and the sea that changes, and the hills and the green trees and the towns and cities shining in the sun. Think of a wet roof at sunset, Cavor! Think of the windows of a westward house!" He made no answer.

"Here we are burrowing in this beastly world that isn't a world, with its inky ocean hidden in some abominable blackness below, and outside that torrid day and that death stillness of night. And all these things that are chasing us now, beastly men of leather – insect men, that come out of a nightmare! After all, they're right! What business have we here smashing them and disturbing their world! For all we know the whole planet is up and after us already. In a minute we may hear them whimpering, and their gongs going. What are we to do? Where are we to go? Here we are as comfortable as snakes from Jamrach's loose in a Surbiton villa!"

"It was your fault," said Cavor.

"My fault!" I shouted. "Good Lord!"

"I had an idea!"

"Curse your ideas!"

"If we had refused to budge—"

"Under those goads?"

"Yes. They would have carried us!"

"Over that bridge?"

"Yes. They must have carried us from outside."

"I'd rather be carried by a fly across a ceiling."

"Good Heavens!"

I resumed my destruction of the fungi. Then suddenly I saw something that struck me even then. "Cavor," I said, "these chains are of gold!"

He was thinking intently, with his hands gripping his cheeks. He turned his head slowly and stared at me, and when I had repeated my words, at the twisted chain about his right hand. "So they are," he said, "so they are." His face lost its transitory interest even as he looked. He hesitated for a moment, then went on with his interrupted meditation. I sat for a space puzzling over the fact that I had only just observed this, until I considered the blue light in which we had been, and which had taken all the colour out of the metal. And from that discovery I also started upon a train of thought that carried me wide and far. I forgot that I had just been asking what business we had in the moon. Gold....

It was Cavor who spoke first. "It seems to me that there are two courses open to us."

"Well?"

"Either we can attempt to make our way – fight our way if necessary – out to the exterior again, and then hunt for our sphere until we find it, or the cold of the night comes to kill us, or else—"

He paused. "Yes?" I said, though I knew what was coming.

"We might attempt once more to establish some sort of understanding with the minds of the people in the moon."

"So far as I'm concerned – it's the first."

"I doubt."

"I don't."

"You see," said Cavor, "I do not think we can judge the Selenites by what we have seen of them. Their central world, their civilised world will be far below in the profounder caverns about their sea. This region of the crust in which we are is an outlying district, a pastoral region. At any rate, that is my interpretation. These Selenites we have seen may be only the equivalent of cowboys and engine-tenders. Their use of goads – in all probability mooncalf goads – the lack of imagination they show in expecting us to be able to do just what they can do, their indisputable brutality, all seem to point to something of that sort. But if we endured—"

"Neither of us could endure a six-inch plank across the bottomless pit for very long."

"No," said Cavor; "but then—"

"I *won't*," I said.

He discovered a new line of possibilities. "Well, suppose we got ourselves into some corner, where we could defend ourselves against these hinds and labourers. If, for example, we could hold out for a week or so, it is probable that the news of our appearance would filter down to the more intelligent and populous parts—"

"If they exist."

"They must exist, or whence came those tremendous machines?"

"That's possible, but it's the worst of the two chances."

"We might write up inscriptions on walls—"

"How do we know their eyes would see the sort of marks we made?"

"If we cut them—"

"That's possible, of course."

I took up a new thread of thought. "After all," I said, "I suppose you don't think these Selenites so infinitely wiser than men."

"They must know a lot more - or at least a lot of different things."

"Yes, but—" I hesitated.

"I think you'll quite admit, Cavor, that you're rather an exceptional man."

"How?"

"Well, you - you're a rather lonely man - have been, that is. You haven't married."

"Never wanted to. But why—"

"And you never grew richer than you happened to be?"

"Never wanted that either."

"You've just rooted after knowledge?"

"Well, a certain curiosity is natural—"

"You think so. That's just it. You think every other mind wants to *know*. I remember once, when I asked you why you conducted all these researches, you said you wanted your F.R.S., and to have the stuff called Cavorite, and things like that. You know perfectly well you didn't do it for that; but at the time my question took you by surprise, and you felt you ought to have something to look like a motive. Really you conducted researches because you *had* to. It's your twist."

"Perhaps it is—"

"It isn't one man in a million has that twist. Most men want – well, various things, but very few want knowledge for its own sake. *I* don't, I know perfectly well. Now, these Selenites seem to be a driving, busy sort of being, but how do you know that even the most intelligent will take an interest in us or our world? I don't believe they'll even know we have a world. They never come out at night – they'd freeze if they did. They've probably never seen any heavenly body at all except the blazing sun. How are they to know there *is* another world? What does it matter to them if they do? Well, even if they *have* had a glimpse of a few stars, or even of the earth crescent, what of that? Why should people living *inside* a planet trouble to observe that sort of thing? Men wouldn't have done it except for the seasons and sailing; why should the moon people?...

"Well, suppose there are a few philosophers like yourself. They are just the very Selenites who'll never have heard of our existence. Suppose a Selenite had dropped on the earth when you were at Lympne, you'd have been the last man in the world to hear he had come. You never read a newspaper! You see the chances against you. Well, it's for these chances we're sitting here doing nothing while precious time is flying. I tell you we've got into a fix. We've come unarmed, we've lost our sphere, we've got no food, we've shown ourselves to the Selenites, and made them think we're strange, strong, dangerous animals; and unless these Selenites are perfect fools, they'll set about now and hunt us till they find us, and when they find us they'll try to take us if they can, and kill us if they can't, and that's the end of the matter. If they take us, they'll probably kill us, through some misunderstanding. After we're done for, they may discuss us perhaps, but we shan't get much fun out of that."

"Go on."

"On the other hand, here's gold knocking about like cast iron at home. If only we can get some of it back, if only we can find our sphere again before they do, and get back, then—"

"Yes?"

"We might put the thing on a sounder footing. Come back in a bigger sphere with guns."

"Good Lord!" cried Cavor, as though that was horrible.

I shied another luminous fungus down the cleft.

"Look here, Cavor," I said, "I've half the voting power anyhow in this affair, and this is a case for a practical man. I'm a practical man, and you are not. I'm not going to trust to Selenites and geometrical diagrams if I can help it. That's all. Get back. Drop all this secrecy – or most of it. And come again."

He reflected. "When I came to the moon," he said, "I ought to have come alone."

"The question before the meeting," I said, "is how to get back to the sphere."

For a time we nursed our knees in silence. Then he seemed to decide for my reasons.

"I think," he said, "one can get data. It is clear that while the sun is on this side of the moon the air will be blowing through this planet sponge from the dark side hither. On this side, at any rate, the air will

be expanding and flowing out of the moon caverns into the craters....
Very well, there's a draught here."

"So there is."

"And that means that this is not a dead end; somewhere behind
us this cleft goes on and up. The draught is blowing up, and that is
the way we have to go. If we try to get up any sort of chimney or gully
there is, we shall not only get out of these passages where they are
hunting for us—"

"But suppose the gully is too narrow?"

"We'll come down again."

"Ssh!" I said suddenly; "what's that?"

We listened. At first it was an indistinct murmur, and then one
picked out the clang of a gong. "They must think we are mooncalves,"
said I, "to be frightened at that."

"They're coming along that passage," said Cavor.

"They must be."

"They'll not think of the cleft. They'll go past."

I listened again for a space. "This time," I whispered, "they're likely
to have some sort of weapon."

Then suddenly I sprang to my feet. "Good heavens, Cavor!"
I cried. "But they *will*! They'll see the fungi I have been pitching
down. They'll—"

I didn't finish my sentence. I turned about and made a leap over
the fungus tops towards the upper end of the cavity. I saw that the
space turned upward and became a draughty cleft again, ascending to
impenetrable darkness. I was about to clamber up into this, and then
with a happy inspiration turned back.

"What are you doing?" asked Cavor.

"Go on!" said I, and went back and got two of the shining fungi,
and putting one into the breast pocket of my flannel jacket, so that it

stuck out to light our climbing, went back with the other for Cavor. The noise of the Selenites was now so loud that it seemed they must be already beneath the cleft. But it might be they would have difficulty in clambering in to it, or might hesitate to ascend it against our possible resistance. At any rate, we had now the comforting knowledge of the enormous muscular superiority our birth in another planet gave us. In other minute I was clambering with gigantic vigour after Cavor's blue-lit heels.

CHAPTER 17

The Fight in the Cave of the Moon Butchers

I do not know how far we clambered before we came to the grating. It may be we ascended only a few hundred feet, but at the time it seemed to me we might have hauled and jammed and hopped and wedged ourselves through a mile or more of vertical ascent. Whenever I recall that time, there comes into my head the heavy clank of our golden chains that followed every movement. Very soon my knuckles and knees were raw, and I had a bruise on one cheek. After a time the first violence of our efforts diminished, and our movements became more deliberate and less painful. The noise of the pursuing Selenites had died away altogether. It seemed almost as though they had not traced us up the crack after all, in spite of the tell-tale heap of broken fungi that must have lain beneath it. At times the cleft narrowed so much that we could scarce squeeze up it; at others it expanded into great drusy cavities, studded with prickly crystals or thickly beset with dull, shining fungoid pimples. Sometimes it twisted spirally, and at other times slanted down nearly to the horizontal direction. Ever and again there was the intermittent drip and trickle of water by us. Once or twice it seemed to us that small living things had rustled out of our reach, but what they were we never saw. They may have been venomous beasts for all I know, but they did us no harm, and we were now tuned to a pitch when a weird creeping thing more or less mattered little. And at last, far above, came the familiar bluish light again, and then we saw that it filtered through a grating that barred our way.

We whispered as we pointed this out to one another, and became more and more cautious in our ascent. Presently we were close under the grating, and by pressing my face against its bars I could see a limited portion of the cavern beyond. It was clearly a large space, and lit no doubt by some rivulet of the same blue light that we had seen flow from the beating machinery. An intermittent trickle of water dropped ever and again between the bars near my face.

My first endeavour was naturally to see what might be upon the floor of the cavern, but our grating lay in a depression whose rim hid all this from our eyes. Our foiled attention then fell back upon the suggestion of the various sounds we heard, and presently my eye caught a number of faint shadows that played across the dim roof far overhead.

Indisputably there were several Selenites, perhaps a considerable number, in this space, for we could hear the noises of their intercourse, and faint sounds that I identified as their footfalls. There was also a succession of regularly repeated sounds – chid, chid, chid – which began and ceased, suggestive of a knife or spade hacking at some soft substance. Then came a clank as if of chains, a whistle and a rumble as of a truck running over a hollowed place, and then again that chid, chid, chid resumed. The shadows told of shapes that moved quickly and rhythmically, in agreement with that regular sound, and rested when it ceased.

We put our heads close together, and began to discuss these things in noiseless whispers.

"They are occupied," I said, "they are occupied in some way."

"Yes."

"They're not seeking us, or thinking of us."

"Perhaps they have not heard of us."

"Those others are hunting about below. If suddenly we appeared here—"

We looked at one another.

"There might be a chance to parley," said Cavor.

"No," I said. "Not as we are."

For a space we remained, each occupied by his own thoughts.

Chid, chid, chid went the chipping, and the shadows moved to and fro.

I looked at the grating. "It's flimsy," I said. "We might bend two of the bars and crawl through."

We wasted a little time in vague discussion. Then I took one of the bars in both hands, and got my feet up against the rock until they were almost on a level with my head, and so thrust against the bar. It bent so suddenly that I almost slipped. I clambered about and bent the adjacent bar in the opposite direction, and then took the luminous fungus from my pocket and dropped it down the fissure.

"Don't do anything hastily," whispered Cavor, as I twisted myself up through the opening I had enlarged. I had a glimpse of busy figures as I came through the grating, and immediately bent down, so that the rim of the depression in which the grating lay hid me from their eyes, and so lay flat, signalling advice to Cavor as he also prepared to come through. Presently we were side by side in the depression, peering over the edge at the cavern and its occupants.

It was a much larger cavern than we had supposed from our first glimpse of it, and we looked up from the lowest portion of its sloping floor. It widened out as it receded from us, and its roof came down and hid the remoter portion altogether. And lying in a line along its length, vanishing at last far away in that tremendous perspective, were a number of huge shapes, huge pallid hulls, upon which the Selenites were busy. At first they seemed big white cylinders of vague import. Then I noted the heads upon them lying towards us, eyeless and skinless like the heads of sheep at a butcher's, and perceived they were the carcasses of mooncalves being cut up, much as the crew of a whaler might cut up a moored whale. They were cutting off the flesh in strips, and on some of the farther trunks the white ribs were showing. It was the sound of their hatchets that made that chid, chid, chid. Some way away a thing like a trolley cable, drawn and loaded with chunks of lax meat, was running up the slope of the cavern floor. This enormous long avenue of hulls that were destined to be food gave us a sense of the vast populousness of the moon world second only to the effect of our first glimpse down the shaft.

It seemed to me at first that the Selenites must be standing on trestle-supported planks,* and then I saw that the planks and supports and the hatchets were really of the same leaden hue as my fetters had seemed before white light came to bear on them. A number of very thick-looking crowbars lay about the floor, and had apparently assisted to turn the dead mooncalf over on its side. They were perhaps six feet long, with shaped handles, very tempting-looking weapons. The whole place was lit by three transverse streams of the blue fluid.

[* Footnote: I do not remember seeing any wooden things on the moon; doors tables, everything corresponding to our terrestrial joinery was made of metal, and I believe for the most part of gold, which as a metal would, of course, naturally recommend itself – other things being equal – on account of the ease in working it, and its toughness and durability.]

We lay for a long time noting all these things in silence. "Well?" said Cavor at last.

I crouched over and turned to him. I had come upon a brilliant idea. "Unless they lowered those bodies by a crane," I said, "we must be nearer the surface than I thought."

"Why?"

"The mooncalf doesn't hop, and it hasn't got wings."

He peered over the edge of the hollow again. "I wonder now—" he began. "After all, we have never gone far from the surface—"

I stopped him by a grip on his arm. I had heard a noise from the cleft below us!

We twisted ourselves about, and lay as still as death, with every sense alert. In a little while I did not doubt that something was quietly ascending the cleft. Very slowly and quite noiselessly I assured myself of a good grip on my chain, and waited for that something to appear.

"Just look at those chaps with the hatchets again," I said.

"They're all right," said Cavor.

I took a sort of provisional aim at the gap in the grating. I could hear now quite distinctly the soft twittering of the ascending Selenites, the dab of their hands against the rock, and the falling of dust from their grips as they clambered.

Then I could see that there was something moving dimly in the blackness below the grating, but what it might be I could not distinguish. The whole thing seemed to hang fire just for a moment – then smash! I had sprung to my feet, struck savagely at something that had flashed out at me. It was the keen point of a spear. I have thought since that its length in the narrowness of the cleft must have prevented its being sloped to reach me. Anyhow, it shot out from the grating like the tongue of a snake, and missed and flew back and flashed again. But the second time I snatched and caught it, and wrenched it away, but not before another had darted ineffectually at me.

I shouted with triumph as I felt the hold of the Selenite resist my pull for a moment and give, and then I was jabbing down through the bars, amidst squeals from the darkness, and Cavor had snapped off the other spear, and was leaping and flourishing it beside me, and making inefficient jabs. Clang, clang, came up through the grating, and then an axe hurtled through the air and whacked against the rocks beyond, to remind me of the fleshers at the carcasses up the cavern.

I turned, and they were all coming towards us in open order waving their axes. They were short, thick, little beggars, with long arms, strikingly different from the ones we had seen before. If they had not heard of us before, they must have realised the situation with incredible swiftness. I stared at them for a moment, spear in hand. "Guard that grating, Cavor," I cried, howled to intimidate them, and rushed to meet them. Two of them missed with their hatchets, and the rest fled incontinently. Then the two also were sprinting away up the cavern, with hands clenched and heads down. I never saw men run like them!

I knew the spear I had was no good for me. It was thin and flimsy, only effectual for a thrust, and too long for a quick recover. So I only chased the Selenites as far as the first carcass, and stopped there and picked up one of the crowbars that were lying about. It felt comfortingly heavy, and equal to smashing any number of Selenites. I threw away my spear, and picked up a second crowbar for the other hand. I felt five times better than I had with the spear. I shook the two threateningly at the Selenites, who had come to a halt in a little crowd far away up the cavern, and then turned about to look at Cavor.

He was leaping from side to side of the grating, making threatening jabs with his broken spear. That was all right. It would keep the Selenites down – for a time at any rate. I looked up the cavern again. What on earth were we going to do now?

We were cornered in a sort of way already. But these butchers up the cavern had been surprised, they were probably scared, and they had no special weapons, only those little hatchets of theirs. And that way lay escape. Their sturdy little forms – ever so much shorter and thicker than the mooncalf herds – were scattered up the slope in a way that was eloquent of indecision. I had the moral advantage of a mad bull in a street. But for all that, there seemed a tremendous crowd of them. Very probably there was. Those Selenites down the cleft had certainly some infernally long spears. It might be they had other surprises for us.... But, confound it! if we charged up the cave we should let them up behind us, and if we didn't those little brutes up the cave would probably get reinforced. Heaven alone knew what tremendous engines of warfare – guns, bombs, terrestrial torpedoes – this unknown world below our feet, this vaster world of which we had only pricked the outer cuticle, might not presently send up to our destruction. It became clear the only thing to do was to charge! It became clearer as the legs of a number of fresh Selenites appeared running down the cavern towards us.

"Bedford!" cried Cavor, and behold! he was halfway between me and the grating.

"Go back!" I cried. "What are you doing—"

"They've got – it's like a gun!"

And struggling in the grating between those defensive spears appeared the head and shoulders of a singularly lean and angular Selenite, bearing some complicated apparatus.

I realised Cavor's utter incapacity for the fight we had in hand. For a moment I hesitated. Then I rushed past him whirling my crowbars, and shouting to confound the aim of the Selenite. He was aiming in the queerest way with the thing against his stomach. "*Chuzz!*" The thing wasn't a gun; it went off like cross-bow more, and dropped me in the middle of a leap.

I didn't fall down, I simply came down a little shorter than I should have done if I hadn't been hit, and from the feel of my shoulder the thing might have tapped me and glanced off. Then my left hand hit again the shaft, and I perceived there was a sort of spear sticking half through my shoulder. The moment after I got home with the crowbar in my right hand, and hit the Selenite fair and square. He collapsed – he crushed and crumpled – his head smashed like an egg.

I dropped a crowbar, pulled the spear out of my shoulder, and began to jab it down the grating into the darkness. At each jab came a shriek and twitter. Finally I hurled the spear down upon them with all my strength, leapt up, picked up the crowbar again, and started for the multitude up the cavern.

"Bedford!" cried Cavor. "Bedford!" as I flew past him.

I seem to remember his footsteps coming on behind me.

Step, leap...whack, step, leap.... Each leap seemed to last ages. With each, the cave opened out and the number of Selenites visible increased. At first they seemed all running about like ants in a disturbed ant-hill, one or two waving hatchets and coming to meet me, more running away, some bolting sideways into the avenue of carcasses, then presently others came in sight carrying spears, and then others. I saw a most extraordinary thing, all hands and feet, bolting for cover. The cavern grew darker farther up.

Flick! something flew over my head. Flick! As I soared in mid-stride I saw a spear hit and quiver in one of the carcasses to my left. Then, as I came down, one hit the ground before me, and I heard the remote chuzz! with which their things were fired. Flick, flick! for a moment it was a shower. They were volleying!

I stopped dead.

I don't think I thought clearly then. I seem to remember a kind of stereotyped phrase running through my mind: "Zone of fire, seek cover!" I know I made a dash for the space between two of the carcasses, and stood there panting and feeling very wicked.

I looked round for Cavor, and for a moment it seemed as if he had vanished from the world. Then he came out of the darkness between the row of the carcasses and the rocky wall of the cavern. I saw his little face, dark and blue, and shining with perspiration and emotion.

He was saying something, but what it was I did not heed. I had realised that we might work from mooncalf to mooncalf up the cave until we were near enough to charge home. It was charge or nothing. "Come on!" I said, and led the way.

"Bedford!" he cried unavailingly.

My mind was busy as we went up that narrow alley between the dead bodies and the wall of the cavern. The rocks curved about – they could not enfilade us. Though in that narrow space we could not leap, yet with our earth-born strength we were still able to go very much faster than the Selenites. I reckoned we should presently come right among them. Once we were on them, they would be nearly as formidable as black beetles. Only there would first of all be a volley. I thought of a stratagem. I whipped off my flannel jacket as I ran.

"Bedford!" panted Cavor behind me.

I glanced back. "What?" said I.

He was pointing upward over the carcasses. "White light!" he said. "White light again!"

I looked, and it was even so; a faint white ghost of light in the remoter cavern roof. That seemed to give me double strength.

"Keep close," I said. A flat, long Selenite dashed out of the darkness, and squealed and fled. I halted, and stopped Cavor with my hand. I hung my jacket over my crowbar, ducked round the next carcass, dropped jacket and crowbar, showed myself, and darted back.

"Chuzz-flick," just one arrow came. We were close on the Selenites, and they were standing in a crowd, broad, short, and tall together, with a little battery of their shooting implements pointing down the cave. Three or four other arrows followed the first, then their fire ceased.

I stuck out my head, and escaped by a hair's-breadth. This time I drew a dozen shots or more, and heard the Selenites shouting and twittering as if with excitement as they shot. I picked up jacket and crowbar again.

"*Now!*" said I, and thrust out the jacket.

"Chuzz-zz-zz-zz! Chuzz!" In an instant my jacket had grown a thick beard of arrows, and they were quivering all over the carcass behind us. Instantly I slipped the crowbar out of the jacket, dropped the jacket – for all I know to the contrary it is lying up there in the moon now – and rushed out upon them.

For a minute perhaps it was massacre. I was too fierce to discriminate, and the Selenites were probably too scared to fight. At any rate they made no sort of fight against me. I saw scarlet, as the saying is. I remember I seemed to be wading among those leathery, thin things as a man wades through tall grass, mowing and hitting, first right, then left; smash. Little drops of moisture flew about. I trod on things that crushed and piped and went slippery. The crowd seemed to open and close and flow like water. They seemed to have no combined plan whatever. There were spears flew about me, I was grazed over the ear by one. I was stabbed once in the arm and once in the cheek, but I only found that out afterwards, when the blood had had time to run and cool and feel wet.

What Cavor did I do not know. For a space it seemed that this fighting had lasted for an age, and must needs go on for ever. Then suddenly it was all over, and there was nothing to be seen but the backs of heads bobbing up and down as their owners ran in all directions.... I seemed altogether unhurt. I ran forward some paces, shouting, then turned about. I was amazed.

I had come right through them in vast flying strides, they were all behind me, and running hither and thither to hide.

I felt an enormous astonishment at the evaporation of the great fight into which I had hurled myself, and not a little exultation. It did not seem to me that I had discovered the Selenites were unexpectedly flimsy, but that I was unexpectedly strong. I laughed stupidly. This fantastic moon!

I glanced for a moment at the smashed and writhing bodies that were scattered over the cavern floor, with a vague idea of further violence, then hurried on after Cavor.

CHAPTER 18

In the Sunlight

Presently we saw that the cavern before us opened upon a hazy void. In another moment we had emerged upon a sort of slanting gallery, that projected into a vast circular space, a huge cylindrical pit running vertically up and down. Round this pit the slanting gallery ran without any parapet or protection for a turn and a half, and then plunged high above into the rock again. Somehow it reminded me then one of those spiral turns of the railway through the Saint Gothard. It was all tremendously huge. I can scarcely hope to convey to you the Titanic proportion of all that place, the Titanic effect of it. Our eyes followed up the vast declivity of the pit wall, and overhead and far above we beheld a round opening set with faint stars, and half of the lip about it well nigh blinding with the white light of the sun. At that we cried aloud simultaneously.

"Come on!" I said, leading the way.

"But there?" said Cavor, and very carefully stepped nearer the edge of the gallery. I followed his example, and craned forward and looked down, but I was dazzled by that gleam of light above, and I could see only a bottomless darkness with spectral patches of crimson and purple floating therein. Yet if I could not see, I could hear. Out of this darkness came a sound, a sound like the angry hum one can hear if one puts one's ear outside a hive of bees, a sound out of that enormous hollow, it may be, four miles beneath our feet...

For a moment I listened, then tightened my grip on my crowbar, and led the way up the gallery.

"This must be the shaft we looked down upon," said Cavor. "Under that lid."

"And below there, is where we saw the lights."

"The lights!" said he. "Yes – the lights of the world that now we shall never see."

"We'll come back," I said, for now we had escaped so much I was rashly sanguine that we should recover the sphere.

His answer I did not catch.

"Eh?" I asked.

"It doesn't matter," he answered, and we hurried on in silence.

I suppose that slanting lateral way was four or five miles long, allowing for its curvature, and it ascended at a slope that would have made it almost impossibly steep on earth, but which one strode up easily under lunar conditions. We saw only two Selenites during all that portion of our flight, and directly they became aware of us they ran headlong. It was clear that the knowledge of our strength and violence had reached them. Our way to the exterior was unexpectedly plain. The spiral gallery straightened into a steeply ascendent tunnel, its floor bearing abundant traces of the mooncalves, and so straight and short in proportion to its vast arch, that no part of it was absolutely dark. Almost immediately it began to lighten, and then far off and high up, and quite blindingly brilliant, appeared its opening on the exterior, a slope of Alpine steepness surmounted by a crest of bayonet shrub, tall and broken down now, and dry and dead, in spiky silhouette against the sun.

And it is strange that we men, to whom this very vegetation had seemed so weird and horrible a little time ago, should now behold it with the emotion a home-coming exile might feel at sight of his native land. We welcomed even the rareness of the air that made us pant as we ran, and which rendered speaking no longer the easy thing that it had been, but an effort to make oneself heard. Larger grew the sunlit circle above us, and larger, and all the nearer tunnel sank into a rim of indistinguishable black. We saw the dead bayonet shrub no longer with any touch of green in it, but brown and dry and thick, and the shadow of its upper branches high out of sight made a densely interlaced pattern upon the tumbled rocks. And at the immediate mouth of the tunnel was a wide trampled space where the mooncalves had come and gone.

We came out upon this space at last into a light and heat that hit and pressed upon us. We traversed the exposed area painfully, and clambered up a slope among the scrub stems, and sat down at last panting in a high place beneath the shadow of a mass of twisted lava. Even in the shade the rock felt hot.

The air was intensely hot, and we were in great physical discomfort, but for all that we were no longer in a nightmare. We seemed to have come to our own province again, beneath the stars. All the fear and stress of our flight through the dim passages and fissures below had fallen from us. That last fight had filled us with an enormous confidence in ourselves so far as the Selenites were concerned. We looked back almost incredulously at the black opening from which we had just emerged. Down there it was, in a blue glow that now in our memories seemed the next thing to absolute darkness, we had met with things like mad mockeries of men, helmet-headed creatures, and had walked in fear before them, and had submitted to them until we could submit no longer. And behold, they had smashed like wax and scattered like chaff, and fled and vanished like the creatures of a dream!

I rubbed my eyes, doubting whether we had not slept and dreamt these things by reason of the fungus we had eaten, and suddenly discovered the blood upon my face, and then that my shirt was sticking painfully to my shoulder and arm.

"Confound it!" I said, gauging my injuries with an investigatory hand, and suddenly that distant tunnel mouth became, as it were, a watching eye.

"Cavor!" I said; "what are they going to do now? And what are we going to do?"

He shook his head, with his eyes fixed upon the tunnel. "How can one tell what they will do?"

"It depends on what they think of us, and I don't see how we can begin to guess that. And it depends upon what they have in reserve. It's as you say, Cavor, we have touched the merest outside of this world. They may have all sorts of things inside here. Even with those shooting things they might make it bad for us....

"Yet after all," I said, "even if we *don't* find the sphere at once, there is a chance for us. We might hold out. Even through the night. We might go down there again and make a fight for it."

I stared about me with speculative eyes. The character of the scenery had altered altogether by reason of the enormous growth and subsequent drying of the scrub. The crest on which we sat was high, and commanded a wide prospect of the crater landscape, and we saw it now all sere and dry in the late autumn of the lunar afternoon. Rising one behind the other were long slopes and fields of trampled brown where the mooncalves had pastured, and far away in the full blaze of the sun a drove of them basked slumberously, scattered shapes, each with a blot of shadow against it like sheep on the side of a down. But never a sign of a Selenite was to be seen. Whether they had fled on our emergence from the interior passages, or whether they were accustomed to retire after driving out the mooncalves, I cannot guess. At the time I believed the former was the case.

"If we were to set fire to all this stuff," I said, "we might find the sphere among the ashes."

Cavor did not seem to hear me. He was peering under his hand at the stars, that still, in spite of the intense sunlight, were abundantly visible in the sky. "How long do you think we've have been here?" he asked at last.

"Been where?"

"On the moon."

"Two earthly days, perhaps."

"More nearly ten. Do you know, the sun is past its zenith, and sinking in the west. In four days' time or less it will be night."

"But – we've only eaten once!"

"I know that. And— But there are the stars!"

"But why should time seem different because we are on a smaller planet?"

"I don't know. There it is!"

"How does one tell time?"

"Hunger – fatigue – all those things are different. Everything is different – everything. To me it seems that since first we came out of the sphere has been only a question of hours – long hours – at most."

"Ten days," I said; "that leaves—" I looked up at the sun for a moment, and then saw that it was halfway from the zenith to the western edge of things. "Four days! ... Cavor, we mustn't sit here and dream. How do you think we may begin?"

I stood up. "We must get a fixed point we can recognise – we might hoist a flag, or a handkerchief, or something – and quarter the ground, and work round that."

He stood up beside me.

"Yes," he said, "there is nothing for it but to hunt the sphere. Nothing. We may find it - certainly we may find it. And if not—"

"We must keep on looking."

He look this way and that, glanced up at the sky and down at the tunnel, and astonished me by a sudden gesture of impatience. "Oh! but we have done foolishly! To have come to this pass! Think how it might have been, and the things we might have done!"

"We might do something yet."

"Never the thing we might have done. Here below out feet is a world. Think of what that world must be! Think of that machine we saw, and the lid and the shaft! They were just remote outlying things, and those creatures we have seen and fought with no more than ignorant peasants, dwellers in the outskirts, yokels and labourers half akin to brutes. Down below! Caverns beneath caverns, tunnels, structures, ways... It must open out, and be greater and wider and more populous as one descends. Assuredly. Right down at the last the central sea that washes round the core of the moon. Think of its inky waters under the spare lights - if, indeed, their eyes *need* lights! Think of the cascading tributaries pouring down their channels to feed it! Think of the tides upon its surface, and the rush and swirl of its ebb and flow! Perhaps they have ships that go upon it, perhaps down there are mighty cities and swarming ways, and wisdom and order passing the wit of man. And we may die here upon it, and never see the masters who *must* be - ruling over these things! We may freeze and die here, and the air will freeze and thaw upon us, and then—! Then they will come upon us, come on our stiff and silent bodies, and find the sphere we cannot find, and they will understand at last too late all the thought and effort that ended here in vain!"

His voice for all that speech sounded like the voice of someone heard in a telephone, weak and far away.

"But the darkness," I said.

"One might get over that."

"How?"

"I don't know. How am I to know? One might carry a torch, one might have a lamp— The others – might understand."

He stood for a moment with his hands held down and a rueful face, staring out over the waste that defied him. Then with a gesture of renunciation he turned towards me with proposals for the systematic hunting of the sphere.

"We can return," I said.

He looked about him. "First of all we shall have to get to earth."

"We could bring back lamps to carry and climbing irons, and a hundred necessary things."

"Yes," he said.

"We can take back an earnest of success in this gold."

He looked at my golden crowbars, and said nothing for a space. He stood with his hands clasped behind his back, staring across the crater. At last he signed and spoke. "It was *I* found the way here, but to find a way isn't always to be master of a way. If I take my secret back to earth, what will happen? I do not see how I can keep my secret for a year, for even a part of a year. Sooner or later it must come out, even if other men rediscover it. And then ... Governments and powers will struggle to get hither, they will fight against one another, and against these moon people; it will only spread warfare and multiply the occasions of war. In a little while, in a very little while, if I tell my secret, this planet to its deepest galleries will be strewn with human dead. Other things are doubtful, but that is certain. It is not as though man had any use for the moon. What good would the moon be to men? Even of their own planet what have they made but a battle-ground and theatre of infinite folly? Small as his world is, and short as his time, he has still in his little life down there far more than he can do. No! Science has toiled too long forging weapons for fools to use. It is time she held her hand. Let him find it out for himself again – in a thousand years' time."

"There are methods of secrecy," I said.

He looked up at me and smiled. "After all," he said, "why should one worry? There is little chance of our finding the sphere, and down below things are brewing. It's simply the human habit of hoping till we die that makes us think of return. Our troubles are only beginning. We have shown these moon folk violence, we have given them a taste of our quality, and our chances are about as good as a tiger's that has got loose and killed a man in Hyde Park. The news of us must be running down from gallery to gallery, down towards the central parts.... No sane beings will ever let us take that sphere back to earth after so much as they have seen of us."

"We aren't improving our chances," said I, "by sitting here."

We stood up side by side.

"After all," he said, "we must separate. We must stick up a handkerchief on these tall spikes here and fasten it firmly, and from this as a centre we must work over the crater. You must go westward, moving out in semicircles to and fro towards the setting sun. You must move first with your shadow on your right until it is at right angles with the direction of your handkerchief, and then with your shadow on your left. And I will do the same to the east. We will look into every gully, examine every skerry of rocks; we will do all we can to find my sphere. If we see the Selenites we will hide from them as well as we can. For drink we must take snow, and if we feel the need of food, we must kill a mooncalf if we can, and eat such flesh as it has – raw – and so each will go his own way."

"And if one of us comes upon the sphere?"

"He must come back to the white handkerchief, and stand by it and signal to the other."

"And if neither?"

Cavor glanced up at the sun. "We go on seeking until the night and cold overtake us."

"Suppose the Selenites have found the sphere and hidden it?"

He shrugged his shoulders.

"Or if presently they come hunting us?"

He made no answer.

"You had better take a club," I said.

He shook his head, and stared away from me across the waste.

But for a moment he did not start. He looked round at me shyly, hesitated. "*Au revoir*," he said.

I felt an odd stab of emotion. A sense of how we had galled each other, and particularly how I must have galled him, came to me. "Confound it," thought I, "we might have done better!" I was on the point of asking him to shake hands – for that, somehow, was how I felt just then – when he put his feet together and leapt away from me towards the north. He seemed to drift through the air as a dead leaf would do, fell lightly, and leapt again. I stood for a moment watching him, then faced westward reluctantly, pulled myself together, and with something of the feeling of a man who leaps into icy water, selected a leaping point, and plunged forward to explore my solitary half of the moon world. I dropped rather clumsily among rocks, stood up and looked about me, clambered on to a rocky slab, and leapt again....

When presently I looked for Cavor he was hidden from my eyes, but the handkerchief showed out bravely on its headland, white in the blaze of the sun.

I determined not to lose sight of that handkerchief whatever might betide.

CHAPTER 19

Mr. Bedford Alone

In a little while it seemed to me as though I had always been alone on the moon. I hunted for a time with a certain intentness, but the heat was still very great, and the thinness of the air felt like a hoop about one's chest. I came presently into a hollow basin bristling with tall, brown, dry fronds about its edge, and I sat down under these to rest and cool. I intended to rest for only a little while. I put down my clubs beside me, and sat resting my chin on my hands. I saw with a sort of colourless interest that the rocks of the basin, where here and there the crackling dry lichens had shrunk away to show them, were all veined and splattered with gold, that here and there bosses of rounded and wrinkled gold projected from among the litter. What did that matter now? A sort of languor had possession of my limbs and mind, I did not believe for a moment that we should ever find the sphere in that vast desiccated wilderness. I seemed to lack a motive for effort until the Selenites should come. Then I supposed I should exert myself, obeying that unreasonable imperative that urges a man before all things to preserve and defend his life, albeit he may preserve it only to die more painfully in a little while.

Why had we come to the moon?

The thing presented itself to me as a perplexing problem. What is this spirit in man that urges him for ever to depart from happiness and security, to toil, to place himself in danger, to risk even a reasonable certainty of death? It dawned upon me up there in the moon as a thing I ought always to have known, that man is not made simply to go about being safe and comfortable and well fed and amused. Almost any man, if you put the thing to him, not in words, but in the shape of opportunities, will show that he knows as much. Against his interest, against his happiness, he is constantly being driven to do unreasonable things. Some force not himself impels him, and go he must. But why? Why? Sitting there in the midst of that useless moon gold, amidst the things of another world, I took count of all my life. Assuming I was to die a castaway upon the moon, I failed altogether to see what purpose I had served. I got no light on that point, but at any rate it was clearer to me than it had ever been in my life before that I was not serving my own purpose, that all my life I had in truth never served the purposes of my private life. Whose purposes, what purposes, was I serving?... I ceased to speculate on why we had come to the moon, and took a wider sweep. Why had I come to the earth? Why had I a private life at all?...I lost myself at last in bottomless speculations....

My thoughts became vague and cloudy, no longer leading in definite directions. I had not felt heavy or weary – I cannot imagine one doing so upon the moon – but I suppose I was greatly fatigued. At any rate I slept.

Slumbering there rested me greatly, I think, and the sun was setting and the violence of the heat abating, through all the time I slumbered. When at last I was roused from my slumbers by a remote clamour, I felt active and capable again. I rubbed my eyes and stretched my arms. I rose to my feet – I was a little stiff – and at once prepared to resume my search. I shouldered my golden clubs, one on each shoulder, and went on out of the ravine of the gold-veined rocks.

The sun was certainly lower, much lower than it had been; the air was very much cooler. I perceived I must have slept some time.

It seemed to me that a faint touch of misty blueness hung about the western cliff I leapt to a little boss of rock and surveyed the crater. I could see no signs of mooncalves or Selenites, nor could I see Cavor, but I could see my handkerchief far off, spread out on its thicket of thorns. I looked bout me, and then leapt forward to the next convenient view-point.

I beat my round in a semicircle, and back again in a still remoter crescent. It was very fatiguing and hopeless. The air was really very much cooler, and it seemed to me that the shadow under the westward cliff was growing broad. Ever and again I stopped and reconnoitred, but there was no sign of Cavor, no sign of Selenites; and it seemed to me the mooncalves must have been driven into the interior again – I could see none of them. I became more and more desirous of seeing Cavor. The winged outline of the sun had sunk now, until it was scarcely the distance of its diameter from the rim of the sky. I was oppressed by the idea that the Selenites would presently close their lids and valves, and shut us out under the inexorable onrush of the lunar night. It seemed to me high time that he abandoned his search, and that we took counsel together. I felt how urgent it was that we should decide soon upon our course. We had failed to find the sphere, we no longer had time to seek it, and once these valves were closed with us outside, we were lost men. The great night of space would descend upon us – that blackness of the void which is the only absolute death. All my being shrank from that approach. We must get into the moon again, though we were slain in doing it. I was haunted by a vision of our freezing to death, of our hammering with our last strength on the valve of the great pit.

I took no thought any more of the sphere. I thought only of finding Cavor again. I was half inclined to go back into the moon without him, rather than seek him until it was too late. I was already half-way back towards our handkerchief, when suddenly—

I saw the sphere!

I did not find it so much as it found me. It was lying much farther to the westward than I had gone, and the sloping rays of the sinking sun reflected from its glass had suddenly proclaimed its presence in a dazzling beam. For an instant I thought this was some new device of the Selenites against us, and then I understood.

I threw up my arms, shouted a ghostly shout, and set off in vast leaps towards it. I missed one of my leaps and dropped into a deep ravine and twisted my ankle, and after that I stumbled at almost every leap. I was in a state of hysterical agitation, trembling violently, and quite breathless long before I got to it. Three times at least I had to stop with my hands resting on my side and in spite of the thin dryness of the air, the perspiration was wet upon my face.

I thought of nothing but the sphere until I reached it, I forgot even my trouble of Cavor's whereabouts. My last leap flung me with my hands hard against its glass; then I lay against it panting, and trying vainly to shout, "Cavor! here is the sphere!" When I had recovered a little I peered through the thick glass, and the things inside seemed tumbled. I stooped to peer closer. Then I attempted to get in. I had to hoist it over a little to get my head through the manhole. The screw stopper was inside, and I could see now that nothing had been touched, nothing had suffered. It lay there as we had left it when we had dropped out amidst the snow. For a time I was wholly occupied in making and remaking this inventory. I found I was trembling violently. It was good to see that familiar dark interior again! I cannot tell you how good. Presently I crept inside and sat down among the things. I looked through the glass at the moon world and shivered. I placed my gold clubs upon the table, and sought out and took a little food; not so much because I wanted it, but because it was there. Then it occurred to me that it was time to go out and signal for Cavor. But I did not go out and signal for Cavor forthwith. Something held me to the sphere.

After all, everything was coming right. There would be still time for us to get more of the magic stone that gives one mastery over men. Away there, close handy, was gold for the picking up; and the sphere would travel as well half full of gold as though it were empty. We could go back now, masters of ourselves and our world, and then—

I roused myself at last, and with an effort got myself out of the sphere. I shivered as I emerged, for the evening air was growing very cold. I stood in the hollow staring about me. I scrutinised the bushes round me very carefully before I leapt to the rocky shelf hard by, and took once more what had been my first leap in the moon. But now I made it with no effort whatever.

The growth and decay of the vegetation had gone on apace, and the whole aspect of the rocks had changed, but still it was possible to make out the slope on which the seeds had germinated, and the rocky mass from which we had taken our first view of the crater. But the spiky shrub on the slope stood brown and sere now, and thirty feet high, and cast long shadows that stretched out of sight, and the little seeds that clustered in its upper branches were brown and ripe. Its work was done, and it was brittle and ready to fall and crumple under the freezing air, so soon as the nightfall came. And the huge cacti, that had swollen as we watched them, had long since burst and scattered their spores to the four quarters of the moon. Amazing little corner in the universe – the landing place of men!

Some day, thought I, I will have an inscription standing there right in the midst of the hollow. It came to me, if only this teeming world within knew of the full import of the moment, how furious its tumult would become!

But as yet it could scarcely be dreaming of the significance of our coming. For if it did, the crater would surely be an uproar of pursuit, instead of as still as death! I looked about for some place from which I might signal Cavor, and saw that same patch of rock to which he had leapt from my present standpoint, still bare and barren in the sun. For a moment I hesitated at going so far from the sphere. Then with a pang of shame at that hesitation, I leapt....

From this vantage point I surveyed the crater again. Far away at the top of the enormous shadow I cast was the little white handkerchief fluttering on the bushes. It was very little and very far, and Cavor was not in sight. It seemed to me that by this time he ought to be looking for me. That was the agreement. But he was nowhere to be seen.

I stood waiting and watching, hands shading my eyes, expecting every moment to distinguish him. Very probably I stood there for quite a long time. I tried to shout, and was reminded of the thinness of the air. I made an undecided step back towards the sphere. But a lurking dread of the Selenites made me hesitate to signal my whereabouts by hoisting one of our sleeping-blankets on to the adjacent scrub. I searched the crater again.

It had an effect of emptiness that chilled me. And it was still. Any sound from the Selenites in the world beneath had died away. It was as still as death. Save for the faint stir of the shrub about me in the little breeze that was rising, there was no sound nor shadow of a sound. And the breeze blew chill.

Confound Cavor!

I took a deep breath. I put my hands to the sides of my mouth. "Cavor!" I bawled, and the sound was like some manikin shouting far away.

I looked at the handkerchief, I looked behind me at the broadening shadow of the westward cliff, I looked under my hand at the sun. It seemed to me that almost visibly it was creeping down the sky.

I felt I must act instantly if I was to save Cavor. I whipped off my vest and flung it as a mark on the sere bayonets of the shrubs behind me, and then set off in a straight line towards the handkerchief. Perhaps it was a couple of miles away – a matter of a few hundred leaps and strides. I have already told how one seemed to hang through those lunar leaps. In each suspense I sought Cavor, and marvelled why he should be hidden. In each leap I could feel the sun setting behind me. Each time I touched the ground I was tempted to go back.

A last leap and I was in the depression below our handkerchief, a stride, and I stood on our former vantage point within arms' reach of it. I stood up straight and scanned the world about me, between its lengthening bars of shadow. Far away, down a long declivity, was the opening of the tunnel up which we had fled, and my shadow reached towards it, stretched towards it, and touched it, like a finger of the night.

Not a sign of Cavor, not a sound in all the stillness, only the stir and waving of the scrub and of the shadows increased. And suddenly and violently I shivered. "Cav–" I began, and realised once more the uselessness of the human voice in that thin air. Silence. The silence of death.

Then it was my eye caught something – a little thing lying, perhaps fifty yards away down the slope, amidst a litter of bent and broken branches. What was it? I knew, and yet for some reason I would not know. I went nearer to it. It was the little cricket-cap Cavor had worn. I did not touch it, I stood looking at it.

I saw then that the scattered branches about it had been forcibly smashed and trampled. I hesitated, stepped forward, and picked it up.

I stood with Cavor's cap in my hand, staring at the trampled reeds and thorns about me. On some, of them were little smears of something dark, something that I dared not touch. A dozen yards away, perhaps, the rising breeze dragged something into view, something small and vividly white.

It was a little piece of paper crumpled tightly, as though it had been clutched tightly. I picked it up, and on it were smears of red. My eye caught faint pencil marks. I smoothed it out, and saw uneven and broken writing ending at last in a crooked streak up on the paper.

I set myself to decipher this.

"I have been injured about the knee, I think my kneecap is hurt, and I cannot run or crawl," it began – pretty distinctly written.

Then less legibly: "They have been chasing me for some time, and it is only a question of" – the word "time" seemed to have been written here and erased in favour of something illegible – "before they get me. They are beating all about me."

Then the writing became convulsive. "I can hear them," I guessed the tracing meant, and then it was quite unreadable for a space. Then came a little string of words that were quite distinct: "a different sort of Selenite altogether, who appears to be directing the—" The writing became a mere hasty confusion again.

"They have larger brain cases - much larger, and slenderer bodies, and very short legs. They make gentle noises, and move with organized deliberation...

"And though I am wounded and helpless here, their appearance still gives me hope." That was like Cavor. "They have not shot at me or attempted... injury. I intend—"

Then came the sudden streak of the pencil across the paper, and on the back and edges - blood!

And as I stood there stupid, and perplexed, with this dumbfounding relic in my hand, something very soft and light and chill touched my hand for a moment and ceased to be, and then a thing, a little white speck, drifted athwart a shadow. It was a tiny snowflake, the first snowflake, the herald of the night.

I looked up with a start, and the sky had darkened almost to blackness, and was thick with a gathering multitude of coldly watchful stars. I looked eastward, and the light of that shrivelled world was touched with sombre bronze; westward, and the sun robbed now by a thickening white mist of half its heat and splendour, was touching the crater rim, was sinking out of sight, and all the shrubs and jagged and tumbled rocks stood out against it in a bristling disorder of black shapes. Into the great lake of darkness westward, a vast wreath of mist was sinking. A cold wind set all the crater shivering. Suddenly, for a moment, I was in a puff of falling snow, and all the world about me gray and dim.

And then it was I heard, not loud and penetrating as at first, but faint and dim like a dying voice, that tolling, that same tolling that had welcomed the coming of the day: Boom!... Boom!... Boom!...

It echoed about the crater, it seemed to throb with the throbbing of the greater stars, the blood-red crescent of the sun's disc sank as it tolled out: Boom!... Boom!... Boom!...

What had happened to Cavor? All through that tolling I stood there stupidly, and at last the tolling ceased.

And suddenly the open mouth of the tunnel down below there, shut like an eye and vanished out of sight.

Then indeed was I alone.

Over me, around me, closing in on me, embracing me ever nearer, was the Eternal; that which was before the beginning, and that which triumphs over the end; that enormous void in which all light and life and being is but the thin and vanishing splendour of a falling star, the cold, the stillness, the silence – the infinite and final Night of space.

The sense of solitude and desolation became the sense of an overwhelming presence that stooped towards me, that almost touched me.

"No," I cried. "*No!* Not yet! not yet! Wait! Wait! Oh, wait!" My voice went up to a shriek. I flung the crumpled paper from me, scrambled back to the crest to take my bearings, and then, with all the will that was in me, leapt out towards the mark I had left, dim and distant now in the very margin of the shadow.

Leap, leap, leap, and each leap was seven ages.

Before me the pale serpent-girdled section of the sun sank and sank, and the advancing shadow swept to seize the sphere before I could reach it. I was two miles away, a hundred leaps or more, and the air about me was thinning out as it thins under an air-pump, and the cold was gripping at my joints. But had I died, I should have died leaping. Once, and then again my foot slipped on the gathering snow as I leapt and shortened my leap; once I fell short into bushes that crashed and smashed into dusty chips and nothingness, and once I stumbled as I dropped and rolled head over heels into a gully, and rose bruised and bleeding and confused as to my direction.

But such incidents were as nothing to the intervals, those awful pauses when one drifted through the air towards that pouring tide of night. My breathing made a piping noise, and it was as though knives were whirling in my lungs. My heart seemed to beat against the top of my brain. "Shall I reach it? O Heaven! Shall I reach it?"

My whole being became anguish.

"Lie down!" screamed my pain and despair; "lie down!"

The nearer I struggled, the more awfully remote it seemed. I was numb, I stumbled, I bruised and cut myself and did not bleed.

It was in sight.

I fell on all fours, and my lungs whooped.

I crawled. The frost gathered on my lips, icicles hung from my moustache, I was white with the freezing atmosphere.

I was a dozen yards from it. My eyes had become dim. "Lie down!" screamed despair; "lie down!"

I touched it, and halted. "Too late!" screamed despair; "lie down!"

I fought stiffly with it. I was on the manhole lip, a stupefied, half-dead being. The snow was all about me. I pulled myself in. There lurked within a little warmer air.

The snowflakes – the airflakes – danced in about me, as I tried with chilling hands to thrust the valve in and spun it tight and hard. I sobbed. "I will," I chattered in my teeth. And then, with fingers that quivered and felt brittle, I turned to the shutter studs.

As I fumbled with the switches – for I had never controlled them before – I could see dimly through the steaming glass the blazing red streamers of the sinking sun, dancing and flickering through the snowstorm, and the black forms of the scrub thickening and bending and breaking beneath the accumulating snow. Thicker whirled the snow and thicker, black against the light. What if even now the switches overcame me? Then something clicked under my hands, and in an instant that last vision of the moon world was hidden from my eyes. I was in the silence and darkness of the inter-planetary sphere.

CHAPTER 20

Mr. Bedford in Infinite Space

It was almost as though I had been killed. Indeed, I could imagine a man suddenly and violently killed would feel very much as I did. One moment, a passion of agonising existence and fear; the next darkness and stillness, neither light nor life nor sun, moon nor stars, the blank infinite. Although the thing was done by my own act, although I had already tasted this very of effect in Cavor's company, I felt astonished, dumbfounded, and overwhelmed. I seemed to be borne upward into an enormous darkness. My fingers floated off the studs, I hung as if I were annihilated, and at last very softly and gently I came against the bale and the golden chain, and the crowbars that had drifted to the middle of the sphere.

I do not know how long that drifting took. In the sphere of course, even more than on the moon, one's earthly time sense was ineffectual. At the touch of the bale it was as if I had awakened from a dreamless sleep. I immediately perceived that if I wanted to keep awake and alive I must get a light or open a window, so as to get a grip of something with my eyes. And besides, I was cold. I kicked off from the bale, therefore, clawed on to the thin cords within the glass, crawled along until I got to the manhole rim, and so got my bearings for the light and blind studs, took a shove off, and flying once round the bale, and getting a scare from something big and flimsy that was drifting loose, I got my hand on the cord quite close to the studs, and reached them. I lit the little lamp first of all to see what it was I had collided with, and discovered that old copy of *Lloyd's News* had slipped its moorings, and was adrift in the void. That brought me out of the infinite to my own proper dimensions again. It made me laugh and pant for a time, and suggested the idea of a little oxygen from one of the cylinders. After that I lit the heater until I felt warm, and then I took food. Then I set to work in a very gingerly fashion on the Cavorite blinds, to see if I could guess by any means how the sphere was travelling.

The first blind I opened I shut at once, and hung for a time flattened and blinded by the sunlight that had hit me. After thinking a little I started upon the windows at right angles to this one, and got the huge crescent moon and the little crescent earth behind it, the second time. I was amazed to find how far I was from the moon. I had reckoned that not only should I have little or none of the "kick-off" that the earth's atmosphere had given us at our start, but that the tangential "fly off" of the moon's spin would be at least twenty-eight times less than the earth's. I had expected to discover myself hanging over our crater, and on the edge of the night, but all that was now only a part of the outline of the white crescent that filled the sky. And Cavor—?

He was already infinitesimal.

I tried to imagine what could have happened to him. But at that time I could think of nothing but death. I seemed to see him, bent and smashed at the foot of some interminably high cascade of blue. And all about him the stupid insects stared...

Under the inspiring touch of the drifting newspaper I became practical again for a while. It was quite clear to me that what I had to do was to get back to earth, but as far as I could see I was drifting away from it. Whatever had happened to Cavor, even if he was still alive, which seemed to me incredible after that blood-stained scrap, I was powerless to help him. There he was, living or dead behind the mantle of that rayless night, and there he must remain at least until I could summon our fellow men to his assistance. Should I do that? Something of the sort I had in my mind; to come back to earth if it were possible, and then as maturer consideration might determine, either to show and explain the sphere to a few discreet persons, and act with them, or else to keep my secret, sell my gold, obtain weapons, provisions, and an assistant, and return with these advantages to deal on equal terms with the flimsy people of the moon, to rescue Cavor, if that were still possible, and at any rate to procure a sufficient supply of gold to place my subsequent proceedings on a firmer basis. But that was hoping far; I had first to get back.

I set myself to decide just exactly how the return to earth could be contrived. As I struggled with that problem I ceased to worry about what I should do when I got there. At last my only care was to get back.

I puzzled out at last that my best chance would be to drop back towards the moon as near as I dared in order to gather velocity, then to shut my windows, and fly behind it, and when I was past to open my earthward windows, and so get off at a good pace homeward. But whether I should ever reach the earth by that device, or whether I might not simply find myself spinning about it in some hyperbolic or parabolic curve or other, I could not tell. Later I had a happy inspiration, and by opening certain windows to the moon, which had appeared in the sky in front of the earth, I turned my course aside so as to head off the earth, which it had become evident to me I must pass behind without some such expedient. I did a very great deal of complicated thinking over these problems – for I am no mathematician – and in the end I am certain it was much more my good luck than my reasoning that enabled me to hit the earth. Had I known then, as I know now, the mathematical chances there were against me, I doubt if I should have troubled even to touch the studs to make any attempt. And having puzzled out what I considered to be the thing to do, I opened all my moonward windows, and squatted down – the effort lifted me for a time some feet or so into the air, and I hung there in the oddest way – and waited for the crescent to get bigger and bigger until I felt I was near enough for safety. Then I would shut the windows, fly past the moon with the velocity I had got from it – if I did not smash upon it – and so go on towards the earth.

And that is what I did.

At last I felt my moonward start was sufficient. I shut out the sight of the moon from my eyes, and in a state of mind that was, I now recall, incredibly free from anxiety or any distressful quality, I sat down to begin a vigil in that little speck of matter in infinite space that would last until I should strike the earth. The heater had made the sphere tolerably warm, the air had been refreshed by the oxygen, and except for that faint congestion of the head that was always with me while I was away from earth, I felt entire physical comfort. I had extinguished the light again, lest it should fail me in the end; I was in darkness, save for the earthshine and the glitter of the stars below me. Everything was so absolutely silent and still that I might indeed have been the only being in the universe, and yet, strangely enough, I had no more feeling of loneliness or fear than if I had been lying in bed on earth. Now, this seems all the stranger to me, since during my last hours in that crater of the moon, the sense of my utter loneliness had been an agony....

Incredible as it will seem, this interval of time that I spent in space has no sort of proportion to any other interval of time in my life. Sometimes it seemed as though I sat through immeasurable eternities like some god upon a lotus leaf, and again as though there was a momentary pause as I leapt from moon to earth. In truth, it was altogether some weeks of earthly time. But I had done with care and anxiety, hunger or fear, for that space. I floated, thinking with a strange breadth and freedom of all that we had undergone, and of all my life and motives, and the secret issues of my being. I seemed to myself to have grown greater and greater, to have lost all sense of movement; to be floating amidst the stars, and always the sense of earth's littleness and the infinite littleness of my life upon it, was implicit in my thoughts.

I can't profess to explain the things that happened in my mind. No doubt they could all be traced directly or indirectly to the curious physical conditions under which I was living. I set them down here just for what they are worth, and without any comment. The most prominent quality of it was a pervading doubt of my own identity. I became, if I may so express it, dissociate from Bedford; I looked down on Bedford as a trivial, incidental thing with which I chanced to be connected. I saw Bedford in many relations – as an ass or as a poor beast, where I had hitherto been inclined to regard him with a quiet pride as a very spirited or rather forcible person. I saw him not only as an ass, but as the son of many generations of asses. I reviewed his school-days and his early manhood, and his first encounter with love, very much as one might review the proceedings of an ant in the sand. Something of that period of lucidity I regret still hangs about me, and I doubt if I shall ever recover the full-bodied self satisfaction of my early days. But at the time the thing was not in the least painful, because I had that extraordinary persuasion that, as a matter of fact, I was no more Bedford than I was any one else, but only a mind floating in the still serenity of space. Why should I be disturbed about this Bedford's shortcomings? I was not responsible for him or them.

For a time I struggled against this really very grotesque delusion.
I tried to summon the memory of vivid moments, of tender or
intense emotions to my assistance; I felt that if I could recall one
genuine twinge of feeling the growing severance would be stopped.
But I could not do it. I saw Bedford rushing down Chancery Lane,
hat on the back of his head, coat tails flying out, *en route* for his
public examination. I saw him dodging and bumping against, and
even saluting, other similar little creatures in that swarming gutter of
people. Me? I saw Bedford that same evening in the sitting-room of a
certain lady, and his hat was on the table beside him, and it wanted
brushing badly, and he was in tears. Me? I saw him with that lady in
various attitudes and emotions – I never felt so detached before....
I saw him hurrying off to Lympne to write a play, and accosting
Cavor, and in his shirt sleeves working at the sphere, and walking
out to Canterbury because he was afraid to come! Me? I did not
believe it.

I still reasoned that all this was hallucination due to my solitude,
and the fact that I had lost all weight and sense of resistance. I
endeavoured to recover that sense by banging myself about the
sphere, by pinching my hands and clasping them together. Among
other things, I lit the light, captured that torn copy of *Lloyd's*, and
read those convincingly realistic advertisements about the Cutaway
bicycle, and the gentleman of private means, and the lady in distress
who was selling those "forks and spoons." There was no doubt *they*
existed surely enough, and, said I, "This is your world, and you are
Bedford, and you are going back to live among things like that for all
the rest of your life." But the doubts within me could still argue: "It
is not you that is reading, it is Bedford, but you are not Bedford, you
know. That's just where the mistake comes in."

"Confound it!" I cried; "and if I am not Bedford, what am I?"

But in that direction no light was forthcoming, though the strangest fancies came drifting into my brain, queer remote suspicions, like shadows seen from away. Do you know, I had a sort of idea that really I was something quite outside not only the world, but all worlds, and out of space and time, and that this poor Bedford was just a peephole through which I looked at life? ...

Bedford! However I disavowed him, there I was most certainly bound up with him, and I knew that wherever or whatever I might be, I must needs feel the stress of his desires, and sympathise with all his joys and sorrows until his life should end. And with the dying of Bedford – what then? ...

Enough of this remarkable phase of my experiences! I tell it here simply to show how one's isolation and departure from this planet touched not only the functions and feeling of every organ of the body, but indeed also the very fabric of the mind, with strange and unanticipated disturbances. All through the major portion of that vast space journey I hung thinking of such immaterial things as these, hung dissociated and apathetic, a cloudy megalomaniac, as it were, amidst the stars and planets in the void of space; and not only the world to which I was returning, but the blue-lit caverns of the Selenites, their helmet faces, their gigantic and wonderful machines, and the fate of Cavor, dragged helpless into that world, seemed infinitely minute and altogether trivial things to me.

Until at last I began to feel the pull of the earth upon my being, drawing me back again to the life that is real for men. And then, indeed, it grew clearer and clearer to me that I was quite certainly Bedford after all, and returning after amazing adventures to this world of ours, and with a life that I was very likely to lose in this return. I set myself to puzzle out the conditions under which I must fall to earth.

CHAPTER 21

Mr. Bedford at Littlestone

My line of flight was about parallel with the surface as I came into the upper air. The temperature of sphere began to rise forthwith. I knew it behoved me to drop at once. Far below me, in a darkling twilight, stretched a great expanse of sea. I opened every window I could, and fell – out of sunshine into evening, and out of evening into night. Vaster grew the earth and vaster, swallowing up the stars, and the silvery translucent starlit veil of cloud it wore spread out to catch me. At last the world seemed no longer a sphere but flat, and then concave. It was no longer a planet in the sky, but the world of Man. I shut all but an inch or so of earthward window, and dropped with a slackening velocity. The broadening water, now so near that I could see the dark glitter of the waves, rushed up to meet me. The sphere became very hot. I snapped the last strip of window, and sat scowling and biting my knuckles, waiting for the impact....

The sphere hit the water with a huge splash: it must have sent it fathoms high. At the splash I flung the Cavorite shutters open. Down I went, but slower and slower, and then I felt the sphere pressing against my feet, and so drove up again as a bubble drives. And at the last I was floating and rocking upon the surface of the sea, and my journey in space was at an end.

The night was dark and overcast. Two yellow pinpoints far away showed the passing of a ship, and nearer was a red glare that came and went. Had not the electricity of my glow-lamp exhausted itself, I could have got picked up that night. In spite of the inordinate fatigue I was beginning to feel, I was excited now, and for a time hopeful, in a feverish, impatient way, that so my travelling might end.

But at last I ceased to move about, and sat, wrists on knees, staring at a distant red light. It swayed up and down, rocking, rocking. My excitement passed. I realised I had yet to spend another night at least in the sphere. I perceived myself infinitely heavy and fatigued. And so I fell asleep.

A change in my rhythmic motion awakened me. I peered through the refracting glass, and saw that I had come aground upon a huge shallow of sand. Far away I seemed to see houses and trees, and seaward a curve, vague distortion of a ship hung between sea and sky.

I stood up and staggered. My one desire was to emerge. The manhole was upward, and I wrestled with the screw. Slowly I opened the manhole. At last the air was singing in again as once it had sung out. But this time I did not wait until the pressure was adjusted. In another moment I had the weight of the window on my hands, and I was open, wide open, to the old familiar sky of earth.

The air hit me on the chest so that I gasped. I dropped the glass screw. I cried out, put my hands to my chest, and sat down. For a time I was in pain. Then I took deep breaths. At last I could rise and move about again.

I tried to thrust my head through the manhole, and the sphere rolled over. It was as though something had lugged my head down directly it emerged. I ducked back sharply, or I should have been pinned face under water. After some wriggling and shoving I managed to crawl out upon sand, over which the retreating waves still came and went.

I did not attempt to stand up. It seemed to me that my body must be suddenly changed to lead. Mother Earth had her grip on me now – no Cavorite intervening. I sat down heedless of the water that came over my feet.

It was dawn, a gray dawn, rather overcast but showing here and there a long patch of greenish gray. Some way out a ship was lying at anchor, a pale silhouette of a ship with one yellow light. The water came rippling in in long shallow waves. Away to the right curved the land, a shingle bank with little hovels, and at last a lighthouse, a sailing mark and a point. Inland stretched a space of level sand, broken here and there by pools of water, and ending a mile away perhaps in a low shore of scrub. To the north-east some isolated watering-place was visible, a row of gaunt lodging-houses, the tallest things that I could see on earth, dull dabs against the brightening sky. What strange men can have reared these vertical piles in such an amplitude of space I do not know. There they are, like pieces of Brighton lost in the waste.

For a long time I sat there, yawning and rubbing my face. At last I struggled to rise. It made me feel that I was lifting a weight. I stood up.

I stared at the distant houses. For the first time since our starvation in the crater I thought of earthly food. "Bacon," I whispered, "eggs. Good toast and good coffee.... And how the devil am I going to get all this stuff to Lympne?" I wondered where I was. It was an east shore anyhow, and I had seen Europe before I dropped.

I heard footsteps crunching in the sand, and a little round-faced, friendly-looking man in flannels, with a bathing towel wrapped about his shoulders, and his bathing dress over his arm, appeared up the beach. I knew instantly that I must be in England. He was staring most intently at the sphere and me. He advanced staring. I dare say I looked a ferocious savage enough – dirty, unkempt, to an indescribable degree; but it did not occur to me at the time. He stopped at a distance of twenty yards. "Hul-lo, my man!" he said doubtfully.

"Hullo yourself!" said I.

He advanced, reassured by that. "What on earth is that thing?" he asked.

"Can you tell me where I am?" I asked.

"That's Littlestone," he said, pointing to the houses; "and that's Dungeness! Have you just landed? What's that thing you've got? Some sort of machine?"

"Yes."

"Have you floated ashore? Have you been wrecked or something? What is it?"

I meditated swiftly. I made an estimate of the little man's appearance as he drew nearer. "By Jove!" he said, "you've had a time of it! I thought you— Well— Where were you cast away? Is that thing a sort of floating thing for saving life?"

I decided to take that line for the present. I made a few vague affirmatives. "I want help," I said hoarsely. "I want to get some stuff up the beach – stuff I can't very well leave about." I became aware of three other pleasant-looking young men with towels, blazers, and straw hats, coming down the sands towards me. Evidently the early bathing section of this Littlestone.

"Help!" said the young man: "rather!" He became vaguely active. "What particularly do you want done?" He turned round and gesticulated. The three young men accelerated their pace. In a minute they there about me, plying me with questions I was indisposed to answer. "I'll tell all that later," I said. "I'm dead beat. I'm a rag."

"Come up to the hotel," said the foremost little man. "We'll look after that thing there."

I hesitated. "I can't," I said. "In that sphere there's two big bars of gold."

They looked incredulously at one another, then at me with a new inquiry. I went to the sphere, stooped, crept in, and presently they had the Selenites' crowbars and the broken chain before them. If I had not been so horribly fagged I could have laughed at them. It was like kittens round a beetle. They didn't know what to do with the stuff. The fat little man stooped and lifted the end of one of the bars, and then dropped it with a grunt. Then they all did.

"It's lead, or gold!" said one.

"Oh, it's *gold*!" said another.

"Gold, right enough," said the third.

Then they all stared at me, and then they all stared at the ship lying at anchor.

"I say!" cried the little man. "But where did you get that?"

I was too tired to keep up a lie. "I got it in the moon."

I saw them stare at one another.

"Look here!" said I, "I'm not going to argue now. Help me carry these lumps of gold up to the hotel – I guess, with rests, two of you can manage one, and I'll trail this chain thing – and I'll tell you more when I've had some food."

"And how about that thing?"

"It won't hurt there," I said. "Anyhow – confound it! – it must stop there now. If the tide comes up, it will float all right."

And in a state of enormous wonderment, these young men most obediently hoisted my treasures on their shoulders, and with limbs that felt like lead I headed a sort of procession towards that distant fragment of "sea-front." Half-way there we were reinforced by two awe-stricken little girls with spades, and later a lean little boy, with a penetrating sniff, appeared. He was, I remember, wheeling a bicycle, and he accompanied us at a distance of about a hundred yards on our right flank, and then I suppose, gave us up as uninteresting, mounted his bicycle and rode off over the level sands in the direction of the sphere.

I glanced back after him.

"*He* won't touch it," said the stout young man reassuringly, and I was only too willing to be reassured.

At first something of the gray of the morning was in my mind, but presently the sun disengaged itself from the level clouds of the horizon and lit the world, and turned the leaden sea to glittering waters. My spirits rose. A sense of the vast importance of the things I had done and had yet to do came with the sunlight into my mind. I laughed aloud as the foremost man staggered under my gold. When indeed I took my place in the world, how amazed the world would be!

If it had not been for my inordinate fatigue, the landlord of the Littlestone hotel would have been amusing, as he hesitated between my gold and my respectable company on the one and my filthy appearance on the other. But at last I found myself in a terrestrial bathroom once more with warm water to wash myself with, and a change of raiment, preposterously small indeed, but anyhow clean, that the genial little man had lent me. He lent me a razor too, but I could not screw up my resolution to attack even the outposts of the bristling beard that covered my face.

I sat down to an English breakfast and ate with a sort of languid appetite – an appetite many weeks old and very decrepit – and stirred myself to answer the questions of the four young men. And I told them the truth.

"Well," said I, "as you press me – I got it in the moon."

"The moon?"

"Yes, the moon in the sky."

"But how do you mean?"

"What I say, confound it!"

"Then you have just come from the moon?"

"Exactly! through space – in that ball." And I took a delicious mouthful of egg. I made a private note that when I went back to the moon I would take a box of eggs.

I could see clearly that they did not believe one word what I told them, but evidently they considered me the most respectable liar they had ever met. They glanced at one another, and then concentrated the fire of their eyes on me. I fancy they expected a clue to me in the way I helped myself to salt. They seemed to find something significant in my peppering my egg. These strangely shaped masses of gold they had staggered under held their minds. There the lumps lay in front of me, each worth thousands of pounds, and as impossible for any one to steal as a house or a piece of land. As I looked at their curious faces over my coffee-cup, I realised something of the enormous wilderness of explanations into which I should have to wander to render myself comprehensible again.

"You don't *really* mean—" began the youngest young man, in the tone of one who speaks to an obstinate child.

"Just pass me that toast-rack," I said, and shut him up completely.

"But look here, I say," began one of the others. "We're not going to believe that, you know."

"Ah, well," said I, and shrugged my shoulders.

"He doesn't want to tell us," said the youngest young man in a stage aside; and then, with an appearance of great *sang-froid*, "You don't mind if I take a cigarette?"

I waved him a cordial assent, and proceeded with my breakfast. Two of the others went and looked out of the farther window and talked inaudibly. I was struck by a thought. "The tide," I said, "is running out?"

There was a pause, a doubt who should answer me.

"It's near the ebb," said the fat little man.

"Well, anyhow," I said, "it won't float far."

I decapitated my third egg, and began a little speech. "Look here," I said. "Please don't imagine I'm surly or telling you uncivil lies, or anything of that sort. I'm forced almost, to be a little short and mysterious. I can quite understand this is as queer as it can be, and that your imaginations must be going it. I can assure you, you're in at a memorable time. But I can't make it clear to you now – it's impossible. I give you my word of honour I've come from the moon, and that's all I can tell you.... All the same, I'm tremendously obliged to you, you know, tremendously. I hope that my manner hasn't in any way given you offence."

"Oh, not in the least!" said the youngest young man affably. "We can quite understand," and staring hard at me all the time, he heeled his chair back until it very nearly upset, and recovered with some exertion. "Not a bit of it," said the fat young man.

"Don't you imagine *that*!" and they all got up and dispersed, and walked about and lit cigarettes, and generally tried to show they were perfectly amiable and disengaged, and entirely free from the slightest curiosity about me and the sphere. "I'm going to keep an eye on that ship out there all the same," I heard one of them remarking in an undertone. If only they could have forced themselves to it, they would, I believe, even have gone out and left me. I went on with my third egg.

"The weather," the fat little man remarked presently, "has been immense, has it not? I don't know *when* we have had such a summer."

Phoo-whizz! Like a tremendous rocket!

And somewhere a window was broken....

"What's that?" said I.

"It isn't—?" cried the little man, and rushed to the corner window. All the others rushed to the window likewise. I sat staring at them.

Suddenly I leapt up, knocked over my third egg, rushed for the window also. I had just thought of something. "Nothing to be seen there," cried the little man, rushing for the door.

"It's that boy!" I cried, bawling in hoarse fury; "it's that accursed boy!" and turning about I pushed the waiter aside – he was just bring me some more toast – and rushed violently out of the room and down and out upon the queer little esplanade in front of the hotel.

The sea, which had been smooth, was rough now with hurrying cat's-paws, and all about where the sphere had been was tumbled water like the wake of a ship. Above, a little puff of cloud whirled like dispersing smoke, and the three or four people on the beach were staring up with interrogative faces towards the point of that unexpected report. And that was all! Boots and waiter and the four young men in blazers came rushing out behind me. Shouts came from windows and doors, and all sorts of worrying people came into sight – agape.

For a time I stood there, too overwhelmed by this new development to think of the people.

At first I was too stunned to see the thing as any definite disaster – I was just stunned, as a man is by some accidental violent blow. It is only afterwards he begins to appreciate his specific injury.

"Good Lord!"

I felt as though somebody was pouring funk out of a can down the back of my neck. My legs became feeble. I had got the first intimation of what the disaster meant for me. There was that confounded boy – sky high! I was utterly left. There was the gold in the coffee-room – my only possession on earth. How would it all work out? The general effect was of a gigantic unmanageable confusion.

THE FIRST MEN IN THE MOON

"I say," said the voice of the little man behind. "I *say*, you know."

I wheeled about, and there were twenty or thirty people, a sort of irregular investment of people, all bombarding me with dumb interrogation, with infinite doubt and suspicion. I felt the compulsion of their eyes intolerably. I groaned aloud.

"I *can't*," I shouted. "I tell you I can't! I'm not equal to it! You must puzzle and – and be damned to you!"

I gesticulated convulsively. He receded a step as though I had threatened him. I made a bolt through them into the hotel. I charged back into the coffee-room, rang the bell furiously. I gripped the waiter as he entered. "D'ye hear?" I shouted. "Get help and carry these bars up to my room right away."

He failed to understand me, and I shouted and raved at him. A scared-looking little old man in a green apron appeared, and further two of the young men in flannels. I made a dash at them and commandeered their services. As soon as the gold was in my room I felt free to quarrel. "Now get out," I shouted; "all of you get out if you don't want to see a man go mad before your eyes!" And I helped the waiter by the shoulder as he hesitated in the doorway. And then, as soon as I had the door locked on them all, I tore off the little man's clothes again, shied them right and left, and got into bed forthwith. And there I lay swearing and panting and cooling for a very long time.

At last I was calm enough to get out of bed and ring up the round-eyed waiter for a flannel nightshirt, a soda and whisky, and some good cigars. And these things being procured me, after an exasperating delay that drove me several times to the bell, I locked the door again and proceeded very deliberately to look the entire situation in the face.

The net result of the great experiment presented itself as an absolute failure. It was a rout, and I was the sole survivor. It was an absolute collapse, and this was the final disaster. There was nothing for it but to save myself, and as much as I could in the way of prospects from our *débâcle*. At one fatal crowning blow all my vague resolutions of return and recovery had vanished. My intention of going back to the moon, of getting a sphereful of gold, and afterwards of having a fragment of Cavorite analysed and so recovering the great secret – perhaps, finally, even of recovering Cavor's body – all these ideas vanished altogether.

I was the sole survivor, and that was all.

I think that going to bed was one of the luckiest ideas I have ever had in an emergency. I really believe I should either have got loose-headed or done some indiscreet thing. But there, locked in and secure from all interruptions, I could think out the position in all its bearings and make my arrangements at leisure.

Of course, it was quite clear to me what had happened to the boy. He had crawled into the sphere, meddled with the studs, shut the Cavorite windows, and gone up. It was highly improbable he had screwed the manhole stopper, and, even if he had, the chances were a thousand to one against his getting back. It was fairly evident that he would gravitate with my bales to somewhere near the middle of the sphere and remain there, and so cease to be a legitimate terrestrial interest, however remarkable he might seem to the inhabitants of some remote quarter of space. I very speedily convinced myself on that point. And as for any responsibility I might have in the matter, the more I reflected upon that, the clearer it became that if only I kept quiet about things, I need not trouble myself about that. If I was faced by sorrowing parents demanding their lost boy, I had merely to demand my lost sphere – or ask them what they meant. At first I had had a vision of weeping parents and guardians, and all sorts of complications; but now I saw that I simply had to keep my mouth shut, and nothing in that way could arise. And, indeed, the more I lay and smoked and thought, the more evident became the wisdom of impenetrability.

It is within the right of every British citizen, provided he does not commit damage nor indecorum, to appear suddenly wherever he pleases, and as ragged and filthy as he pleases, and with whatever amount of virgin gold he sees fit to encumber himself, and no one has any right at all to hinder and detain him in this procedure. I formulated that at last to myself, and repeated it over as a sort of private Magna Charta of my liberty.

Once I had put that issue on one side, I could take up and consider in an equable manner certain considerations I had scarcely dared to think of before, namely, those arising out of the circumstances of my bankruptcy. But now, looking at this matter calmly and at leisure, I could see that if only I suppressed my identity by a temporary assumption of some less well-known name, and if I retained the two months' beard that had grown upon me, the risks of any annoyance from the spiteful creditor to whom I have already alluded became very small indeed. From that to a definite course of rational worldly action was plain sailing. It was all amazingly petty, no doubt, but what was there remaining for me to do?

Whatever I did I was resolved that I would keep myself level and right side up.

I ordered up writing materials, and addressed a letter to the New Romney Bank – the nearest, the waiter informed me – telling the manager I wished to open an account with him, and requesting him to send two trustworthy persons properly authenticated in a cab with a good horse to fetch some hundredweight of gold with which I happened to be encumbered. I signed the letter "Blake," which seemed to me to be a thoroughly respectable sort of name. This done, I got a Folkstone Blue Book, picked out an outfitter, and asked him to send a cutter to measure me for a dark tweed suit, ordering at the same time a valise, dressing bag, brown boots, shirts, hat (to fit), and so forth; and from a watchmaker I also ordered a watch. And these letters being despatched, I had up as good a lunch as the hotel could give, and then lay smoking a cigar, as calm and ordinary as possible, until in accordance with my instructions two duly authenticated clerks came from the bank and weighed and took away my gold. After which I pulled the clothes over my ears in order to drown any knocking, and went very comfortably to sleep.

I went to sleep. No doubt it was a prosaic thing for the first man back from the moon to do, and I can imagine that the young and imaginative reader will find my behaviour disappointing. But I was horribly fatigued and bothered, and, confound it! what else was there to do? There certainly was not the remotest chance of my being believed, if I had told my story then, and it would certainly have subjected me to intolerable annoyances. I went to sleep. When at last I woke up again I was ready to face the world as I have always been accustomed to face it since I came to years of discretion. And so I got away to Italy, and there it is I am writing this story. If the world will not have it as fact, then the world may take it as fiction. It is no concern of mine.

And now that the account is finished, I am amazed to think how completely this adventure is gone and done with. Everybody believes that Cavor was a not very brilliant scientific experimenter who blew up his house and himself at Lympne, and they explain the bang that followed my arrival at Littlestone by a reference to the experiments with explosives that are going on continually at the government establishment of Lydd, two miles away. I must confess that hitherto I have not acknowledged my share in the disappearance of Master Tommy Simmons, which was that little boy's name. That, perhaps, may prove a difficult item of corroboration to explain away. They account for my appearance in rags with two bars of indisputable gold upon the Littlestone beach in various ingenious ways – it doesn't worry me what they think of me. They say I have strung all these things together to avoid being questioned too closely as to the source of my wealth. I would like to see the man who could invent a story that would hold together like this one. Well, they must take it as fiction – there it is.

I have told my story – and now, I suppose, I have to take up the worries of this terrestrial life again. Even if one has been to the moon, one has still to earn a living. So I am working here at Amalfi, on the scenario of that play I sketched before Cavor came walking into my world, and I am trying to piece my life together as it was before ever I saw him. I must confess that I find it hard to keep my mind on the play when the moonshine comes into my room. It is full moon here, and last night I was out on the pergola for hours, staring away at the shining blankness that hides so much. Imagine it! tables and chairs, and trestles and bars of gold! Confound it! – if only one could hit on that Cavorite again! But a thing like that doesn't come twice in a life. Here I am, a little better off than I was at Lympne, and that is all. And Cavor has committed suicide in a more elaborate way than any human being ever did before. So the story closes as finally and completely as a dream. It fits in so little with all the other things of life, so much of it is so utterly remote from all human experience, the leaping, the eating, the breathing, and these weightless times, that indeed there are moments when, in spite of my moon gold, I do more than half believe myself that the whole thing was a dream....

CHAPTER 22

The Astonishing Communication of
Mr. Julius Wendigee

When I had finished my account of my return to the earth at Littlestone, I wrote, "The End," made a flourish, and threw my pen aside, fully believing that the whole story of the First Men in the Moon was done. Not only had I done this, but I had placed my manuscript in the hands of a literary agent, had permitted it to be sold, had seen the greater portion of it appear in the *Strand Magazine*, and was setting to work again upon the scenario of the play I had commenced at Lympne before I realised that the end was not yet. And then, following me from Amalfi to Algiers, there reached me (it is now about six months ago) one of the most astounding communications I have ever been fated to receive. Briefly, it informed me that Mr. Julius Wendigee, a Dutch electrician, who has been experimenting with certain apparatus akin to the apparatus used by Mr. Tesla in America, in the hope of discovering some method of communication with Mars, was receiving day by day a curiously fragmentary message in English, which was indisputably emanating from Mr. Cavor in the moon.

At first I thought the thing was an elaborate practical joke by some one who had seen the manuscript of my narrative. I answered Mr. Wendigee jestingly, but he replied in a manner that put such suspicion altogether aside, and in a state of inconceivable excitement I hurried from Algiers to the little observatory upon the Monte Rosa in which he was working. In the presence of his record and his appliances – and above all of the messages from Cavor that were coming to hand – my lingering doubts vanished. I decided at once to accept a proposal he made to me to remain with him, assisting him to take down the record from day to day, and endeavouring with him to send a message back to the moon. Cavor, we learnt, was not only alive, but free, in the midst of an almost inconceivable community of these ant-like beings, these ant-men, in the blue darkness of the lunar caves. He was lamed, it seemed, but otherwise in quite good health – in better health, he distinctly said, than he usually enjoyed on earth. He had had a fever, but it had left no bad effects. But curiously enough he seemed to be labouring under a conviction that I was either dead in the moon crater or lost in the deep of space.

His message began to be received by Mr. Wendigee when that gentleman was engaged in quite a different investigation. The reader will no doubt recall the little excitement that began the century, arising out of an announcement by Mr. Nikola Tesla, the American electrical celebrity, that he had received a message from Mars. His announcement renewed attention to fact that had long been familiar to scientific people, namely: that from some unknown source in space, waves of electromagnetic disturbance, entirely similar those used by Signor Marconi for his wireless telegraphy, are constantly reaching the earth. Besides Tesla quite a number of other observers have been engaged in perfecting apparatus for receiving and recording these vibrations, though few would go so far to consider them actual messages from some extraterrestrial sender. Among that few, however, we must certainly count Mr. Wendigee. Ever since 1898 he had devoted himself almost entirely to this subject, and being a man of ample means he had erected an observatory on the flanks of Monte Rosa, in a position singularly adapted in every way for such observations.

My scientific attainments, I must admit, are not great, but so far as they enable me to judge, Mr. Wendigee's contrivances for detecting and recording any disturbances in the electromagnetic conditions of space are singularly original and ingenious. And by a happy combination of circumstances they were set up and in operation about two months before Cavor made his first attempt to call up the earth. Consequently we have fragments of his communication even from the beginning. Unhappily, they are only fragments, and the most momentous of all the things that he had to tell humanity – the instructions, that is, for the making of Cavorite, if, indeed, he ever transmitted them – have throbbed themselves away unrecorded into space. We never succeeded in getting a response back to Cavor. He was unable to tell, therefore, what we had received or what we had missed; nor, indeed, did he certainly know that any one on earth was really aware of his efforts to reach us. And the persistence he displayed in sending eighteen long descriptions of lunar affairs – as they would be if we had them complete – shows how much his mind must have turned back towards his native planet since he left it two years ago.

You can imagine how amazed Mr. Wendigee must have been when he discovered his record of electromagnetic disturbances interlaced by Cavor's straightforward English. Mr. Wendigee knew nothing of our wild journey moonward, and suddenly – this English out of the void!

It is well the reader should understand the conditions under which it would seem these messages were sent. Somewhere within the moon Cavor certainly had access for a time to a considerable amount of electrical apparatus, and it would seem he rigged up – perhaps furtively – a transmitting arrangement of the Marconi type.

This he was able to operate at irregular intervals: sometimes for only half an hour or so, sometimes for three or four hours at a stretch. At these times he transmitted his earthward message, regardless of the fact that the relative position of the moon and points upon the earth's surface is constantly altering. As a consequence of this and of the necessary imperfections of our recording instruments his communication comes and goes in our records in an extremely fitful manner; it becomes blurred; it "fades out" in a mysterious and altogether exasperating way. And added to this is the fact that he was not an expert operator; he had partly forgotten, or never completely mastered, the code in general use, and as he became fatigued he dropped words and misspelt in a curious manner.

Altogether we have probably lost quite half of the communications he made, and much we have is damaged, broken, and partly effaced. In the abstract that follows the reader must be prepared therefore for a considerable amount of break, hiatus, and change of topic. Mr. Wendigee and I are collaborating in a complete and annotated edition of the Cavor record, which we hope to publish, together with a detailed account of the instruments employed, beginning with the first volume in January next. That will be the full and scientific report, of which this is only the popular transcript. But here we give at least sufficient to complete the story I have told, and to give the broad outlines of the state of that other world so near, so akin, and yet so dissimilar to our own.

CHAPTER 23

An Abstract of the Six Messages
First Received from Mr. Cavor

The two earlier messages of Mr. Cavor may very well be reserved for that larger volume. They simply tell, with greater brevity and with a difference in several details that is interesting, but not of any vital importance, the bare facts of the making of the sphere and our departure from the world. Throughout, Cavor speaks of me as a man who is dead, but with a curious change of temper as he approaches our landing on the moon. "Poor Bedford," he says of me, and "this poor young man," and he blames himself for inducing a young man, "by no means well equipped for such adventures," to leave a planet "on which he was indisputably fitted to succeed" on so precarious a mission. I think he underrates the part my energy and practical capacity played in bringing about the realisation of his theoretical sphere. "We arrived," he says, with no more account of our passage through space than if we had made a journey of common occurrence in a railway train.

And then he becomes increasingly unfair to me. Unfair, indeed, to an extent I should not have expected in a man trained in the search for truth. Looking back over my previously written account of these things, I must insist that I have been altogether juster to Cavor than he has been to me. I have extenuated little and suppressed nothing. But his account is:

"It speedily became apparent that the entire strangeness of our circumstances and surroundings – great loss of weight, attenuated but highly oxygenated air, consequent exaggeration of the results of muscular effort, rapid development of weird plants from obscure spores, lurid sky – was exciting my companion unduly. On the moon his character seemed to deteriorate. He became impulsive, rash, and quarrelsome. In a little while his folly in devouring some gigantic vesicles and his consequent intoxication led to our capture by the Selenites – before we had had the slightest opportunity of properly observing their ways...."

(He says, you observe, nothing of his own concession to these same "vesicles.")

And he goes on from that point to say that "We came to a difficult passage with them, and Bedford mistaking certain gestures of theirs" – pretty gestures they were! – "gave way to a panic violence. He ran amuck, killed three, and perforce I had to flee with him after the outrage. Subsequently we fought with a number who endeavoured to bar our way, and slew seven or eight more. It says much for the tolerance of these beings that on my recapture I was not instantly slain. We made our way to the exterior and separated in the crater of our arrival, to increase our chances of recovering our sphere. But presently I came upon a body of Selenites, led by two who were curiously different, even in form, from any of these we had seen hitherto, with larger heads and smaller bodies, and much more elaborately wrapped about. And after evading them for some time I fell into a crevasse, cut my head rather badly, and displaced my patella, and, finding crawling very painful, decided to surrender – if they would still permit me to do so. This they did, and, perceiving my helpless condition, carried me with them again into the moon. And of Bedford I have heard or seen nothing more, nor, so far as I can gather, any Selenite. Either the night overtook him in the crater, or else, which is more probable, he found the sphere, and, desiring to steal a march upon me, made off with it – only, I fear, to find it uncontrollable, and to meet a more lingering fate in outer space."

And with that Cavor dismisses me and goes on to more interesting topics. I dislike the idea of seeming to use my position as his editor to deflect his story in my own interest, but I am obliged to protest here against the turn he gives these occurrences. He said nothing about that gasping message on the blood-stained paper in which he told, or attempted to tell, a very different story. The dignified self-surrender is an altogether new view of the affair that has come to him, I must insist, since he began to feel secure among the lunar people; and as for the "stealing a march" conception, I am quite willing to let the reader decide between us on what he has before him. I know I am not a model man – I have made no pretence to be. But am I *that*?

However, that is the sum of my wrongs. From this point I can edit Cavor with an untroubled mind, for he mentions me no more.

It would seem the Selenites who had come upon him carried him to some point in the interior down "a great shaft" by means of what he describes as "a sort of balloon." We gather from the rather confused passage in which he describes this, and from a number of chance allusions and hints in other and subsequent messages, that this "great shaft" is one of an enormous system of artificial shafts that run, each from what is called a lunar "crater," downwards for very nearly a hundred miles towards the central portion of our satellite. These shafts communicate by transverse tunnels, they throw out abysmal caverns and expand into great globular places; the whole of the moon's substance for a hundred miles inward, indeed, is a mere sponge of rock. "Partly," says Cavor, "this sponginess is natural, but very largely it is due to the enormous industry of the Selenites in the past. The enormous circular mounds of the excavated rock and earth it is that form these great circles about the tunnels known to earthly astronomers (misled by a false analogy) as volcanoes."

It was down this shaft they took him, in this "sort of balloon" he speaks of, at first into an inky blackness and then into a region of continually increasing phosphorescence. Cavor's despatches show him to be curiously regardless of detail for a scientific man, but we gather that this light was due to the streams and cascades of water – "no doubt containing some phosphorescent organism" – that flowed ever more abundantly downward towards the Central Sea. And as he descended, he says, "The Selenites also became luminous." And at last far below him he saw, as it were, a lake of heatless fire, the waters of the Central Sea, glowing and eddying in strange perturbation, "like luminous blue milk that is just on the boil."

"This Lunar Sea," says Cavor, in a later passage "is not a stagnant ocean; a solar tide sends it in a perpetual flow around the lunar axis, and strange storms and boilings and rushings of its waters occur, and at times cold winds and thunderings that ascend out of it into the busy ways of the great ant-hill above. It is only when the water is in motion that it gives out light; in its rare seasons of calm it is black. Commonly, when one sees it, its waters rise and fall in an oily swell, and flakes and big rafts of shining, bubbly foam drift with the sluggish, faintly glowing current. The Selenites navigate its cavernous straits and lagoons in little shallow boats of a canoe-like shape; and even before my journey to the galleries about the Grand Lunar, who is Master of the Moon, I was permitted to make a brief excursion on its waters.

"The caverns and passages are naturally very tortuous. A large proportion of these ways are known only to expert pilots among the fishermen, and not infrequently Selenites are lost for ever in their labyrinths. In their remoter recesses, I am told, strange creatures lurk, some of them terrible and dangerous creatures that all the science of the moon has been unable to exterminate. There is particularly the Rapha, an inextricable mass of clutching tentacles that one hacks to pieces only to multiply; and the Tzee, a darting creature that is never seen, so subtly and suddenly does it slay..."

He gives us a gleam of description.

"I was reminded on this excursion of what I have read of the Mammoth Caves; if only I had had a yellow flambeau instead of the pervading blue light, and a solid-looking boatman with an oar instead of a scuttle-faced Selenite working an engine at the back of the canoe, I could have imagined I had suddenly got back to earth. The rocks about us were very various, sometimes black, sometimes pale blue and veined, and once they flashed and glittered as though we had come into a mine of sapphires. And below one saw the ghostly phosphorescent fishes flash and vanish in the hardly less phosphorescent deep. Then, presently, a long ultra-marine vista down the turgid stream of one of the channels of traffic, and a landing stage, and then, perhaps, a glimpse up the enormous crowded shaft of one of the vertical ways.

"In one great place heavy with glistening stalactites a number of boats were fishing. We went alongside one of these and watched the long-armed Selenites winding in a net. They were little, hunchbacked insects, with very strong arms, short, bandy legs, and crinkled face-masks. As they pulled at it that net seemed the heaviest thing I had come upon in the moon; it was loaded with weights – no doubt of gold – and it took a long time to draw, for in those waters the larger and more edible fish lurk deep. The fish in the net came up like a blue moonrise – a blaze of darting, tossing blue.

"Among their catch was a many-tentaculate, evil-eyed black thing, ferociously active, whose appearance they greeted with shrieks and twitters, and which with quick, nervous movements they hacked to pieces by means of little hatchets. All its dissevered limbs continued to lash and writhe in a vicious manner. Afterwards, when fever had hold of me, I dreamt again and again of that bitter, furious creature rising so vigorous and active out of the unknown sea. It was the most active and malignant thing of all the living creatures I have yet seen in this world inside the moon....

"The surface of this sea must be very nearly two hundred miles (if not more) below the level of the moon's exterior; all the cities of the moon lie, I learnt, immediately above this Central Sea, in such cavernous spaces and artificial galleries as I have described, and they communicate with the exterior by enormous vertical shafts which open invariably in what are called by earthly astronomers the 'craters' of the moon. The lid covering one such aperture I had already seen during the wanderings that had preceded my capture.

"Upon the condition of the less central portion of the moon I have not yet arrived at very precise knowledge. There is an enormous system of caverns in which the mooncalves shelter during the night; and there are abattoirs and the like – in one of these it was that I and Bedford fought with the Selenite butchers – and I have since seen balloons laden with meat descending out of the upper dark. I have as yet scarcely learnt as much of these things as a Zulu in London would learn about the British corn supplies in the same time. It is clear, however, that these vertical shafts and the vegetation of the surface must play an essential role in ventilating and keeping fresh the atmosphere of the moon. At one time, and particularly on my first emergence from my prison, there was certainly a cold wind blowing *down* the shaft, and later there was a kind of sirocco upward that corresponded with my fever. For at the end of about three weeks I fell ill of an indefinable sort of fever, and in spite of sleep and the quinine tabloids that very fortunately I had brought in my pocket, I remained ill and fretting miserably, almost to the time when I was taken into the presence of the Grand Lunar, who is Master of the Moon.

"I will not dilate on the wretchedness of my condition," he remarks, "during those days of ill-health." And he goes on with great amplitude with details I omit here. "My temperature," he concludes, "kept abnormally high for a long time, and I lost all desire for food. I had stagnant waking intervals, and sleep tormented by dreams, and at one phase I was, I remember, so weak as to be earth-sick and almost hysterical. I longed almost intolerably for colour to break the everlasting blue..."

He reverts again presently to the topic of this sponge-caught lunar atmosphere. I am told by astronomers and physicists that all he tells is in absolute accordance with what was already known of the moon's condition. Had earthly astronomers had the courage and imagination to push home a bold induction, says Mr. Wendigee, they might have foretold almost everything that Cavor has to say of the general structure of the moon. They know now pretty certainly that moon and earth are not so much satellite and primary as smaller and greater sisters, made out of one mass, and consequently made of the same material. And since the density of the moon is only three-fifths that of the earth, there can be nothing for it but that she is hollowed out by a great system of caverns. There was no necessity, said Sir Jabez Flap, F.R.S., that most entertaining exponent of the facetious side of the stars, that we should ever have gone to the moon to find out such easy inferences, and points the pun with an allusion to Gruyere, but he certainly might have announced his knowledge of the hollowness of the moon before. And if the moon is hollow, then the apparent absence of air and water is, of course, quite easily explained. The sea lies within at the bottom of the caverns, and the air travels through the great sponge of galleries, in accordance with simple physical laws. The caverns of the moon, on the whole, are very windy places. As the sunlight comes round the moon the air in the outer galleries on that side is heated, its pressure increases, some flows out on the exterior and mingles with the evaporating air of the craters (where the plants remove its carbonic acid), while the greater portion flows round through the galleries to replace the shrinking air of the cooling side that the sunlight has left. There is, therefore, a constant eastward breeze in the air of the outer galleries, and an upflow during the lunar day up the shafts, complicated, of course, very greatly by the varying shape of the galleries, and the ingenious contrivances of the Selenite mind....

CHAPTER 24

The Natural History of the Selenites

The **messages** of Cavor from the sixth up to the sixteenth are for the most part so much broken, and they abound so in repetitions, that they scarcely form a consecutive narrative. They will be given in full, of course, in the scientific report, but here it will be far more convenient to continue simply to abstract and quote as in the former chapter. We have subjected every word to a keen critical scrutiny, and my own brief memories and impressions of lunar things have been of inestimable help in interpreting what would otherwise have been impenetrably dark. And, naturally, as living beings, our interest centres far more upon the strange community of lunar insects in which he was living, it would seem, as an honoured guest than upon the mere physical condition of their world.

I have already made it clear, I think, that the Selenites I saw resembled man in maintaining the erect attitude, and in having four limbs, and I have compared the general appearance of their heads and the jointing of their limbs to that of insects. I have mentioned, too, the peculiar consequence of the smaller gravitation of the moon on their fragile slightness. Cavor confirms me upon all these points. He calls them "animals," though of course they fall under no division of the classification of earthly creatures, and he points out "the insect type of anatomy had, fortunately for men, never exceeded a relatively very small size on earth." The largest terrestrial insects, living or extinct, do not, as a matter of fact, measure six inches in length; "but here, against the lesser gravitation of the moon, a creature certainly as much an insect as vertebrate seems to have been able to attain to human and ultra-human dimensions."

He does not mention the ant, but throughout his allusions the ant is continually being brought before my mind, in its sleepless activity, in its intelligence and social organisation, in its structure, and more particularly in the fact that it displays, in addition to the two forms, the male and the female form, that almost all other animals possess, a number of other sexless creatures, workers, soldiers, and the like, differing from one another in structure, character, power, and use, and yet all members of the same species. For these Selenites, also, have a great variety of forms. Of course, they are not only colossally greater in size than ants, but also, in Cavor's opinion at least, in intelligence, morality, and social wisdom are they colossally greater than men. And instead of the four or five different forms of ant that are found, there are almost innumerably different forms of Selenite. I had endeavoured to indicate the very considerable difference observable in such Selenites of the outer crust as I happened to encounter; the differences in size and proportions were certainly as wide as the differences between the most widely separated races of men. But such differences as I saw fade absolutely to nothing in comparison with the huge distinctions of which Cavor tells. It would seem the exterior Selenites I saw were, indeed, mostly engaged in kindred occupations – mooncalf herds, butchers, fleshers, and the like. But within the moon, practically unsuspected by me, there are, it seems, a number of other sorts of Selenite, differing in size, differing in the relative size of part to part, differing in power and appearance, and yet not different species of creatures, but only different forms of one species, and retaining through all their variations a certain common likeness that marks their specific unity. The moon is, indeed, a sort of vast ant-hill, only, instead of there being only four or five sorts of ant, there are many hundred different sorts of Selenite, and almost every gradation between one sort and another.

It would seem the discovery came upon Cavor very speedily. I infer rather than learn from his narrative that he was captured by the mooncalf herds under the direction of these other Selenites who "have larger brain cases (heads?) and very much shorter legs." Finding he would not walk even under the goad, they carried him into darkness, crossed a narrow, plank-like bridge that may have been the identical bridge I had refused, and put him down in something that must have seemed at first to be some sort of lift. This was the balloon – it had certainly been absolutely invisible to us in the darkness – and what had seemed to me a mere plank-walking into the void was really, no doubt, the passage of the gangway. In this he descended towards constantly more luminous caverns of the moon. At first they descended in silence – save for the twitterings of the Selenites – and then into a stir of windy movement. In a little while the profound blackness had made his eyes so sensitive that he began to see more and more of the things about him, and at last the vague took shape.

"Conceive an enormous cylindrical space," says Cavor, in his seventh message, "a quarter of a mile across, perhaps; very dimly lit at first and then brighter, with big platforms twisting down its sides in a spiral that vanishes at last below in a blue profundity; and lit even more brightly – one could not tell how or why. Think of the well of the very largest spiral staircase or lift-shaft that you have ever looked down, and magnify that by a hundred. Imagine it at twilight seen through blue glass. Imagine yourself looking down that; only imagine also that you feel extraordinarily light, and have got rid of any giddy feeling you might have on earth, and you will have the first conditions of my impression. Round this enormous shaft imagine a broad gallery running in a much steeper spiral than would be credible on earth, and forming a steep road protected from the gulf only by a little parapet that vanishes at last in perspective a couple of miles below.

"Looking up, I saw the very fellow of the downward vision; it had, of course, the effect of looking into a very steep cone. A wind was blowing down the shaft, and far above I fancy I heard, growing fainter and fainter, the bellowing of the mooncalves that were being driven down again from their evening pasturage on the exterior. And up and down the spiral galleries were scattered numerous moon people, pallid, faintly luminous beings, regarding our appearance or busied on unknown errands.

"Either I fancied it or a flake of snow came drifting down on the icy breeze. And then, falling like a snowflake, a little figure, a little man-insect, clinging to a parachute, drove down very swiftly towards the central places of the moon.

"The big-headed Selenite sitting beside me, seeing me move my head with the gesture of one who saw, pointed with his trunk-like 'hand' and indicated a sort of jetty coming into sight very far below: a little landing-stage, as it were, hanging into the void. As it swept up towards us our pace diminished very rapidly, and in a few moments, as it seemed, we were abreast of it, and at rest. A mooring-rope was flung and grasped, and I found myself pulled down to a level with a great crowd of Selenites, who jostled to see me.

"It was an incredible crowd. Suddenly and violently there was forced upon my attention the vast amount of difference there is amongst these beings of the moon.

"Indeed, there seemed not two alike in all that jostling multitude. They differed in shape, they differed in size, they rang all the horrible changes on the theme of Selenite form! Some bulged and overhung, some ran about among the feet of their fellows. All of them had a grotesque and disquieting suggestion of an insect that has somehow contrived to mock humanity; but all seemed to present an incredible exaggeration of some particular feature: one had a vast right fore-limb, an enormous antennal arm, as it were; one seemed all leg, poised, as it were, on stilts; another protruded the edge of his face mask into a nose-like organ that made him startlingly human until one saw his expressionless gaping mouth. The strange and (except for the want of mandibles and palps) most insect-like head of the mooncalf-minders underwent, indeed, the most incredible transformations: here it was broad and low, here high and narrow; here its leathery brow was drawn out into horns and strange features; here it was whiskered and divided, and there with a grotesquely human profile. One distortion was particularly conspicuous. There were several brain cases distended like bladders to a huge size, with the face mask reduced to quite small proportions. There were several amazing forms, with heads reduced to microscopic proportions and blobby bodies; and fantastic, flimsy things that existed, it would seem, only as a basis for vast, trumpet-like protrusions of the lower part of the mask. And oddest of all, as it seemed to me for the moment, two or three of these weird inhabitants of a subterranean world, a world sheltered by innumerable miles of rock from sun or rain, *carried umbrellas* in their tentaculate hands – real terrestrial looking umbrellas! And then I thought of the parachutist I had watched descend.

"These moon people behaved exactly as a human crowd might have done in similar circumstances: they jostled and thrust one another, they shoved one another aside, they even clambered upon one another to get a glimpse of me. Every moment they increased in numbers, and pressed more urgently upon the discs of my ushers"

– Cavor does not explain what he means by this – "every moment fresh shapes emerged from the shadows and forced themselves upon my astounded attention. And presently I was signed and helped into a sort of litter, and lifted up on the shoulders of strong-armed bearers, and so borne through the twilight over this seething multitude towards the apartments that were provided for me in the moon. All about me were eyes, faces, masks, a leathery noise like the rustling of beetle wings, and a great bleating and cricket-like twittering of Selenite voices."

We gather he was taken to a "hexagonal apartment," and there for a space he was confined. Afterwards he was given a much more considerable liberty; indeed, almost as much freedom as one has in a civilised town on earth. And it would appear that the mysterious being who is the ruler and master of the moon appointed two Selenites "with large heads" to guard and study him, and to establish whatever mental communications were possible with him. And, amazing and incredible as it may seem, these two creatures, these fantastic men insects, these beings of other world, were presently communicating with Cavor by means of terrestrial speech.

Cavor speaks of them as Phi-oo and Tsi-puff. Phi-oo, he says, was about 5 feet high; he had small slender legs about 18 inches long, and slight feet of the common lunar pattern. On these balanced a little body, throbbing with the pulsations of his heart. He had long, soft, many-jointed arms ending in a tentacled grip, and his neck was many-jointed in the usual way, but exceptionally short and thick. His head, says Cavor – apparently alluding to some previous description that has gone astray in space – "is of the common lunar type, but strangely modified. The mouth has the usual expressionless gape, but it is unusually small and pointing downward, and the mask is reduced to the size of a large flat nose-flap. On either side are the little eyes.

"The rest of the head is distended into a huge globe and the chitinous leathery cuticle of the mooncalf herds thins out to a mere membrane, through which the pulsating brain movements are distinctly visible. He is a creature, indeed, with a tremendously hypertrophied brain, and with the rest of his organism both relatively and absolutely dwarfed."

In another passage Cavor compares the back view of him to Atlas supporting the world. Tsi-puff it seems was a very similar insect, but his "face" was drawn out to a considerable length, and the brain hypertrophy being in different regions, his head was not round but pear-shaped, with the stalk downward. There were also litter-carriers, lopsided beings, with enormous shoulders, very spidery ushers, and a squat foot attendant in Cavor's retinue.

The manner in which Phi-oo and Tsi-puff attacked the problem of speech was fairly obvious. They came into this "hexagonal cell" in which Cavor was confined, and began imitating every sound he made, beginning with a cough. He seems to have grasped their intention with great quickness, and to have begun repeating words to them and pointing to indicate the application. The procedure was probably always the same. Phi-oo would attend to Cavor for a space, then point also and say the word he had heard.

The first word he mastered was "man," and the second "Mooney" – which Cavor on the spur of the moment seems to have used instead of "Selenite" for the moon race. As soon as Phi-oo was assured of the meaning of a word he repeated it to Tsi-puff, who remembered it infallibly. They mastered over one hundred English nouns at their first session.

Subsequently it seems they brought an artist with them to assist the work of explanation with sketches and diagrams – Cavor's drawings being rather crude. "He was," says Cavor, "a being with an active arm and an arresting eye," and he seemed to draw with incredible swiftness.

The eleventh message is undoubtedly only a fragment of a longer communication. After some broken sentences, the record of which is unintelligible, it goes on:

"But it will interest only linguists, and delay me too long, to give the details of the series of intent parleys of which these were the beginning, and, indeed, I very much doubt if I could give in anything like the proper order all the twistings and turnings that we made in our pursuit of mutual comprehension. Verbs were soon plain sailing – at least, such active verbs as I could express by drawings; some adjectives were easy, but when it came to abstract nouns, to prepositions, and the sort of hackneyed figures of speech, by means of which so much is expressed on earth, it was like diving in cork-jackets. Indeed, these difficulties were insurmountable until to the sixth lesson came a fourth assistant, a being with a huge football-shaped head, whose *forte* was clearly the pursuit of intricate analogy. He entered in a preoccupied manner, stumbling against a stool, and the difficulties that arose had to be presented to him with a certain amount of clamour and hitting and pricking before they reached his apprehension. But once he was involved his penetration was amazing. Whenever there came a need of thinking beyond Phi-oo's by no means limited scope, this prolate-headed person was in request, but he invariably told the conclusion to Tsi-puff, in order that it might be remembered; Tsi-puff was ever the arsenal for facts. And so we advanced again.

"It seemed long and yet brief – a matter of days – before I was positively talking with these insects of the moon. Of course, at first it was an intercourse infinitely tedious and exasperating, but imperceptibly it has grown to comprehension. And my patience has grown to meet its limitations, Phi-oo it is who does all the talking. He does it with a vast amount of meditative provisional 'M'm – M'm' and has caught up one or two phrases, If I may say,' 'If you understand,' and beads all his speech with them.

"Thus he would discourse. Imagine him explaining his artist.

"'M'm – M'm – he – if I may say – draw. Eat little – drink little – draw. Love draw. No other thing. Hate all who not draw like him. Angry. Hate all who draw like him better. Hate most people. Hate all who not think all world for to draw. Angry. M'm. All things mean nothing to him – only draw. He like you ... if you understand.... New thing to draw. Ugly – striking. Eh?

"'He' – turning to Tsi-puff – 'love remember words. Remember wonderful more than any. Think no, draw no – remember. Say' – here he referred to his gifted assistant for a word – 'histories – all things. He hear once – say ever.'

"It is more wonderful to me than I dreamt that anything ever could be again, to hear, in this perpetual obscurity, these extraordinary creatures – for even familiarity fails to weaken the inhuman effect of their appearance – continually piping a nearer approach to coherent earthly speech – asking questions, giving answers. I feel that I am casting back to the fable-hearing period of childhood again, when the ant and the grasshopper talked together and the bee judged between them..."

And while these linguistic exercises were going on Cavor seems to have experienced a considerable relaxation of his confinement. "The first dread and distrust our unfortunate conflict aroused is being," he said, "continually effaced by the deliberate rationality of all I do.... I am now able to come and go as I please, or I am restricted only for my own good. So it is I have been able to get at this apparatus, and, assisted by a happy find among the material that is littered in this enormous store-cave, I have contrived to despatch these messages. So far not the slightest attempt has been made to interfere with me in this, though I have made it quite clear to Phi-oo that I am signalling to the earth.

"'You talk to other?' he asked, watching me.

"'Others,' said I.

"'Others,' he said. 'Oh yes, Men?'

"And I went on transmitting."

Cavor was continually making corrections in his previous accounts of the Selenites as fresh facts flowed upon him to modify his conclusions, and accordingly one gives the quotations that follow with a certain amount of reservation. They are quoted from the ninth, thirteenth, and sixteenth messages, and, altogether vague and fragmentary as they are, they probably give as complete a picture of the social life of this strange community as mankind can now hope to have for many generations.

"In the moon," says Cavor, "every citizen knows his place. He is born to that place, and the elaborate discipline of training and education and surgery he undergoes fits him at last so completely to it that he has neither ideas nor organs for any purpose beyond it. 'Why should he?' Phi-oo would ask. If, for example, a Selenite is destined to be a mathematician, his teachers and trainers set out at once to that end. They check any incipient disposition to other pursuits, they encourage his mathematical bias with a perfect psychological skill. His brain grows, or at least the mathematical faculties of his brain grow, and the rest of him only so much as is necessary to sustain this essential part of him. At last, save for rest and food, his one delight lies in the exercise and display of his faculty, his one interest in its application, his sole society with other specialists in his own line. His brain grows continually larger, at least so far as the portions engaging in mathematics are concerned; they bulge ever larger and seem to suck all life and vigour from the rest of his frame. His limbs shrivel, his heart and digestive organs diminish, his insect face is hidden under its bulging contours. His voice becomes a mere stridulation for the stating of formula; he seems deaf to all but properly enunciated problems. The faculty of laughter, save for the sudden discovery of some paradox, is lost to him; his deepest emotion is the evolution of a novel computation. And so he attains his end.

"Or, again, a Selenite appointed to be a minder of mooncalves is from his earliest years induced to think and live mooncalf, to find his pleasure in mooncalf lore, his exercise in their tending and pursuit. He is trained to become wiry and active, his eye is indurated to the tight wrappings, the angular contours that constitute a 'smart mooncalfishness.' He takes at last no interest in the deeper part of the moon; he regards all Selenites not equally versed in mooncalves with indifference, derision, or hostility. His thoughts are of mooncalf pastures, and his dialect an accomplished mooncalf technique. So also he loves his work, and discharges in perfect happiness the duty that justifies his being. And so it is with all sorts and conditions of Selenites – each is a perfect unit in a world machine....

"These beings with big heads, on whom the intellectual labours fall, form a sort of aristocracy in this strange society, and at the head of them, quintessential of the moon, is that marvellous gigantic ganglion the Grand Lunar, into whose presence I am finally to come. The unlimited development of the minds of the intellectual class is rendered possible by the absence of any bony skull in the lunar anatomy, that strange box of bone that clamps about the developing brain of man, imperiously insisting 'thus far and no farther' to all his possibilities. They fall into three main classes differing greatly in influence and respect. There are administrators, of whom Phi-oo is one, Selenites of considerable initiative and versatility, responsible each for a certain cubic content of the moon's bulk; the experts like the football-headed thinker, who are trained to perform certain special operations; and the erudite, who are the repositories of all knowledge. To the latter class belongs Tsi-puff, the first lunar professor of terrestrial languages. With regard to these latter, it is a curious little thing to note that the unlimited growth of the lunar brain has rendered unnecessary the invention of all those mechanical aids to brain work which have distinguished the career of man. There are no books, no records of any sort, no libraries or inscriptions. All knowledge is stored in distended brains much as the honey-ants of Texas store honey in their distended abdomens. The lunar Somerset House and the lunar British Museum Library are collections of living brains...

"The less specialised administrators, I note, do for the most part take a very lively interest in me whenever they encounter me. They will come out of the way and stare at me and ask questions to which Phi-oo will reply. I see them going hither and thither with a retinue of bearers, attendants, shouters, parachute-carriers, and so forth – queer groups to see. The experts for the most part ignore me completely, even as they ignore each other, or notice me only to begin a clamorous exhibition of their distinctive skill. The erudite for the most part are rapt in an impervious and apoplectic complacency, from which only a denial of their erudition can rouse them. Usually they are led about by little watchers and attendants, and often there are small and active-looking creatures, small females usually, that I am inclined to think are a sort of wife to them; but some of the profounder scholars are altogether too great for locomotion, and are carried from place to place in a sort of sedan tub, wabbling jellies of knowledge that enlist my respectful astonishment. I have just passed one in coming to this place where I am permitted to amuse myself with these electrical toys, a vast, shaven, shaky head, bald and thin-skinned, carried on his grotesque stretcher. In front and behind came his bearers, and curious, almost trumpet-faced, news disseminators shrieked his fame.

"I have already mentioned the retinues that accompany most of the intellectuals: ushers, bearers, valets, extraneous tentacles and muscles, as it were, to replace the abortive physical powers of these hypertrophied minds. Porters almost invariably accompany them. There are also extremely swift messengers with spider-like legs and 'hands' for grasping parachutes, and attendants with vocal organs that could well nigh wake the dead. Apart from their controlling intelligence these subordinates are as inert and helpless as umbrellas in a stand. They exist only in relation to the orders they have to obey, the duties they have to perform.

"The bulk of these insects, however, who go to and fro upon the spiral ways, who fill the ascending balloons and drop past me clinging to flimsy parachutes are, I gather, of the operative class. 'Machine hands,' indeed, some of these are in actual nature – it is not figure of speech, the single tentacle of the mooncalf herd is profoundly modified for clawing, lifting, guiding, the rest of them no more than necessary subordinate appendages to these important mechanisms, have enormously developed auditory organs; some whose work lies in delicate chemical operations project a vast olfactory organ; others again have flat feet for treadles with anchylosed joints; and others – who I have been told are glassblowers – seem mere lung-bellows. But every one of these common Selenites I have seen at work is exquisitely adapted to the social need it meets. Fine work is done by fined-down workers, amazingly dwarfed and neat. Some I could hold on the palm of my hand. There is even a sort of turnspit Selenite, very common, whose duty and only delight it is to apply the motive power for various small appliances. And to rule over these things and order any erring tendency there might be in some aberrant natures are the most muscular beings I have seen in the moon, a sort of lunar police, who must have been trained from their earliest years to give a perfect respect and obedience to the swollen heads.

"The making of these various sorts of operative must be a very curious and interesting process. I am very much in the dark about it, but quite recently I came upon a number of young Selenites confined in jars from which only the fore-limbs protruded, who were being compressed to become machine-minders of a special sort. The extended 'hand' in this highly developed system of technical education is stimulated by irritants and nourished by injection, while the rest of the body is starved. Phi-oo, unless I misunderstood him, explained that in the earlier stages these queer little creatures are apt to display signs of suffering in their various cramped situations, but they easily become indurated to their lot; and he took me on to where a number of flexible-minded messengers were being drawn out and broken in. It is quite unreasonable, I know, but such glimpses of the educational methods of these beings affect me disagreeably. I hope, however, that may pass off, and I may be able to see more of this aspect of their wonderful social order. That wretched-looking hand-tentacle sticking out of its jar seemed to have a sort of limp appeal for lost possibilities; it haunts me still, although, of course it is really in the end a far more humane proceeding than our earthly method of leaving children to grow into human beings, and then making machines of them.

"Quite recently, too – I think it was on the eleventh or twelfth visit I made to this apparatus – I had a curious light upon the lives of these operatives. I was being guided through a short cut hither, instead of going down the spiral, and by the quays to the Central Sea. From the devious windings of a long, dark gallery, we emerged into a vast, low cavern, pervaded by an earthy smell, and as things go in this darkness, rather brightly lit. The light came from a tumultuous growth of livid fungoid shapes – some indeed singularly like our terrestrial mushrooms, but standing as high or higher than a man.

"'Mooneys eat these?' said I to Phi-oo.

"'Yes, food.'

"'Goodness me!' I cried; 'what's that?'

"My eye had just caught the figure of an exceptionally big and ungainly Selenite lying motionless among the stems, face downward. We stopped.

"'Dead?' I asked. (For as yet I have seen no dead in the moon, and I have grown curious.)

"'No!' exclaimed Phi-oo. 'Him – worker – no work to do. Get little drink then – make sleep – till we him want. What good him wake, eh? No want him walking about.'

"'There's another!' cried I.

"And indeed all that huge extent of mushroom ground was, I found, peppered with these prostrate figures sleeping under an opiate until the moon had need of them. There were scores of them of all sorts, and we were able to turn over some of them, and examine them more precisely than I had been able to previously. They breathed noisily at my doing so, but did not wake. One, I remember very distinctly: he left a strong impression, I think, because some trick the light and of his attitude was strongly suggestive a drawn-up human figure. His fore-limbs were long, delicate tentacles – he was some kind of refined manipulator – and the pose of his slumber suggested a submissive suffering. No doubt it was a mistake for me to interpret his expression in that way, but I did. And as Phi-oo rolled him over into the darkness among the livid fleshiness again I felt a distinctly unpleasant sensation, although as he rolled the insect in him was confessed.

"It simply illustrates the unthinking way in which one acquires habits of feeling. To drug the worker one does not want and toss him aside is surely far better than to expel him from his factory to wander starving in the streets. In every complicated social community there is necessarily a certain intermittency of employment for all specialised labour, and in this way the trouble of an 'unemployed' problem is altogether anticipated. And yet, so unreasonable are even scientifically trained minds, I still do not like the memory of those prostrate forms amidst those quiet, luminous arcades of fleshy growth, and I avoid that short cut in spite of the inconveniences of the longer, more noisy, and more crowded alternative.

"My alternative route takes me round by a huge, shadowy cavern, very crowded and clamorous, and here it is I see peering out of the hexagonal openings of a sort of honeycomb wall, or parading a large open space behind, or selecting the toys and amulets made to please them by the dainty-tentacled jewellers who work in kennels below, the mothers of the moon world – the queen bees, as it were, of the hive. They are noble-looking beings, fantastically and sometimes quite beautifully adorned, with a proud carriage, and, save for their mouths, almost microscopic heads.

"Of the condition of the moon sexes, marrying and giving in marriage, and of birth and so forth among the Selenites, I have as yet been able to learn very little. With the steady progress of Phi-oo in English, however, my ignorance will no doubt as steadily disappear. I am of opinion that, as with the ants and bees, there is a large majority of the members in this community of the neuter sex. Of course on earth in our cities there are now many who never live that life of parentage which is the natural life of man. Here, as with the ants, this thing has become a normal condition of the race, and the whole of such replacement as is necessary falls upon this special and by no means numerous class of matrons, the mothers of the moon-world, large and stately beings beautifully fitted to bear the larval Selenite. Unless I misunderstand an explanation of Phi-oo's, they are absolutely incapable of cherishing the young they bring into the moon; periods of foolish indulgence alternate with moods of aggressive violence, and as soon as possible the little creatures, who are quite soft and flabby and pale coloured, are transferred to the charge of celibate females, women 'workers' as it were, who in some cases possess brains of almost masculine dimensions."

Just at this point, unhappily, this message broke off. Fragmentary and tantalising as the matter constituting this chapter is, it does nevertheless give a vague, broad impression of an altogether strange and wonderful world – a world with which our own may have to reckon we know not how speedily. This intermittent trickle of messages, this whispering of a record needle in the stillness of the mountain slopes, is the first warning of such a change in human conditions as mankind has scarcely imagined heretofore. In that satellite of ours there are new elements, new appliances, traditions, an overwhelming avalanche of new ideas, a strange race with whom we must inevitably struggle for mastery – gold as common as iron or wood...

CHAPTER 25

The Grand Lunar

The penultimate message describes, with occasionally elaborate detail, the encounter between Cavor and the Grand Lunar, who is the ruler or master of the moon. Cavor seems to have sent most of it without interference, but to have been interrupted in the concluding portion. The second came after an interval of a week.

The first message begins: "At last I am able to resume this—" it then becomes illegible for a space, and after a time resumed in mid-sentence.

The missing words of the following sentence are probably "the crowd." There follows quite clearly: "grew ever denser as we drew near the palace of the Grand Lunar – if I may call a series of excavations a palace. Everywhere faces stared at me – blank, chitinous gapes and masks, eyes peering over tremendous olfactory developments, eyes beneath monstrous forehead plates; and undergrowth of smaller creatures dodged and yelped, and helmet faces poised on sinuous, long-jointed necks appeared craning over shoulders and beneath armpits. Keeping a welcome space about me marched a cordon of stolid, scuttle-headed guards, who had joined us on our leaving the boat in which we had come along the channels of the Central Sea. The quick-eyed artist with the little brain joined us also, and a thick bunch of lean porter-insects swayed and struggled under the multitude of conveniences that were considered essential to my state.

I was carried in a litter during the final stage of our journey. This litter was made of some very ductile metal that looked dark to me, meshed and woven, and with bars of paler metal, and about me as I advanced there grouped itself a long and complicated procession.

"In front, after the manner of heralds, marched four trumpet-faced creatures making a devastating bray; and then came squat, resolute-moving ushers before and behind, and on either hand a galaxy of learned heads, a sort of animated encyclopedia, who were, Phi-oo explained, to stand about the Grand Lunar for purposes of reference. (Not a thing in lunar science, not a point of view or method of thinking, that these wonderful beings did not carry in their heads!) Followed guards and porters, and then Phi-oo's shivering brain borne also on a litter. Then came Tsi-puff in a slightly less important litter; then myself on a litter of greater elegance than any other, and surrounded by my food and drink attendants. More trumpeters came next, splitting the ear with vehement outcries, and then several big brains, special correspondents one might well call them, or historiographers, charged with the task of observing and remembering every detail of this epoch-making interview. A company of attendants, bearing and dragging banners and masses of scented fungus and curious symbols, vanished in the darkness behind. The way was lined by ushers and officers in caparisons that gleamed like steel, and beyond their line, so far as my eyes could pierce the gloom, the heads of that enormous crowd extended.

"I will own that I am still by no means indurated to the peculiar effect of the Selenite appearance, and to find myself, as it were, adrift on this broad sea of excited entomology was by no means agreeable. Just for a space I had something very like what I should imagine people mean when they speak of the 'horrors.' It had come to me before in these lunar caverns, when on occasion I have found myself weaponless and with an undefended back, amidst a crowd of these Selenites, but never quite so vividly. It is, of course, as absolutely irrational a feeling as one could well have, and I hope gradually to subdue it. But just for a moment, as I swept forward into the welter of the vast crowd, it was only by gripping my litter tightly and summoning all my will-power that I succeeded in avoiding an outcry or some such manifestation. It lasted perhaps three minutes; then I had myself in hand again.

"We ascended the spiral of a vertical way for some time, and then passed through a series of huge halls dome-roofed and elaborately decorated. The approach to the Grand Lunar was certainly contrived to give one a vivid impression of his greatness. Each cavern one entered seemed greater and more boldly arched than its predecessor. This effect of progressive size was enhanced by a thin haze of faintly phosphorescent blue incense that thickened as one advanced, and robbed even the nearer figures of clearness. I seemed to advance continually to something larger, dimmer, and less material.

"I must confess that all this multitude made me feel extremely shabby and unworthy. I was unshaven and unkempt; I had brought no razor; I had a coarse beard over my mouth. On earth I have always been inclined to despise any attention to my person beyond a proper care for cleanliness; but under the exceptional circumstances in which I found myself, representing, as I did, my planet and my kind, and depending very largely upon the attractiveness of my appearance for a proper reception, I could have given much for something a little more artistic and dignified than the husks I wore. I had been so serene in the belief that the moon was uninhabited as to overlook such precautions altogether. As it was I was dressed in a flannel jacket, knickerbockers, and golfing stockings, stained with every sort of dirt the moon offered, slippers (of which the left heel was wanting), and a blanket, through a hole in which I thrust my head. (These clothes, indeed, I still wear.)

Sharp bristles are anything but an improvement to my cast of features, and there was an unmended tear at the knee of my knickerbockers that showed conspicuously as I squatted in my litter; my right stocking, too, persisted in getting about my ankle. I am fully alive to the injustice my appearance did humanity, and if by any expedient I could have improvised something a little out of the way and imposing I would have done so. But I could hit upon nothing. I did what I could with my blanket – folding it somewhat after the fashion of a toga, and for the rest I sat as upright as the swaying of my litter permitted.

"Imagine the largest hall you have ever been in, imperfectly lit with blue light and obscured by a gray-blue fog, surging with metallic or livid-gray creatures of such a mad diversity as I have hinted. Imagine this hall to end in an open archway beyond which is a still larger hall, and beyond this yet another and still larger one, and so on. At the end of the vista, dimly seen, a flight of steps, like the steps of Ara Coeli at Rome, ascend out of sight. Higher and higher these steps appear to go as one draws nearer their base. But at last I came under a huge archway and beheld the summit of these steps, and upon it the Grand Lunar exalted on his throne.

"He was seated in what was relatively a blaze of incandescent blue. This, and the darkness about him gave him an effect of floating in a blue-black void. He seemed a small, self-luminous cloud at first, brooding on his sombre throne; his brain case must have measured many yards in diameter. For some reason that I cannot fathom a number of blue search-lights radiated from behind the throne on which he sat, and immediately encircling him was a halo. About him, and little and indistinct in this glow, a number of body-servants sustained and supported him, and overshadowed and standing in a huge semicircle beneath him were his intellectual subordinates, his remembrancers and computators and searchers and servants, and all the distinguished insects of the court of the moon. Still lower stood ushers and messengers, and then all down the countless steps of the throne were guards, and at the base, enormous, various, indistinct, vanishing at last into an absolute black, a vast swaying multitude of the minor dignitaries of the moon. Their feet made a perpetual scraping whisper on the rocky floor, as their limbs moved with a rustling murmur.

"As I entered the penultimate hall the music rose and expanded into an imperial magnificence of sound, and the shrieks of the news-bearers died away....

"I entered the last and greatest hall....

"My procession opened out like a fan. My ushers and guards went right and left, and the three litters bearing myself and Phi-oo and Tsi-puff marched across a shiny darkness of floor to the foot of the giant stairs. Then began a vast throbbing hum, that mingled with the music. The two Selenites dismounted, but I was bidden remain seated – I imagine as a special honour. The music ceased, but not that humming, and by a simultaneous movement of ten thousand respectful heads my attention was directed to the enhaloed supreme intelligence that hovered above me.

"At first as I peered into the radiating glow this quintessential brain looked very much like an opaque, featureless bladder with dim, undulating ghosts of convolutions writhing visibly within. Then beneath its enormity and just above the edge of the throne one saw with a start minute elfin eyes peering out of the glow. No face, but eyes, as if they peered through holes. At first I could see no more than these two staring little eyes, and then below I distinguished the little dwarfed body and its insect-jointed limbs shrivelled and white. The eyes stared down at me with a strange intensity, and the lower part of the swollen globe was wrinkled.

Ineffectual-looking little hand-tentacles steadied this shape on the throne....

"It was great. It was pitiful. One forgot the hall and the crowd.

"I ascended the staircase by jerks. It seemed to me that this darkly glowing brain case above us spread over me, and took more and more of the whole effect into itself as I drew nearer. The tiers of attendants and helpers grouped about their master seemed to dwindle and fade into the night. I saw that shadowy attendants were busy spraying that great brain with a cooling spray, and patting and sustaining it. For my own part, I sat gripping my swaying litter and staring at the Grand Lunar, unable to turn my gaze aside. And at last, as I reached a little landing that was separated only by ten steps or so from the supreme seat, the woven splendour of the music reached a climax and ceased, and I was left naked, as it were, in that vastness, beneath the still scrutiny of the Grand Lunar's eyes.

"He was scrutinising the first man he had ever seen....

"My eyes dropped at last from his greatness to the ant figures in the blue mist about him, and then down the steps to the massed Selenites, still and expectant in their thousands, packed on the floor below. Once again an unreasonable horror reached out towards me.... And passed.

"After the pause came the salutation. I was assisted from my litter, and stood awkwardly while a number of curious and no doubt deeply symbolical gestures were vicariously performed for me by two slender officials. The encyclopaedic galaxy of the learned that had accompanied me to the entrance of the last hall appeared two steps above me and left and right of me, in readiness for the Grand Lunar's need, and Phi-oo's pale brain placed itself about half-way up to the throne in such a position as to communicate easily between us without turning his back on either the Grand Lunar or myself. Tsi-puff took up position behind him. Dexterous ushers sidled sideways towards me, keeping a full face to the Presence. I seated myself Turkish fashion, and Phi-oo and Tsi-puff also knelt down above me. There came a pause. The eyes of the nearer court went from me to the Grand Lunar and came back to me, and a hissing and piping of expectation passed across the hidden multitudes below and ceased.

"That humming ceased.

"For the first and last time in my experience the moon was silent.

"I became aware of a faint wheezy noise. The Grand Lunar was addressing me. It was like the rubbing of a finger upon a pane of glass.

"I watched him attentively for a time, and then glanced at the alert Phi-oo. I felt amidst these slender beings ridiculously thick and fleshy and solid; my head all jaw and black hair. My eyes went back to the Grand Lunar. He had ceased; his attendants were busy, and his shining superfices was glistening and running with cooling spray.

"Phi-oo meditated through an interval. He consulted Tsi-puff. Then he began piping his recognisable English – at first a little nervously, so that he was not very clear.

"'M'm – the Grand Lunar – wished to say – wishes to say – he gathers you are – m'm – men – that you are a man from the planet earth. He wishes to say that he welcomes you – welcomes you – and wishes to learn – learn, if I may use the word – the state of your world, and the reason why you came to this.'

"He paused. I was about to reply when he resumed. He proceeded to remarks of which the drift was not very clear, though I am inclined to think they were intended to be complimentary. He told me that the earth was to the moon what the sun is to the earth, and that the Selenites desired very greatly to learn about the earth and men. He then told me no doubt in compliment also, the relative magnitude and diameter of earth and moon, and the perpetual wonder and speculation with which the Selenites had regarded our planet. I meditated with downcast eyes, and decided to reply that men too had wondered what might lie in the moon, and had judged it dead, little recking of such magnificence as I had seen that day. The Grand Lunar, in token of recognition, caused his long blue rays to rotate in a very confusing manner, and all about the great hall ran the pipings and whisperings and rustlings of the report of what I had said. He then proceeded to put to Phi-oo a number of inquiries which were easier to answer.

"He understood, he explained, that we lived on the surface of the earth, that our air and sea were outside the globe; the latter part, indeed, he already knew from his astronomical specialists. He was very anxious to have more detailed information of what he called this extraordinary state of affairs, for from the solidity of the earth there had always been a disposition regard it as uninhabitable. He endeavoured first to ascertain the extremes of temperature to which we earth beings were exposed, and he was deeply interested by my descriptive treatment of clouds and rain. His imagination was assisted by the fact that the lunar atmosphere in the outer galleries of the night side is not infrequently very foggy. He seemed inclined to marvel that we did not find the sunlight too intense for our eyes, and was interested in my attempt to explain that the sky was tempered to a bluish colour through the refraction of the air, though I doubt if he clearly understood that. I explained how the iris of the human eyes can contract the pupil and save the delicate internal structure from the excess of sunlight, and was allowed to approach within a few feet of the Presence in order that this structure might be seen. This led to a comparison of the lunar and terrestrial eyes. The former is not only excessively sensitive to such light as men can see, but it can also *see* heat, and every difference in temperature within the moon renders objects visible to it.

"The iris was quite a new organ to the Grand Lunar. For a time he amused himself by flashing his rays into my face and watching my pupils contract. As a consequence, I was dazzled and blinded for some little time....

"But in spite of that discomfort I found something reassuring by insensible degrees in the rationality of this business of question and answer. I could shut my eyes, think of my answer, and almost forget that the the Grand Lunar has no face....

"When I had descended again to my proper place the Grand Lunar asked how we sheltered ourselves from heat and storms, and I expounded to him the arts of building and furnishing. Here we wandered into misunderstandings and cross-purposes, due largely, I must admit, to the looseness of my expressions. For a long time I had great difficulty in making him understand the nature of a house. To him and his attendant Selenites it seemed, no doubt, the most whimsical thing in the world that men should build houses when they might descend into excavations, and an additional complication was introduced by the attempt I made to explain that men had originally begun their homes in caves, and that they were now taking their railways and many establishments beneath the surface. Here I think a desire for intellectual completeness betrayed me. There was also a considerable tangle due to an equally unwise attempt on my part to explain about mines. Dismissing this topic at last in an incomplete state, the Grand Lunar inquired what we did with the interior of our globe.

"A tide of twittering and piping swept into the remotest corners of that great assembly when it was at last made clear that we men know absolutely nothing of the contents of the world upon which the immemorial generations of our ancestors had been evolved. Three times had I to repeat that of all the 4000 miles of distance between the earth and its centre men knew only to the depth of a mile, and that very vaguely. I understood the Grand Lunar to ask why had I come to the moon seeing we had scarcely touched our own planet yet, but he did not trouble me at that time to proceed to an explanation, being too anxious to pursue the details of this mad inversion of all his ideas.

"He reverted to the question of weather, and I tried to describe the perpetually changing sky, and snow, and frost and hurricanes. 'But when the night comes,' he asked, 'is it not cold?'

"I told him it was colder than by day.

"'And does not your atmosphere freeze?'

"I told him not; that it was never cold enough for that, because our nights were so short.

"'Not even liquefy?'

"I was about to say 'No,' but then it occurred to me that one part at least of our atmosphere, the water vapour of it, does sometimes liquefy and form dew, and sometimes freeze and form frost – a process perfectly analogous to the freezing of all the external atmosphere of the moon during its longer night. I made myself clear on this point, and from that the Grand Lunar went on to speak with me of sleep. For the need of sleep that comes so regularly every twenty-four hours to all things is part also of our earthly inheritance. On the moon they rest only at rare intervals, and after exceptional exertions. Then I tried to describe to him the soft splendours of a summer night, and from that I passed to a description of those animals that prowl by night and sleep by day. I told him of lions and tigers, and here it seemed as though we had come to a deadlock. For, save in their waters, there are no creatures in the moon not absolutely domestic and subject to his will, and so it has been for immemorial years. They have monstrous water creatures, but no evil beasts, and the idea of anything strong and large existing 'outside' in the night is very difficult for them...."

[The record is here too broken to transcribe for the space of perhaps twenty words or more.]

"He talked with his attendants, as I suppose, upon the strange superficiality and unreasonableness of (man) who lives on the mere surface of a world, a creature of waves and winds, and all the chances of space, who cannot even unite to overcome the beasts that prey upon his kind, and yet who dares to invade another planet. During this aside I sat thinking, and then at his desire I told him of the different sorts of men. He searched me with questions. 'And for all sorts of work you have the same sort of men. But who thinks? Who governs?'

"I gave him an outline of the democratic method.

"When I had done he ordered cooling sprays upon his brow, and then requested me to repeat my explanation conceiving something had miscarried.

"'Do they not do different things, then?' said Phi-oo.

"Some, I admitted, were thinkers and some officials; some hunted, some were mechanics, some artists, some toilers. 'But *all* rule,' I said.

"'And have they not different shapes to fit them to their different duties?'

"'None that you can see,' I said, 'except perhaps, for clothes. Their minds perhaps differ a little,' I reflected.

"'Their minds must differ a great deal,' said the Grand Lunar, 'or they would all want to do the same things.'

"In order to bring myself into a closer harmony with his preconceptions, I said that his surmise was right. 'It was all hidden in the brain,' I said; but the difference was there. Perhaps if one could see the minds and souls of men they would be as varied and unequal as the Selenites. There were great men and small men, men who could reach out far and wide, men who could go swiftly; noisy, trumpet-minded men, and men who could remember without thinking....'"

[The record is indistinct for three words.]

"He interrupted me to recall me to my previous statements. 'But you said all men rule?' he pressed.

"'To a certain extent,' I said, and made, I fear, a denser fog with my explanation.

"He reached out to a salient fact. 'Do you mean,' asked, 'that there is no Grand Earthly?'

"I thought of several people, but assured him finally there was none. I explained that such autocrats and emperors as we had tried upon earth had usually ended in drink, or vice, or violence, and that the large and influential section of the people of the earth to which I belonged, the Anglo-Saxons, did not mean to try that sort of thing again. At which the Grand Lunar was even more amazed.

"'But how do you keep even such wisdom as you have?' he asked; and I explained to him the way we helped our limited"

[A word omitted here, probably "brains."]

"with libraries of books. I explained to him how our science was growing by the united labours of innumerable little men, and on that he made no comment save that it was evident we had mastered much in spite of our social savagery, or we could not have come to the moon. Yet the contrast was very marked. With knowledge the Selenites grew and changed; mankind stored their knowledge about them and remained brutes – equipped. He said this..."

[Here there is a short piece of the record indistinct.]

"He then caused me to describe how we went about this earth of ours, and I described to him our railways and ships. For a time he could not understand that we had had the use of steam only one hundred years, but when he did he was clearly amazed. (I may mention as a singular thing, that the Selenites use years to count by, just as we do on earth, though I can make nothing of their numeral system. That, however, does not matter, because Phi-oo understands ours.) From that I went on to tell him that mankind had dwelt in cities only for nine or ten thousand years, and that we were still not united in one brotherhood, but under many different forms of government. This astonished the Grand Lunar very much, when it was made clear to him. At first he thought we referred merely to administrative areas.

"'Our States and Empires are still the rawest sketches of what order will some day be,' I said, and so I came to tell him...."

[At this point a length of record that probably represents thirty or forty words is totally illegible.]

"The Grand Lunar was greatly impressed by the folly of men in clinging to the inconvenience of diverse tongues. 'They want to communicate, and yet not to communicate,' he said, and then for a long time he questioned me closely concerning war.

"He was at first perplexed and incredulous. 'You mean to say,' he asked, seeking confirmation, 'that you run about over the surface of your world – this world, whose riches you have scarcely begun to scrape – killing one another for beasts to eat?'

"I told him that was perfectly correct.

"He asked for particulars to assist his imagination.

"'But do not ships and your poor little cities get injured?' he asked, and I found the waste of property and conveniences seemed to impress him almost as much as the killing. 'Tell me more,' said the Grand Lunar; 'make me see pictures. I cannot conceive these things.'

"And so, for a space, though something loath, I told him the story of earthly War.

"I told him of the first orders and ceremonies of war, of warnings and ultimatums, and the marshalling and marching of troops. I gave him an idea of manoeuvres and positions and battle joined. I told him of sieges and assaults, of starvation and hardship in trenches, and of sentinels freezing in the snow. I told him of routs and surprises, and desperate last stands and faint hopes, and the pitiless pursuit of fugitives and the dead upon the field. I told, too, of the past, of invasions and massacres, of the Huns and Tartars, and the wars of Mahomet and the Caliphs, and of the Crusades. And as I went on, and Phi-oo translated, and the Selenites cooed and murmured in a steadily intensified emotion.

"I told them an ironclad could fire a shot of a ton twelve miles, and go through 20 feet of iron – and how we could steer torpedoes under water. I went on to describe a Maxim gun in action, and what I could imagine of the Battle of Colenso. The Grand Lunar was so incredulous that he interrupted the translation of what I had said in order to have my verification of my account. They particularly doubted my description of the men cheering and rejoicing as they went into battle.

"'But surely they do not like it!' translated Phi-oo.

"I assured them men of my race considered battle the most glorious experience of life, at which the whole assembly was stricken with amazement.

"'But what good is this war?' asked the Grand Lunar, sticking to his theme.

"'Oh! as for *good*!' said I; 'it thins the population!'

"'But why should there be a need—?'

"There came a pause, the cooling sprays impinged upon his brow, and then he spoke again."

[At this point a series of undulations that have been apparent as a perplexing complication as far back as Cavor's description of the silence that fell before the first speaking of the Grand Lunar become confusingly predominant in the record. These undulations are evidently the result of radiations proceeding from a lunar source, and their persistent approximation to the alternating signals of Cavor is curiously suggestive of some operator deliberately seeking to mix them in with his message and render it illegible. At first they are small and regular, so that with a little care and the loss of very few words we have been able to disentangle Cavor's message; then they become broad and larger, then suddenly they are irregular, with an irregularity that gives the effect at last of some one scribbling through a line of writing. For a long time nothing can be made of this madly zigzagging trace; then quite abruptly the interruption ceases, leaves a few words clear, and then resumes and continues for the rest of the message, completely obliterating whatever Cavor was attempting to transmit. Why, if this is indeed a deliberate intervention, the Selenites should have preferred to let Cavor go on transmitting his message in happy ignorance of their obliteration of its record, when it was clearly quite in their power and much more easy and convenient for them to stop his proceedings at any time, is a problem to which I can contribute nothing. The thing seems to have happened so, and that is all I can say. This last rag of his description of the Grand Lunar begins in mid-sentence.]

"...interrogated me very closely upon my secret. I was able in a little while to get to an understanding with them, and at last to elucidate what has been a puzzle to me ever since I realised the vastness of their science, namely, how it is they themselves have never discovered Cavorite.' I find they know of it as a theoretical substance, but they have always regarded it as a practical impossibility, because for some reason there is no helium in the moon, and helium..."

[Across the last letters of helium slashes the resumption of that obliterating trace. Note that word "secret," for that, and that alone, I base my interpretation of the message that follows, the last message, as both Mr. Wendigee and myself now believe it to be, that he is ever likely to send us.]

CHAPTER 26

The Last Message Cavor Sent to the Earth

In this unsatisfactory manner the penultimate message of Cavor dies out. One seems to see him away there in the blue obscurity amidst his apparatus intently signalling us to the last, all unaware of the curtain of confusion that drops between us; all unaware, too, of the final dangers that even then must have been creeping upon him. His disastrous want of vulgar common sense had utterly betrayed him. He had talked of war, he had talked of all the strength and irrational violence of men, of their insatiable aggressions, their tireless futility of conflict. He had filled the whole moon world with this impression of our race, and then I think it is plain that he made the most fatal admission that upon himself alone hung the possibility – at least for a long time – of any further men reaching the moon. The line the cold, inhuman reason of the moon would take seems plain enough to me, and a suspicion of it, and then perhaps some sudden sharp realisation of it, must have come to him. One imagines him about the moon with the remorse of this fatal indiscretion growing in his mind. During a certain time I am inclined to guess the Grand Lunar was deliberating the new situation, and for all that time Cavor may have gone as free as ever he had gone. But obstacles of some sort prevented his getting to his electromagnetic apparatus again after that message I have just given. For some days we received nothing. Perhaps he was having fresh audiences, and trying to evade his previous admissions. Who can hope to guess?

And then suddenly, like a cry in the night, like a cry that is followed by a stillness, came the last message. It is the briefest fragment, the broken beginnings of two sentences.

The first was: "I was mad to let the Grand Lunar know—"

There was an interval of perhaps a minute. One imagines some interruption from without. A departure from the instrument – a dreadful hesitation among the looming masses of apparatus in that dim, blue-lit cavern – a sudden rush back to it, full of a resolve that came too late. Then, as if it were hastily transmitted came: "Cavorite made as follows: take—"

There followed one word, a quite unmeaning word as it stands: "uless."

And that is all.

It may be he made a hasty attempt to spell "useless" when his fate was close upon him. Whatever it was that was happening about that apparatus we cannot tell. Whatever it was we shall never, I know, receive another message from the moon. For my own part a vivid dream has come to my help, and I see, almost as plainly as though I had seen it in actual fact, a blue-lit shadowy dishevelled Cavor struggling in the grip of these insect Selenites, struggling ever more desperately and hopelessly as they press upon him, shouting, expostulating, perhaps even at last fighting, and being forced backwards step by step out of all speech or sign of his fellows, for evermore into the Unknown – into the dark, into that silence that has no end....

LIFE & WORKS
H.G. WELLS

Herbert George (H.G.) Wells (1866–1946) has been inspiring awe with his novels ever since their publication in the late nineteenth century. The shocking, ground-breaking content has never appeared more graphic than in the first radio adaptation of *The War of the Worlds* (1898), broadcast on Halloween night in 1938. Some of the audience actually believed that the narrated events – presented as a factual news bulletin – were true and that Martians were indeed invading Earth. The ensuing panic led to an increased interest in Wells's work, which has hardly diminished to this day.

THE BOY WITH BIG IDEAS

Wells was a prolific writer of both fiction and nonfiction essays on society, government and world history, but it is his science-fiction novels for which he is best known and remembered. His childhood had a great influence on both his political leanings and choice of career. Wells was born in Kent into an industrious, self-sufficient family; his father ran a shop and also played professional cricket for Kent county. A broken leg at age eight meant that Wells junior was bedridden for months, and during convalescence he devoured as many books as he could from the local library, inspiring a dream of becoming a writer.

After attempting several jobs with little enjoyment – including a punishing three-year apprenticeship at a draper's firm from the age of fourteen – Wells secured a pupil-teacher job at Midhurst Grammar School, where he had briefly studied. He then won a scholarship to the Normal School of Science, London, where he studied Biology. Wells flourished at writing, becoming a founder of *The Science Schools Journal*, in which some of his short stories were published, but he failed his final year, meaning that he lost his scholarship. Nevertheless, he went on to complete a Zoology degree in 1890, before resuming teaching (one of his students was A.A. Milne). Married twice – first to his cousin, Isabel, then to one his students, Amy, known as Jane – Wells had numerous affairs and fathered a total of four children, two with Jane and two with other women.

Wells's science-fiction novels were among his earliest works. It was here that Wells began to explore the nature-nurture debate and ideas of evolution and a utopian society, stating in *The War of the Worlds* that 'life is an incessant struggle for existence'. He also wrote several nonfiction works including *The Outline of History* (1920) and *A Short History of the World* (1922), aiming to make material often saved for academics accessible to an interested general public. In many ways he remained the small boy eagerly reading library books.

THE FATHER OF SCIENCE FICTION

Although 'the Father of Science Fiction' designation is often used to describe others, especially Jules Verne (1828-1905), Wells is certainly a strong contender for the title. His science-fiction novels remain durably popular, inspiring countless adaptations, and are still drawn upon in literature, plays and films today. Wells was a massive influence on early science-fiction literature, even coining the term 'time machine' in one of his earliest and best-loved novels, *The Time Machine* (1895). This novel, partly inspired by his own short story, 'The Chronic Argonauts' (1888), charts the tale of the Time Traveller (no other name is given for the character; Wells often sacrifices well-rounded characters for innovative plots). The Time Traveller journeys to the future to discover that life on Earth has evolved into two species: the Eloi – intelligent, peaceful and technological, living above the ground – and the Morlocks – ape-like creatures living underground whose labour allows the Eloi to enjoy their lives of leisure. The Time Traveller concludes that the Eloi represent the upper class, living off the industry of the Morlocks. Only on closer analysis does he find that the Morlocks live off Eloi flesh, both species dependent on the other in very different ways. He escapes and travels onwards, seeing the Earth slowly die, returning home only three hours after he left (just in time for an after-dinner smoke). What became of him on his final journey is never discovered.

The Time Machine was followed by *The Invisible Man* (1897), in which Wells fused his knowledge of science with his capacity for invention, this time in the familiar setting of the England of his childhood. The main protagonist, Griffin, is a scientist who is able to make himself invisible. Unable to return his body to normal, Griffin lays low in a village (covered in a long coat, hat and bandages to hide his affliction) where he terrorises the villagers until his secret is exposed. He seeks help from a local doctor, but when Griffin, by now a mad and menacing character, talks of his 'homicidal' reign of terror, Dr. Kemp plots to trap Griffin and thwart his plan. Griffin is captured while trying to kill Dr. Kemp and is himself killed by the villagers, his body and the wounds inflicted upon him finally becoming visible as he dies.

In *The War of the Worlds*, Wells again touched upon the theme of evolution, with the invading Martians being forced to leave their own dying world. The Martians quickly take over London, forcing humans to flee with little or no resistance. It is only the fact that people have become immune to certain forms of bacteria that saves them, as opposed to the Martians, who have built up no immunity (there was no bacteria on Wells's Mars). The novel also addresses concerns the British had in the late nineteenth century about invasion from 'alien' countries. This novel – and several of Wells's other books – ends in a teasing enigma. Will more Martians invade Earth, this time successfully? Did Thomas Marvel ever figure out the secrets in the Invisible Man's notes? Where did the Time Traveller end up?

Wells's themes, characters and ideas have become a firm fixture of science fiction, appearing everywhere from the infamous *The War of the Worlds* radio broadcast to modern popular culture, such as *The League of Extraordinary Gentlemen* (1999 onwards) comic books, films and television shows. Many of the futuristic ideas in his novels, including world war, robots and nuclear power, have come to pass and even today, with the current plethora of science fiction available, his influence shows no sign of diminishing.

A GLOSSARY
OF GOTHIC, VICTORIAN
& LITERARY TERMS

A

abbess: nun in charge of a convent; female brothel keeper, a madame

abhorrence: feeling of loathing or revulsion

abode: place where people live; period of living somewhere

abominable: causing revulsion or disgust

air-blebs: air heads, empty-headed people

afterlife: existence after death; eternal life

alchemy: mythical practice of turning base metals into gold, prolonging life or finding a universal remedy for disease

alderman: term for a half-Crown; senior local government official

ale: alcoholic drink made from hops and fermented malt, stronger and heavier than beer

almanac: annual calendar which contains information on important dates, tides, astronomical data, etc.

almshouse: lodgings for the poor, privately funded (often by the church), as opposed to the workhouse, which was publicly funded

anatomical: relating to the structure of the body

antagonist: enemy or adversary

apoplexy: a crippling cerebral stroke, sometimes fatal; a fit of anger

apothecary: pharmacist; one who prepares drugs and medicines and gives medical advice; lowest order of medical man

apprentice: someone who works under a skilled professional for a specific amount of time (usually seven years) in order to learn a trade. When one finished his apprenticeship, he became a journeyman and would get paid for work himself

Armageddon: the final battle between good and evil

asylum: institution for people with mental health problems, often referred to as lunatic asylums

automaton: someone who resembles a machine by going through motions repetitively, but without feeling or emotion

B

Babylonian finger: that which spells out the writing on the wall; delivering a judgment

balderdash: nonsense, senseless or exaggerated speech or writing

banns: announcement or notice of a forthcoming marriage in a parish church, proclaimed on three consecutive Sundays

beak: magistrate

bearer up: thief with a female accomplice who would distract the victim so the crime could be performed

beating: repeatedly hitting someone; scaring birds from bushes out into the open for shooting parties

Bedlam: nickname for the Hospital of St Mary of Bethlehem, a London psychiatric hospital; place or situation full of noise, frenzy and confusion

beg to: wish to

berserker: traditionally an ancient and ferocious Norse warrior known for savagery

Black Smoke: poisonous gas used by the Martians in *The War of the Worlds* to kill humans

blackleg: someone who works during a strike, often criticised by those who obey the strike (also known as a 'scab')

blag: to steal something, often by smash-and-grab; to trick or con someone

blasphemy: sacrilegious talk concerning God or religion

bloodletting: reducing the volume of blood in the body by either opening a vein or applying leeches as a way of restoring health, used from ancient times up to the nineteenth century

bloofer: vampire, usually female; term possibly comes from the mispronunciation of 'beautiful'

bludger: violent criminal who often used a bludgeon or heavy, stout weapon

blue bottle: policeman

boarder: person paying rent for a bed, a room and usually meals in a private home or boarding house

bob: cockney slang for a shilling or five-pence piece

body-snatching: the act of stealing corpses from graves, tombs or morgues, usually for dissection or scientific study

borough: town that had been given the right to self-govern by royal charter; in Victorian London, Southwark was referred to as 'the borough'

Bow Street Runners: detective force in London who pre-dated the police, organized by novelist Henry Fielding and his brother John in 1750 up to 1829, when Robert Peel founded London's first police force

buck cabbie: dishonest cab driver

bug hunting: stealing from or cheating drunks, especially at night in drinking dens

bull: cockney slang for five shillings

C

calamity: accident or distressing event

cant: a free meal; language or vocabulary spoken by thieves or groups of people perceived to be common

caper: criminal act; dangerous activity

cash carrier: pimp or whore's minder, who would literally hold the money earned by soliciting

census: official list of the British population, including address and details of age, gender, occupation and birthplace, carried out every ten years since 1841

charnel-house: vault containing the remains of dead bodies or skeletons

chilblains: red, itchy swelling to parts of face, fingers and toes caused by exposure to cold and damp

chimera: something wished for but impossible; a fire-breathing monster from Greek mythology

chink: money (from the noise coins make when they knock against each other)

chiv/shiv: knife, razor or sharpened stick used as a weapon

choker: clergyman, referring to the clerical collar worn around the neck

cholera: disease of the small intestine, often fatal, marked by symptoms of thirst, cramps, vomiting and diarrhoea, caused by drinking water tainted with human waste. Victorians were hit with several cholera epidemics before sanitation conditions were improved

choused: to have been cheated

christen: to remove identifying marks from; to use for the first time; to make something like new again

chronometer: tool for measuring accurate time

claustrophobia: abnormal dread of being imprisoned or confined in a close or narrow space

cly faking: to pick someone's pocket

coal scuttle: metal pail for carrying and pouring coal

commencement: the beginning or start of something

contagion: spread of disease caused by close contact

cop/copper: policeman

costermonger: street peddler, usually selling fruits or vegetables

cracksman: safecracker, someone who cracks or breaks locks

cravat: scarf or band of fabric worn around the neck and tied in a bow

creator: someone who makes something come alive

crib: building, house or lodging; location of a gaol

crow: lookout during criminal activities; doctor

crusher: policeman

cudgel: heavy stick used as a weapon

cursory: quick, superficial and not very thorough

D

daresay: venture to say; think probable

day boarder: someone who spends the day at school but lives at home, as opposed to someone who boards at the school

deadlurk: empty premises

deaner: shilling

deformity: disfigurement or malformation, often of a body part but can also refer to morals or the mind

deity: god or goddess; supreme being

deputation: group of people charged with a mission or to represent other people

despatch: send something; to send someone to carry out a task

deuce hog: two shillings

device: tuppence; an emblem or motto

Devil: the Devil, as depicted in Christianity and some other religions, stands as the enemy or opposite to God and tempts people to sin so that they go to Hell; the actual term 'Devil' comes from the Latin *diabolus*, meaning slanderous. Gothic characters are often tempted by agents of the Devil

dewskitch: a beating (bodily assault)

diligence: public stagecoach; taking care or attention over something

ding: to throw something away; to take something that has been thrown away

diphtheria: infectious disease caused by germs in the throat, causing difficulty in breathing, fever and damage to the heart and nervous system

dirge: funeral hymn, mournful lament for the dead

dispatches: loaded dice; sends someone to carry out a task

do down: to beat someone with fists, especially as a punishment

dogmatism: emphatic belief presented as fact without consideration of truth or others' opinions

dollyshop: unlicensed, often cheap, loan or pawn shop

don: eminent, professional or clever person; leader or head of a group

Doppelgänger: literally translated from German as 'doublegoer'; the ghostly apparition of another, living person; double or alter ego

double-knock: applied to the door by a confident visitor, one who was known to the family and comfortable with the purpose of his visit (a single-knock signified a more timid caller, often of an inferior class)

dowager: widow with an inherited title or property from her deceased husband; distinguished, respected older woman

down: cause suspicion or doubt; to inform on a person, when used in the expression 'to put down on someone'

dragsman: someone who steals from carriages or coaches

draught: cheque or bill of exchange; a small quantity of liquid drunk in one mouthful

duckett: street dealer or vendor's licence

duffer: someone who sells allegedly stolen or worthless goods, also known as a 'hawker'

E

ecod: mild curse, most likely derived from 'My God'

economy: cheapness; giving better value

employ: to hire someone to work for you; if you were in the employ of or employed by someone, you worked for them

entrapment: imprisoning someone; incarcerating or trapping someone, often in dark, strange or claustrophobic surroundings

epidemic: illness that spreads rapidly and extensively, affecting most of the people who come in contact with it

epoch: period of time marked by particular events

erethism: extreme excitement or stimulation

escop/eslop: policeman

establishment: shop, place of business

exorcism: act of forcing the Devil, a demon or evil spirits from the body of someone who is possessed, done through religious prayer or rituals

expectations: chance of coming into an inheritance, property or money

extermination: destruction of an entire group or civilization

extra-terrestrial: existing outside of the earth's atmosphere

F

fadge: slang term for farthing

fakement: sham or trick, often used when begging

fan: to feel surreptitiously under someone's clothing while they are wearing it, searching for objects to steal

farthing: monetary unit worth a quarter of a penny; something almost worthless or of the lowest value

fawney-dropping: trick where a criminal pretends to find a ring (which has no actual value) and sells it as an item of possible worth

fiend: evil demon; evil or wicked person

finny: slang term for five-pound note

flam: lie or deception

flash: to show off or try to impress; something special or expensive-looking

flash house: public house with criminals as clientele

flimp: snatch stealing or pickpocketing from a crowd

flue faker: chimney sweep, usually young boys

footman: servant in livery, usually in a mansion or palace; a servant who serves at table, tends the door or carriage, runs errands

forebodings: feelings of apprehension or anxiety

forfeits: parlour games where each player needs to supply a correct answer and has a forfeit if the answer is not given

foundling: orphan or abandoned child raised by someone else

furlong: unit of measurement equal to 201 m (660 ft), the length of the traditional furrow or plough trench on a farm

furtherance: helping or advancing the progress of something

fusillade: volleys of shots fired simultaneously or in rapid succession

G

gaff: show or exhibition; cheap, smutty theatre; hoax or trick

galvanize: to shock someone or something into action

gammon: misleading comment, meant to deceive

gammy: someone false who is not to be trusted

gaol: jail

garret: fob pocket in a waistcoat; room at the top of the house

gattering: public house

general post: mail that was sent from the London Post Office to the rest of England

ghost: phantom or spirit of somebody who has died and who has possibly not gone on to the afterlife, which often inspires fear or terror

gibbet: post with a projecting beam for hanging executed criminals, often done publicly as a warning to the public

gig: light, open, two-wheeled carriage drawn by a single horse

gill: unit of liquid equalling a quarter of a pint

glock: slow, half-witted person

gonoph: petty, small-time criminal

Gorgon: female monster from Greek mythology with snakes for hair

gothic: style of architecture, music, art or fiction generally associated with strange, frightening occurrences and mysterious or supernatural plots, characters or locations

gout: disease mainly affecting men, causing inflammation and swelling of the hands and feet, arthritis and deformity; caused by excess uric acid production

governess: woman employed to teach and care for children in a school or home

greatcoat: long, heavy overcoat worn outdoors, often with a short cape worn over the shoulders

grog: mixture of alcohol, often rum, and water, named after an English admiral who diluted sailors' rum

grotesque: misshapen or mutated character; something or someone unexpected, monstrous or bizarre

gruel: watery, unappetizing porridge, popular with the owners of the workhouse or orphanage due to its cheapness

guinea: gold coin, monetary value of twenty-one shillings or one pound and one shilling

gulpy: someone gullible or easy to fool

H

haberdasher: someone who sells personal items, often accessories such as thread or ribbons

hackney coach: carriage for hire

hansom cab: two-wheeled, horse-drawn carriage where the driver sat on a high seat at the back so that the passengers had a clear view of the road

haunted: visited by a ghost or supernatural being

haybag: derogatory term for a woman

Heat-Ray: infrared ray, used by the Martians in *The War of the Worlds*

heliograph: signalling device that works by moving a mirror to reflect sunlight

heresy: belief that contradicts generally accepted or official religious teaching

hob: metal shelf or rack over a fireplace where the pans or kettle could be warmed

hoisting: shoplifting; to lift something up

hopping: picking hops, used for making beer

humbug: something insincere or nonsensical, meant to deceive or cheat people; used to express disbelief or disgust; a hoax or fraud

hykey: pride, arrogance

I

incubus: name for a male demon, thought to be a fallen angel, who forces himself sexually upon sleeping women, which often resulted in the birth of a demon or deformed, half-human child

infusoria: single-celled organisms

indefatigable: tirelessly persistent; not giving in to fatigue

influenza/flu: viral illness causing aching joints, fever, headaches, sore throat, cough and sneezing, even followed by death in Victorian times

inmate: someone confined to an institution such as a lunatic asylum or prison

Inquisition: organization founded by the Catholic Church charged with the eradication of heresy or acting against God, by which those found guilty were often put to death

insensate: lacking understanding, sense or reason; without sensitivity or feeling

insurrection: uprising in revolt or rebellion, usually against an established government or authority

integument: tough, protective outer layer

interred: buried

ironclad: armoured warship

ironmonger: someone who sells metal goods, tools and hardware

irons: guns, usually pistols or revolvers

J

jolly: disturbance or brawl; to be cheerful or happy

journeyman: skilled worker who has finished an apprenticeship and is qualified to hire himself out for work

Judgment Day: the end of the world when God judges humanity and the dead come back to life; also known as doomsday

Judy: term for a woman, usually a prostitute

juggernaut: massive and destructive force that is almost impossible to stop

jump: ground-floor window, or a burglary committed by entering through the window

K

kecks: slang term for trousers

ken: house, lodging or public house

kidsman: organizer of child thieves

kith: someone's friends, neighbours or relatives

knaves: jacks in a deck of cards

knee breeches: trousers that reach the knee

knock up: to bang loudly on someone's door to wake them up

know life, to: to be familiar with criminal ways; to be street-wise

kopjes: small hill, South African term meaning 'little head'

L

lag: convict; someone sentenced to transportation or gaol

lassitude: feeling of weariness, lack of energy

laudanum: solution of opium and alcohol used as pain relief or to aid sleep, highly addictive

lavender, in: to hide from the police; to pawn something for money; to be dead

leg: dishonest person, cheat

leviathan: sea monster; large and powerful object or thing

liberal: generous; tolerant or open-minded

link boy: boy who carries a torch to light a person's way through the dark streets

lodger: person paying rent to stay in a room (or bed) in somebody else's house

logbook: book in which a teacher would comment on pupils' attendance, behaviour, learning progress, etc.

lumber: wood used for building or woodworking, often second-hand furniture; to pawn something; to go to gaol

lurker: criminal; beggar or someone who dresses as a beggar for money

lush: alcoholic drink; someone who drinks too much alcohol; luxurious

M

macer: cheat

mag: slang term for a ha'pence piece

magistrate: judge over trials of misdemeanours; civil officer who upholds the law

maid-of-all-work: usually a young girl, hired as the only servant in the house and required to do any job asked of her

mail coach: carrier of the mail and a limited number of passengers, replaced in the mid-nineteenth century by the railroad

malefactor: someone who commits a crime or wrongdoing

malignity: malevolence, bad feeling towards someone

malt: grain, such as barley, that has been allowed to ferment, used for brewing beer and sometimes whisky

mandrake: homosexual; type of plant

mania: mental obsession or abnormality which can cause mood swings

mark: the victim of a crime

market day: the regular day each week when country people would bring their livestock and goods to sell in town

market town: town that regularly held a market, usually the largest town of a farming area

masochism: psychosexual perversion where someone gains erotic pleasure by having pain, abuse or humiliation inflicted on them

materially reduced: having your circumstances and/or finances reduced or lessened

maxim: statement or saying

mead: fermented alcoholic drink made of water, honey, malt, yeast and sometimes spices

mecks: alcohol, usually wine or spirits

Messrs: plural of Mr., used when referring to more than one man

metamorphosis: change or complete transformation in physical form, shape or structure, thought to be caused by supernatural powers

miasma: unpleasant smell or vapour, often related to disease or death

Michaelmas: Christian festival celebrating the archangel Michael, celebrated on 29 September, one of the four quarters of the year

middle class: people who earn enough money to live comfortably, often in a skilled profession, such as doctors and lawyers

mist: cloud of water particles that condense in the atmosphere, often used in Gothic literature to obscure objects or to prelude something or someone terrifying

mizzle: steal or disappear; fine rain

moniker/monniker: signature; first name

mortality: death rate; the number of deaths in a given time or given group

moucher/moocher: rural vagrant or beggar, someone who lives on the road

mourning clothes: black garments worn after a relative dies, the length of which depended on your relationship to the deceased

muck snipe: someone down on their luck

muffler: scarf

mug-hunter: street thief or pickpocket, from which the modern term 'mugger' comes

mutcher: pickpocket who usually steals from drunks

N

nail: steal; to catch someone who is guilty of a crime

natural philosophy: the science of nature

necromancy: black art of conversing with the spirits of the dead, usually done to predict or influence the future, also for making the dead perform tasks for you; witchcraft or sorcery

nethers: charges or rent for lodgings

netherskens: cheap, unsavoury lodging houses, flophouses

new-fangled: new or original, not necessarily an improvement over a previous version

nib: point of a pen, often a fountain pen

nibbed: arrested

nickey: slow or simple-minded

nightmare: frightening or unsettling dream, often used in Gothic literature to heighten drama or fear; a malign spirit thought to haunt or suffocate people during sleep

nobble: to inflict severe pain or bodily harm

nose: informant or spy; to try to find something out

O

occult: relating to the supernatural, witchcraft or magic; something not capable of being understood by ordinary people, but known only by the initiated

occupation: job, means of earning a living

odour: smell

omnibus: single or double-decker bus which was pulled by horses, capable of carrying lots of people

omnipotent: having unlimited power, god-like, infinite

on the fly: while in motion, moving quickly; something done quickly or spontaneously

opium: drug extracted from the dried juice and seeds of the opium poppy which is highly addictive

orthodox: following established rules of religion or society; proper way of behaving

outdoor relief: charity for the poor which did not require them to enter the workhouse, eliminated in 1834 by the New Poor Law to stop people playing the system

outsider: instrument used for opening a lock from the wrong side; stranger or interloper

P

page: boy or young man working as a servant or running errands

pall: detect; become dull or fade; gloomy atmosphere or mood

palmer: shoplifter; someone who 'palms' items to steal them

palsy: medical condition producing uncontrollable shaking of the muscles

pandemonium: wild disorder, chaos

panegyric: impassioned speech or text praising something or someone

parlour: living room, usually for guests

patterer: someone who earns a living by recitation or hawker's sales talk, convincing people to buy goods

peach: inform against someone or give information against someone, often leading to imprisonment

pea-coat: short, heavy, double-breasted overcoat worn by seamen, usually dark blue or black

peelers: nickname for the new London police force, organized by Sir Robert Peel in 1829

pertaining to: concerning or to do with

phantasm: ghost or apparition

phenomenon: fact or occurrence that is out of the ordinary or hard to believe, even though it can be seen, felt, heard, etc.

phonograph: gramophone, machine for recording or playing sound

picnic: any informal social gathering for which each guest provided a share of the food; informal meal eaten outside

pidgeon: victim; also known as a plant

pig: policeman, usually a detective

pig in a poke: something for sale at more than its true value

pleurisy: inflammation of the lungs producing a fever, hacking cough, sharp chest pain and difficulty in breathing

polyglot: someone who can speak or understand several languages

poorhouse: place where poor, old or sick people lived, where anyone able was put to work; also known as the workhouse

portrait: likeness of an individual or group created through photography or in paintings

possession: being controlled by an evil, demonic, supernatural force

post chaise: enclosed, four-wheeled, horse-drawn carriage, used to transport mail and passengers

premonitory: premonition or warning

prig: self-righteous or superior person

proctor: court officer who manages the affairs of others, answering to an attorney or solicitor

prodigious: great in amount or size; a lot

profane: disrespectful of religious beliefs

Prometheus: a Titan who stole fire from the Greek god, Zeus, in order to give it to humankind

proprietor: owner of a commercial or business enterprise

puckering: jabbering; speaking in an incomprehensible manner

pugilistic: relating to the practice of boxing or fist fighting

punishers: men hired to give beatings or 'nobblings'

pursuit: the act of chasing after someone, usually to attack or catch them, often inspiring fear

push: slang term for money

putrefactive: causing decay or putrefaction

Q

quadrille: card game for four players using forty cards; dance

quarter days: four days of the year when quarterly payments were made: Lady Day (25 March), Midsummer (24 June), Michaelmas (29 September) and Christmas (25 December)

quay: wharf or platform in a port or harbour where ships are loaded or unloaded

quick-lime: white, corrosive, alkaline substance consisting of calcium oxide, acquired by heating limestone

quid: slang term for pound

R

racket: illicit or dishonest occupation or activity

ream: someone superior, real or genuine

red planet: name for the planet Mars, given due to its red colour

red weed: fictional plant found in *The War of the Worlds*, which gives the planet Mars its red colour

remembrance: memory

repeater: pocket watch that chimed on the hour or quarter past the hour, making it easier to tell the time in the dark

reservist: reserve member of the military

resurrectionist: body snatcher; someone who steals corpses from graves, usually to sell to medical students. Legally, only the bodies of criminals could be used, but demand for corpses was so high that resurrectionists dug up the graves of the recently dead

revenant: dead person who has returned to terrorize or to avenge a score with someone living

revenge: act of avenging or repaying someone for a harm that the person has caused; to punish someone in retaliation for something done to them or to a loved one, carried out by humans or by spirits; a popular theme in Gothic literature

ribald: description for vulgar, lewd humour, often involving jokes about sex

roller: thief who robs drunks; prostitute who steals from her (usually drunk) customers

Romanticism: arts and literature of the Romantic movement, characterized by the passion, emotion and often danger of love and associated feelings

Romany: gypsy or traveller; language spoken by gypsies

rookery: urban slum or ghetto; nesting place for rooks

rozzers: policemen

ruffles: slang term for handcuffs

ruin: to go out of business; lose all your money or possessions

S

saddle: loaf; cut of meat

sadism: perversion where one person gains sexual gratification by causing others physical or mental pain, first coined to describe the writings of the Marquis de Sade; delight in torment or excessive cruelty

salubrity: health or well-being

Salvation Army: worldwide religious organization founded by William Booth in 1865; it provided aid to the poor, helped those in need and sought to bring people back to God

sapper: military engineer

sawbones: physician or surgeon

scarlet fever: infection usually suffered by children, causing a red rash and high fever; also called Scarlatina

screever: forger; writer of fake documents

sealing wax: wax that is soft when heated, used to seal letters – red for business letters, black for mourning and other colours for general correspondence

sentinel: guard or soldier who keeps watch

servant's lurk: public house used primarily by crooked or dismissed servants

sharp: conman, card swindler

shilling: unit of money equal to five pence in today's money

shirkster: layabout, work-shy

shofulman: someone who makes or passes bad money

silicious: consisting of silica, a crystalline compound

slap-bang job: public house frequented by thieves, where no credit is given

slate: used to teach children to write; they would write on black slates with white chalk, instead of the paper used today

slum: ghetto; false or faked document; to cheat someone or pass money you know to be bad or false

smasher: someone who passes bad or false money

snakesman: small boy used for housebreaking, as they could enter a house through a small gap

snoozer: someone who steals from sleeping guests in hotels

snowing: stealing clothes that have been hung out on a washing line to dry

somnambulism: sleepwalking, a dissociated mental state that occurs during deep sleep during which, in Gothic literature, people would do things they would not normally do

spectroscope: tool for recording and measuring spectra of light or radiation

spike: slang term for the workhouse

sponging-house: temporary prison for those who cannot pay their debts, prior to them being sent to a prison such as Marshalsea in London

srew: skeleton key, for use in burglaries

stricken: affected by; suffering or struck by

sublime: the concept of being awed, moved or transported by something, such as religion, beauty or emotions; used in Gothic literature for the thrill of being terrified, because fear inspires such strong emotions

substratum: underlying layer

succubus: female demon, counterpart of the incubus (*q.v.*)

supernatural: used to describe phenomena or events that seem unbelievable or cannot be explained by natural laws or occurrences relating to magic or the occult

superstition: deep-seated but often irrational belief in something, such as an action or ritual, that is thought to bring good or bad luck

sweetmeat: sweet treat, such as candy or candied fruit, often served at the end of a meal

swell: elegantly or stylishly dressed gentleman; expensive dress

T

tallow: hard, fatty substance from sheep or oxen, used to make candles or soap

taper: small, slim wax candle, narrower at the top than at the bottom

taproom: bar room in a public house where working-class people ate and drank, as opposed to the parlour, used by the middle classes

terrestrial: an inhabitant of, or relating to, the earth

thick 'un: slang term for sovereign

thicker: slang for sovereign or pound

Thing, the: name given to the Martian spacecraft in *The War of the Worlds*

thriving: to be profitable or successful; flourishing

thwart: to prevent someone from doing something

timorous: timid or nervous

Titan: name for the giants from Greek mythology; one of Saturn's moons

tocsin: warning signal or bell

toff: elegant or stylish gentleman; someone rich or upper-class

toffken: house in which well-to-do, upper-class people lived

topped: to be hung

tradesman: man in a skilled trade, such as a carpenter or plumber; shopkeeper; someone who buys and sells goods

transfigure: to transform

transportation: when exiled British criminals were sent to the colonies, usually Australia, as punishment

trephining: surgery on the skull to remove sections of bone, sometimes used to treat mental illness

troglodytic: to describe a cave-dweller; bestial or brutal of character

turnkey: jailor; keeper of keys

typhoid: serious, often fatal, illness caused by drinking polluted water (contaminated by sewage)

U

ululation: howling or crying out, often from pain

unanimity: consensus or agreement

uncanny: something or someone too strange, weird or eerie to be natural or human; supernatural

unclean: dirty, impure

union workhouse: workhouse for the poor, which parishes were obligated to provide after the 1834 New Poor Law

unhallowed: unholy or not consecrated ground

unprovided for: left with no money or security

upper class: people from rich, moneyed families, such as landowners or aristocracy

V

vamp: to steal; to pawn something; to seduce or manipulate someone

vampire: supernatural being of a malignant nature, believed to leave its coffin at night to suck the blood of the living for sustenance, from European folklore

vapour: steam

venal: corrupt, capable of being bribed

vespers: evening church service, prayers

vintner: wine maker or merchant

vivisection: surgery performed upon living organisms for scientific research or investigation

W

watch: men chosen to guard the streets at night, periodically calling out the time and ensuring that no crimes were being committed

werewolf: someone who is human by day and turns into a wolf at night, living off humans, animals or even corpses, from European folklore

whist: popular card game, now known as bridge

witchcraft: spells and magic performed by a witch; in Gothic fiction the witch is usually depicted as an old, hag-like crone or a beautiful, seductive young woman

without: outside, usually referring to outside the house in which someone is

woe-begone: sad or miserable in appearance

work capitol: crime punishable by death

workhouse: place where the sick, poor, old and those in debt went or were sent for food and shelter. The New Poor Law (1834) made the workhouse almost a prison for the poor, who had to work hard in miserable conditions, often fed on gruel only and separated from their families

working class: those in heavy manual labour, usually for low, hourly wages, such as farm labourers, factory workers and builders

worrit: worry; worry-wort

wretch: miserable or unhappy person

Y

yack: slang term for a watch

Z

zoophagous: carnivorous, feeding on animal flesh

COLLECTOR'S EDITIONS

FLAME TREE

A wide range of new and classic
fiction, including short story
anthologies, *Collectable Classics*,
Gothic Fantasy collections and
Epic Tales of mythology.

•

Available at all good
bookstores, and online at
flametreepublishing.com

FLAME TREE PUBLISHING